—A—
FAITHFUL GATHERING

Books by Leslie Gould

THE COURTSHIPS OF LANCASTER COUNTY

Courting Cate

Adoring Addie

Minding Molly

Becoming Bea

NEIGHBORS OF LANCASTER COUNTY

Amish Promises

Amish Sweethearts

Amish Weddings

THE SISTERS OF LANCASTER COUNTY

A Plain Leaving

A Simple Singing

A Faithful Gathering

A

FAITHFUL GATHERING

LESLIE GOULD

BETHANYHOUSE
a division of Baker Publishing Group
Minneapolis, Minnesota

Published by Bethany House Publishers
11400 Hampshire Avenue South
Bloomington, Minnesota 55438
www.bethanyhouse.com

Bethany House Publishers is a division of
Baker Publishing Group, Grand Rapids, Michigan

Printed in the United States of America

Library of Congress Cataloging-in-Publication Data
Names: Gould, Leslie, author.
Title: A faithful gathering / Leslie Gould.
Description: Minneapolis, Minnesota : Bethany House Publishers, a division of
  Baker Publishing Group, [2019] | Series: The sisters of Lancaster county ; Book 3
Identifiers: LCCN 2018033952| ISBN 9780764219719 (trade paper) | ISBN
  9781493417322 (ebook) | ISBN 9780764233159 (cloth)
Subjects: | GSAFD: Christian fiction.
Classification: LCC PS3607.O89 F35 2019 | DDC 813/.6—dc23
LC record available at https://lccn.loc.gov/2018033952

Cover design by LOOK Design Studio
Cover photography by Mike Habermann Photography, LLC

Author is represented by MacGregor Literary, Inc.

18   19   20   21   22   23   24   7   6   5   4   3   2   1

To all those in health care.
You aid, serve, and heal.
Thank you.

For where two or three are gathered together in my name,
there am I in the midst of them.

Matthew 18:20

—1—

Leisel Bachmann

APRIL 2017

A crash yanked me out of my cleaning routine at the care facility. *4:32 A.M.* I dropped the sponge on the kitchen counter and hurried down the hall.

Earl Weber's door was open a crack. I pushed into the room. A man wearing pajamas and a robe was sprawled across the floor.

I flicked the light on. "Are you all right, Mr. Weber?" I crouched beside him, taking his wrist. He had a pulse, but his eyes were closed.

As I reached for my phone in the pocket of my smock, he grabbed my wrist. "I'm all right." His eyes flew open. "I felt light-headed, is all. I got myself on the floor before I fell."

"Did you lose consciousness?" I needed to call the nurse if he did.

"No." He rolled to his side.

"I'll help you up," I said. He was my favorite resident in the

9

entire center, although I tried not to let it show. He was ninety-two, mostly lucid, and always kind.

Once I had him back in bed, I asked him why he'd gotten up in the first place.

"I heard Betty call my name."

Betty was his wife. She'd passed away six years ago.

When I didn't respond, he reached for my hand. "I was sure she was at the door, waiting for me. That I'd just come home from the war, that she had our baby girl in her arms. I could hear both of them. It all seemed so real."

"That happens sometimes." I'd felt my *Dat's* presence a few times after he'd died.

"Thank you," he said, "for being such a good friend to me. You're the best nurse I've ever had."

I didn't remind him—again—that I wasn't a nurse. Instead, I tucked him in, told him I'd check on him soon, and slipped out of the room.

I wasn't a nurse yet, but I would be soon. Graduation was tomorrow. And in less than a month, I'd take my state boards—the licensing exam all nursing graduates had to pass to practice nursing.

Growing up Amish, I'd been warned about being prideful, and I took the warning seriously. But Mr. Weber was right. I was a good nurse. I had the problem-solving skills, emotional stability, and empathy needed to do the job.

As I returned to my cleaning, I thought of Mr. Weber and the stories he'd told me about being a fighter pilot in Europe during the final months of World War II. "I had it easy," he often said. "I couldn't see the fine details of the destruction I caused."

That might have been true, but it was still a dangerous job, and I was grateful he'd survived. He'd be celebrating his ninety-third birthday in a week.

Dat had told me once that my grandfather, who died before I was born, had served as a conscientious objector during World War II. Sadly, Dat passed before he told me more. Honestly, I wasn't that interested at the time, but getting to know Mr. Weber had made me curious. I'd have to ask my *Aenti* Suz for the story.

My phone dinged with an incoming text. It had to be Nick, since no one else texted me at such an early hour. He'd graduated the year before and was a nurse in the emergency department at the University of Pittsburgh Medical Center—Mercy, located in Uptown. We'd been dating for nearly three years.

I pulled my phone out of my pocket. *Looking forward to dinner.*

I smiled. He was taking me out tonight to celebrate my graduation—after we both got some sleep.

Ditto, I texted back, sending a smiling emoji along with the word.

A half hour later, I checked on Mr. Weber. He was sound asleep. Just as I started to do my charting for the night, a yell came from across the hall. Mrs. O'Sullivan was probably having a nightmare.

I sat with her, speaking in a soothing voice until she drifted back to sleep. By then it was nearly six, and the early risers were beginning to wake. I started a pot of coffee and then began getting the residents ready for the day. I always tried to get as many dressed as possible before the day shift—and my supervisor, Rita—arrived. I'd do my charting before I left.

At 7:15, the staff met for the shift change. Rita had a big mug of coffee in her hand and a bleary look in her eyes. I reported that the evening had been mostly calm, but Mrs. O'Sullivan had a nightmare and Mr. Weber had fallen.

"He didn't lose consciousness," I quickly added.

"You charted what happened?" Rita asked.

"Not yet. I didn't have time."

"You said it was a calm night."

"It was, mostly. It got busy though, and I started my charting later than usual."

Rita pursed her lips. "That's not like you, Leisel."

My face grew warm, but there was no need to react—I hadn't done anything wrong.

After the shift change, I headed to the nursing station to chart. Just as I finished documenting Mr. Weber's fall, I heard another aide call out Rita's name, and then say, "He's not breathing."

I stepped into the hall. Mr. Weber's door was wide open. I rushed into his room.

The man was just as I last saw him, except his mouth was slightly open. I took his wrist in my hand. No pulse. I knew he had a Do Not Resuscitate order in his file, and by the temperature of his skin, it was too late anyway.

As Rita hurried back into the room, I raised my head. "He's gone."

She crossed her arms. "Well, I certainly hope this wasn't caused by his fall."

"It wasn't," I said. "He didn't lose consciousness or have a bump on his head or anything like that." More likely, he'd dreamt about hearing his wife's voice because his time was near. I was sure he was ready to go and was thankful he hadn't suffered.

Rita made a throaty noise, and then said, "I'll call the undertaker and his daughter. You'd better get the fall charted."

"I already did." I turned toward her. "I'd like to stay and see his daughter." I wanted to tell her about what he'd said.

Rita shook her head. "There's no need for that. Go on home."

"I'd rather stay."

"No," she said. "Go home. We can talk more about all of this tomorrow."

"I graduate tomorrow," I said. "I'm taking a few days off, remember?"

She wrinkled her nose. "No, I don't remember. Are you going out of town?"

"No." I didn't give her any details, but I was going to spend those few days looking for a new apartment. I'd already given notice on mine.

Not wanting to clash with Rita anymore, I placed my hand on Mr. Weber's forehead and said a silent thank-you for his life and then a final good-bye. At least for now. He'd had a quiet faith that played out in the way he treated people and the way he spoke about God. Mr. Weber certainly wasn't the first resident who'd died on my watch, but he was the one I'd miss the most.

By the time I turned to leave the room, Rita was gone. I grabbed my things and headed down the hall. Rita was on the phone in her office, so I gave her a quick wave and headed out the door.

I contemplated calling Nick to tell him about Mr. Weber but decided not to. It could wait until dinner. He'd mourn with me, I knew. Growing to truly care about your patients was both the blessing and the heartbreak of working in health care.

The morning was cold and overcast, and I quickened my pace through the neighborhood. I'd lived in what Nick called "the dive" for the last four years, as long as I'd been in Pittsburgh. It was a furnished studio basement apartment. Could there be anything worse?

Of course, when I signed the lease, I was thrilled. It wasn't far from the University of Pittsburgh, and there was a grocery store and café within walking distance. Then I'd found the job at the care facility, which was in the neighborhood too.

The apartment was the first step in my *Englisch* life. But now I was ready for the second step: graduation. And then a bigger apartment with some natural light that I'd be able to afford because I'd soon secure my first nursing job. I figured I'd only sign a six-month lease on a new place though—I didn't want to commit to anything long-term. Just in case.

I hadn't given notice to Rita about quitting my job yet, but surely she knew it was coming. If she could actually remember that I was graduating from nursing school.

My phone dinged again as I started down the stairs to my apartment. *See you tonight!*

I answered Nick with a thumbs-up and a heart. After a moment of thought, I added, *Can you talk?* Why wait until tonight to tell him about Mr. Weber? Within a split second my phone rang. I sat down on the bottom step as I answered it.

"Hey, what's up?"

Once I'd relayed the whole story, he said, "I'm sorry that he's gone, but it sounds like it was his time. What a great way to go."

"That's exactly what I thought."

Nick's voice grew even more tender. "I know you'll miss him though."

"I will." But death was part of life. I'd never been shielded from that as a child, and then as an eighteen-year-old I'd nursed my father as he died from cancer.

Nick reassured me that I'd handled the situation correctly. Already I felt better. After we said good-bye, I dug my keys out of my backpack and unlocked my front door. A musty smell greeted me, one that lingered no matter how much I cleaned and persisted even though the apartment was icy cold. I'd spent my entire childhood in a freezing bedroom—I didn't need to give in to anything as luxurious as heat now. I kicked off my shoes, bumping against my waist-high stack of nursing textbooks as I did.

For the first time in four years I didn't need to study. All I had to do today was sleep a little, look online for a new apartment, research nursing jobs in the area, and then get ready for my celebratory date with Nick.

I knelt beside my bed as I always did before I slept, another practice I hadn't given up from my childhood. I prayed for my family, about my upcoming boards, for Nick, and then for the two of us. "Please guide us, Lord," I prayed. "And thank you for how you've led us so far."

The restaurant, located on Mount Washington, was the most upscale I'd ever been to—linen tablecloths and napkins, crystal glasses, and fresh flowers. I was both enchanted and alarmed, which pretty much summed up the last four years of my life. The Englisch ways enticed me, but at the same time, I believed them to be extravagant.

Fine dining wasn't part of my Amish upbringing. Neither was the picturesque view outside the window. Below us was Point State Park, where the Ohio, Allegheny, and Monongahela Rivers joined together.

Nick took my hand from across the table. "What are you going to order?" he asked.

"The chicken."

He shook his head. "That's the cheapest thing on the menu. You should order something else."

What was Nick thinking? The chicken entrée was still thirty bucks. We both had student loans to pay back and old vehicles that broke down every other month.

"I like chicken." I gave him a sassy look, which made him smile. His dark wavy hair was newly trimmed, and his brown eyes shone. He wore a suit and tie and looked as handsome as ever. I glanced down at my lap and the dress I'd borrowed from my friend Paisley for the occasion. I had no idea what the fabric was called, but it was flimsy and flowing, and I felt fancy wearing it.

Nick patted the pocket of his jacket absentmindedly as he said, "I talked with a recruiter yesterday."

A job recruiter? Hospitals were so desperate to hire nurses that many contracted with companies to find the personnel they needed. My stomach lurched. "Are you leaving the medical center?" I managed to sputter, wondering if I'd misread our plans for the future.

"Eventually." His hand felt warm. I was afraid mine was icy cold. "It's the best way to get my student loans paid off."

I'd heard some hospitals helped pay off student loans, which would be great for him. "Where will you go?"

"It depends on what happens after officer training school— what assignment I get."

"Assignment?" Slowly, it dawned on me. He'd brought up joining the Air Force in passing, but I thought he'd dropped the idea. Apparently he hadn't.

"Leisel?" His voice was so low I hardly heard it.

I lifted my head and met his eyes. "I didn't know you were still thinking about joining the Air Force."

An unsettled look fell across his face. "I never stopped thinking about it. I don't want to struggle financially the way my parents did for years. I don't want student loan debt hanging over us."

Us.

"We could concentrate on paying off your loans first," Nick said. "Or you could join up too, and—"

"Join the military?" I choked out, interrupting him.

He nodded, but then our waiter appeared before he could say more.

16

I ordered the chicken breast. Nick ordered the lump crab and Asian pear appetizer for us to share and the salmon for his dinner.

"How about a glass of our house sauvignon blanc or chardonnay to go with the chicken and salmon?" the waiter asked.

"I'll just have water," I quickly answered.

"Me too," Nick added.

After the waiter left, I hoped the conversation wouldn't go back to the Air Force. But it did.

"I've done my research. Joining the Air Force would pay off our student loans. And there are a lot of training opportunities for our master's degrees or even doctorates. Nurse practitioner programs. Nurse anesthetist programs." He smiled. "They'd need a commitment for more training. Probably six years is all."

My stomach fell. Six years? I hoped we might be married within a year, or at least a couple of years.

But maybe we wouldn't marry at all now.

The scent of coffee mixed with the scent of grilled meat and fish and freshly laundered linens. It all distracted me for half a second. Until Nick cleared his throat. "You don't seem very enthused."

I blinked. "I'm not interested in joining the military."

Still holding on to my hand, he quickly responded, "That's cool."

"I may have left the Amish church, but I still agree with the nonresistance ideology. I can't support war."

"But you'd be caring for the medical needs of people—not just soldiers. You'd be taking care of their families too. Not supporting war."

"Indirectly I would be." And he would be too. And if I married him, I'd be supporting him, and therefore supporting war.

I'd given up a lot in leaving my Amish family and community, but I wasn't willing to give up everything.

He cocked his head. "I don't understand."

I slipped my hand from his. "I can't support the military," I said. "It goes against my principles."

He exhaled slowly. "Principles of homeland security? Of protecting our citizens?"

I shook my head. "Of killing other people."

His eyebrows arched. "Right. But we wouldn't be killing people."

I tried again. "But we would be caring for and supporting soldiers—"

Nick interrupted me. "In the Air Force they're called airmen."

"—so they could kill if needed . . ." My voice trailed off.

"But you already do support the military," he said. "With your taxes. By simply being a US citizen."

"But we don't have a choice when it comes to paying taxes. We do have a choice as far as joining the military."

Perhaps he was catching on because he nodded. "You're right."

Many people didn't understand Amish nonresistance ideology, how opposed we were to serving in the military. *We.* Even now, I still couldn't stop identifying with the Anabaptist movement—which originated in the early 1500s and led to the Mennonite, Hutterite, Amish, Brethren, and Apostolic churches.

Our ancestors fled Europe for America for freedom of religion. Freedom to follow our faith, based on Jesus's Sermon on the Mount. Freedom to turn the other cheek instead of striking back. Freedom to pledge our allegiance to God alone. Because of that, we didn't even have American flags in our schools.

Nick leaned closer. "Would you be okay with me joining, though?"

My head began to spin. What if I wasn't?

Before I could figure out what to say, the waiter approached with our appetizer. And then a speedboat racing down the Ohio River caught our attention. Perhaps Nick realized how uncomfortable the topic was for me because he shifted the conversation to my graduation ceremony the next afternoon. I was thankful my brother-in-law Gordon was willing to miss a day of work to come with my sister Marie and their fifteen-month-old son, Caden. Besides them, Nick would be the only other person there for me.

Nick then told me a story about something that had happened at work the night before. Many people still viewed nursing as a woman's profession because that was the way the media portrayed it. But more and more men were entering the profession, and many who did went into specialty fields, such as emergency, like Nick.

Plus, many had no idea about the rigorous training and expectations. While a doctor can go in and out of a hospital room, nurses provide constant care—dressing wounds, administering medicine, and providing life-saving treatment hour after hour.

"My supervisor said for you to come in and talk with her," Nick said. "We could stop by tonight."

"Oh, I don't want you to have to go into work, not on your night off." I took the last bite of appetizer, realizing I'd hardly tasted it.

"What better way to end the evening?" Nick smiled, but not as broadly as usual. "Each step forward is worth a little bit of a detour." I couldn't help but think he was talking about more than stopping by the hospital.

An hour and a half later, Nick pulled into the parking garage of the medical center. After he parked, he quickly walked around to my door and opened it.

As we walked toward the hospital, his earlier talk of joining the Air Force continued to nag at me, but I didn't say anything. My sisters often accused me of avoiding conflict, and they were right. I did. Even as he was dying of cancer, Dat cautioned me not to keep so much inside. "*Find someone in life you can talk with,*" he'd said to me. "*And talk things through with the Lord. He wants us to be honest—with Him, with ourselves, and with others.*"

It wasn't that I was dishonest with myself. I knew what I was thinking. I just didn't share it with others unless I absolutely had to. That typically led people to see me as calm and capable—and I was. Both characteristics helped me in caring for others.

As we headed toward the emergency department, we were silent, which was one of the things I appreciated about Nick. We could be together and not feel as if we needed to talk, yet there were other times we talked nonstop.

We'd met when we both took a certified nursing course back in Lancaster County. I was the Amish girl in class, wearing a cape dress, apron, and *Kapp*. He was the confident young man who drove an old Chevy pickup truck and never balked at holding a bedpan or cleaning a pressure sore. I'd noticed him right away.

For two years we were strictly friends. He was the one who taught me how to drive. He was the one who told me about the University of Pittsburgh's registered nurse program. He never encouraged me to leave the Amish, but told me—if I decided to—he'd do whatever he could to help.

It was at the end of his first year of nursing school that he gave me a ride to Pittsburgh, got me settled in my apartment, and helped me find a job at the care facility. Nick was the one who took me to thrift shops to buy jeans and sweaters. He was the one who helped me through chemistry and anatomy. He was the one who took me to the nondenominational church he attended. *Jah*, it was very different from what I was used to, but I found God and community and fellowship there, just in a different form.

A year after I'd moved to Pittsburgh, on a Sunday afternoon, he reached for my hand. It felt like the most natural thing in the world. Step by step, our relationship grew and progressed. Once he'd graduated and began working in the emergency department, our conversations shifted to the future. To places we'd both like to live and work. To master's and maybe even doctorate degrees. To the idea of marriage. To the possibility of children.

And yes, to that one time before tonight when he'd casually brought up the possibility of his joining the Air Force to quickly pay off his student loans. But then he'd made a joke out of it, comparing it to winning the lottery, and I hadn't taken him seriously.

As we stepped from the garage into the hospital, I let go of his arm. He patted his jacket pocket again as we both faced the hall. What if he had a ring in his pocket? I couldn't imagine being married to a military man.

I quickened my pace toward the emergency department. Although I'd done my emergency rotation at a smaller hospital, I had done several clinicals at the medical center and was familiar with the ED. I craned my neck as we passed each partition. A small boy getting his forehead stitched up. A teenage girl with a leg injury. An elderly man hooked up to an IV.

I followed Nick to the nurses' station. Several people greeted him. I could tell I wasn't the only one who was fond of him. Nick nodded toward a middle-aged woman who stood at a computer, squinting at the screen.

"Hi Sue," he said.

The woman looked up and beamed at Nick. "You sure look spiffy."

He grinned back. "This is Leisel. She's the one I was telling you about. Leisel, this is Sue, my supervisor."

She shook my hand and then said, "And you're looking for a job?"

"Yes," I answered. "I graduate tomorrow, and then I'm taking my boards in a couple of weeks."

"Sounds like you're a go-getter, just like Nick."

I smiled and said I hoped so.

"We don't hire many new grads, but it does happen." She pulled a card from her pocket. "Send me your résumé and then let me know when you pass your boards."

I took the card and thanked her profusely, wondering when exactly I should send my résumé. Not tonight. But tomorrow? Next week? The week after?

On the way back to the car, I thanked Nick for introducing me to Sue.

"Could we talk more soon?" he asked. "About the Air Force?"

I nodded. "After I take my boards." I didn't want to face such a big decision before then. I wanted to marry Nick, but if I didn't want to become a military wife, would he still want to marry me? I couldn't bear the thought of losing him. It was the last thing I needed to worry about before taking such a huge test.

As we walked toward the elevator, he put his arm around me and pulled me close. I breathed in his cologne, and then the antiseptic smell of the hospital. Two of my favorite things—Nick and medicine.

The graduation ceremony wasn't until three the next afternoon. Marie and Gordon planned to drive straight there and sit with Nick.

At one, I dressed in the white nursing uniform I'd purchased for graduation, not sure if I'd ever wear it again. It all depended on where I worked, but most hospital nurses wore scrubs.

I stood in my tiny bathroom and stared at myself in the mirror. Even though I usually pulled my hair back into a ponytail, I left it long. Not because I wanted to, but because I guessed most of the other girls would. My blue eyes seemed sad considering the happy occasion, and I realized how much I was missing Dat. He would have come to my graduation, but *Mamm* wouldn't have come with him. No part of me fantasized she'd show up with Marie. And I wouldn't want her to. She'd feel so uncomfortable, so out of place.

But Dat would have loved it.

It had been four years now since he'd passed, but it felt like yesterday.

I turned away from the mirror, grabbed my bag, and headed for my 1999 Ford Focus.

The day was overcast but fairly warm. A few drops of rain fell as I drove to Carnegie Music Hall, where the ceremony was being held, but it stopped by the time I arrived, which was, of course, early. Hopefully Marie and Gordon had arrived too, and we'd have a chance to chat.

I texted Marie and then climbed out of my car. As I passed through the front doors of the building, I marveled at the green marble and pillars in the foyer. I thought of the Carnegies in the late 1800s making their fortune in steel while my Anabaptist ancestors, the Bachmanns, continued to farm the land they'd owned since 1752. The families couldn't have been more different.

"Leisel!"

Paisley and her best friend, Autumn, came running toward me. The two had grown up together in Philadelphia, been best friends all through school, gone off to nursing school together, and would no doubt find jobs in the same hospital too.

"Your uniform looks so cute!" Autumn called out.

Paisley swung the honors cord around her neck. "Where's yours?"

After they both hugged me, I pulled my cord out of my purse. Paisley took it out of my hands and tenderly draped it around my neck.

The hardest thing for me in nursing school was figuring out how to interact with the other students. I felt so reserved and awkward and had no idea what to talk about. Studying with a group was what really forged friendships though. I had a gift for cementing facts to memory and being able to teach others.

And thanks to Paisley and Autumn, over the years I'd grown a little more comfortable. They'd made it their mission to acclimate me to the real world. With their help, I'd trained myself to compliment someone's purse or shoes. And then I'd listen when that person gave me details about brands and shops and costs even though I wasn't interested.

Over time, Paisley, Autumn, and the other students all learned about my past. Several said they thought I had an accent, although they couldn't place it. Others asked why I wore jeans instead of dresses. Several asked if I'd return to Lancaster County and practice nursing there.

I always patiently answered that I'd never go back to wearing dresses all the time and, no, I'd never return to Lancaster County to work or live, only to visit. And I tried as hard as I could not to speak with an accent.

Through it all, Paisley and Autumn were the two who seemed to accept me for who I was. And I felt I could ask them about confusing slang, such as *bae*, which stood for "before anyone else," which I found out when Autumn asked me, "So is Nick your bae?" She'd laughed at my confused expression and told me no one really used the term *bae* anymore, so not to worry about it. That left me even more baffled. I had to keep up with past slang, as well as current, and then remember not to use it? At least I thought that was what she meant.

And then there was *bye Felicia*, which seemed to mean waving good-bye to someone or something unimportant. And *throwing shade*, which meant to talk poorly about someone. Jah, Englisch slang was like another language altogether.

As I followed Paisley and Autumn toward our staging area, I checked my phone one more time. Nothing from Marie. I did have a text from Nick though. *So proud of you!* he wrote, adding three hearts after it.

When we entered the auditorium, I scanned the crowd and found Nick, but couldn't find Marie, Gordon, and Caden. I hoped they hadn't had car trouble on the four-hour trip from Lancaster County.

The ceremony went fairly quickly. To my surprise, I won the Compassionate Student Nurse Award. To my horror, I had to go up front to accept it, but I managed to remain composed, although my face must have been bright red.

When I walked across the stage for my diploma, I could hear Nick shout. Others clapped too, and several of my classmates cheered and called out my name. My face grew warm again as I took my diploma. But inside I was thrilled. I'd just realized my biggest dream.

I returned to my chair and searched the crowd again. Marie and her family definitely weren't in the audience.

I sat in a middle row of students and had to wait awhile to march out during the recessional. I called Marie as soon as I reached the marble floor of the lobby, surrounded by my classmates and their families hugging and snapping photos. But she didn't answer.

As I slipped my phone back into my pocket, Nick found me and gave me a hug. As he let go, he said, "I couldn't find Marie and Gordon."

"They're not here." I pulled my phone from my pocket again. "I just called Marie, but she didn't answer. I'll call Gordon." Just when I thought it was going to voicemail, my brother-in-law answered, sounding a little out of breath.

"We're in Lancaster," he said. "Marie is in the hospital. She's having stomach issues. They're running tests."

"When were you going to tell me?" I couldn't hide the hurt in my voice.

"I thought Jessica or your Mamm would have called last night."

"Last night? Marie's been in the hospital since then?"

"Actually since yesterday morning." He paused a moment and then said, "I'm sorry. Things have been a little crazy."

"Do you need me to come home? To help?"

"I'll talk to Marie," Gordon said.

"Where's Caden?" I asked.

"With my mom. She took the day off from school, but tomorrow she's playing piano in a wedding. . . ." His voice trailed off. "Sorry. I'm having a hard time keeping track of everything. I'll figure it out and call you back."

"All right." Once I ended the call, I told Nick what was going on.

"When will you leave?"

"I'll wait until Gordon calls me back."

"Are you sure?" I knew Nick would be halfway down the interstate by now if anyone in his family was in the hospital.

"Do you think I should go?" I did have a few days off after all.

He put his arm around me. "What do you want to do?"

I swallowed hard. I wasn't sure.

My phone rang again. It was Jessica. "Sorry I didn't call you last night. I thought Marie would." She must have just talked to Gordon. "We were hoping it wasn't a big deal, but now I'm not so sure. Can you come home? We need you."

– 2 –

Before I could slip out the front doors of the Carnegie Music Hall, Paisley and Autumn found me.

I always felt awkward in these Englisch group-hug situations, but I did my best to act as normal as possible and hug them back.

Paisley asked, "Are you coming to my graduation party tonight?"

I shook my head. "I need to go home. My sister is in the hospital."

"Uh-oh," Paisley said. "What's wrong?"

I quickly shared the information I had and added, "She was supposed to be here today. I just found out why she didn't come."

"Keep us posted," Autumn said. "And let us know when you get back. We'll get together and celebrate then."

I nodded. I wasn't sure what the two of them saw in me, but they always seemed sincere. "I'll be in touch," I said. "For sure." I hugged each of them again and told them good-bye. As I turned to go, Nick moved to my side.

"What can I do to help?" he asked as we jogged down the steps.

My mind spun in a million different directions.

"I could fill up your car with gas while you pack."

"That would be great," I said. "Would you check the air in the tires too?"

He nodded. "I can take your car right now—you take my pickup. I'll meet you back at your apartment. And then we should get something to eat before you leave."

"All right." I'd planned to make a couple of peanut butter sandwiches for the road, but maybe we could go to the little café near my place. That would be quick.

I drove Nick's pickup back to my apartment, and then, as soon as I was in the front door, changed into jeans and a sweatshirt. The first thing I threw into my bag was my state board study book. I'd done well on all of the practice tests and felt sure I'd pass but planned to review everything. I zipped up my bag just as Nick knocked on the door.

A half hour later, after doing my best to eat half a sandwich and a cup of soup, I told Nick good-bye on the sidewalk beside my car. "Let me know how Marie is," he said.

"I will."

He smiled, leaned down, and kissed me. I kissed him back. As we pulled away, Nick said, "Think about rescheduling your state boards."

I shook my head. "I won't need to. They're still over two weeks away. I'll be back long before then," I said. "Marie is young. This can't be anything too serious, right?" Marie had always been healthy. Hopefully the doctor who ordered the tests was simply being proactive.

He smiled at me, but we both knew there were no certainties, no matter one's age. We'd both seen horrible, unpredictable tragedies in our training and work.

I climbed into my car and waved. As I headed for the interstate and began the four-hour drive home, I thought of Marie's phone calls from about a month ago. She hadn't been feeling well. At first I suspected she was pregnant again, but she assured me she wasn't. I asked if she was having indigestion. Then I wondered if she had a food allergy. Or perhaps even an ulcer. I passively suggested she go to the doctor. I'd been so absorbed in finishing up my classes and clinicals and work that I hadn't followed up to see if she had.

As I sped over the bridge spanning the Ohio River and then on to I-376, I took a couple of deep breaths, and then finally said a prayer for Marie, Gordon, and Caden. Then for Jessica and her husband, Silas, and their little girl, Ruby, named after one of our ancestors from the Revolutionary War.

Then I said a prayer for my Mamm and our strained relationship. It had gotten a little better after Marie left the church and joined Gordon's Mennonite congregation because, to Mamm and the church, what Marie did was worse than my never joining the Amish at all. Jah, Mamm was annoyed with me, but she wasn't shunning me. Of course I took no joy in Mamm treating me better because she was now treating Marie worse.

After watching Mamm constantly push Jessica away while she held Marie too tightly, I'd learned early in life to avoid my mother. I spent as much time as I could with Dat and sidestepped Mamm whenever possible.

Now, each time I came home, she'd chastise me about leaving and admonish me to come home, sometimes even saying I was in danger of God's wrath and that I'd been created to be with family, in my community. She told me more than once *Englischers* would never "be there for me" the way my family and the Amish would have been if I hadn't left. She was still predicting God would punish me and someday, once I acknowledged the truth, I'd come to my senses and return to both my church and family.

"You'll never make it on your own," she'd say. *"God will do whatever it takes to bring you back. And if you marry an Englischer, God will never bless your marriage."*

Each time, I would ignore her. I didn't believe God was as punitive as Mamm, but honestly her words made me doubt. When I was tired or discouraged or overwhelmed, there were times when her words played over and over, like a podcast streaming in my brain. Maybe I couldn't make it on my own. Maybe she was right.

As a result, I'd gradually built my world atop an invisible line that I tried to navigate. I would keep my faith and some beliefs particular to the Anabaptists—nonresistance being the biggie—but I would also embrace my education and my future professional life.

And in the end Mamm's predictions of my failure simply made me want to be as self-sufficient as possible and not rely on anyone. I could make it on my own—well, with a little help from Nick.

Because I was so close to becoming a nurse, I guessed that now she might be even more direct about me abandoning my dream and joining the church. It was ironic that Jessica, the daughter Mamm had never gotten along with, was now the only one who was Amish. And that it was Marie and I who'd so thoroughly disappointed our mother.

Outside of Pittsburgh, the landscape quickly changed to emerald green hillsides and the occasional farmhouse and barn. It wasn't quite as idyllic as Lancaster County, but it was beautiful, and even with my anxiety about Marie, I felt myself relax.

Still, I'd loved living in Pittsburgh from the very beginning. It was so vibrant, so alive in a different way. So different from my childhood. Mamm didn't understand how I could tolerate the sound of traffic and living in such close proximity to hundreds of thousands of other people. But the constant hum of cars and trucks and people gave me energy—especially the people. Almost everything about humans fascinated me. Their bodies. Their genetics. Their histories.

Based on my social awkwardness, one might think others fascinated me in only a clinical way, but that wasn't true. Their motivations, responses, emotions, and reactions also intrigued me. I'd never met a person for whom I didn't feel compassion, which I think I learned from my father.

Dat had had no formal medical training, but he had lots of experience, first in a Mennonite clinic in Vietnam back in 1967, then as a sort of healthcare consultant. Now, as a trained nurse, I couldn't recommend freelancing the way he did, although he had never had any problems with his practice. He'd done a lot of research on vitamins, supplements, and natural remedies, and he eventually began sharing them with friends and relatives. Soon, friends of friends and friends of relatives started asking him for advice. They'd come to the house and he'd talk them through their ailments and then either recommend vitamins and supplements or encourage them to see a chiropractor or a physician. Most took his advice, and it seemed he always erred on the side of caution.

By the time I was eight or so, I was trying to eavesdrop on his conversations with people. Eventually, he brought me into his study as a helper. At first I'd inventoried his vitamins and supplements. Later he had me doing research for him.

When I was seventeen, he allowed me to take the certified nursing course. When I decided to get my GED, I told him and he didn't forbid it. Even though I never told him about my aspirations to become a nurse, I think he suspected it. I'd planned to tell him about my dream to go to college—and that I'd applied and been accepted—but then he fell ill.

He'd denied it, saying his cough was just allergies. After far too long, I convinced him to go to the doctor.

He was diagnosed with lung cancer and died four months later. I'd cared for him, delaying my admission to nursing school by a semester. I didn't tell him my plan, not wanting to add to his worries.

Caring for him cemented my desire to go into nursing. I knew it was my calling.

Traffic was light, and my trip was going quickly, but by the time I reached the Somerset exit I was drowsy. I'd worked nights and gone to school during the day and slept weird hours for the last four years. It had gotten me through school with fewer student loans than I would have otherwise; however, I was almost always sleepy.

I pulled into the parking lot of a diner where I sometimes stopped on my way to Lancaster County. Dusk was falling and the evening had grown cool. I walked into the diner, inhaling the strong scent of coffee. I already felt more alert as I ordered a cup to go at the counter.

As the waitress took my money, someone called out from the back of the diner. "Terri!"

One of the other waitresses headed toward the voice and then yelled, "Call 9-1-1!"

I started to dial but then realized I had no idea what the address of the diner was.

"I've got it." The waitress pulled her phone from her apron pocket.

I jumped off the stool and headed toward the back. A man in the last booth had his head slumped to the side, propped against the wall. A woman with long dark hair had her hands on either side of his face. Two children sat on the other bench, frozen.

"My name is Leisel. I'm a nurse," I said as I approached. *Almost a nurse, anyway*, I thought. "May I check on him?"

The woman nodded and slid out of the booth, her big brown eyes wild. "He was talking with us a second ago and then he just stopped."

My own heart raced as I slid into the booth and felt for a carotid pulse. I couldn't find one. "Did he mention anything? Chest pains? A headache? Does he have a medical condition?"

The woman shook her head. "His blood pressure runs a little high, that's all."

I caught sight of the children's faces. A boy and girl, probably ten and eight or so. They seemed more confused than frightened.

I pointed to the two men in the next booth. I hoped my voice was calmer than I felt. "Could you help me?" I was five feet three inches and one hundred pounds. I'd never get the guy out of the booth on my own. "We need to get him on the floor."

As the men moved him, I asked Terri, the waitress who had called 9-1-1 if there was an AED on-site.

She gave me a puzzled look.

"An automated external defibrillator," I explained.

She shook her head.

That was a shame. I asked Terri to take the children to the front of the restaurant, and thankfully the kids followed her without protesting. The woman told me her husband's name was Sonny. "He's only forty-one." As she spoke, my palms grew sweaty and my pulse quickened even more. He was too young to die.

Once he was flat on the linoleum, my training took over, and I recruited the two men to help with the chest compressions.

I showed the first exactly how to position his hands, hoping it wasn't obvious mine were shaking. Then I did the breathing, two to every fifteen compressions, thinking of four years ago when my brother Arden had had a heart attack at Dat's burial and Jessica and I performed CPR. I'd only done it twice since then, both on residents in the care facility without DNR orders.

At the center, I could get up on the bed and get a good bounce going, but not on a diner floor. I didn't have the strength these men did. I had to coach them to push harder and faster. I knew it was possible they might break the man's ribs, but better that than not getting his heart started. All the while I was aware of the man's wife standing to the side.

I gave the man two more breaths. It was probably my imagination, but it seemed Sonny's lips were already cooling. Even with compressions shifting his body around, he was lifeless.

I checked his pulse again.

I'd never felt anything so beautiful. Sonny's heart had started beating. As the emergency team arrived, a seed of hope began to grow in my own chest. After the next cycle of CPR, the two men and I moved back so the paramedics could get to work.

Immediately, they started bagging him, forcing oxygen into his lungs through a bag-valve mask. As they readied to transport him to the ambulance, I asked Sonny's wife if she wanted someone to drive her and the kids to the hospital.

"No, I'll do it," she said.

"Do you live around here?" I asked.

She nodded.

"Can you call someone to meet you?" I nodded toward the children, who still stood beside Terri near the front door of the restaurant. It was always good to have another adult around in an emergency.

"Yes, my parents." She appeared calm, but I could recognize the signs of shock. She certainly wasn't frozen, but she had that deer-in-the-headlights look. "Will he be all right?"

"His heart is beating." I knew nearly ninety percent of people who suffered out-of-hospital cardiac arrests died, but if the cardiac chain of survival was enacted in the first few minutes, it could double or triple a person's chance of survival. Then again, maybe he hadn't had a heart attack. Maybe he'd had a stroke or an aneurysm or something else. "I'll pray he'll be all right," I said.

She nodded and then moved toward her children. She urged them through the door to the parking lot before the paramedics would pass by them with their dad on a stretcher.

I thanked the two men, who had returned to their booth. They nodded. Both seemed a little dazed.

The waitress came toward me with my cup of coffee and change, and then we both watched out the window as the paramedics loaded Sonny into the ambulance and the mom and kids climbed into their car.

"Hopefully he'll make it," Terri said.

I nodded.

"Where are you headed?" she asked.

"Lancaster."

"Can I get you another cup of coffee?"

"No, thank you," I answered. Now that my adrenaline levels were soaring, I hardly needed the first. But I took it anyway.

As I walked out the door, Sonny's wife drove off and the little girl waved at me. I waved back. I'd probably never know how things turned out for their family. But no matter a girl's age, losing her father could change her life forever. I prayed that wouldn't be the case.

It wasn't until an hour later, as darkness swallowed the landscape, that it hit me. The man in the diner—Sonny—might be dead now. His wife, a widow. His children, fatherless. He was young. And yet, in the moment it took for his head to hit his shoulder, his whole life might have changed. And his family's.

My clammy hands gripped the steering wheel. I wasn't one to cry, and I didn't now. Instead, I swallowed several times and then took a deep breath, willing my trembling chin to stop. It wasn't just Sonny. It was Mr. Weber too.

And it was Marie. She had to be all right. She had a husband and baby. I contemplated calling Nick and talking with him as I drove, but I didn't want the conversation to land on the Air Force. Instead, I continued on in the dark, passing trucks and cars, zipping down the interstate. The darkness felt so heavy, so oppressive.

It was nearly eleven o'clock by the time I reached the hospital in Lancaster. Once I parked in the garage, I texted Nick to let him know I'd arrived. He texted me back right away, asking what took so long. I hadn't been delayed that much, but I texted back about the man at the diner. *Sonny.* But it was easier if I thought of him as *the man.*

A half second later, Nick called as I entered the hospital lobby and marched across the polished linoleum toward the elevators.

"Leisel," he said, after I'd told him the whole story, "that's crazy."

"I know, right?"

"Do you think he made it?"

I paused before the elevator bank. "He had a pulse by the time the paramedics arrived, so maybe."

"I hope so," Nick said. "This is too much. With what's going on with Marie and Mr. Weber dying too." Nick's voice calmed me. He knew me so well.

"I know, right?" I said again. "I'll text you tomorrow," I added, "once I find out how Marie is."

"Thanks," he said. "I hope you get some rest."

"You too," I answered.

After we said our farewells, I slipped my phone into my sweatshirt pocket and hit the Up button for the elevator. A few minutes later, I poked my head into Marie's room. Gordon slept in a recliner next to the window. For the moment, Marie was asleep in the bed, a white sheet pulled up to her chin.

I asked the nurse in the hall for an extra blanket, set my alarm for six, and knelt to say my prayers, concentrating mostly on Marie, although I said one for Sonny too. And Mr. Weber's daughter. Then I settled in a chair in the waiting room. I'd always had the gift of being able to fall asleep anywhere and anytime—it was the only way I'd made it through the last four years—but this time it took me quite a while. Marie was just down the hall. Sonny had either lived—or died. Mr. Weber's daughter was now planning his funeral instead of his ninety-third birthday party. Nick was in Pittsburgh, wanting to join the Air Force. I felt unsettled to my core.

When my alarm buzzed, it took me a minute to remember where I was, then it all came back to me. I unfolded myself from the chair and headed to the bathroom, where I brushed my teeth and washed my face.

When I entered Marie's room, a nurse was checking her vitals and Gordon was gone. Hopefully he was grabbing a cup of coffee and some breakfast from the cafeteria.

I stepped up to the bed. "Marie," I said. "I'm here."

"Leisel?"

I reached for her free hand. "What's going on?"

Her long hair was pulled back in a low ponytail and draped over her shoulder. Her face was pale and her dark eyes dull. "My stomach problems got really bad Thursday night. I couldn't keep anything down. Gordon took me to urgent care. We thought I had appendicitis, but the doctor said that wasn't what it was and sent me here."

"What tests have they done?"

"Some blood work. An endoscopy," she answered.

"What are they checking for?"

"Cancer."

I gripped her hand. From what she'd told me before, I hadn't expected that at all. Stomach cancer could be swift and furious. What if I'd checked back with her about going to the doctor a month ago? "When will they have the results of the endoscopy back?"

"It could be a week but hopefully a little sooner. They'll call with the results."

That sounded like forever.

"I was dehydrated," she said, "but hopefully I can go home today."

Marie introduced me to her nurse. "This is my sister, Leisel. I want her to have access to my chart."

The nurse said she'd get the form to make that possible.

"I'm so glad you're here." Marie squeezed my hand. "I'm sorry I didn't make it to your graduation and that you had to leave right after. But thank you. Just having you here makes me feel better."

— 3 —

Later in the morning, Gordon went home to shower and pick up Caden. I said I could go hang out with the little guy, but Marie insisted I stay with her. "Jessica is at Mamm's with Ruby." The children were a year apart and becoming the best of friends. "Gordon will take Caden over there."

"Is Mamm all right with that?" I asked.

"Well, she's never thrilled when I stop by, but I don't think she'll take that out on Caden."

I hoped not.

Marie had signed the paper giving me permission to read her chart, so I scanned through the electronic document as she slept. She first started having stomach pains two months ago. I winced. She'd had them for a month before she'd called me. And then she hadn't gone to her doctor until two weeks ago. Why hadn't I followed up with her?

She'd lost ten pounds, but the doctor thought perhaps it was postpartum weight. He did a pregnancy test, as any good provider would. It was negative. He also ordered tests for H. pylori bacteria, which can cause ulcers. That test had come back negative also. He asked her to make a follow-up appointment, but she hadn't. Instead, Gordon had taken her to urgent care. At that point, she'd been vomiting for twelve hours and had stomach pains, which is why they thought it might be her appendix.

The urgent care doctor gave her another pregnancy test, which also came back negative, and prescribed anti-nausea meds. The doctor then sent her on to the emergency room, thinking it might be her appendix too. However, the emergency room doctor ruled that out right away. The chart said that Marie hadn't had much appetite for "a few months." By the time she was weighed yesterday, she'd lost another five pounds in the last two weeks.

The hospitalist had then ordered an ultrasound, which showed a small mass in her stomach. That was why he'd ordered the test for cancer.

The rest of the chart listed her vitals, along with the anti-nausea meds and painkillers that had been administered. Her blood pressure ran low, but her heartbeat and oxygen levels were normal.

I watched Marie as she slept, praying that she didn't have cancer.

God had some lesson for all of us in this. Perhaps one of the purposes of this scare was to get me in that diner, to care for the husband and father.

Surely Marie didn't have cancer. The mass could easily be benign.

I took the opportunity to text Nick, bringing him up to date. When I didn't hear back from him, I figured he was sleeping.

When Marie woke, she said she felt much better. "When will they let me go home?"

I told her I didn't know, but when the nurse returned, she said the doctor wanted Marie to spend another night. Her eyes filled with tears, but she agreed. I knew how much she wanted to get home to Caden, but her health was far more important right now.

After the nurse left, Marie asked me to call Gordon on my cell. "Then when he returns, you should go home," Marie said. "Get some food. Get some sleep. Hug Caden for me and sing him a song."

"How about I hum to him? No one wants to hear me sing, not even a baby. I wasn't blessed with your beautiful voice," I joked, trying to lighten her mood.

She barely smiled. As I stepped out into the hall to call Gordon, I wondered how long it had been since she felt well enough to sing.

Two hours later, I drove east toward the Bachmann farm, dreading seeing Mamm. Would she blame Marie's illness on her leaving the church? And predict something as bad—or worse—for me?

As I left the city and then reached the farmland, the fields sparkled with new growth. I relaxed a little, turning off the highway toward home.

Home. Even though I dreaded Mamm's reaction to me, my soul stirred as I drove around the curve in the lane and our white house came into view. Tulips bloomed in the front flowerbeds, and Mamm had already filled the pots on the porch with geraniums. Two black rocking chairs, Mamm's and Dat's, sat on the porch. As children, we played around their feet on warm evenings while Mamm read the latest edition of the *Budget* and Dat read one of his medical journals. There was never a question of us being physically safe, getting enough food, or having a warm house. We were well cared for—not like some children I'd seen during my training rotations.

Of course, Mamm's negativity hung all around us. We had an older sister, Rebecca, who died when she was five, shortly after Jessica was born. Our brothers, who were teenagers at the time, were left in charge of her. Mamm was in the hospital with newborn Jessica, and Dat was on his way home.

Rebecca had floundered in the pond and was rescued by our brother, Amos. No one realized she'd taken water into her lungs—she'd seemed absolutely fine. But then she'd died in the middle of the night, and it wasn't until the next morning that Amos and his twin Arden discovered she was gone. *Dry drowning* was the term. I'd researched it in the set of encyclopedias Dat kept in his study.

I wanted to know how common dry drowning was and what could be done to prevent it. The medical term was *pulmonary edema*. It was rare—only one to two percent of drownings. And from what I'd read, the victim usually had trouble breathing right away, which Rebecca hadn't. From what I'd heard, she'd gone to sleep soon after the incident in the pond. The other symptoms were coughing, chest pain, trouble breathing, and feeling extremely tired. Perhaps the last one had been predominant and had sent her to bed early. To her fate.

I shivered. A life could be lost so easily. Dat had seemed to accept Rebecca's death as most Amish would—after all, the Lord giveth and the Lord taketh away—but I sensed Mamm had struggled with it her entire life. We all agreed that it broke her heart. I felt sad about that, and through the years I realized the event had not only hurt Mamm deeply, but it had shaped our lives too. Jessica constantly wondered what our lives, and specifically our mother's, would have been like if Rebecca hadn't died.

Mamm blamed Amos for Rebecca's death, which eventually led him to leave both our home and the Amish. That had been another tragedy in our family. While Jessica dug for answers about Mamm's behavior, I'd done my best not to bring up

Rebecca or Amos at all. Better to avoid those topics than cause more conflict.

I parked my car to the left of the house and then sat for a moment, my eyes shifting from the windmill to the woods to the barn. Finally, I climbed out and grabbed my bag out of the back seat. A bird chirped in the pine tree, and I turned my head toward the sun. The day was warm and bright. A perfect spring day, accented with the scent of soil and cows, and a cool breeze.

Off to my right, my nephew Milton drove a team of mules, plowing the field. As I started toward the porch, I heard voices from the backyard and headed around the side of the house. Jessica stood with her hands on her hips. "Ruby, share with Caden."

The two children sat in a sandbox, both with their hands on a red bucket. Both had honey-blond hair and dark eyes. Ruby's hair was divided into two pigtails and she wore a miniature Amish dress, while Caden wore sweatpants and a sweatshirt.

Jessica bent down and picked up a blue bucket, handing it to Ruby.

The little girl shook her head and stuck out her lower lip.

"Hi!" I called out, hoping to distract my niece and nephew. "How is everyone?"

Caden grinned and Ruby yanked the bucket away. My nephew's smile turned to a pout and then a sputter.

I dropped my bag, hurried to the sandbox, and scooped him up, brushing my face over his flyaway hair. But then Ruby started reaching for me and crying. I didn't get home a lot, but it was often enough that the children remembered me now. Jessica picked up her daughter, shaking her head as she did. She put her arm around me.

I'd always admired my oldest sister. She'd been kind and

caring toward me growing up. She pursued her love of farming even when everyone but Dat discouraged her, and she'd stood up to our brother, Arden, and Bishop Jacobs when not even a man in her position would have. Then she left the Amish and lived an Englisch life for a time, only to return and marry her sweetheart, Silas. Jessica was one of the strongest people I knew.

I told her hello and put my arm around her too, giving her a hug.

Aenti Suz's door was open, and she must have heard me because she came out of her *Dawdi Haus* onto her little porch and called out a hello. She wore a pale blue dress and a Kapp over her silvery hair. She shielded her eyes as she asked, "How is Marie doing?"

"They're keeping her another night," I said. "She's on an IV—fluids and pain meds."

"What about the tests?"

"It will be a few days before they know the results."

Aenti Suz made a *tsk* sound and stepped out onto the lawn. Ruby reached for her and giggled. Everyone loved Aenti Suz.

Jessica let the little girl fall into our aunt's arms.

I bounced Caden up and down and said, "I'm going to get a shower and some sleep. Then I'll see if Gordon wants me to spend the night at the hospital. Maybe this little guy needs some time with one of his parents."

"He seems to be doing okay," Jessica said. "But jah, he's probably starting to feel pretty confused. This is the first time he's ever been away from Marie."

He reached for my mouth. "Oh no you don't," I said, grabbing his sandy hand. "Let's brush you off first."

"I was just going to take them in for a snack." Jessica turned toward Aenti Suz. "Want to come in with us?"

She nodded. As I picked up my bag with my free hand, Jessica stepped to the sandbox and put the cover over the top. Silas had added a few kid-friendly activities to Mamm's yard for the younger grandkids. The sandbox. A small play structure. And a swing set.

As Jessica and I washed the sand off the kids in the downstairs bathroom, she told me Mamm was resting. Mixed emotions filled me as I carried Caden into the kitchen. I always felt that way when I came home. It still felt like home, and yet it wasn't. Someday Arden and his family would move into it. Perhaps Mamm would live with them, but it would never be the home it was to my sisters and me when Dat was alive.

I breathed deeply—Mamm's lavender lotion, along with hints of cinnamon and coffee and scouring cleanser. The countertops in the kitchen sparkled, as did the linoleum floor.

There were two high chairs at the end of the long oak table, where we deposited the kids. Jessica quickly gave each a cracker to chew on while she made peanut butter and grape jelly sandwiches for them.

Aenti Suz had started a fresh pot of coffee. Perhaps the strong smell of it brought Mamm down the stairs.

"Leisel?" she said as she rounded the corner from the staircase.

"Jah, Mamm, it's me." I stayed put. If people thought I wasn't affectionate, they'd think my Mamm was the coldest person they'd ever met. Dat would hug us, which wasn't really the Amish way, but Mamm rarely would. Most Amish felt hugging was too demonstrative. Others saw it as indulgent. I remember sitting on Mamm's lap as a child while she read to us, but that was the only kind of physical contact I could recall. I didn't even remember her brushing my hair—Jessica did that for me.

When Jessica left the church, Mamm felt shamed, as if others were judging her for not being able to keep her daughter from leaving. When Marie left the church, it wasn't that Mamm felt responsible. It was more that she felt devastated that she'd lost a friend, probably her best friend. I imagine she felt betrayed too.

There were many Amish people who lived a kind life, but the same teaching that inspired most to serve others led some to self-righteousness. They strove so hard to live apart from the world that they measured every difference and then held it up for everyone to see. Marie had learned that straight from Mamm. Our mother had Marie under her influence for all of those years, which had made Marie self-righteous, petty, and hard to live with. When Marie left the Amish, she became the caring and compassionate person she'd been as a child.

Mamm stepped into the kitchen and asked about Marie, and I repeated what I'd told Aenti Suz.

"Well, I expected the news wouldn't be good," Mamm said. "There had to be some sort of consequences after she turned her back on God."

"That's not what happened," Jessica said.

Mamm made a noise in the back of her throat.

I pressed my lips together.

Aenti Suz spoke up, changing the topic. "Bethel, how about a cup of coffee?" She pulled a mug out of the cupboard.

"*Denki*," Mamm answered. She turned back toward Jessica. "Is Caden staying with you tonight?"

"We're not sure yet." Jessica took the sandwiches to the kids and put them on their trays. "Leisel will talk to Gordon, and we'll figure it out."

Mamm sat down at the table. "Just to make this clear, I'm not up to caring for Caden."

"Is something wrong?" I asked.

Mamm wrinkled her nose. "I've been tired, is all. I can't keep up with him."

"He can stay with me," Aenti Suz said. She was at least ten years older than Mamm.

"Denki," Jessica said. "Or he can come home with me. We'll figure it out once we find out what Gordon wants."

"What about Marie?" I asked. "Where do you think she should stay, once she's released?"

"Wherever you are." Jessica wrinkled her brow and sighed. "I'm assuming a lot. That's if you can stay."

"I can," I answered.

"It's not that I don't want her at my house," Jessica continued. "It's just that I don't have the gift of taking care of others like you do. You've always been able to assess a situation and figure out what needs to be done without ever losing your cool. I'm still amazed at how well you nursed Dat, essentially all by yourself."

Caring for Dat had been such a tender time for me. I wouldn't have had it any other way.

"If you can take care of Marie the way you did Dat," Jessica said, "that would certainly be what's best for her."

I nodded. Determined to stick around for at least a couple of days, I excused myself to take a shower. After I said my prayers, I crawled into the bed I used to share with Marie when we were little. I'd sleep for an hour and then call Gordon.

Caden and I spent the night in the old upstairs sewing room, where there was a crib and a bed, and Gordon stayed with Marie at the hospital. The next day, Gordon and I made the decision that the best place for Marie to recover would be the farm. Gordon, Marie, and Caden lived in a one-room apartment up three flights of stairs in downtown Lancaster, in a building with no elevator. Space-wise, it made the most sense to have her come home to the farm so I could take care of her.

It was Sunday morning, but it was an "off" Sunday, so there were no services. Mamm wasn't one to visit another district's service or really even visit anyone at all. After I spoke with Gordon and found out that Marie was getting out of the hospital for sure, I headed over to Mamm's, leaving Caden with Aenti Suz.

"That's not a good idea," Mamm said immediately when I told her Marie would be coming out to the farm. "Marie will want to be at home, where she's comfortable."

"No," I said. "She needs our help."

"You can go stay there. Or women from their church will help."

I bit my tongue.

"She can't expect to come home just because she's ill. She should have thought this through three years ago, before she left."

"Mamm—"

"Don't 'Mamm' me." She stood in front of me with her arms crossed. "I'm still your mother and this is still my home. I decide who stays here and who doesn't. If you press me on this, I'll talk with Arden. He won't want Marie here either. She left—she can't come back at her convenience. Bishop Jacobs will support my decision too."

My nostrils flared, but I didn't respond. Why had I expected anything else from her? Of course Mamm wouldn't let Marie come home. She'd left the church. She'd been shunned.

I headed out the back door to Aenti Suz's. She sat on her little porch, Caden on her lap. She was stroking his arm as she sang to him. He leaned against her, his eyes growing heavy.

Speaking softly, I told my aunt what Mamm had said.

"Then Marie will stay here," she said. "And Caden and Gordon too. I'll take care of Marie."

For the second time in the last twenty-four hours, tears stung my eyes. I swallowed hard. "But what about Mamm? And Arden? And the bishop?"

"I'm not worried about any of them," Aenti Suz said. "Don't you worry either."

I couldn't imagine what Aenti Suz would say to change Bishop Jacobs's mind if he was against Marie staying on the farm. Avoiding the subject, I offered, "I'll sleep on your couch and care for Marie."

"You need to go back to Pittsburgh."

"I have a couple more days off work."

"All right," Aenti Suz answered. "I do have a couple of commitments coming up. Between the two of us, we should be able to care for Marie and Caden."

I left a message for Jessica on the answering machine located in their barn and asked if she, Silas, and Ruby wanted to come over in the afternoon to see Marie. I figured having Jessica around to keep Mamm in line might be a good idea, especially if Arden and Vi decided to stop by and make trouble.

My intuition paid off. Not long after Gordon arrived with Marie and she was settled in Aenti Suz's spare bedroom with Gordon and Caden at her side, Arden and Vi did stop by. Unfortunately Jessica, Silas, and Ruby hadn't arrived yet. I could hear Arden and Vi through the open door on the porch, talking with Aenti Suz and Mamm.

"Why is she staying here?" Arden asked.

"Why wouldn't she stay here?" Aenti Suz replied.

"Bishop Jacobs won't allow it."

I stepped closer to the door.

Aenti Suz exhaled and smiled sweetly.

Vi's eyes narrowed. "Where is Caden?"

"Inside, with Marie."

"Do they know what's wrong yet?" she asked.

"*Nee*," Mamm answered.

Vi's voice dropped as she said, "I'm still thinking she's pregnant—"

I stepped to the door. "She's definitely not. That's been ruled out quite a few times."

Vi just shrugged as if she didn't believe me and knew more than the doctors. If Marie hadn't left the church, Arden and Vi's daughter Brenda, who was thirteen, would help with Caden, but they wouldn't allow any of their five children to be around Marie.

Thankfully, Jessica and Silas arrived right then, and Arden told Jessica they had farm business to discuss. My mouth dropped open, but I quickly closed it. Normally Amish folk didn't talk about business on Sundays.

"What's up?" Jessica asked.

"The price of milk keeps going down. We're no longer making a profit."

"We already talked about this."

"Not really," Arden answered. "We didn't come up with a solution."

"Then let's do some brainstorming, but later."

"Sell the herd," he said. "It's the only thing we can do."

Jessica sighed. "And then what?"

"Figure out a crop that will make a profit."

"Well, I hope we don't have to sell the herd." Jessica set Ruby down, and she toddled into the Dawdi Haus to find Caden. "Do you want to talk more later?"

Arden nodded sharply.

He and Silas headed toward the barn, while Vi went back over to her house. Neither she nor Arden had said hello to Marie and Gordon.

Aenti Suz slipped back into her house, and I gave Jessica a questioning look.

She shrugged. "Several area farmers have sold their herds. It's been this way for a year. I just keep thinking maybe if we hang on . . ." Her expression was as serious as I'd ever seen it. I guessed if our Dat hadn't set up a system through his lawyer that Arden and Jessica had to agree on farm decisions that Arden would have sold the herd by now. And the woods. And leased the pasture for fracking. Thank goodness Jessica was looking out for the land.

When Silas returned from the milking, Arden wasn't with him. "I thought he wanted to talk," Jessica said.

Silas shrugged. "He said he was tired and wanted to go home. He'll talk with you soon." I hoped he wasn't headed over to the bishop's to talk about Marie staying at Aenti Suz's. I wouldn't put it past him. He certainly seemed willing to choose what rules he wanted to follow.

The old Jessica would have been eager to hash things out as soon as possible. But the new Jessica just shook her head a little and scooped Ruby into her arms. Motherhood had softened her fiery temper.

Over the next two days, I cared for Marie and Caden, texted Nick now and then, and tried to stay out of Mamm's way. Gordon returned to work, not wanting to use up all his sick and vacation days in case he needed them later.

It took both Aenti Suz and me to care for Caden and Marie. I was also trying to help Mamm with her housework and cooking so she would be more amenable to having Marie on the farm, but I still expected Bishop Jacobs to show up at the Dawdi Haus door at any moment.

On Tuesday, I called Rita, telling her I needed another couple of days off. She wasn't happy with me, so I kept the call short and professional and managed to get off the phone before she started to complain.

On Wednesday morning, as I colored with Caden at the table while Aenti Suz was off helping a widow in the district, Marie had a call on her cell phone. She glanced down at the screen and then up at me. "It's the doctor."

I held my breath as she answered it.

She said "I see" a couple of times and then looked up and made a writing motion with her hand.

I stood, scooping up Caden and the coloring book and the red crayon, and went to Marie's side, handing her the book and crayon.

Marie jotted a few things down on the last page and then said, "Thank you."

After she ended the call, she met my eyes. "They have the results back from the endoscopy. It's cancer."

"Oh, Marie." I collapsed beside her. She took Caden from me and held him tight. His eyes grew wide, but he didn't fuss, as if sensing the seriousness of the moment.

I pointed toward the coloring book, which had fallen to the floor. "What's next?"

"The hospital doctor referred me to an oncologist. Someone from his office will call me today to make an appointment. They may do surgery and then chemo. Maybe even radiation. We'll have to see what the oncologist recommends."

I reached for my sister's hand. I wanted to say, *"You'll get through this. You're young."* But there were no guarantees. So much depended on whether the cancer had spread.

A sob rose up in Marie, and I let go of her hand and pulled her close.

She leaned her head on my shoulder. Another sob shook her, but then she was still. Softly she said, "I want to go home."

"Why?"

She looked toward the front door and said, "Mamm's coldness is getting really hard to take. Vi and Arden's too. I could hear them the other day when they were on the porch, but none of them have come to see me."

"Aenti Suz and I want you here." The farm wasn't where I wanted to be either, but I did want to take care of Marie. And Aenti Suz made the aloofness of the other family members bearable.

She met my eyes again. "You have your boards to take. I don't want you giving them up for me."

"Don't worry, I'll still take them." Belatedly, I remembered that I needed to send my résumé to Nick's boss.

"What about your job?"

"I called my supervisor and took a few more days off. I'll probably go ahead and quit—I'll have a nursing job soon anyway."

"I don't want you to quit before you have another job," Marie said. "I'll be all right."

She couldn't take care of Caden and get any rest, let alone have surgery and go through chemo. I squeezed Marie's shoulder. "Let's take it one day at a time."

Marie dropped her voice and glanced toward the front door as if Mamm might come charging through it. "If it's not practical to go home, I'm wondering if we should go to Randi's house." That was Gordon's mother. "It wouldn't be as stressful there."

If Marie decided to go there, would Randi be okay with me staying too, or would I need to stay at Aenti Suz's and drive back and forth? On one hand, the practical one, it made no sense that Mamm had a six-bedroom house to herself while we were all crowded in the small Dawdi Haus. Of course, on the other hand, the Amish one, it made perfect sense.

"I'm sorry this is so stressful," I said. I was. Marie had never had a strained relationship with Mamm, never given Mamm a moment of worry, until she left the Amish, joined the Mennonites, got a job at the shelter in downtown Lancaster, and married Gordon.

"I'm not going to call Gordon and tell him about the cancer yet. I'll wait until after work."

"He'd want to know," I said. "As soon as possible."

"I'll wait and see if he calls during his lunch break then."

Caden began to fuss.

"What about Mamm? When will you tell her?"

Marie frowned. "After I tell Gordon, I guess."

After lunch, as I put Caden down for his nap, Gordon called Marie. When I came out of the bedroom, Marie was off the phone but resting on the couch with her eyes closed.

I'd never missed Dat more than I did as I stared down at her. I stepped out onto the front porch, closed the front door softly, and sat down on Aenti Suz's single step, turning my head toward the sun.

Tears stabbed at my eyes, but I wasn't one to cry. I quickly blinked them away, but a lump formed in my throat. A wad of emotions. It wasn't like a *globus pharyngeus* that could leave a scratchy or throbbing sensation in a person's throat.

As early as I can remember, science and medicine fascinated me. When I was eight or nine, Dat taught me the periodic table. He told me that everything on earth was made from those elements. *"God gave us what we needed for building everything from tables to barns to feeding and caring for our bodies."*

As he taught me the elements, I named the chickens after them. *Hydrogen. Helium. Lithium. Beryllium. Boron. Carbon.* The names went on and on. I began reading about the individual elements in our set of encyclopedias. Then about food in Dat's nutritional magazines. Then I started reading his medical journals.

For my twelfth Christmas, he gave me an oversized *Gray's Anatomy*, which he'd found at a secondhand store. Mamm, her face pinched, clearly hadn't approved. When she wasn't around, Dat and I studied bones—long, short, flat, irregular, pneumatic, and sesamoid. Then joints. And muscles. The cardiovascular, lymphatic, respiratory, and nervous systems. Endocrine, digestive, and urinary systems. Skin, fascia, and connective tissue.

During the day, Dat would point to different bones on his body and I'd give him the name. *Clavicle. Tibia. Scapula.* He'd talk about the larynx, trachea, and bronchi as we walked through the woods. One time at supper, he began talking about the digestive system, but Mamm put a stop to it, insisting it wasn't "table talk." I'd laughed. How could it not be? Our bodies were digesting our food as we spoke!

She was not amused.

Every bit of information fascinated me, especially blood. It delivered nutrients, the elements our body needed, through our body, and then it carried away metabolic waste from those very same cells. It also carried electrolytes, gases, proteins, glucose, and hormones. Red blood cells carried oxygen, while white blood cells fought bacteria, viruses, cancer cells, and infectious diseases. And platelets helped blood to clot.

We were wonderfully made.

Every time someone in the family had a cut or a scrape, I was there to clean and bandage the wound, satisfying my curiosity of what happened to the skin, how much the wound bled, and how long it would take to heal.

Dat taught me all he knew and checked out books from the library to feed my insatiable appetite. He shared his love of the land with Jessica, his love of music with Marie, and his love of medicine with me. He nurtured each of our interests and did all he could to encourage us. No doubt that was why he allowed me to take the CNA course. Perhaps he thought it would be enough for me—or maybe he knew it wouldn't.

I'd never know.

When I packed for Pittsburgh after Dat died, I searched everywhere for the copy of *Gray's Anatomy*. I'd kept it in Dat's study, on the same shelf as his set of encyclopedias. It wasn't there. I asked Mamm if she'd seen it, but she acted as if she didn't know what I was talking about. I chalked it up to her grief. I hoped someone hadn't given it away or, worse, disposed of it. I was devastated that the book was missing and that I'd have to leave for Pittsburgh without it.

The clopping of a horse's hooves interrupted my thoughts. Aenti Suz was coming up the drive.

She stopped the buggy on the way to the barn and called out, "Stay there. I'll join you in a minute."

Instead, I followed the buggy and helped Aenti Suz unharness her horse. Then we fed him, and I brushed him down. The feel of the brush in my hand and the rhythmic motion of it against the horse's flanks calmed me, along with the comforting smell of the barn.

As we worked, I updated Aenti Suz on Marie's condition. When I finished, I said, "I'm really missing Dat right now."

When I'd finished and put the brush away, Aenti Suz put an arm around me and pulled me close. "You three girls are stronger than you think."

When I didn't answer, not sure if I agreed, she said, "Two generations ago, there were three other Bachmann sisters who faced uncertain times together, without the assistance of their parents. Well, their father was alive at the beginning, but he soon fell ill."

We walked together out of the barn into the afternoon sun. A flock of starlings swooped upward, startling me.

"Do you remember your great-aunts Faith, Hope, and Charity?" Aenti Suz asked.

I shook my head.

"All were married and lived in different locations around the county. They came to visit when they could."

I remembered hearing their names before but had no memory of them. "Are you sure I ever met them? Was I even alive?"

"Let's see." Aenti Suz wrinkled her brow. "I guess not. You were born in 1995, right?"

I nodded.

"Charity lived the longest, and she passed away in 1994, just before you were born."

"What's their story?" I asked.

"Well, it's actually my father's story—Joseph Bachmann."

An image of Mr. Weber flashed through my mind. "You know, I've wanted to hear more about *Dawdi* Joe. Dat told me he served during World War II."

"That's right," Aenti Suz said. "He was the youngest in the family and the only boy. My grandmother was sure he was another girl and chose the name *Joy* for him. When he was born, they decided on Joseph and called him *Joe*." She smiled. "It's my father's story, but his sisters were a part of it as well. Their mother had died, and he'd just been drafted."

"Drafted? Into the military?" I thought of Nick's desire to join the Air Force. *Join.* He certainly wasn't being drafted.

"Joe went into the Civilian Public Service as a conscientious objector to avoid having to fight. As a CO, he didn't have to join the military, but it was still a big deal for a farm boy who'd never been outside Lancaster County." We'd reached her front porch. "Would you like to hear the story?" Aenti Suz asked.

"Jah." I opened the front door a crack so I could hear Caden when he awoke and Marie if she needed me.

"First, some background information," Aenti Suz said as I sat down in the chair next to her. "Some Anabaptist men of fighting age faced horrible experiences during the War to End All Wars, which was later deemed World War I." She explained that there were cases of men being imprisoned, but the worst account was of four Hutterites from South Dakota who reported to serve at Fort Lewis in Washington State. However, when they refused to wear army uniforms, they were imprisoned in Alcatraz and thrown into solitary confinement. Later, they were sent to Fort Leavenworth, Kansas, where two of the men died from exposure.

That particular Hutterite group, fearing the war wouldn't actually be the one to end all wars, fled to Canada to avoid any future military conflicts. Other Anabaptist groups, in response to the persecution that had taken place, did all they could to come up with a future program for those with nonresistance beliefs.

"In October 1940, the United States, in response to the war in Europe, reinstated the draft, and by December of that year a group of Anabaptists had worked with the government to create the Civilian Public Service," Aenti Suz said. "By the time Pearl Harbor was bombed a year later, there were already CPS camps around the nation. Two years later, Joe Bachmann turned eighteen and was drafted."

— 4 —

Joe Bachmann

APRIL 1944

When Joe's draft number came up in the spring of 1944, his father drove him in the family wagon to a church in Lancaster to meet with the Selective Service Board. Joe had only been to town a few times in his life, but Dat seemed to know exactly where he was going. Automobiles zipped around the wagon, and a few blocks away a trolley clanged along its track. In the distance, a train whistle blew. Joe's head turned from side to side, taking in all of the sights and sounds. He loved the family farm and land, but he found the city exciting.

Soon, his father parked the wagon next to a flowering lilac bush, and Joe jumped down and tied the horse to a hitch. Together they walked toward the church.

Joe was quite a bit taller than Dat now, and he noticed his father's shoulders hunched more than ever. Dat's beard had been completely gray for as long as Joe could remember, and he walked with a limp from an accident two years before. A Model T had run the wagon off the road, and Dat had been tossed into a ditch on his hip. Thankfully Dat and the horse had survived.

Dat was seventy, much older than Joe's friends' fathers. Dat had married as a young man, but he and his first wife never had children. After she died, he married again and had three daughters and then Joe. For years, Dat had seemed ageless, but since Mamm passed away three years prior, Dat had seemed to grow old quickly. The accident hadn't helped.

Dat hadn't said much about Joe being drafted into the service except that, as in everything, Joe should aim to serve the Lord and do his very best.

Over the last two years, several of the other young men from their district, located in the heart of Lancaster County, had headed west to work in CPS camps—some in logging operations, some on farms, some to fight fires. A few had turned their backs on the teachings of their church and joined the army, but Joe knew he'd never do that.

Joe glanced down at his documents as they neared the church and said, "The board meets in a place called the 'fellowship hall.'" The building was made of bricks, with a tall white steeple that reached up to the blue sky.

When they reached the front door, Joe took his hat off and held it in his hand as a middle-aged man with a round belly and a bald head swung the door open. "So you're a Dutchy who won't fight."

Joe simply said, "I'm here to get my orders for the CPS."

The man told Dat he wouldn't be allowed in the meeting.

"All right." He turned toward Joe. "I'll wait in the wagon."

Joe followed the Englisch man down a hallway and then into a large room where four other men sat behind a table. The fifth man joined them.

He was thankful for the CPS and hoped to be assigned to an agriculture camp. He'd been farming his entire life and had a knack for it. There were woods on his family farm, and he enjoyed caring for the trees almost as much as growing the crops. Anything in agriculture would suit him just fine.

But it was soon clear the Selective Service Board had a different idea for him.

"How do you feel about working in medicine?" a man wearing a suit coat and tie asked.

Working in a hospital certainly wasn't his first choice. Joe was sure he was going to be sent to work on a psychiatric ward, like others in his district had been. He squared his shoulders. "I've cared for the sick before but never the mentally ill." He'd helped his sisters nurse their mother in the months before she passed.

"There's a general hospital in Chicago, a Catholic one, that's been turned into a hospital for"—Joe expected to hear *the insane*, but instead the man said—"for soldiers. They're currently short-staffed and looking for orderlies. We're sending you there. There's a staff of Civilian Public Service men who stay in barracks on-site."

They explained that Joe would be under the direction of an army officer, most likely a doctor, but that all of his assignments and transfers would be ratified by the Selective Service Board. "You will cease to have any rights, but you may be granted privileges," the man with the tie explained. "Ones that can be taken away at any moment. You will have no choice as far as where you are assigned or for how long you will be at any one location. You will be transferred as needed for the good of our country."

"Understood?" The man who'd greeted him at the front door had his arms crossed over his wide chest.

Joe nodded.

"Speak up," the man said.

"Yes, sir," Joe answered.

The man in the tie stamped a document. "Here are your orders and train ticket. Arrive at the station early. You can take a streetcar to the hospital once you reach Chicago."

Joe must have had a puzzled expression on his face because the man said, "A streetcar is a trolley. You'll find the right one outside of the train station."

The man slid the paperwork across the table toward Joe. He took the documents and then thanked all of the men on the board.

They simply nodded their heads in return.

Joe didn't look at the paperwork until he reached the sidewalk. He was to arrive in Chicago in two weeks and report to the hospital immediately. *Chicago.* He never expected to be sent to a city. He was a country boy, and a Plain one at that.

Once he reached the wagon, he squinted up at his father, shading his eyes, although he didn't say anything, and hopped up to the bench.

"How'd it go?" Dat asked.

"I'm being sent to Chicago." Joe tried to hide the excitement in his voice, but he must have failed because Dat had a confused expression on his face.

"I'll be working in a hospital for soldiers. As an orderly."

He showed the document to his father. Together, they leafed through the papers. There was a packing list, obviously the same one they gave to everyone. One suit with a white shirt and a tie. Three changes of denim pants and shirts. Two good pairs of work shoes plus Sunday shoes. Several pairs of Sunday socks. Two pairs of pajamas. Toiletries.

Joe folded the orders as Dat pursed his lips and snapped the reins. Their old horse lurched forward. Joe guessed his father was thinking that caring for wounded soldiers would come mighty close to supporting the war, but Joe didn't see how it was any worse than growing food to feed soldiers.

Was it all right to provide services that made it possible for others to employ force? That was the constant question in his mind. Being nonresistant, holding the conviction that it was always wrong to employ force against another human being, was a complicated concept.

But at least Joe had a place to serve and didn't have to worry about being arrested for evading the draft. He'd heard of some Englisch people who resented nonresistant men for not fighting. But Joe wasn't acquainted well enough with any Englisch people to know—or care—if they were critical of the CPS.

Dat didn't say anything, but he slumped a little more as he drove the wagon out of town. Joe felt a tinge of guilt about his excitement at going to Chicago. Now Dat would have to farm alone. Well, that wasn't true. Joe's sisters—Faith, Hope, and Charity—would help. None were married, and all three were strong and capable.

His heart fell, and he swallowed hard as reality set in. He'd miss his sisters, including Faith, even though he didn't have a great relationship with her. He'd miss his Dat most of all. He'd spent more time with his father than anyone on earth, and although the man didn't speak much, he'd led by example and had cared for his family in a loving way.

Jah, he felt bad about leaving, but it couldn't be helped. He'd have to make the most of the days he had left with his family.

It was a long ride to the farm, first on pavement and then gravel and then up the dirt road. As they rounded the curve, the newly whitewashed farmhouse gleamed in the sunlight. The pink blooms of tulips swayed in the wind.

But it was the two women waving at him on the porch who made him smile. Hope and Charity. Faith was most likely busy in the house.

In some families, the youngest might have been spoiled, but not in his. Hope and Charity had high expectations for their little brother, and they never let him forget it. Faith, on the other hand, could be downright mean to him.

Hope leaned against the rail, and Charity skipped down the steps. Both were thin and tall, with dark hair and brown eyes.

Joe reached for the reins from his father. "Go on into the house and rest. I'll take care of the horse and get started on the chores."

"Denki," his father said as Joe pulled on the reins. Dat climbed down, but before Joe started the wagon back up, Charity came running toward him. She was the youngest of the sisters and the most cheerful.

"Wait!" she called out. "It's my turn to help." Charity and Hope took turns with the chores while Faith took charge of the house. The younger sisters helped with that too, but Faith never worked in the barn or fields. Joe knew she would have to soon, which wouldn't make her happy.

Charity boosted herself up into the back of the wagon, swinging her legs off the back. "Giddy up!" she yelled.

The horse started toward the barn before Joe snapped the reins.

"How'd it go?" Charity called out to him.

"Just fine."

She scrambled up the bed of the wagon and knelt behind him. "Were our prayers answered? Are they letting you stay here to farm instead of sending you away?"

He shook his head. "Dat's here to farm—that's enough for them."

Her voice dropped in tone but not volume. "Where are they sending you?"

"Chicago."

"Why a city?"

"I'm going to work in a hospital."

"That doesn't make any sense."

He shrugged again. "That's where they need me."

"Oh, Joe," Charity said. "What are we going to do without you?"

He laughed. "Get married?"

She pushed against his shoulder. "I'm not getting married until Faith and Hope do, and we all know there's a shortage of men around here with all of them going off with the CPS."

"Oh, there are plenty of old widowers around. Like Abe Yoder." The man wasn't that old—only thirty. And, unlike many widowers, he didn't have any children.

She laughed. "Jah, Abe's perfect for Faith—not me."

Faith was twenty-eight. Most Amish women married by their early twenties, if not sooner. But Faith was picky. Then Mamm got sick. Then all the young men her age were already married or had gone off to serve.

"I'll take care of the horse while you get started on the milking," Charity said as Joe pulled to a stop.

Joe let his sister take over and headed toward the pasture for the cow. They only kept one, although Dat talked about starting another dairy herd. They'd gotten rid of their milk cows during the Depression. However, milk was more profitable now.

Dat wouldn't buy dairy cows with Joe leaving, though. It would be hard enough for him to keep up with the crops, let alone a herd.

That evening after the dishes were done, Dat told Joe to give Faith his packing list. He did, reluctantly. She took it from him, sat at the far end of the oak table their father had made a decade earlier, and pulled the lamp close. She was rounder than her sisters and a little shorter too.

Faith harrumphed a few times as she read. Joe wished he could collect the needed clothing himself, but she was in charge of the household budget and would have to decide what could be made and what would have to be purchased.

"I don't know why you need the denim pants," Faith said. "You have plenty of other work pants."

Joe didn't respond. He disagreed more with Faith than anyone, but he didn't want to argue now, especially not with Dat at the other end of the table.

"Sister, buy one pair of denim pants and a denim shirt too," Dat said. "And sew a new white shirt to go with Joe's suit."

Faith wrinkled her nose. Joe was sure she would have said his old clothes would work just fine if Dat hadn't been in the room.

Joe supposed he deserved her wrath. He'd been a mischievous boy, playing tricks and putting off his chores up until a few years ago. She'd told him, more than once, that he'd never amount to anything. "You'll never be worthy of this farm," she'd said when he was fourteen and the slash fire near the woods got away from him. He'd yelled for help and Dat and the girls had all come running. They'd extinguished it before any of the trees caught fire, and everyone had been relieved. Except for Faith. She'd berated him about it for days.

Not long after that, Mamm was diagnosed with cancer and Joe stopped his foolish ways, but Faith hadn't seemed to notice. She still thought of him as the irresponsible fourteen-year-old boy.

Dat pushed himself up from the table and headed to the back door, on his way to the outhouse. Once the door closed, Faith turned toward Joe and said, "You're looking forward to leaving, aren't you?"

Joe hung his head, ashamed that his excitement was obvious. He'd never choose to go, but, jah, he planned to make the most of the adventure ahead of him. He didn't tell Faith that though.

"I'm worried for your soul," she said. "You haven't joined the church and here you are going off on your own, to a city, with no accountability. I wouldn't be surprised if you never come back."

He raised his head. "No, I will. I promise." He'd join the church and take over the farming, God willing. That was all he'd ever wanted.

She crossed her arms as her eyes drilled through him.

He was tempted to drop his head again, but he didn't. Nor did he say anything more.

Finally, she said, "Only God can know for sure, but I won't be holding my breath."

Regardless of Faith's predictions about her brother, she followed Dat's orders about the clothes and gave them to him in a bundle the night before he left. He packed everything in a leather satchel of Dat's. He'd make do with what he had.

The next morning, Joe dressed in the new white shirt, carefully pinning the opening. Then he pulled on his trousers and suit jacket.

When he sat at the oak table to eat one last breakfast with his family, Dat led the silent prayer. Joe asked God to care for his father and sisters and to look over the land. Then Joe prayed that God would use him to serve others and give him the strength to remain true to his faith and upbringing.

After Dat ended the prayer, they ate mostly in silence. Hope had cooked hotcakes, Joe's favorite, but even with butter and maple syrup they stuck in his throat. After Dat said the closing prayer, Joe snuck out the back door onto the enclosed porch that was the original Bachmann cabin, built back in 1752. The river rock fireplace still existed, although no one used it anymore. He strode across the wood floor, through the door, and down the back steps. To his right was the barn, and to his left was the pasture with the old oak tree, and then beyond it, the woods. He breathed in the cool spring air. Would he come home someday and be worthy to farm the land? Or would Faith's predictions come true?

Dat hired an Englisch neighbor with a Ford pickup truck to drive all of them to the station. As the neighbor pulled up, Faith said she had too many chores to do to traipse into town and told Joe a quick good-bye, adding, "Don't do anything foolish."

Charity gave their oldest sister a wilting look but didn't say anything.

As Dat climbed into the passenger seat, Joe placed his bag in the bed of the truck first and then helped Hope and Charity over the tailgate. At least there were benches around the bed of the truck. After he jumped up, the neighbor accelerated down the lane. Joe stayed on his feet, holding on to the high side rail. He thought Faith might be watching from the porch, waving good-bye, but she'd already stepped back inside. He stood until the house, barn, and farm disappeared, thinking of soldiers leaving to go to Europe or the South Pacific who wondered if they'd ever return. At least he had no worries of that. Jah, the idea of going away and seeing a little bit of the world appealed to him, but he was happy he would be returning to the land that had been in his family for nearly two hundred years.

As the farm faded from his sight, Charity grabbed his hand and tugged on it. "Sit down."

He did. Soon the truck reached the highway and gained speed, and the spring air cooled even more. Joe grabbed his hat, holding it to his head, and his sisters tied their black bonnets. The closer they grew to town, the more expressionless Hope and Charity's faces became, and Joe guessed he appeared the same.

The truck slowed as they reached the city limits. Soon the large brick houses on the edge of town gave way to row houses. Englisch children played in front of the homes, and old men sat on the stoops.

When they reached the city center, the driver drove past the train station and then found a parking place a block away. Once the truck stopped, Joe helped his sisters down and grabbed his bag. The neighbor climbed out of the cab and extended his hand. The man's grip was firm, and he pumped Joe's hand several times. "Some think you boys are taking the easy way out, and I can't say that I don't agree, but just the same I'm grateful for the effort you're making. I know it'll be a hardship for your family to have you gone." The man nodded toward Dat. "I'll wait out here."

Dat tipped his hat to the man and led the way toward the station.

Several soldiers walked with their families too. Joe thought of the Englisch boys he'd gone to school with through the eighth grade. He knew the older ones had all been drafted. Some were in the South Pacific. A few others were in England and North Africa. Many more were in training and would be deployed soon. Now his classmates were being drafted too. Those students had gone on to high school while Joe, who was six feet tall by then, had gone to work with his Dat. But he still thought of them often.

As soon as they entered the lobby, Dat checked with the stationmaster about the train to Chicago. When he returned, he said, "The train's on time. It's boarding now."

Dat shook Joe's hand. "Write to us," he said. "Remember who you are and whom you belong to."

Joe nodded. He belonged to God. He'd been taught that his entire life. He clung to his Dat's hand for a long moment but then let it go.

Hope patted him on the back. "I put paper, envelopes, and stamps in your bag. Follow Dat's instructions and use them, as soon as you arrive."

Charity patted his other shoulder. "Don't forget us."

His voice caught as he spoke. "Never."

Even though they didn't hug, and especially not in public, the tears in Charity's eyes gave away her emotions.

Joe didn't dare say anything more, afraid his voice would break. He gripped his bag and headed toward the platform, glancing down at his ticket. Once he reached his train, he looked back. His family stood in the middle of the lobby, the only Plain people in the place, as the crowd flowed around them. His father and sisters all appeared forlorn, but then they waved in unison. He raised his hand in response and then bolted up the steps to the train.

The crowds in the Lancaster station were nothing compared to the hordes of people in Union Station in Chicago. He'd never seen so many people. He'd been on the train for nearly twenty-four hours, but the energy of the station revived him. Englisch girls told soldiers and sailors good-bye. The smells of eggs and coffee from nearby food vendors filled the air. Shoe-shine boys and paperboys shouted out to those passing by. A man sold single stems of roses, and a soldier quickly bought one and then rushed toward a woman waiting for him at the far end of the station.

The Selective Service Board member had told him to take the streetcar to the hospital. He asked a vendor for directions, but the man laughed and said, "There's a streetcar out there for every direction. Just go hop on the right one."

Puzzled, Joe didn't press the man for more details. From the paperwork he had, it seemed the hospital was near the train station, not more than a few miles. He found a kiosk that sold maps and bought one, then sat in a chair and spread it over his lap. Once he found the hospital, he decided to walk. It wasn't far.

"Why aren't you in uniform?" an older man sitting next to him asked.

"I'm with the CPS," Joe answered. No doubt the man noticed his accent. Perhaps he thought Joe was German.

"What's that?"

"The Civilian Public Service. I'm working in a hospital."

The man sneered, "Oh, you're one of those pacifists."

Joe folded his map. "I'm happy to serve my country as I can."

The man shook his head. "While others die."

Joe slipped the map into the pocket of his jacket, grabbed his bag, and wished the man a good day. Then he quickly walked away. Perhaps the man had a son or grandson who'd been killed. One never knew what might be at the heart of someone's criticism. He tried not to take it personally.

He bought an egg sandwich before he left the station. There were no meat sandwiches available—the woman selling them said she'd sold out hours ago. Living in a city would be quite a bit different from the country. His family had to live on rations like everyone else, but they raised steers and chickens. Granted, they sold most of what they butchered, but they still had more than most. He ate as he walked, heading out the east door toward Lake Michigan. He'd seen it from the train and wanted a closer look.

He walked across a couple of streets to the seawall. The wind tugged at his hat. He finished his sandwich and put his free hand on top of his head. He'd never seen such a mass of water. He'd actually never seen anything bigger than the Susquehanna River. The body of water he was most familiar with was the pond back home.

He breathed in deeply, smelling fish from the nearby dock, diesel fuel from the boats, and smoke from the factories. Several fishing vessels were within sight, and a few ships chugged toward the city. Beyond them was the endless lake with no shore in view.

Several couples strolled along the lake, and Joe stepped back, taking it all in. He'd courted several girls back home, a few who were older than he was. Faith had commented more than once that she wasn't sure what all those girls saw in him. He wasn't sure either, but he did his best not to dwell on that.

He did know, however, that he hadn't courted—or met—a girl he thought he could marry. And it certainly wouldn't happen now. Marriage could be years away for him.

In the meantime, he'd see all he could.

He turned back toward the station and then headed northwest toward the hospital. The city bustled around him. He'd never seen such tall buildings or so many vehicles—and streetcars too. They did seem to be going every direction.

People rushed past him, going this way and that. Women wore fancy dresses, high heels, and red lipstick. The men were dressed in tailored suits and wore fashionable hats. He touched his old straw hat and sighed. One of the men on the Selective Service Board had told him to blend in as best he could and not draw attention to himself, but he stuck out like a sore thumb in Chicago.

Even though the late April day was cool, Joe had broken a sweat by the time he reached the hospital, a large multistory brick building that covered at least a few blocks. He took out his orders and marched up the front steps. Once he entered the building, he stopped for a moment, squinting as his eyes adjusted to the dim light. On one side of the lobby were several chairs clustered together. On the other was a statue of a woman with a baby—Mary with baby Jesus, he assumed.

Once his eyes adjusted, he approached a woman sitting behind a desk and told her his name and that he was reporting for the Civilian Public Service.

"Goodness, I didn't know we were expecting a new orderly," she said. "I think Captain Russell is away for the day. I'll call Lieutenant Shaw and see if she can put you to work."

She? Joe didn't know that women could be officers.

"Wait over there." The woman gestured toward the chairs.

He did as he was told, but he waited so long that he began to grow drowsy. He was too tall to rest his head on the back of his chair. Afraid he might fall asleep and topple over, he stood and walked to a window that looked out onto the street. A horn honked and then a taxi stopped. An older woman climbed out, her face worn and weary. Joe's heart lurched. Perhaps she had an injured son inside the hospital. The woman reminded him of his Mamm, and the ache of losing her washed over him all over again. So many people were hurting in the world. A mother for a son. A son for a mother. Joe hoped he'd be able to ease a measure of pain in his work at the hospital.

A voice behind him called out, "Joseph Bachmann?"

He turned. A young woman with intense blue eyes stood by the receptionist's desk, a file in her hand. Her blond hair was tucked under a nurse's cap, and she wore a white dress and a frown.

"I am Joseph." He stepped forward. "But you can call me Joe."

"I'm Lt. Shaw," she said. "And you can call me *ma'am*."

− 5 −

Leisel

Caden's cries interrupted us, but Marie called out, "I'll get him." I stayed on the porch with Aenti Suz.

"Why have I never heard this story before?" I asked.

"Well," she said, "I thought your father would have told it to you."

I shook my head. "He talked about his father some. I remember him saying Amish scholars went to public schools back then."

"Your grandfather stopped going to school after the eighth grade," Aenti Suz said. "Some Amish students continued after that, but his help was needed on the farm. Your Dat and I went to Englisch schools too, but in the 1960s we were required to go until we were sixteen. The law didn't change until the Supreme Court decision in 1972 that exempted the Amish and other groups from compulsory education beyond the eighth grade."

I nodded. "Dat also talked about farming with his Dat. And about caring for him when he was ill." In fact, that story had inspired me to be courageous as I cared for Dat.

"Jah, he was very gentle with our father. There were some who were surprised a man could provide such loving care."

"I know you helped too," I said quickly.

"I did," Aenti Suz said. "We cared for him in the Dawdi Haus. Our Mamm had already passed, or else she would have been a big help too."

I could imagine Dat and Aenti Suz nursing their father. He was a fortunate man to have two children who were so compassionate. But then again, maybe they were that way because of the way he'd raised them.

Marie came out on the porch with Caden. He pressed his face against her chest when he saw us. I stood, offering her my chair.

As she sat, I spotted Milton at the mailboxes. Then he started toward us.

There was nothing as uplifting as a beautiful spring day on the farm. I turned my face toward the sun and soaked in the warmth until Milton started up the steps.

"Aenti Suz, you have a letter." His eyes sparkled. "From your boyfriend."

"What?" I belted out.

Marie smiled. "David still writes to you?"

Aenti Suz ignored us both. "Denki," she said to Milton as she took the letter.

"Who's David?" I knew my voice sounded as betrayed as I felt. Why had no one told me that Aenti Suz had a man in her life?

"He's just a friend," Aenti Suz said.

"You remember him," Marie said to me. "David Herschberger. Aenti Suz knew him when they were young, and then we spent time with him down in Pinecraft. He helped get us on the bus home after Jessica was hospitalized. I'm sure I told you about him."

I remembered her mentioning him three years ago, but that was all.

Marie turned toward Aenti Suz. "And then he visited here."

"Indeed he did," Aenti Suz said.

I clapped my hands together, vaguely remembering that as well. "And then what happened?"

"Nothing," Aenti Suz said. "Absolutely nothing."

"Why not?" Again, my voice betrayed my emotions. This time it was frustration.

Aenti Suz met my eyes. "It's not like you to be so nosy. You're usually so reserved about this sort of thing."

My face grew warm. "I'm just thinking it would be so nice for you to have a boyfriend."

She shook her head. "I'm completely content with my life." She slipped the letter into her pocket.

"Will you write him back?" I asked.

She shrugged. "It depends on what he's written."

"David really cared for Aenti Suz," Marie said. "He was very clear about how he felt."

Aenti Suz stood. "I'll leave you two to your unsolicited fascination about my life."

I cringed. We'd offended her. "Wait," I said. "What about Dawdi's story?"

"That will have to wait, I'm afraid." She started toward the door.

Was she punishing me? That wasn't like Aenti Suz. It wasn't like her to be offended either.

Once she was inside, I sat down in her chair. "What was that all about?"

Marie shook her head. "I'm not sure, but I'm guessing David has been pursuing her. You know, in an older-Amish-man-sort-of-way. And for some reason, she's not interested."

"Do you know what happened, exactly?"

She shrugged. "It seemed they had a great time together in Florida. Don't you remember me telling you they spent every day together?"

"Somewhat . . ." Had I really been so absorbed with school and studying and work and Nick that I hadn't really listened? Just like I hadn't about Marie's stomach pains?

"When Gordon called about Jessica," Marie continued, "it was David who helped get us on the bus and on our way. After he came back home to Chester County he came down for dinner, but Aenti Suz seemed distant with him. Afterward, she told me she didn't want to rush into anything." She shrugged. "That was three years ago. I didn't even know they were still in contact."

"So, she decided he wasn't right for her. That's not surprising, right? She would have married long ago if she wanted to."

Caden pulled his face away from Marie's chest and gave me a sleepy smile. I put out my arms and he scrambled into them, totally distracting me from our conversation until Marie said, "Except they seemed absolutely perfect together. The way Jessica and Silas are for each other. The way Gordon and I are." She gave me a teasing glance. "The way you and Nick are—at least from what I've seen. You really should bring him around more."

I ignored her comment. Nick—and his desire to join the Air Force—was the last thing I wanted to think about. "What do you think happened, as far as Aenti Suz?"

"I don't know. Maybe it was the bus accident. Or coming back home." She shrugged again.

"She does seem happy." There was no reason to worry about Aenti Suz. She knew what she was doing. "Maybe she really never wanted to marry."

"Oh, no. She did." Marie said. "The love of her life was killed in Vietnam. When Dat was there."

Dat had told me about the clinic he worked in for a year in Vietnam, but he never said anything about anyone being killed. It dawned on me that he could have been killed too.

Just then, Caden began to cry and Marie said she was feeling nauseated and needed to take her meds. "Caden probably needs a snack." She stood. "You should ask Aenti Suz about her boyfriend—fiancé, actually. Maybe she'd tell you about him."

I wasn't so sure she would, but I would definitely ask. After she finished telling me Dawdi Joe's story.

The next day, I called Rita and asked for more time off. "A couple of weeks," I said.

She wasn't happy and told me so. When I didn't respond, she said, "Mr. Weber's daughter wants to speak with you."

"About what?"

"She read through his chart. She wants to hear about his last night."

I held back from reminding Rita I'd wanted to stay that morning and speak with his daughter. "Give her my cell number. She can give me a call."

Rita sighed. "I'll give you her number when you get back. I'll tell her you'll be out of town a few more days."

"A couple of weeks—"

"See you soon. Bye." The line clicked as she hung up. I doubted Mr. Weber's daughter was upset over his fall. At least I certainly hoped not. She probably just wanted to know what his last words were, that sort of thing. I put it out of my mind.

I took Marie to the oncologist the next day. He recommended surgery before chemotherapy, which wasn't what I'd read when

I researched treatments. "You're right," he told me. "But it's not unheard of to do the surgery first—and in this case we don't want to wait." He diagnosed her as having Stage 2 cancer. I kicked myself that we hadn't found it at Stage 1.

A couple of days later, we went to see her surgeon, Dr. Turner. He was tall and wore his blond hair short. He addressed Marie first and then me. I introduced myself as Marie's sister.

Then, commenting on Marie's Kapp, he said he knew she was Mennonite because it was rounded instead of heart-shaped, like the Amish in Lancaster County wore. She told him she'd grown up Amish but had left to become Mennonite before she married.

He turned to me, his gray eyes lively. "So you're her sister, but you're not Amish or Mennonite?"

I nodded. "I've left altogether. I go to a nondenominational church now."

"Here in Lancaster?"

"No, in Pittsburgh. I just graduated from nursing school."

"Fascinating. I'm looking for an office nurse, but I'm guessing you have something more exciting in mind."

I smiled and assured him that I did, although I had nothing against office nurses.

"I figured." He grinned. "You don't seem the type to be satisfied with weighing people and taking their blood pressure."

"Yeah, I'm more interested in blood and guts." Suddenly I felt embarrassed talking that way in front of Marie. "I'm sorry," I said, turning toward her.

She shook her head. "It's alright."

Dr. Turner appeared confused. He didn't get it.

"Blood and guts," I said. "She's having stomach surgery."

He slapped his forehead. "You're much more astute—and empathetic—than I am."

"Not really," I responded. "I'm the one who made the faux pas in the first place."

He grimaced.

Thankfully, Marie changed the topic, saying to Dr. Turner, "Tell us about yourself," and saved us both from further embarrassment.

I almost fell off my chair when he said he'd grown up Mennonite in Michigan. To think this doctor had Anabaptist roots too! He quickly explained that his family wasn't Old Order. "It wasn't a big deal for me to go to med school, not really."

He continued, saying that he'd graduated from Johns Hopkins University with extensive surgery experience and that he'd been working in Lancaster for the last three years. He seemed fairly young, early thirties probably, but competent and willing to answer every single question I had, including how much of Marie's stomach would have to be removed and if any other organs would too. He was hoping for a minimal amount of removal, of course, and he was eighty percent certain from the diagnostic tests that no other organs were affected.

He also scheduled the surgery for as soon as possible—a week away, the second week of May. He agreed with the oncologist that the surgery should be performed first before the chemotherapy. "The tumor is small enough to be removed first," he said. "Then the chemo can do its job."

As Marie discussed scheduling details with the nurse, I made up my mind to still take my state boards on May 17 since Marie would be in the hospital, recovering from her surgery. I would simply slip away to Pittsburgh, take the boards, and then return to her side. I could have rescheduled the test in Lancaster, but I believed going to Pittsburgh would put me in a better place to concentrate on my test.

But for the time being there were far more important things

for me to do than worry about passing my test. Besides, I felt completely confident that I would, so I put it out of my mind.

When we got back to the farm, while Marie went to rest, I called Rita again and gave her my notice, saying I wouldn't be back to work.

"Do you expect me to give you a good recommendation?" she asked.

"Yes," I answered. "There's no reason you shouldn't. I can't help it that my sister has cancer."

Her voice softened a little. "We're really short-staffed. Couldn't you come back after her surgery? Just for a month or so, until you find your next job?"

"I'm sorry," I said. "I can't." Thankfully I had my savings, and I wouldn't have to start paying back my student loans for six months. "But what about Mr. Weber's daughter? Could you give me her number or give her mine?"

"I'll give her yours," Rita said. "She might not call though. The funeral was yesterday."

I held in a sigh. I had wanted to talk with her the morning her father died, but now I only wanted what was best for her in her grief.

I tried not to worry about Marie as I went through my day caring for her and Caden. For someone used to having a microwave, dishwasher, washer and dryer, and grocery store nearby, it was quite the adjustment. Of course Aenti Suz helped as much as she could, although she did have commitments to helping her widowed friends in the district.

I'd been doing a poor job of keeping Nick up-to-date on what was going on, but he texted me and asked me to call him that afternoon.

I took Caden outside with me, plopping him down in the sandbox and piling the bucket and little shovels and rakes all around him. Then I stepped to the garden, called Nick, and began to weed between the tomato plants, positioned so I could keep an eye on Caden.

Nick sounded groggy when he answered.

"Oh no," I said. "I woke you up."

"I ended up working last night," he said.

"You should have texted me not to call."

"No." He sounded a little perkier. "I wanted you to. I don't work tonight. How are things going?"

I gave him an update about Marie's appointments. He asked me what I thought of the doctors, and I told him I was especially impressed with Dr. Turner and then mentioned that he'd grown up Mennonite.

"Interesting," Nick said. "Marie and Gordon are really fortunate to have you there. How long will you be able to stay?"

"Hopefully until she's had a couple weeks of chemo. I quit my job, so that's not an issue, and the lease will be up on my apartment at the end of this month."

"Have you applied for any nursing jobs yet?"

"I will," I said, "after I pass my boards."

"You'll pass your boards," he said.

I thought so too, but it would be prideful to say that. "I hope so."

"There's a neuro floor position open here," he said.

I would have liked to go straight to emergency or intensive care, but that wasn't always possible. Nick had started as a floor nurse but then quickly got a job in emergency. Hopefully something like that would work for me too.

"Apply online," he said. "And send Sue your résumé. She asked about it. Do you have your references lined up?"

I assured him I did. I'd already talked with two of my professors and my clinical supervisor. I had all of the necessary information, but I just needed Wi-Fi and time on my laptop. I'd have to sneak away to a coffee shop during Caden's naptime.

"I have a stretch of days off coming up soon," Nick said. "I was thinking about coming to Lancaster."

I held my breath for a second. Did I want him to come? Jah, of course I did. I just didn't want him to talk about joining the Air Force.

"I talked with the recruiter again, and—"

"Do we have to talk about this now?"

"Leisel . . ." He paused and then said, "Is this a deal breaker for you?"

I exhaled. Was it? "I can't think about it right now," I said. "Not when Marie is facing . . ." I couldn't say it.

"That's fair," he said. "But can we talk in person? When I come in two weeks?"

"All right," I managed to squeak. I was sure by then I'd be able to make Nick understand that he couldn't join the Air Force, that it wasn't right for our future.

"I'm praying for Marie," he said. "And for you."

"Denki," I answered. "I mean, thank you." In truth, I was having a hard time praying myself. When I knelt beside Aenti Suz's couch at night, it seemed as if my prayers became lodged in my throat. I had to force them out, one word at a time.

Nick asked, "Is it good to be home?"

"It is and it isn't," I answered. "It will be good to see you when I'm in Pittsburgh."

"Ditto." We talked for a few more minutes, but then Caden looked my way and started to cry. I dropped the weeds in my hand in the pile at the edge of the garden and started toward the sandbox.

"Who's crying?" Nick asked.

"Caden. The sandbox trick was short lived."

"Aww," Nick said. "Poor guy."

As I scooped up Caden, he reached for my phone. But then Arden came out of the barn and I told Nick I needed to go.

"Just a minute—"

"No, Arden's coming. You know how he feels about phones on the farm. I'll text you. Bye." I ended the call and slipped the phone into my pocket. I needed to be back on the Bachmann farm. I knew that. But it wasn't always easy.

The Sunday night before the surgery Jessica came over with Ruby to spend the night at Mamm's. The plan was for Jessica to care for Caden so Aenti Suz could leave for the hospital with Gordon's mother by the time Marie was in recovery.

Caden was still asleep in his travel crib in the spare bedroom when we got ready to leave the next morning. I stood in the doorway and watched Marie stare at him. I could only guess how much she wanted to scoop him up in her arms, but it was only four thirty and she probably hoped, for Aenti Suz's sake, that he'd sleep for another couple of hours. She blew him a kiss and turned toward the hallway.

Gordon was already on the porch with Marie's bag. Together, we all stepped out into the dark, and then I followed Gordon and Marie to the hospital so I'd have my car available.

The night air was cold, and I turned on the heat in my car. A star twinkled in the dark sky. I hoped Marie could see it. I wondered what she and Gordon were talking about. I felt a sudden pang of longing for Nick.

We stayed with Marie as long as we could in pre-op. Dr. Turner, dressed in blue scrubs, came in to talk with Marie before they wheeled her into surgery. I quickly introduced him to Gordon and the two shook hands.

"I'll keep you updated on the surgery," Dr. Turner said. Then he bowed his head a little and added, "I've been praying for you, Marie." He turned toward Gordon and me. "And for all of you."

I could tell that we were all touched by his remark. I managed to say thank you because Marie and Gordon didn't seem able to speak at all.

Gordon kissed Marie good-bye, and then an OR nurse wheeled Marie's gurney through the double doors and into surgery. Gordon and I headed to the cafeteria for breakfast, and then we settled in the waiting room with our cups of coffee. Although I'd brought my study book with me, I didn't open it. I couldn't concentrate on studying, not now.

Just before ten, a nurse came out and told us that Dr. Turner said the surgery was going well and was nearly finished. Hopefully Marie would be in recovery soon, but Dr. Turner would come out and talk to us in person first.

Gordon texted his mom and suggested she go get Aenti Suz. We waited for Dr. Turner, but he didn't come out. After an hour, I was beginning to worry.

Finally, he came out, a grim expression on his face.

I wanted to shout, "Is she all right?!" but refrained.

"How is she?" Gordon asked before Dr. Turner could speak.

"Overall, fine. But her blood pressure crashed on the table just as we ended. She's stabilized now. They'll monitor her extra closely in recovery."

I asked about the surgery.

"It was all textbook," he answered. "No surprises. We'll have to wait for the pathology report, of course, to find out if the cancer spread. She's going to be in a lot of pain, but the meds should manage it. We need her to heal as quickly as possible so she can get started on her chemo."

Gordon and I both nodded.

"I'll check on her later this afternoon, after my office appointments," Dr. Turner added.

By the time we reached the recovery waiting room, both Randi and Aenti Suz were there. We waited again for what seemed like an eternity, but then the nurse called for Gordon.

He turned toward me and said, "Come with me."

Marie was groggy and in and out of consciousness. "Where's Caden? Is he all right?" she asked in Pennsylvania Dutch.

"Yes. He's with Jessica. On the farm," I answered in English.

She opened her eyes wider and threw a leg over the side of the bed. "I should get up."

"No." I stepped forward and moved her leg back. "You need to stay right here." I talked through what was going on with her, telling her that Dr. Turner said the surgery went well.

She seemed to respond to that. Once she was ready to be moved to a room on the post-op floor, I collected Aenti Suz and Randi, and we took the elevator up.

Trying to make small talk, I asked Randi how she was doing.

"A little frazzled. Of course, this is minor compared to what Marie is going through, but I had quite the surprise yesterday," she said. "I've had a pipe burst in my kitchen. I'm afraid I'm going to need quite a bit of repair work done. A new floor. Maybe even a new cabinet under the sink. I have a call in to my insurance company."

Poor woman. That sounded like a hassle. It also sounded like one less place where Marie could recover. Aenti Suz's truly was the best option.

Later in the afternoon, while Aenti Suz and Randi were getting a bite to eat, Dr. Turner came into Marie's room to check on her. She was as pale as her sheets and didn't look well.

He took a look at the incision. Gordon glanced away, but I stepped closer. It wasn't hard for me to look at Marie's body, even as cut and wounded as it was, but I didn't blame him for being shocked. From what I could see, everything looked all right. Of course, it was essential that the wound be cleaned and cared for to keep it from becoming infected.

After Aenti Suz and Randi returned, Gordon said he would spend the night at the hospital and I should go get something to eat and then head home.

"I'll ride with you when you're ready," Aenti Suz said.

I nodded.

Marie reached for my hand. "Thank you for being here."

I squeezed her hand as I told her good-bye, in case she was asleep when I returned, and excused myself while Aenti Suz stayed in the room. I ate a sandwich in the cafeteria and then started back. On the way, I noticed the sign to the chapel and decided to stop there.

As I entered, I squinted in the dim light. In the first pew sat a woman wearing a Kapp. Aenti Suz.

"How's Marie doing?" I asked as I slipped in beside her.

"She's asleep. Did Gordon tell you I'd be waiting in here?"

I shook my head. "I just decided to step inside on my way to Marie's room. And here you are."

She reached for my hand. "I thought when I was younger that life would get easier. First I lost Jake. And then my parents. I thought the hard part was over. Then Rebecca died and Amos left and then Jessica. Then we lost your father."

"We're not going to lose Marie," I said.

She sighed wearily. "It's just so hard to have her ill, to have her suffering. I'd take her place in a moment if I could."

I squeezed my Aenti's hand. "I know you would. So would I."

We sat there silently for a long moment until I decided, even though I longed to hear more about my grandfather's story, to ask her about Jake. "Would you tell me about your fiancé?"

She shook her head. "No. But I will tell you more about my father."

"Here? Now?"

She nodded. "Chapels aren't a place common to our people. And the hospital in Chicago was definitely an environment my father hadn't even imagined existed. What better place than right here to tell you more about his time during World War II."

— 6 —

Joe

Lieutenant Shaw said the elevator was too slow, so Joe followed her up the stairs to the third floor, still carrying his bag. He stayed three steps behind her, fearing she might yell at him if he got too close.

When they reached the double doors, he hurried in front of her and opened one.

She stopped a moment and asked, "Where are you from?"

"Pennsylvania."

"What area?"

Joe squared his shoulders, worried that she judged him harshly for being a conscientious objector, but then immediately chastised himself. He'd never cared before what others thought of him. "I'm from Lancaster County," he answered.

She frowned a little and said, "I wondered." She gestured toward the hall and led the way. "Have you worked in a hospital before?"

"No," he answered. He'd never even been in a hospital.

She exhaled.

90

"I'm a fast learner," he quickly added.

"Let's hope so." She turned and pushed through the second double door and stepped into the ward. Joe followed. A mix of smells—blood, urine, and even linoleum wax—hung heavy in the air. Beds were lined up on both sides of the ward, filled with soldiers. Some had bandages wrapped around stumps of arms and legs. Others were in body casts. Many had bandages wrapped around their heads.

"You'll be bathing and feeding soldiers, dressing wounds, and moving patients. You'll learn by doing. Don't take the trauma of each soldier onto yourself or you'll soon be discouraged and then overwhelmed. Stay upbeat. It's good for everyone."

Joe searched the woman's eyes and saw a flicker of pain.

One of the patients, a young man with an amputated leg, said loudly, "Nurse. Where have you been?"

"Not far." Her voice had changed. It was more lighthearted now. "You know I'd never leave you."

"That's good," he replied.

Lt. Shaw motioned toward Joe. "We have a new orderly. This is Joe Bachmann from Lancaster County, Pennsylvania."

"A Dutchy," a man with both arms in casts called out.

"Be nice. He's going to be feeding you," Lt. Shaw countered. "And I'm guessing"—she glanced toward him—"he's a good man."

Joe's face grew warm. Maybe she wasn't as harsh as he'd feared. But then she added, "Like all of you! Now, we'll finish dressing your wounds so everyone will be ready for their supper."

After he stashed his bag and jacket at the nurses' station, Joe rolled up his sleeves, washed his hands, and followed Lt. Shaw to the supply cabinet. They gathered basins, sponges, gauze, and tape.

"Fill the basins and follow me," she said, taking the sponges, gauze, and tape in her hands.

He retreated back to the sink, did as he was told, and then carried a basin in each of his big hands, passing the elevator doors. At least he guessed it was the elevator. He'd never been on one—he'd only heard about them. He joined Lt. Shaw at the back of the ward. They were the only nurse and orderly for around forty patients.

"Half of the soldiers had their dressings changed this morning," she explained. "But now we need to get the rest done."

The ward was warm and stuffy, even with the south windows open. The sharp scent of the antiseptic turned Joe's stomach at first, but after a while he became accustomed to it. They worked on the first few patients together as Lt. Shaw showed Joe how to change the dressings. He'd seen plenty of gore on the farm and had attended to animal wounds and injuries in the family, but amputations and open wounds stopped him. He thought of Faith telling him he'd never amount to anything, but he hoped he could do the right thing here. He prayed silently, asking God to give him the strength he needed. He knew he'd try his best, at least.

After assisting Lt. Shaw with several dressings, she sent him to the other side of the room to work on those soldiers.

Once he was away from the lieutenant, Joe chatted with the men, asking where they were from. The first, Bennie, was from Maine. He had an amputated leg. "The bullet hit me in the knee, right in the joint. I waited out on a battlefield in Italy, on the western seaboard, for a couple of hours before the ambulance driver could get to me," he said. "Our medic had been killed, so I was entirely dependent on the driver to care for me. I've always wondered if they would have gotten to me earlier, if they could have saved my leg. I sure do miss it."

Joe listened attentively to Bennie.

The man continued. "But I was one of the lucky ones. Others all around me died. If we'd had more medics and ambulance drivers they might have been saved." Joe couldn't even imagine what the man had gone through, along with so many others. As Joe unwound the bandages around Bennie's leg, he kept himself from shuddering. The wound was festering and hadn't seemed to heal properly. Joe didn't feel qualified to tend it, but he did the best he could, praying the soldier couldn't discern his horror at the sight of it. The soldier winced, and Joe apologized.

"Not your fault." He shook like a scared calf, which made Joe feel all the worse.

When Joe finished, Bennie thanked him. Perhaps he could tell Joe was nervous about his work because he said, "You're doing just fine."

Next, Joe changed the dressing on a man who had lost his arm at his elbow. His face was hard and his disposition angry. "My brother went down with the *Arizona* during Pearl Harbor," he said. "You should be ashamed for not fighting."

Joe made sure his voice was steady before he spoke. "I'm sorry about your brother. And I'm sorry about your arm."

"Don't be," the man said.

Joe continued on. By the time he finished, he'd forgotten his initial queasiness. In fact, his stomach was growling, but it was time to feed the soldiers their supper. As he washed his hands, Lt. Shaw joined him. He told her Bennie's wound didn't look good, and she responded that she'd note it in his chart and ask the doctor to take a look.

The elevator opened, and two orderlies wearing white pants and white shirts pushed carts out onto the floor. The shallow shelves were filled with trays of chicken noodle soup and slices of bread.

"You distribute the food," Lt. Shaw said, "and I'll start feeding those who need help. Then you can help me finish up."

Joe wondered who would have been helping her all afternoon if he hadn't arrived when he did, but he didn't ask. Instead, he delivered meal after meal. The slices of bread were all thin, store-bought it seemed, and covered with what Joe guessed was margarine. He'd read about it in the newspaper but hadn't seen it before. By the time Joe started the second row, men on the first row were already done eating. Bennie asked for more. Joe turned toward Lt. Shaw, but she shook her head without raising it before he even asked.

Joe figured Bennie knew the policy but was hoping he could get more food out of the new guy.

The soup smelled better than it looked. Joe thought of his Mamm's chicken noodle soup. His sisters made it now, but it was never as good as their mother's. Of course he'd never tell them that. Here, however, he'd more than welcome his sisters' soup.

He exhaled after he served the last of the capable patients and then returned the tray. He picked up another one and headed toward the man with both arms in casts.

"Where are you from?" Joe asked.

The man grunted.

Joe dipped the spoon into the bowl. The man was eager to eat and cooperated, taking in spoonful after spoonful. Joe fed him the bread too, all without saying any more.

When he was finished, he smiled at the man, but didn't receive one in return. Joe took care of the bowl and tray and then moved on to feed the next patient.

The light outside the ward grew darker. Just as Joe finished feeding the last soldier, another nurse came onto the unit.

"Lt. Shaw," she called out from the nurses' station. "Who's helping you?"

"We have a new orderly."

"Another CO?"

"That's right."

Lt. Shaw started toward the nurses' station while Joe returned the tray and bowl back to the cart.

"I'm going to put you back on nights," the other nurse said to Lt. Shaw. "And the new orderly—what did you say his name is?"

"Joe Bachmann."

"I'll put him on nights too. Starting tomorrow evening."

"All right." Lt. Shaw sounded exhausted.

"You can stay and help me get everyone ready for bed," the other nurse said, "since you won't have to report in the morning. The orderly too."

"Oh, don't make him," Lt. Shaw said. "He's been traveling. He just arrived this afternoon."

"I'll stay," Joe said. "Why don't you let Lt. Shaw go rest?"

"Well." The other nurse put her hand on her hip. "A real gentleman." She extended her hand. "I'm Lt. Madison."

"Pleased to meet you," Joe said.

"Thank you for your offer, but you should go on down to the basement and find your room. Captain Russell should be back by now. He'll show you around. Report back here tomorrow at 2200, sharp. In fact, be a few minutes early. We prefer that."

"Yes, ma'am." He feared he'd just made Lt. Shaw's load harder instead of easier, as he'd intended. Joe stepped behind the counter to collect his bag and jacket. He glanced down at his new white shirt. It was splattered with blood.

Lt. Madison turned toward Lt. Shaw. "Get started on the meds. I'll help in a minute."

Lt. Shaw said, "Yes, ma'am" and stepped toward a cabinet. But then she turned toward Joe. "The cafeteria is on the first floor. Go get something to eat before you report to Captain Russell or you might end up going to bed hungry."

Joe thanked her and headed to the stairwell, thankful he'd have a chance to work with Lt. Shaw and get to know her better. There was something both foreign and familiar about her.

The cafeteria was crowded with doctors, nurses, orderlies, and other hospital staff. Joe found an empty seat in the back of the cafeteria, slid his tray onto the table, and placed his bag on the chair beside him. Two nurses sat at the other end of the table, joking with each other over the clatter of dishes and spoons. Neither said hello to him. He suddenly felt a wave of homesickness. Everything was so different here. The people. The setting. The chatter.

He quickly consumed his bowl of soup and a piece of the bread that hardly had any taste. The texture of the margarine was odd too, so he swallowed it quickly.

Once he was done, he watched others take their trays to the far end of the cafeteria and slide them into a small opening. He did likewise and realized a crew was washing dishes behind the wall.

He went back to the stairwell and headed down another flight, gripping his bag. Once he reached the basement, he headed down the hall toward voices. An orderly stepped out of a doorway and started toward him.

"Hallo," Joe said. "I'm looking for Captain Russell."

"His office is the next one down," the man said.

The door was closed so Joe knocked. When no one answered, he knocked again, this time louder.

"What do you want?"

"I'm Joe Bachmann," he called out. "Reporting for duty."

"It's unlocked."

He opened the door and stepped into the small room.

A man wearing a khaki uniform kept his head down as he wrote on a form. Joe stood with his bag in his hand, waiting.

The man looked up. He appeared to be in his mid-thirties and wore his hair short.

Joe extended his orders.

The man read them quickly and then said, "Grab two uniforms, linens, a blanket, a towel, and a pillow from the shelf." He nodded toward the side of the room. "Then find an empty bed in the barracks."

"Where is that?" Joe asked.

"Two doors to your right, down here in the basement," the captain said. "The women have a dormitory on the top floor. No men are allowed up there for any reason. Understand?"

Joe's face warmed. "Of course."

"Report to the third floor at 0700 tomorrow morning."

"Sir," Joe said. "I worked there this afternoon, and Lt. Madison told me to report for night shift tomorrow."

A look of amusement passed over the captain's face. "You'll follow my orders, not Lt. Madison's." The man nodded toward Joe's shirt. "Take that to the laundry—it's at the other end of the basement. They'll get the blood out for you."

Joe nodded, thanked the man, and quickly retrieved the items from the shelves. As he walked through the barracks, several of the men climbed off their beds and shook his hand. One was from New York. He definitely wasn't Amish. Another was a Mennonite man from Ohio. Another was a Quaker from Philadelphia. A dark-skinned man introduced himself as Ali. He was from Newark, New Jersey. "I'm Moslem," he said.

Joe had never met a Moslem person, or someone who was a Quaker either. All of the men were polite and welcoming. He continued on until he found an empty bed.

He didn't mind working the day shift the next morning, but he did regret he wouldn't be working with Lt. Shaw.

Joe didn't sleep well that night even though he was exhausted. The noises from the other men and the honks and sirens outside the basement windows woke him over and over. He rose early before anyone else, showered, and dressed in his all-white uniform. After he ate breakfast, he arrived on the ward a half hour early. Of course, the nurse and orderly who'd worked all night were happy to see him.

But when Lt. Madison arrived, she was annoyed. At first she chastised him for disobeying her, but after he said he was following Captain Russell's orders, she pursed her lips and spun away from him.

She did seem pleased to boss him around, however. Joe started out with managing the bedpans. Next, he and Lt. Madison fed the patients, then distributed the meds, and bathed the soldiers. They dressed the worst of the wounds and assisted several doctors, including Captain Russell, when they came through on their rounds.

They repeated the feeding process at noon. After they'd finished, Lt. Madison grabbed an extra sandwich off the tray and told Joe to do the same.

Then they dressed more of the wounds. At three p.m., another nurse and orderly arrived. Although the tasks were foreign to Joe, and he was definitely learning how to do them under a fair amount of stress, he didn't feel as if he'd put in a whole day's work. At home he was used to being in the fields twelve hours or more in the spring and summer.

He retreated to the barracks and took a piece of paper, an envelope, and a stamp from the trunk at the end of his bed where he'd stored his things. He started a letter home, writing about the train trip, Lake Michigan and Chicago, the hospital, and his first two days of work. *So far, I've been able to do the tasks required of me*, he wrote. *I've met all sorts of interesting people from different places—Ohio, New York, New Jersey, and Philadelphia. Objecting to fighting seems to be what we have in common.* Joe couldn't help but wonder what the other men thought of him.

That evening, he looked for Lt. Shaw in the cafeteria but didn't see her. Afterward, he sat in the barracks across from Ali. He had the darkest skin Joe had ever seen—a color comparable to coffee with just a little bit of cream. He'd been working at the hospital for three months. Joe listened to his story.

"Are all Moslems nonresistant?" Joe asked.

"Nonresistant?"

"Pacifists." Joe knew that was the more common term, although it wasn't a synonym for nonresistant. Not only did the Amish not believe in fighting, they didn't believe in defending themselves either.

Ali shook his head. "There are many beliefs among those who follow Islam, just like with other faiths. Not all Moslems are conscientious objectors." The man said he had a wife and son back home.

Joe wondered who was supporting his family while he was gone but didn't ask. Hopefully Ali had relatives or friends who were helping.

Ali asked Joe if he wanted to go for a walk in the neighborhood surrounding the hospital, and Joe gladly accepted the invitation.

Outside, two boys stopped them, asking if they'd buy war bonds.

Ali said, "No, thank you," and Joe nodded his head in agreement.

One of the boys sneered at them and said, "Don't you care if our soldiers die?"

Ali explained that they worked as orderlies at the hospital and that they very much wanted for the soldiers to live.

The other boy grabbed the first boy's arm and they turned down the street.

At least the doctors and nurses in the hospital seemed to value what the conscientious objectors did. So far, none of them had been negative in any way, at least not in front of Joe.

In fact, Captain Russell had complimented him earlier in the day, saying he had a knack for medicine. "You should join up," he said. "Six weeks of training at Fort Drum and you'd be ready to head to the front line to take care of soldiers there. With your strength and quick feet, you'd be a big help."

Joe just smiled.

Later that night, as Joe finished his letter, he realized that not only did he miss his family, but he also missed speaking Pennsylvania Dutch. Speaking Englisch was a bit of an effort for him. Jah, being away from home was harder than he'd expected.

The next morning, he rose early again. After he'd made his bed, tidied up, and showered, he headed to the cafeteria. As he ate a bowl of oatmeal, he hoped he'd see Lt. Shaw on the ward at the change of shift.

After he finished breakfast, he headed up the stairwell, taking the steps two at a time. As he neared the floor, he heard shouting, which compelled him to run the rest of the way. When he reached the floor, an orderly and Lt. Shaw held a patient on his back, flat against the mattress.

Joe rushed to the side of the bed.

"Grab his arms," Lt. Shaw ordered.

Joe did as he was told, pinning the man down.

"I'll be right back." She ran to the medicine cabinet.

The patient writhed and shouted, "Let me go!" He cursed and tried to yank his arms away.

Joe held on, leaning on the man. "It's all right," Joe murmured.

The man cursed again, his gray eyes wild, pupils dilated.

Without even realizing what he was doing, Joe began to sing one of the few hymns he knew in Englisch, one that Charity had recently taught him. "When peace like a river, attendeth my way . . ."

The man kept thrashing, breaking one leg loose from the other orderly. Joe kept singing as he swung his right leg up and pinned the man down with his knee. As he sang, he prayed Lt. Shaw would hurry up with whatever she went to get. He was afraid if the man broke free, he might throw a punch.

Joe kept singing. "Though Satan should buffet, though trials should come . . ."

Finally, Lt. Shaw returned with a syringe in her hand.

The man yelled again, but she ignored him as she lifted his gown and plunged the needle into the flesh of his backside.

"This will help you." Her face was flushed, but she kept her voice calm. She whispered, "Don't let go, boys, until I tell you."

Joe held on to the man. Within a couple of minutes, the soldier began to relax, and his lids closed over his wild eyes.

"Let go of him. Slowly," Lt. Shaw said.

Joe moved his knee and the other orderly let go of the man's other leg. Joe let go of one arm and then the other.

Lt. Shaw exhaled.

"What happened?" Joe asked.

Bennie, who was in the next bed, piped up. "He's crazy, that's what happened."

Lt. Shaw wrinkled her nose. "I hope he didn't have a reaction to a medication. I'll let Captain Russell know. Or perhaps it's his nerves." She lowered her voice. "Battle fatigue. It hits some out of the blue, or so it seems. Others struggle with it every day."

Joe hadn't ever seen anyone with battle fatigue, but he had heard of it. During the War to End All Wars, he'd been told it was called *shell shock.*

Two other orderlies arrived with the breakfast carts, and then once Lt. Madison arrived, Lt. Shaw finished up her charting while Joe started feeding the patients who couldn't feed themselves and Lt. Madison passed out the bowls of oatmeal to the other patients.

"See you later," Lt. Shaw said to the other nurse.

Lt. Madison turned toward her, a tray in her hands. "I hope you're not upset about being back on nights."

"Not at all." Lt. Shaw smiled, though she looked absolutely spent.

"It's really the easier shift," Lt. Madison continued.

Lt. Shaw nodded. "It's fine. Really." Then she turned toward Joe. "I don't know what we would have done if you hadn't arrived." Her blue eyes glistened. "Denki."

Joe smiled. "Glad I could help."

It wasn't until after she left the ward that he realized she'd thanked him in Pennsylvania Dutch.

— 7 —

Leisel

I t's late," Aenti Suz said. "We should head home."

"Wait," I replied. "You can't stop now."

She yawned. "You need your rest even more than I do. I'm guessing you'll come back here in the morning."

Aenti Suz's yawn was contagious, and my mouth involuntarily opened too. I covered it quickly.

"Besides," she said, "Caden might be out of sorts. We should see if we can help Jessica."

"You're right." I stood quickly.

We stopped by Marie's room, but both she and Gordon were asleep. We didn't want to wake them, so we headed out to the parking garage and to my car.

Aenti Suz could have picked up the story on the drive home but instead we talked about Marie. I'd left a message on the machine out in the barn and hoped Mamm had checked it. Or maybe Arden had and passed on the message.

I turned onto Oak Road at *Sunn-unnah*, just as streaks of

pinks and oranges appeared in the western sky over the emerald green field.

"*Ach*," Aenti Suz said. "That's what miracles look like. I'm confident Marie will completely recover."

It was a sunset with a perfectly scientific explanation based on the wavelength of the light and the size of the particles in the atmosphere. The miracle of Marie's body, the way God created it to heal, was what amazed me. And bodies could heal—or not. But I appreciated the intent behind Aenti Suz's comment. We all hoped Marie would recover, miracle or not.

I parked in my usual spot and followed Aenti Suz to her Dawdi Haus. No one was there.

"They must be over at Mamm's," I said. "Why don't you rest for a while? I'll go help Jessica."

No one was in the kitchen or the living room, and Mamm wasn't in her sewing room, but a baby—Caden, I was sure—cried from the second floor, so I headed upstairs.

Jessica stood in the old sewing room, where the crib was, Caden in her arms and Ruby hanging on to her leg.

"Oh dear. I'll take him." I held out my arms. For a moment I was afraid he wouldn't come to me, but then he did. He kept crying.

"How is Marie?" Jessica asked.

I told her what the doctor had said. "Didn't Mamm check the messages? Or Arden?"

Jessica shook her head. "Not that I know of. At least no one told me."

"Where's Mamm?" I asked.

"Bed. At least that's where I think she is."

It was eight thirty. "Did she help you at all today?"

Jessica shrugged.

My pulse raced. "What's going on with her?"

"I don't know. But something's bugging her."

Caden began to scream, and I started to bounce him. "Did you plan to have him sleep here?"

Jessica nodded and scooped Ruby into her arms. "We're sleeping in our old room."

"I'll take him over to Aenti Suz's," I said. "Where his travel crib is."

Needless to say, Caden hardly slept that night and neither did I. He couldn't settle down, so I took him out to Aenti Suz's living room. But when he continued to be fussy, I finally took him over to Mamm's. Since the house was larger, he wasn't as likely to keep others awake there. I wanted Aenti Suz to get some sleep.

When Mamm came down at five o'clock, I had Caden in his high chair. I'd started a pot of coffee for me and had prepared a bowl of cereal for him.

I was surprised to see Mamm so early. I expected her to ask about Marie but she didn't. "Did you get my message?"

She shook her head.

"Marie came through the surgery all right."

"I figured," Mamm said. "Otherwise you would have woken me up when you got home."

I had a dozen questions for her—starting with why she went to bed before I got home—but Caden began to cry again. I quickly poured myself a cup of coffee and grabbed the bowl of cereal.

"All that child does is cry," Mamm muttered as she poured her own cup of coffee.

I inhaled sharply. Maybe it was better that Mamm wasn't helping Jessica with the children. She'd probably only make things worse.

I had Caden fed, bathed, diapered, and dressed by the time

Jessica and Ruby came down the stairs. Ruby was smiling and laughing, and Jessica seemed well rested too.

"There's our little girl." Mamm held out her arms to Ruby. "Come to your *Mammi*."

I winced. Mamm had played favorites with her daughters—and now she was doing the same with her grandchildren. Dat had never played favorites with anyone.

Ruby didn't take the bait and instead hid her face against Jessica's leg.

"Give her a few minutes." Jessica turned toward me. "How's Caden? How are you?"

I didn't want to complain about a lack of sleep so I simply said, "He's having a rough time."

Mamm harrumphed.

Jessica turned toward me, rolled her eyes, and mouthed, *Ignore her.*

"After everyone's ready for the day, I thought I'd head up to the hospital and see if Gordon wants to get some sleep."

Jessica nodded, slipping Ruby into the high chair. "It'll just take me a few minutes to feed Ruby. Then I can take Caden."

I reminded her that I'd be going to Pittsburgh that night and taking my test the next day.

"I remember," she said. "Ruby and I will sleep over at Aenti Suz's so Caden can sleep in his travel crib."

I thanked her and then sat in Mamm's rocker with the little guy, hoping maybe he'd fall asleep. He didn't. He seemed traumatized to be away from his parents, and I didn't know what to do to help him.

After I arrived at the hospital, Gordon headed to the farm to spend some time with Caden while I stayed with Marie. I brought my review book again, but it stayed in my backpack. I didn't open it once.

Marie's first worry was about Caden. I didn't tell her how upset he was.

"You know how much he likes Ruby," I said. "It's a warm day. They're probably playing in the sandbox and having a great time."

Marie smiled a little. "I'm so grateful for my sisters."

She told me she was doing fine, but I quickly realized she wasn't. By midmorning she was in a lot of pain, long before it was time for her meds, and her blood pressure kept crashing. She was pale and weak, and quite frankly, I was alarmed. Several times I pushed the button when I felt the nurse didn't respond quickly enough to a low blood pressure reading on the machine, even though the alarm went off.

Obviously the nurse had a lot of assignments for the day, but this was Marie. My sister. I hoped I would remember what it was like to be on this side of the bed when I started working as a nurse in a hospital.

I tried to do everything I could to help. As I gave Marie a sponge bath, I thought of my Dawdi Joe doing the same for soldiers all those years ago in Chicago. As I coaxed Marie to eat, I thought of Joe feeding his patients. Like Joe, I'd moved to a city far away from Lancaster County. But unlike Joe, I'd already trained as a CNA when I started working in the nursing home and taking classes. I already knew I wanted a career in medicine. He'd been thrown into it, having had no part in the decision making.

But that was what was done in times of war. I wondered if Nick realized what he'd be signing up for if he joined the Air Force. His life wouldn't be his own, not at all.

He texted me several times during the day. First to make sure

I wanted to return to Pittsburgh to take the test. *You can re-schedule. Or take it in Lancaster, if that would be better.* I texted back that I wanted to take the test the next day, in Pittsburgh.

Then he texted to see what time I would arrive and if he could see me. I told him I wouldn't get in until late.

No worries, he texted back. *The most important thing is that you get a good night's sleep.* He said he could meet me after the test. *I'll take you to lunch to celebrate.* I cringed. I wouldn't even know if I passed or not until two days after I took the test. *Lunch would be nice,* I texted back. *No matter the outcome of the test.* ☺

Mostly, throughout the day, my attention was on Marie. "Hospital time" was an inconsistent animal. Sometimes it was slower than a sloth. Other times it raced like a cheetah. This day sped by and in no time it was late afternoon and Gordon had returned.

"How's Caden?" was the first thing Marie asked.

"He's missing his mama," Gordon answered. "But he's doing all right."

I guessed that meant he spent the day crying.

"I should get going." I hadn't told either of them that I'd planned to take my boards the next day. I'd expected that Marie would be doing better, that it would be her last day in the hospital—that it would be clear sailing. Now I wondered if I should have rescheduled the test.

No. Marie wouldn't want me to do that.

I cleared my throat. Both Marie and Gordon turned toward me. "Jessica is going to be in charge of Caden tonight. I'm taking my state boards tomorrow. I scheduled them back in April, before I graduated. Before I knew . . ."

"Where are you taking the test?"

"In Pittsburgh."

Marie's eyes grew wide. "You're driving there? Tonight?"

I nodded.

"That's crazy," she said.

"I'm sorry I won't be here."

Gordon glanced at Marie. "I wish you would have told us. I could have come sooner so you could get on the road."

"I'll be fine." I grabbed my backpack.

Marie reached for my hand. "I'll be praying."

"Denki," I said. "I'll be back by tomorrow evening. I'll call and see where you are. If you're still in the hospital, I can come here. If you still want to go to the farm, I'll meet you there."

She shook her head. "That's too much for you. Spend another night at your apartment. Then come back."

"We'll see." Not wanting to stay away from her any longer than I absolutely had to, I didn't say any more. I didn't want to add to Marie's stress. I hugged her and then told both of them good-bye.

Stopping by the cafeteria, I purchased a sandwich I could eat in the car and the largest coffee they sold. Then I texted Nick that I was on my way.

As I drove, rain splattered my windshield. I tried to think through the test material, but over and over my mind went blank. I breathed deeply. When panic started to creep up, I logically thought through the chain of events happening in my brain—neurotransmitters sent signals to different brain structures, including the amygdala and hypothalamus. Those signals activated the sympathetic nervous system, which set off my "fight-or-flight" response. In turn, adrenaline was released in the bloodstream, causing the feeling of panic, along with an increased heart rate, shortness of breath, and sweating. Some people even had dizziness. As I thought through the process, I determined for that not to happen.

My trick worked. The threat of panic fled and my heart rate slowed.

Everything I'd learned would come back to me when it was time to take the test. I was sure of it.

I turned up the radio. Both Paisley and Autumn had texted me in the last week, asking how Marie was and wondering when I'd return to Pittsburgh. Both told me to let them know ahead of time so we could make plans to get together, but I hadn't. I felt bad about it, but I didn't feel up to any social interaction. Both were better friends to me than I was to them. Hopefully I could make it up to them someday.

When I passed the exit to Somerset, as the sign for the diner sped by, my heart rate increased again. Had the man lived? If so, how was he doing? If not, how was his family? A few minutes later, my phone rang. I didn't recognize the number and didn't answer it. But then I started to fret about that. Maybe it was Gordon on a hospital line.

I pulled over at the next exit, stopping in the parking lot of a mini-mart, and listened to the voicemail. It was Mr. Weber's daughter, saying she'd like to speak with me. "Please call when you can," she'd said.

I pressed Call. There was no reason to put it off.

"Thank you for calling me right back," she said when she answered. "Rita told me you were working the night my father died. Could you tell me what happened?"

I told her about his fall, what he said about hearing her mother at the door, holding her as a baby, and about tucking him back into bed. I didn't tell her he'd told me I was the best nurse he'd ever had.

"I checked on him a half hour later and he was sleeping soundly, but by the change of shift, he'd passed," I explained. "He probably died soon after the last time I checked on him."

"Goodness," she said. "I wish you would have called me when he fell. I would have come in—and been with him when he died." I could hear the tears in her voice.

I wasn't sure how to respond. Choosing my words carefully, I said, "If we'd known he only had a few hours left, someone would have called you. But we didn't have any idea."

"I asked to be notified whenever anything happened," she said.

"That's the nurse's responsibility." I inhaled. "She would have called you in the morning. I'm an aide, and we're instructed not to call family in the middle of the night." In truth, it wasn't our job to call family at all.

"Well," she said. "I had concerns about you earlier, but I still would have expected more. . . ."

I took a deep breath, shocked at the drastic change in her attitude. I'd always gotten along so well with her. I reminded myself that she was grieving and stressed. I'd seen it before in other family members who grew irrational when a relative grew worse—or died.

"I'm really sorry for your loss," I said. "Your father was a wonderful person."

When she didn't answer, I thought maybe the call had been disconnected. "Hello?"

"I'm here," she said. "You should have given me the chance to *be there*, with my father."

"I understand your pain," I said.

She laughed bitterly. "How could you?"

I hesitated. I didn't want to talk with this woman about my own father and my grief, not now. Instead, I said, "I'm traveling and pulled over to call you. I need to get back on the road."

"I see," she said. "Someone will be in touch once I decide what to do."

"Pardon?"

"I'll talk with my lawyer tomorrow. I don't want this to happen to another family."

I was stunned. I'd followed protocol and done nothing wrong. I didn't owe her any more of an explanation. In retrospect, I probably shouldn't have spoken with her at all. "Have a good evening." I quickly added, "Good-bye," and ended the call.

My hand shook a little as I shifted into Drive. Then I gripped the steering wheel tightly and pulled back onto the freeway. Her lawyer would set her straight. She had no case against me. Still, panic threatened and, again, I logically forced it away. Then I turned up the radio and drove on into the inky darkness.

It was ten thirty by the time I reached my apartment. I half hoped Nick had ignored my request and was waiting for me. He wasn't. But a paper sack sat on my doorstep. I picked it up and peered inside. A small bag of coffee. An apple and an orange. A bag of almonds. Three granola bars. And a card.

I unlocked my door, put everything on the kitchen counter, and opened the card.

Leisel,

You're the strongest person I know. You've got this. Don't think about the test tonight. Get a good night's sleep. Then do your best.

Love and prayers,
Nick

My heart missed a beat. I put on my pajamas, knelt to say my stilted prayers, and then crawled into bed. Against Nick's advice, I started thinking about the test. Panic threatened me for the third time. Once again, I willed it away. I had one last push to get my proverbial boulder to the top of the hill. Then I could go home, care for Marie, and apply for jobs. And figure out my future.

I tossed and turned all night. I'd been a good caregiver to an elderly man, but his daughter was sure I'd done something wrong. But I hadn't helped Marie. I hadn't followed through on my advice to her, and she'd put off going to the doctor. My thoughts turned to the man in the diner. Had I done all I could for him?

I flopped from one side to the other. At midnight, I climbed out of bed and began packing my kitchen. I'd take a couple of boxes home with me and then come back and finish cleaning the apartment some other time. I was glad I'd only browsed for new apartments and hadn't put a deposit down on anything. At least that was one less thing to worry about.

I finally slept between two and four—at least I didn't check the time on my phone between those hours. At five o'clock, I climbed out of bed, started a pot of coffee, and ate one of the granola bars. Even after I showered and dressed, I still had three hours until the test started, so I decided I might as well review my notes. First I stared at the care environment section. And then the psychosocial integrity section.

My eyes began to swim. It was as if I hadn't looked at the material at all, which shouldn't have been surprising—it had been since before I graduated that I last studied. Putting the notes away, I decided to drive to the test-taking site and then take a walk.

The gray light of morning crept over the hills and then the rivers as I drove toward downtown. The wavelengths of light and the size of the particles weren't as optimal for the sunrise as they'd been for the sunset back home. The sun crept over the eastern hills and the sky turned a lighter hue of gray that matched the color of the rivers, foretelling a gloomy day.

There wasn't much traffic yet, and I made good time. I hated to pay extra for parking, but there was nothing else I could do. I parked in a garage, and then headed out for a long walk. It was cold for mid-May, and the rain sputtered on and off.

As I walked, I told myself that there was no need to be negative. I'd had a rough twenty-four hours—actually a rough two weeks—but I felt confident in my knowledge. It was bound to come back as I answered the questions.

I knew the minimum number of questions was seventy-five while the maximum was 265. Some people passed in seventy-five questions. Some passed in 265. And lots failed somewhere in between. If you were doing really well, you could pass in seventy-five. On the other hand, you could also fail in seventy-five. Or you could teeter along all the way to 265 and then pass—or fail. I knew students who'd done extremely well in nursing school who didn't pass on their first try. I knew others who barely passed their classes who aced their licensing exam. Critical thinking was key.

I entered the building and took the elevator to the third floor. When I reached the test-taking office, there was already a line of people ready to check in.

Soon, we were all seated in front of computer screens. Ninety minutes into the test, one of the test takers stood with a smile on her face and checked out with the facilitator. Not long after, another one did.

I was on question eighty now, which meant I hadn't passed in seventy-five questions. I continued on, tackling question after question, trying to stay positive. If I was answering the questions right, they should be getting harder. But I was so anxious

I couldn't track if they were getting harder or easier. Plus I had a six-hour limit. If I went over that, the test would time out.

I ended up finishing with an hour to spare, but I'd gone through all 265 questions. Only one other person was left in the room.

When I reached the hall, I knew I should text Nick but felt too exhausted. I hoped I'd passed, but perhaps I'd been over-confident. Perhaps I should have made time to study, no matter what else was going on.

When I reached my car, my phone pinged with a text from Nick. *Ready for lunch?*

I considered blowing him off. Not answering his text. Going back to my apartment to sleep. Or going back to grab my things and flee to Lancaster County.

But that wouldn't be fair to him. Not after everything he'd done for me.

I texted him back. *Sure. How about the café by my apartment? In twenty minutes?*

See you then, he texted back.

He had a table and a smile on his face when I arrived. He hugged me and pulled out my chair. As soon as I sat, he asked, "So how did it go?"

He must have known by the look on my face that I wasn't happy with how I'd done. He wrapped his arms around me once again.

The boulder I thought I'd pushed to the top of the hill had just come crashing down, landing on top of me.

— 8 —

We sat in the back of the café at our favorite table. It wasn't my style to be self-deprecating. I was never one to say that I'd thought I'd flunked a test when I knew I hadn't. I always kept quiet. But I'd never thought I'd failed a test in my life. Until now.

"If anyone would pass, it's you," Nick reassured me.

I hadn't told him about the two sleepless nights. About my compulsive thoughts about Marie. About the threat from Mr. Weber's daughter. About my flashbacks to the man in the diner.

"You're tired, is all," Nick said. "You're under too much stress. And you lost the board lottery with your two hundred sixty-five questions. Try to chill for the next two days. Everything will be better soon."

I ordered a cup of coffee and a cup of soup, while Nick ordered a salad, sandwich, and chips.

"That's not much lunch," Nick said to me after the waitress left.

I shrugged. I wasn't hungry, which made me remember the food he'd left last night. "Oh hey, thank you for the granola bars and fruit. That was really sweet."

"You're welcome." He leaned forward. "I'd do anything for you."

Anything but not join the Air Force. I didn't say it out loud, but I thought it. Why couldn't he have grown up Anabaptist? I chastised myself at the thought. If he had, neither of us would have pursued nursing, most likely. Then I thought of Dr. Turner. He'd grown up Anabaptist and gone to medical school.

Nick asked about Marie. I told him about her blood pressure crashing and how worried I was about her. He listened attentively.

Once our food arrived, I took a few bites of soup and then forced a few more down while Nick inhaled his food. When we finished eating—or when I pushed my cup forward, still half full—I said I needed to get on the road.

"Are you sure?" he said. "Wouldn't it be better to spend another night? We could go out for breakfast in the morning when I get off work."

"That would be nice," I said. "But hopefully Marie will get out of the hospital tomorrow morning. I'd like to be there to talk with the surgeon again."

He nodded. "You're a good sister. And aunt." He didn't ask how long I thought I'd stay in Lancaster, and I appreciated that. Nick wasn't clingy and needy, not like some of my classmates' boyfriends.

I ordered coffee to go, and then Nick walked me to my car. "We still haven't talked . . . about us."

"I know." My voice fell. "Soon?"

He wrinkled his nose.

"I just can't handle anything else right now," I said. I'd been prematurely relieved he hadn't brought up the topic. It appeared he hadn't changed his mind.

After he helped me carry my kitchen boxes to my trunk, he simply gave me a hug as we said good-bye.

117

As I drove out of the city, I thought of the first time I'd met Nick. It was the first day of our CNA class. I'd hired a driver to take me to the nursing home on the edge of Lancaster where the class was held. Nick had graduated from high school the year before and was taking courses at the community college. He was interested in studying nursing and figured working as a CNA would give him a good idea whether he wanted to take that route or not.

He wasn't the only man in the class, but he was the youngest. I wasn't the only woman in the class, of course, but I was the only Plain one.

Immediately I noticed his root-beer-colored eyes, and then he smiled at me as I slipped into the room.

I didn't smile back.

There was a seat beside him, but I continued to the next row and sat there. We didn't talk the first day or the next. All of my attention was on the nurse teaching the class. She was in her early thirties and had graduated from a nursing school in Philadelphia. "Nursing school was hard—anatomy, physiology, clinicals—but absolutely worth it. There are so many possibilities as far as jobs. I'm thankful every single day that I chose this career."

She'd worked in home health care for a few years after college, and now she worked for the company that owned the nursing home. She said she got her CNA while she was in nursing school and the skills she learned helped her during her clinicals. She added that being a CNA, in itself, was a great career too.

I didn't think I'd particularly enjoy working with elderly patients, but I wouldn't mind it either. In fact, I just hoped I'd be able to work as a CNA at all—a problem I was pretty sure no one else in the room had.

As much as I purposefully avoided Nick, I did notice him. His brown eyes were hard to miss, and he was by far the tallest person in the class. He also knew the answer to almost every question the instructor asked. He wasn't prideful about it, and it wasn't that he raised his hand each time, but it was obvious he knew the material.

It wasn't until we started our clinicals that we talked. We were both in the dining hall feeding patients when he said, "I've been impressed with your answers in class."

I simply thanked him and concentrated on the eighty-seven-year-old man in front of me who was trying to blow bubbles with his applesauce.

"What are your plans after you complete this course?" he asked.

I shrugged. Dat had given me permission to take the class, which only lasted a month, but I still didn't know if I'd get permission to get a CNA job. I hadn't joined the church, so it wasn't as if Bishop Jacobs could say I couldn't do it. Dat thought it was fine, but I figured Mamm wouldn't want me to be around so many Englisch people day in and day out. She had a fear another child of hers would leave the church, and at the time she was sure it wouldn't be Marie. Which left me.

Nick asked me again, but I deflected and asked what his plans were. He answered that he was looking into the nursing program at the University of Pittsburgh. That was all he said, but that, combined with what our teacher had said about her nursing school, got me dreaming.

"Have you thought about going to med school?" I asked the next time we talked.

He'd nodded. "Yeah, I looked into that too. But I decided I'd rather go into nursing. I don't want hundreds of thousands of dollars of student debt. Thousands will be hard enough. Plus I can always get an advanced degree in nursing as a nurse practitioner or nurse anesthetist."

I didn't know what either of those was, but I asked my driver to take me by the public library on the way home so I could look them up. A nurse practitioner could do almost everything a doctor could, including prescribing. A nurse anesthetist performed the same tasks as an anesthesiologist.

My admiration for the nursing profession grew.

It was soon evident that Nick and I were doing the best of all the students. He began sitting by me in the classroom in the morning, and our instructor often assigned us to the same area of the nursing home for our afternoon clinicals. One time, when I was caring for an obese patient, Nick checked in with me several times to help move the man. Even though Nick was lanky, he was strong. I didn't think it was fair of me to depend on him, but I appreciated his willingness to help.

One day after class, the receptionist handed me a note that said my driver wasn't going to be able to pick me up.

"Everything okay?" Nick had asked.

When I told him I needed to call for a ride, he said, "I can take you."

I shook my head but then changed my mind. I'd have him drop me off on the highway and I'd walk up the lane. No one would even know.

He drove a Chevy pickup that was old but clean both inside and out. He opened the passenger door and then I reached over and opened his door for him. That made him smile.

He didn't start the engine until I had my seat belt fastened. He drove responsibly, and we chatted away about what we'd learned that day.

When I asked him to drop me off at the intersection of Oak Road and the highway, he said, "I can take you all the way."

"No, here is fine." When I started to reach for the door, he pulled over, saying, "Oh," as if he understood the situation.

He waited, though, until I was halfway down the lane, until I turned and waved again. After that he drove me home after every class, always dropping me off in the same spot. One day, I jokingly asked if he'd teach me how to drive. He pulled over onto a dirt road and told me to trade places with him. With the patience of a saint, he taught me the basics of driving and let me practice several times after that. When the class ended, he gave me his phone number and asked for mine.

I told him it would be best if I just called him. I didn't at first—I hated talking on the phone—but after a couple of months, I did. I'd gotten my GED and wanted to know more about applying to nursing school. I took my ACTs and aced them. I applied to the same school that Nick had in Pittsburgh and included an essay about growing up Amish and that I was willing to leave to pursue that calling. On the day before he moved to Pittsburgh to start nursing school, Nick took the time to meet me at the library to help me edit the essay and finish my application.

When I received the acceptance letter in the late fall of 2012 with a start date of spring 2013, I called him immediately and we celebrated together on the phone.

When Dat was diagnosed with cancer two weeks later, I called Nick and he told me to contact the college and ask for my admittance to be postponed to fall 2013. It was good advice.

When Dat decided to stop chemo, I called Nick in the middle of the night. When Dat stopped eating, I again called Nick in the middle of the night. When Dat went into a coma, I called Nick for a third time in the middle of the night.

When Dat died, I called Nick as soon as I could. He asked if he could come to the funeral, but I told him no. I didn't have the energy to explain to everyone who he was. The stress of Dat's death, Jessica's homecoming, Amos's unexpected appearance,

Marie's self-righteousness, and Mamm's fragility was more than enough for me to deal with.

After seeing the way Mamm and Marie treated Jessica the week after Dat died, though, I called Nick again. I decided I might as well leave home sooner rather than later. He looked for CNA jobs and apartments for me in Pittsburgh, emailing me the links. I applied online at the library for both.

Once I'd secured a job and a place to live, he met me in Harrisburg at the café in the same building as Jessica's apartment and then took me to Pittsburgh and helped me transition to an Englisch life, including taking me to church with him. I didn't find a community like the one I'd left, but I found kindness and support. A place to learn and worship.

Nick was honestly the best friend I'd ever had. A better friend than even my sisters. My relationship with him had developed step by step, in a natural way.

I clenched my jaw. Now, we were at the first impasse of our relationship.

Even though I couldn't figure out what was coming next, just thinking through my story with Nick made me feel better. I truly believed God had brought Nick into my life and led me to nursing school. And God had a plan for me, even though I'd forgotten that both during the test and afterward. I squared my shoulders as the sun broke through the clouds.

As I drove, I finished the last of my coffee just as I passed the first sign for the upcoming Somerset exit. I hesitated. Could I take any more bad news? Regardless, I decided to stop at the diner for more coffee and ask for an update on the man. Surely someone would know the outcome. And if he'd survived, I could really use the good news.

The lot in front of the diner was nearly full, and I parked along the side. I sat at the counter for a few minutes before a waitress, one I didn't recognize, asked what I needed.

"A large coffee to go," I answered. "And hopefully some information." I quickly explained about the man who'd experienced the cardiac incident a few weeks ago.

"I heard about that." She pursed her lips. "But I'm not sure what happened. Let me get Terri. I think she knows."

A minute later, one of the waitresses from that night walked out of the kitchen.

"Oh, hi," she said, obviously recognizing me.

I introduced myself anyway. "I keep thinking about the man who collapsed the last time I was in," I said. "And I wondered if you have an update."

Her face fell.

My heartbeat quickened.

"I'm sorry," she said. "He didn't make it."

Even though I knew the odds, I still had hoped he'd beaten them. "I'm so sorry too." I swallowed, trying to dislodge the lump in my throat.

"You were so great with all of it," she said. "In fact, his wife came by about a week ago. She was hoping you'd stop in again sometime, and she left her number."

I winced. What if she wanted to sue me too? I took the number that Terri had retrieved from near the cash register and thanked her, but then I stuffed the slip of paper in the pocket of my backpack. I didn't have the resolve to call her, not now. I'd learned my lesson with Mr. Weber's daughter.

I fought back my tears until I reached my car. As I buckled my seat belt, the first sob wracked me, followed by another. Tears streamed down my face. That little boy and girl were without a father. That poor woman had lost her husband.

I reached into the back seat for the tissue box and swiped at my tears and then blew my nose. Here I was, the girl who didn't cry, wallowing in a parking lot in Somerset. It wasn't like me to be so emotional.

I was tired, yes. And for the first time I could remember, scared.

For Marie. And Gordon. And Caden. And me. It was one thing to lose Dat, but he was sixty-seven when he died. Marie was a young woman. A young mother.

Another sob threatened me, but I willed it away.

I called Gordon to see if I should go to the hospital or the farm. "Go on home," he said. "Marie's had a rough evening. I'll stay again tonight."

As I turned onto the ramp, I thought about my emotional reaction at both Sonny's death and Marie's illness. I was raised to believe in God's wisdom, in His will. The rain fell on the just and the unjust. The Lord knew the number of our days. Some lived a long life, some a short one. Blessed be the name of the Lord.

Had my faith changed that much in the last four years? Was I not trusting God? He'd allowed Mr. Weber to live to be nearly ninety-three, but He'd allowed Sonny to die while he was still a young man. Perhaps God would allow Marie to die young too. I'd grown up believing that God worked in mysterious ways, with plans we couldn't understand.

Nick would say that death was never part of God's plan— that it was the result of Adam and Eve's sin. It was the consequence we lived with until heaven.

Death was definitely part of life. I couldn't change what God allowed. Or control when a person died.

As I passed a semi truck, I breathed a prayer for Mr. Weber's daughter, that she would gain clarity with her father's death.

Then I said a prayer for Marie. *Please heal her. Please. Please. Please.*

My thoughts spiraled the way they had last night when I was trying to sleep. I hadn't given Marie the advice she needed. Mr. Weber's daughter might sue me. And I hadn't saved Sonny. Perhaps I wasn't meant for the medical field.

If not, what would I do? Move back home with Mamm? Take a job as a CNA? Give up my car and join the church?

I felt ill.

When I'd first left for Pittsburgh, I was excited, much like my Dawdi Joe had been with his trip to Chicago. Maybe I'd gotten my confidence from him. I couldn't help but wonder if he continued to find his time away from home a big adventure. Had he faltered at some point?

I drove on, sipping my coffee and eating another granola bar. By the time I reached the farm, the sun slipped beyond the horizon, the rain sending it on its way. There were no beautiful streaks of light to bid it farewell. No miracles tonight.

I parked, grabbed my backpack, and was headed toward the Dawdi Haus just as Bishop Jacobs opened the front door and stepped onto the porch.

"Leisel," he said.

I nodded. "Hallo."

He'd never said more than a few words at a time to me, and he didn't change his pattern now. With a quick farewell, he was on his way.

I stepped into the little house. By the lamp burning in the living room, I saw Aenti Suz rocking Caden. He appeared to be asleep.

I nodded toward the door. "What did Bishop Jacobs want?"

"He just had a few questions," Aenti Suz answered.

"About Marie staying here?"

She nodded. "But don't give it another thought."

"What did he decide?"

"He's going to think about it."

I wrinkled my nose.

"How was your test?" she asked.

"Fine."

Aenti Suz smiled at me. "I don't want to get up yet. Every time I've tried, this little one wakes up. Would you make me a cup of peppermint tea? And then come sit with me?"

When I returned with tea for both of us, she said, "Tell me how your test went."

"I won't know the results for a couple of days." I placed her cup of tea on the table beside her rocking chair and held on to mine. Changing the subject, I asked how her day had gone.

After she brought me up to speed—mainly that Caden had been unsettled all day and Jessica needed a break—she asked if I'd like to hear more of my Dawdi Joe's story.

"Please." I cradled my cup in my hand. I couldn't think of anything I'd like more.

"Where were we?" she asked.

"Dawdi Joe had helped Lt. Shaw with a violent patient, and then she thanked him in Pennsylvania Dutch."

"That's right." Aenti Suz's eyes sparkled. She picked up her tea, took a sip, and then replaced it on the table. She tightened her grip on Caden as she rocked in the chair and launched back into the story.

— 9 —

Joe

Time passed quickly on the days Joe worked. Most of the doctors were easy to get along with, but there was one named Karcher who criticized Joe no matter what he did. The doctor was in his late thirties and had a wife and five children back in Maryland. "I'd fight if I wasn't a doctor," he told Joe one day. "I can't imagine why you're not."

When Joe didn't respond, the man grabbed him by the wrist. "Answer me," he demanded.

Joe pressed his arm against the doctor's and, keeping his voice low and calm, said, "Let go of me."

When he didn't, Joe yanked his wrist out of the man's grasp. "If you have a problem with my work, please speak to Captain Russell."

"Oh, believe me, I will." As Joe stepped away, Karcher hissed, "Coward."

Joe couldn't help but wonder if the others viewed him as a coward too. Did Captain Russell, even though he was so amiable? Lt. Madison? Lt. Shaw?

He realized his shoulders were slouching, and he forced himself to stand up straight. But even with the pain of wondering what others thought of him, he'd rather be working than not. Time sped by when he was on shift, but it slowed to a crawl when he had days off. He requested extra shifts whenever possible, which Captain Russell took advantage of, grateful for Joe's work ethic. Several more times, the captain suggested that Joe join the army. Finally, Joe made it clear that he was a conscientious objector and couldn't. "But you wouldn't be fighting," Captain Russell said. "You wouldn't be doing anything different than you are now."

Joe simply smiled at the man. He couldn't be part of the military.

"Think about it," the captain said. "When we're sent overseas, I'd like to have you go with us."

"When are you going?" Joe asked.

"Soon, most likely."

"Who will go?"

"I'm not positive yet." Captain Russell wrinkled his brow. "There's still some discussion about that."

Joe walked down to the lake with Ali often. As they strode along the shore in the rain one day, Ali explained that, along with the sugar, gas, and shoe lines that Joe was familiar with back home, there were also lines for cigarettes, meat, and soap, and that women couldn't find stockings anywhere. All of the silk was going to make parachutes.

Joe's sisters had never worn silk stockings—they'd worn knitted socks—but Joe had noticed the women in Chicago didn't wear anything on their legs. He expected that would change in the winter though.

Another day when he walked with Ali there was brilliant sunshine. The sky and lake were both so blue that Joe was sure he'd never seen anything so peaceful. But his moment of tranquility ended when two soldiers who appeared to have been drinking stopped them. "What branch are you in?" one of the men slurred.

"The CPS," Joe answered.

The second man laughed. "The what?"

"The Civilian Public Service," Joe explained.

The first man poked Ali in the chest. "What about you?" he sneered.

"The same, sir," Ali answered, his head held high.

"Don't get smart with me." The man's words were slurred again.

"We mean you no harm." Joe stepped between the first man and Ali. "We're very grateful for your service." He turned to Ali and mouthed, *Go. Fast.* Then he walked behind his friend, quickening his pace.

He heard steps behind them but didn't turn around. "Come back and face us," the first man yelled.

"Let it go," the second man said to his friend.

Joe and Ali kept walking as quickly as they could without breaking into a run. He felt like a scared calf, but he wasn't about to fight the soldiers. That would go against his faith— and do nothing to better the situation. Escaping as quickly as possible was the best strategy.

After a good half mile, Ali slowed and said, "Maybe we shouldn't come down here again."

"We have as much right to be down here as they do." But it was easier for Joe to state it as a fact than feel it as reality. He was happy to be in Chicago, to be meeting new people and seeing new places, but it wasn't as easy as he'd expected. Everything was so different.

His first letter from home arrived the end of the third week, from Charity. She wrote about the weather and the church service the day before. Then she wrote about Dat. *I believe he's grown weaker since you left. All of us girls are helping in the fields now, even Faith. At least you were able to get all of the planting done—I just hope Dat's health holds, and we can get the crops harvested. I know the food is needed.* She signed her name and then added that she would write more soon. He folded the letter and slipped it back into the envelope, praying for his Dat and sisters as he did. That was all he could do for now.

On a Friday evening in mid-May, several of the nurses, including Lt. Madison, gathered in the lobby of the hospital to go to a dance downtown. Several of the orderlies accompanied them, along with Captain Russell.

He asked Joe why he wasn't dressed and ready to tag along. Joe smiled and said, "I'm going for a walk." A dance was the last place he'd go.

"You should come with us," he said. "Lt. Shaw is, along with everyone else. We're going to have a great time."

Joe thanked him for the invitation. He knew Ali wasn't going. Hopefully he'd want to go for a walk too.

As it turned out, Ali had to work, so Joe headed back up the stairs to the lobby to go for a walk by himself. Lt. Shaw sat in one of the chairs, wearing a skirt and blouse, reading a book. Her blond hair was pulled back in a bun at the nape of her neck. She glanced up and then waved when she saw him.

He approached. "I thought you were going with the others."

She shook her head. "I don't dance, and sitting around watching the others didn't appeal to me. What are you doing this evening?"

"I'm going for a walk." He hesitated for a moment. Would he sound forward to ask her to join him?

"Could I go with you?" she asked.

"I'd like that," he answered, rubbing the back of his neck, hoping he wouldn't embarrass himself in front of her. "I thought I'd head toward the lake."

She took her book back to her room and returned with a sweater.

At first they walked silently as Joe struggled to come up with something to talk about. He was afraid Lt. Shaw might see through his awkwardness. He settled on asking her where she was from.

"I grew up outside of Springfield, Illinois," she said, "with my grandparents, after my parents passed away."

"I'm sorry," Joe said. "What happened?"

"We were visiting my grandparents and my mother and father went into town to do some Christmas shopping. A snowstorm caught them by surprise and on the way home they were involved in a bad accident. Both were killed instantly. I have a few memories of them before they died, but my earliest vivid memory is of Grandmother crying when the sheriff came to the door to give us the news. Did I mention that my grandmother and grandfather were Mennonite?"

"Oh." It was all beginning to make sense. "And they spoke Pennsylvania Dutch?"

"Just a little. I spent the summers with an aunt and uncle south of there who are Amish."

His heart lurched. "What made you decide to become a nurse?"

She ducked under the branch of a flowering crabapple tree. "I needed to support myself somehow. My grandparents both passed away a few years ago."

Of course she wouldn't want to join her aunt and uncle's church and become Amish, not after having grown up Mennonite, which must have been a liberal group if they didn't speak

131

Pennsylvania Dutch in the home. And now she was completely Englisch.

Feeling awkward and not knowing how to respond, he eventually said, "That explains how you know the word *Denki*."

She laughed. "That slipped out. I'm sorry."

"No," he said, stepping over magnolia petals on the sidewalk. "It was nice to hear."

As they walked on, he asked if she was happy to be off the farm and in the city.

"Not entirely," she said. "I don't mind the city, but there's nothing like the smell of freshly cut hay, along with the feeling of working hard all day long. Not that we don't work hard here—we do. But working outside has its own kind of satisfaction."

Joe agreed wholeheartedly.

As they reached the lake, he realized that she'd matched his pace, and he regretted not slowing down. But she wasn't out of breath.

The sun grew lower over the city as they walked along the shore. Lt. Shaw told him that she'd graduated from nursing school a year before and joined the army immediately. He guessed she was at least twenty—two years older than he was.

"Look," she said, pointing. The sky had turned a fiery orange, with yellow closest to the horizon and lavender toward the top, and was setting over the tallest building on the skyline. The building had hundreds of windows and some sort of figure on top that was a silhouette against the setting sun. "That's the Chicago Board of Trade Building."

Joe was reminded of the spectacular sunsets back on the farm that filled his soul. Now, both his soul and heart filled with emotion like never before. Perhaps it was the city, but he guessed it was more likely the company.

He could only imagine what Faith would say to him about his swell of feelings for an Englisch girl—an army officer, at that. *"You're getting too big for your britches. . . . Why would a girl like that want anything to do with you? . . . You'll never amount to anything anyway. Not to mention, you're treading where no Amish boy should go."*

"Isn't it amazing?" Lt. Shaw's face lit up like the sun.

Joe swallowed, found his voice, and started to say, just as Lt. Shaw did, "We only have God to thank—"

They both began to laugh when they realized they were saying the same thing and then together finished "—for such beauty."

"My grandfather used to say that," she said, looking up at him.

"My father too." Joe's heart swelled more, but then as the last of the sun disappeared, he thought of the soldiers who'd stopped him and Ali the week before. "We'd better get going." Could he protect Lt. Shaw if they were accosted? Without resorting to violence?

As he turned west, Lt. Shaw slipped her arm into the crook of his elbow, sending a tingle down his spine. He drew his arm closer to his body and again she matched his stride as they walked in silence. He wished the evening would never end.

They passed several groups of soldiers, but all of them had girls with them, and none of the men paid any attention to Joe and Lt. Shaw. They all seemed to be having fun and were oblivious to anyone else.

Thinking back to their conversation by the lake, Joe asked Lt. Shaw, "Did you ever think about living with your aunt and uncle permanently?"

She shook her head. "They have fourteen children. You'd think one more wouldn't matter, but it was time for me to become independent. So many women were getting jobs building aircraft and making munitions, but I needed something where I could support myself after the war too."

He guessed most women would plan to get married, keep house, and raise children. But of course not all people married.

"I haven't been back to the farm for a couple of years," she said. "I do miss my aunt and uncle and cousins, who are all male. Not one girl in the family."

"Except for you," Joe pointed out.

She smiled wryly. "Well, they were good to me, but I never felt I truly belonged. My uncle and cousins are all good men, don't get me wrong. From what I've witnessed, Amish men are raised to be hard workers, good husbands, and good fathers."

Joe certainly hoped he would be, regardless of Faith's predictions.

Lt. Shaw continued. "My aunt truly cared about me, but there was a division there. She'd been raised Mennonite and married an Amish man. Her sister, my mother, had been raised Mennonite and married an *Englischman*. I was a reminder of that." She shrugged. "My older cousins have married and have families of their own, and my aunt and uncle are growing old, with the responsibility of still caring for the younger ones. It's a lot for them. Perhaps if I had a girl cousin, she and I would be close. I do miss my trips to the farm though. . . ." Her voice trailed off.

Joe regretted his earlier assumption. She wasn't as enamored with the Englisch way of life as he'd guessed. It sounded as if she were simply being pragmatic, although he knew she had a gift for being a nurse. He'd seen it in action.

As they walked in silence for another block, Joe realized he wasn't the only one who felt awkward in conversations. She seemed to also. But he wasn't as worried as he had been before. Perhaps she didn't mind the quiet. He liked that in a person.

After another block, she asked him about Lancaster County. "What is it like?" she asked. "I assume you farm there."

He answered that he did. He told her about his Dat and his sisters, and then that his Mamm had died a few years before.

"I'm sorry," she said.

"I'm sorry about your parents too," he answered. "And that you were so young when they passed."

"Denki," she answered.

When they climbed the stairs to the hospital, she didn't let go of his arm. A strand of hair had fallen from her bun, against her face. He longed to brush it aside.

As they stepped into the lobby, a loud booming voice jerked Joe out of the dreamlike state he'd been in all evening.

"Well, well, well." Karcher stood in the middle of the lobby, his feet spread wide. "Lt. Shaw, you have no business being out with a Dutchy, holding on to him like that."

Lt. Shaw didn't let go of Joe's arm, but he sensed her stiffen. "My personal life is none of your business." Then she spit out, "Second Lieutenant Karcher."

As a first lieutenant she outranked him.

The man's face reddened, right up to his hairline. "I'll report you to Captain Russell."

"By all means," she said. "I've done nothing wrong."

Karcher smirked. "Bachmann's your subordinate."

"No, he's with the CPS."

"That's right. The man is shirking his duty—he's un-American."

"Nothing could be further from the truth," Lt. Shaw retorted, tightening her grip on Joe. "He's a good man and a skilled orderly. And a compassionate human being." She glared at Karcher as if implying he wasn't.

The man didn't seem to register her words or tone. "I'll walk you to your room," he said.

"You absolutely will not." She started toward the staircase, dragging Joe along. When they reached the door to the female dormitory, he swallowed hard, trying to control his anger. "Will you be all right?" He'd never felt like hitting a person before—until now.

She nodded. "He won't follow me."

"I'll wait here," Joe whispered. "Until he leaves."

"Denki. I enjoyed our time together." She turned her face up toward his. "And I meant what I said about you." She let go of his arm and slipped through the door. Joe pulled the door shut and stood with his arms crossed over his chest as Karcher headed out the front door.

Maybe Faith was wrong. Maybe he would amount to something someday. Maybe he did already.

His heart constricted. Even though he hadn't joined the church yet, he knew he would. Karcher was right, but in a way the man wouldn't understand. Joe and Lt. Shaw had no business being interested in each other—not that Joe believed she truly cared for him, but he feared it was too late for him not to care for her.

Karcher did report Lt. Shaw to Captain Russell, but nothing came of it except that Joe feared Lt. Shaw distanced herself some. He couldn't blame her. They still continued to spend time together. They sat by each other in the cafeteria. Took more walks, although they stayed in the neighborhood instead of going down to the lake. But Lt. Shaw didn't loop her arm through his again.

A couple of times, Karcher sneered at them, but Lt. Shaw insisted that Joe just ignore him. On the last Sunday of May, they both had the day off, and Joe tagged along to the Mennonite church Lt. Shaw attended when she could.

She explained on the way that she hadn't told anyone she was a US Army officer. "I've told a few people in the congregation that I work as a nurse, but that's all. The Mennonite church is familiar to me, although this particular one isn't. Still, I don't want to go anywhere else. But they wouldn't understand why I joined the army. I hardly do myself."

"Do you regret it?"

She wrinkled her nose and said, "Not yet."

As they walked, she asked, "How old are you, Joe?"

"Eighteen," he answered.

"Goodness, I thought you were at least my age. Twenty. You seem wise beyond your years." But she didn't react negatively that he was younger. And it increased his confidence that she thought he was at least twenty.

He'd never been to a service inside a church building before. It was a simple structure on the outside, located in a neighborhood with modest houses. There were wooden benches on the inside with a simple pulpit up front. The songs and the sermon were all in Englisch, and Joe found himself missing home.

Yet he appreciated the sermon. The minister read Colossians 3:15: "And let the peace of God rule in your hearts, to the which also ye are called in one body; and be ye thankful." He preached about relying on the peace of Christ even when the entire world was at war. "Pray for peace," he said, "and above all remember that you are called to peace. Live that out in our congregation, in your families, in your neighborhoods, and at your places of work. Those are the best ways we can share the peace of Christ."

Joe thought of the patients he cared for and the nurses and doctors he worked with. He thought of Lt. Shaw. Jah, he wanted the peace of Christ for all of them.

"And don't forget to be thankful," the minister said. "Gratitude makes us aware of all Christ has done for us, of His sacrifices. A grateful heart draws other people to the love of Christ."

Joe thought about that too. He had so much to be thankful for. The Lord. His family. All that he was learning. The people he'd met in Chicago.

After the service ended, several people came up and greeted Lt. Shaw. She introduced Joe to each one, explaining he was from Lancaster County. All of them asked questions about his life there. Some asked if he knew a particular family. One lived close to Leacock, and Joe believed he knew which farm was theirs. The connections between Mennonites and the Amish in some circles were strong, even all the way to Chicago.

On the way to the trolley from the church, Lt. Shaw took Joe's arm again. "That was a good sermon."

He agreed as his nerves jumped up and down his spine.

"I'm thankful for you," she said.

He swallowed hard, wanting to say he was thankful for her too, but the words stuck in his throat. He simply smiled and nodded his head. Lt. Shaw was making his time in Chicago more than bearable.

On a Tuesday morning in early June, Joe had stepped out of the shower room and dressed for his shift when Captain Russell, who stood in the doorway of his office, motioned for him. Joe headed down the hall and into the office, where several other orderlies and doctors were gathered around the radio. Karcher leaned against the far wall, his hands shoved into the pockets of his white coat. It appeared he'd just gotten done with his shift, which meant he'd been working with Lt. Shaw. Joe tried to catch the man's gaze, but Karcher averted his eyes.

Joe turned toward Ali and started to ask what was going on, but his friend hushed him and pointed to the radio. ". . . invasion began at 6:30 local time this morning. The Allied operation began with the landing of airborne troops at the mouth of the Seine River. The Allied armies are on the march!"

Captain Russell let out a *whoop* and most of the doctors clapped. Joe felt his heart sink. Who knew how many were dying right now. But then his heart lifted. Perhaps the war would soon be over. Perhaps the battle would save lives in the long run. How God must mourn what men did to each other.

But after four years, Allied troops were back on European soil. Hopefully they could push the Germans back and hold their ground.

As music came on, several of the men shook hands. Joe didn't want to celebrate a battle, but he couldn't help the surge of emotion he felt. Would he soon be going home? He felt both elated and devastated.

Once he left Chicago, he'd never see Lt. Shaw again.

When he reached the third floor, a radio blared out another news report: "The beaches of Northern France are alive right now with Allied troops. . . ."

Lt. Shaw stood at the narcotics cabinet, counting the medications as she did at the end of every shift. She turned and caught his eye. "Did you hear?" She nodded toward the radio.

He nodded, stepping closer to her.

Her eyes sparkled. "Hopefully this is the beginning of the end."

Joe wanted to reach out and wipe away the tears that had escaped her eyes, but of course he didn't. "God willing," he said.

She smiled and brushed away her own tears, nodding in agreement.

Too soon, she left the floor. The radio stayed on all day, and they all quieted whenever a newscast started. Bennie, whose stump still hadn't healed, was ecstatic. "This is what we've been waiting for!" he shouted whenever an update came on.

Joe tried to calm the soldier down. He was running a fever,

and Joe knew too much excitement wasn't good for him. Toward the end of Joe's shift, Bennie gestured toward his stump and said, "Today made this all worth it."

Joe feared his voice would quake if he spoke, so he simply smiled at Bennie. The boy had sacrificed so much. What had Joe done? Leaving Lancaster County to come to Chicago had been exciting. The little adversity he'd faced was easy to deal with compared to what Bennie had already been through and what was still ahead. After giving Bennie a second serving of soup and bread, he headed to the cafeteria.

Lt. Shaw sat next to him as they listened to the radio that had been dragged into the room. The newscast said Adolf Hitler had personally taken charge of all of the German anti-invasion operations.

"Sounds as if he's frightened," Lt. Shaw said.

Joe hoped so.

The day after the invasion, General Eisenhower released a communiqué stating that the Allied losses were light during the invasion, but it seemed his message was more for Hitler than for the folks back home. Many lost their lives on the beaches and in the fields of Normandy. Joe had been right in fearing the casualty count was high. Over 425,000 Allied and German troops were killed, wounded, or unaccounted for.

In late June, three weeks after the invasion, there were rumors of doctors and nurses at the Chicago hospital being transferred to France as a combat unit. Joe heard about it first from Ali.

"Will orderlies be sent too?" If so, Joe hoped he'd be selected to go.

Ali said, "Only army orderlies as far as I've heard. Not any of us."

Joe woke in the middle of the night worried that Lt. Shaw would be sent to France. It didn't feel right that so much would be required of her, along with the others, while he stayed safe and sound in Chicago.

The first of July, Joe had a letter from Hope. She said they were working hard but doing well. *Dat had a bad spell a couple of weeks ago but is doing better. He says to tell you hello and that he prays for you every day.* Joe's heart constricted as he read. He was relieved Dat was doing better but wondered how bad the spell had been. *I'll let you know the following because I doubt Faith will. Abe Yoder has been stopping by to court her.* Hope, who usually had clarity before anyone else in the family, wrote, *I'm guessing they'll marry in the fall, and I didn't want you to be surprised.*

Joe was happy for his sister—and for Abe Yoder. He hoped she'd learned to be kinder than she had been in the past. He knew it would be a loss to his Dat to not have Faith keeping house and helping with the farming. Perhaps Abe Yoder would move to the farm once they married. Or maybe Joe would be home by then.

Hope continued, *We've had hot, humid weather. The lightning bugs were out last night, and we all laughed as we remembered the joy you found in chasing them—even up until last year.* He smiled at the memory, knowing his family had found pleasure in laughing at his antics his entire life. *We all cherish your letters. Please write when you can. We're praying the war will end soon, and you'll be home before we know it.*

Joe reread the letter and then answered it, saying that he was well and that he too hoped the war would end soon.

The next morning, when he showed up on the ward, Lt. Shaw wasn't there. However, Karcher was. The man avoided making eye contact with Joe, as he had for the last several weeks.

Joe asked Lt. Madison about Lt. Shaw.

"She wasn't feeling well and left about a half hour ago."

Joe hoped Lt. Shaw was all right and looked for her at suppertime in the cafeteria, but he didn't see her. She wasn't on the ward the next morning either.

On Saturday morning, she was back. When he asked how she was feeling, she said, "All right."

Since they both had the next day off, he asked if she'd like to go to church.

"I would," she said.

As they set out at nine o'clock the next morning, the day was already hot and sticky. Lt. Shaw pointed to a bench in a park along the way and asked if they could stop and rest.

Once they'd sat down, Lt. Shaw said she'd received bad news from her uncle. "My aunt died last month."

"Oh no," Joe responded.

"I didn't even know she was ill. And then he waited so long to let me know she'd passed." Lt. Shaw shivered, even in the heat. "She was my last connection to my parents and my grandparents."

Joe told her that he was sorry.

"Denki," she said. "I feel so disconnected, as if I'm floating off by myself. And soon, it seems, I'll be sailing off to Europe." As she exhaled, she looked as if her heart were breaking. "I feel so silly saying this, but it's hard to be going off to war and not have any relatives back home thinking about me and praying for me." Lt. Shaw brushed at her eyes. "This sounds so immature, I know, but if I were to die in France, no one would cry."

"It doesn't sound immature—and it's not true," Joe said. "Surely your uncle and cousins would."

She looked up at him with misty eyes. "It's a nice thought, but they would simply say it was God's will."

He understood that reaction. That's what so many had said when his Mamm passed. True, God had allowed it. But Joe wasn't so sure that He willed tragedies. He certainly didn't believe God had willed this horrible war.

"I'd cry," he said. "If something happened to you."

"Thank you, Joe. You're too kind. But I'm afraid I'm foolish at heart, wanting what I don't have. And I'm tired. I shouldn't even think about this sort of thing when I'm exhausted."

He longed to put his arm around her, to protect her.

Instead, he whispered, "You're not foolish. I haven't seen you, not once, act foolishly or shy away from a dangerous situation on the ward. You're brave and courageous. You have good reason to react the way you are to going to Europe. Perhaps Captain Russell will understand."

"I don't want to say anything," she said. "I shouldn't get special treatment. Others have families—mothers and fathers. Many of the doctors have wives and children. They actually have far more reason to stay than I do."

"Do you feel as if you can talk to God about all of this?" Joe asked.

"I think so." She smiled up at him. "It helps that I've talked it through with you. Thank you for listening—you've been so understanding. I know God is too." She leaned away from him. "I hope I haven't been unfair to you."

"What do you mean?"

She sighed again. "You're expected to join the church. All of this"—her blue eyes met his as she spread her arms wide—"Chicago, the hospital, me. None of this can be a part of your life. Not for more than this season."

Joe's heart lurched.

"I hope I wasn't too forward on our first walk, when Lt. Karcher saw us."

"Not at all," he answered. Was that why she hadn't taken his arm since? "I've worried about Karcher though. Has he behaved poorly toward you?"

Lt. Shaw shrugged her shoulders. "He won't listen to me on the ward. He overrules every idea I have. If I say a patient needs one thing, he'll do everything he can to prove the patient needs something else. But, no, he hasn't behaved badly like he did that night. What about toward you?"

"He won't look me in the eye."

Lt. Shaw smiled a little. "I think Captain Russell pulled him through the wringer about 'reporting' us."

Joe wanted to say something more but not about Karcher. About them. But as he tried to choose the right words, she pushed herself up from the bench. The moment had passed. He'd missed his chance.

Joe thought about Lt. Shaw the next morning when Lt. Madison received her orders. By the end of July she'd be going to training at Fort Drum in upstate New York. Then she'd travel to England and across the Channel to France sometime in September.

The day went from bad to worse when Bennie's fever spiked. "Joe, I don't feel right," Bennie said. "I feel like I'm dying." The soldier's breathing was irregular and the skin on his thigh was patchy.

Karcher was doing the rounds and Joe alerted him. But when the doctor examined Bennie, he simply made a few notes in his chart. After Karcher left, Joe told Lt. Madison he thought they needed to get Bennie more care. She made a phone call and got an older, more experienced doctor on the floor. He examined Bennie and then called for a blood sample. Joe overheard the doctor say he thought Bennie was septic.

Joe had been on the floor long enough to know that wasn't good. It meant Bennie could have a blood infection.

Lt. Madison drew the blood, and Joe delivered it to the lab. When he returned, Bennie was gasping for breath. Joe helped Lt. Madison get an oxygen tent set up as Joe sang hymns and tried to soothe him. But just before the end of the shift, Bennie breathed for the last time as Joe held on to the soldier's hand.

Joe left the floor feeling defeated. Bennie had died. Lt. Shaw was probably going to France. He hadn't felt so low the whole time he'd been in Chicago.

When he returned to the barracks, Captain Russell was waving his orders around gleefully. The captain was going to France too. He'd be the commander of the unit being sent from the hospital. He said there were fifteen of them, including Lt. Shaw. Everyone Joe worked with the most, except the other Civilian Public Service orderlies and Karcher, was going.

"Will you join up now?" Captain Russell asked Joe. "You could do your training at Fort Drum and leave from there with the rest of us."

Joe felt a loyalty he hadn't expected. He asked if civilian orderlies could volunteer. "We're not taking any civilians," the captain said. "You'd need to enlist. The army needs more orderlies. Like I said, I could get you a place at Fort Drum. It wouldn't be a problem."

Joe hadn't joined the Amish church—he wouldn't be shunned if he joined. He could enlist, serve his time in the army, return home after he was discharged, and then join the church. It would break his father's heart though.

But if he enlisted, he'd be able to help Lt. Shaw—and the others too.

Captain Russell must have sensed Joe's grief because he asked, "What's wrong?"

He told him Bennie had just died.

"That's why you need to enlist," Captain Russell said. "If Bennie had been helped right away instead of being left on the field all that time, the docs in the field hospital might have saved his leg." He squeezed Joe's shoulder. "There's important work to be done, and you could play a role in it."

— 10 —

As Joe walked toward the lake with Ali that night, he talked through his dilemma.

His friend shook his head. "Why would you consider joining? You're nonresistant. You'd go through training to learn how to kill another person, and you'd have to do it, if needed. You could end up as a medic on a battlefield—not an orderly in a field hospital. Either way you'd have to wear an army uniform and carry a weapon."

Ali had a point. Joe feared he wouldn't be able to pull the trigger to take another life, which would be a danger to everyone around him.

"Have you heard of the American Field Service?" Ali asked.

Joe shook his head.

"It's a volunteer service with the Allied Forces. I have a friend, a CO who joined a couple of years ago. He drove an ambulance in Northern Africa and now he's in Italy, or at least he was. Maybe he's in France by now."

"I don't know how to drive an ambulance—or any vehicle," Joe said. "I only know how to drive a wagon. And a buggy."

Ali laughed and slapped him on the back. "Well, that won't do you any good."

The next morning, as Joe accompanied Captain Russell on his rounds, he asked the doctor what he knew about the American Field Service.

"We have a doctor here who served in Northern Africa. He said the AFS was invaluable. He doesn't know what they would have done without them." Captain Russell paused before going on to the next patient. "Why do you ask?"

Joe cleared his throat. "I'd like to do more. . . ." He couldn't help but think of Bennie.

"Then the AFS sounds like a good option." Captain Russell grabbed the patient's chart.

"Except . . ."

Captain Russell glanced up.

"First, I don't know how to drive." Joe gripped imaginary reins with his hands.

Captain Russell grinned. "No, I don't suppose you would."

"And say I did learn to drive and then joined the AFS, I'd like to find out where I'd be sent. Would there be any chance I could be assigned to your hospital?"

Captain Russell's expression turned from somber to serious. "Chances are we'd all end up in France—to start with at least—but I can't even guess how many Allied regiments there will be. If we met up at some point, I'd say that would be a miracle."

Joe understood. If he joined the AFS, his sole purpose would have to be to serve the infantry soldiers. Not to support his friends, Lt. Shaw in particular, or to even hope to see her again. His thoughts returned to Bennie and the need for ambulance drivers. In the months to come, it would be as essential as ever to get the wounded to field hospitals as soon as possible. Joe was strong and capable. He could carry a grown man by himself, if need be. And he was fast on his feet. "I'd like to learn to drive and apply to go with the AFS," he said.

Captain Russell's eyes shone. "I'll check around and see what I can find out. And in the meantime, I'll find a car." He smiled again. "And give you a lesson or two."

Just as they finished their rounds, Karcher stepped onto the floor and marched straight toward Captain Russell. "I need to speak with you. In private."

Without looking up, Captain Russell said, "If this is about your lack of orders, there's nothing to talk about. You're not going."

"That's absurd," Karcher bellowed.

Captain Russell looked up and met the man's eyes. "You're untrustworthy as a doctor, ungentlemanly with the nurses, and rude to the orderlies. Why in the world would I want to take you? I'm guessing you'll be receiving other orders shortly—but not in our unit."

Karcher scoffed. "You ask a Dutchy to join the army so he can go with you, yet you're denying me the chance?"

"That's right. But Bachmann isn't your concern, so back off."

Shaking his head in disgust, Karcher plowed between the two of them, heading for the stairwell.

"Ignore him," Captain Russell said. "I really don't care what he says to me. I'm just grateful my superiors heeded my request to leave him behind."

Joe nodded in agreement. He'd rather have Karcher tormenting him in Chicago than treating Lt. Shaw badly during their training in New York, and then overseas too.

Captain Russell approached Joe in the cafeteria the next evening as he was eating with Lt. Shaw.

"Let's go," Captain Russell said, eyes gleaming. "We have the car for an hour."

"The car?" Lt. Shaw turned toward Joe. "What's going on?"

"Maybe not much." Joe stood and grabbed his tray. "We'll see how it goes."

Joe had never shared with anyone in his family that cars and trucks fascinated him, but Faith had noticed and ridiculed him about it, admonishing him to be cautious of "the ways of the world." Still, the few times Joe had been in a vehicle, he'd carefully observed what the driver did. Throttle. Clutch. Accelerator. Shift from first to second to third.

Captain Russell stopped in front of a black 1932 Ford Cabriolet. Joe knew it had a V8, which was a powerful engine.

The captain tossed him the keys. One of the newer cars he'd rode in back home, not long ago, was started with a key—otherwise Joe wasn't sure he'd know what to do with it.

He inhaled and willed himself to be calm. As he slipped it into the ignition, he pushed in the clutch.

"Good," Captain Russell said. "You know the basics."

"I'm not sure that I do, actually," Joe said. "You'd better talk me through everything."

"All right," the captain said. "Let's just take a moment and go over a few things, but first I want to tell you that I grew up in a little town in Minnesota." He cleared his throat. "My parents didn't have a car. With the Depression and all, they couldn't afford one, so I didn't learn to drive until I joined the army. You didn't learn for another reason, but don't think you're alone."

Joe was encouraged by the man's words, and by the time the captain had Joe start the car and pull away from the curb, he felt more confident.

It felt like trial by fire as he lurched through the first few blocks, but by the time he turned right toward the lake, he mostly had the hang of the shifting. Soon they were on Lake Shore Drive with the breeze from the lake blowing through the car.

"You're a natural," Captain Russell said.

Joe shifted into fourth. "Did you have a chance to talk with the doctor who served in North Africa?"

"I did," the captain said. "He said the AFS is a godsend. Far more soldiers would die on the field if it weren't for them. Of course, he reiterated what we already expected—there would be little chance you'd see our unit over there at all."

Joe nodded. He wouldn't expect anything, but if the AFS accepted him, he would still pray that he'd be stationed somewhere near Captain Russell and his unit.

"So if you decide to join, it should be to serve in that way. Not to help me"—Captain Russell cleared his throat—"or anyone serving with me."

Joe shot him a smile as he came around a curve. The captain yelled, "Slow down!" as he braced his hand against the dash.

Joe slammed on the brakes and pushed the clutch in at the same time. At the last minute, he swerved and careened around an old, dilapidated truck in the middle of the road. The driver waved for them to stop, yelling, "Can you give me a push?"

"One thing I forgot to teach you," Captain Russell said as Joe pulled the car over to the side of the road, "is always expect the unexpected."

A few days later, Joe received a letter from Charity saying how much she missed him. *Abe Yoder has been visiting frequently to see Faith. He's a good man, but I'm not sure Faith appreciates him. I didn't think she'd be as critical of him as she's been with all of us, but she's turned out to be even worse. Hope thinks they'll be married by fall, but I'm not so sure.*

Joe's stomach sunk. First, he hadn't realized that Faith treated Hope and Charity the way she treated him, but it sounded as if she did. He never would have expected Faith to treat a prospective husband that way either. For the first time, he wondered what was behind her behavior.

After a second driving lesson the next week, Captain Russell said Joe didn't need any more, but Joe insisted he did. He couldn't go off to Europe to drive an ambulance with so little experience.

As Joe parked the car in front of the hospital, Captain Russell grinned and pointed toward the entrance to the hospital. "Well, maybe one more lesson."

Lt. Shaw headed down the front steps with Lt. Madison. Each carried a basket.

"Look who's here." Captain Russell jumped out of the car. "Lt. Shaw, you sit up front. I'll sit in the back with Lt. Madison."

"What's going on?" Joe asked.

"A picnic," Captain Russell said as he opened the trunk so the women could store the baskets.

Joe glanced at Lt. Shaw as she climbed into the front, seeing if she might tell him what was going on, but she had a questioning expression on her face too.

"How about we go to that park we passed when we were driving along the lake?" Captain Russell asked as he settled into the back seat.

Nervousness washed over Joe. Was this a double date set up by Captain Russell? Was it obvious to everyone how much he admired Lt. Shaw?

He nearly stalled the car but shoved the clutch in all the way and managed to get it moving. He took a deep breath and headed back toward the lake.

Perhaps his anxiety was obvious to the others because no one spoke until Joe turned onto Lake Shore Drive. Then Lt. Shaw asked, "Did you just learn to drive for the fun of it?"

"Something like that," Joe answered.

Captain Russell grabbed the back of Joe's seat. "He wants to go to France. As an ambulance driver."

Lt. Shaw's voice wavered. "What?"

"With the American Field Service," Captain Russell continued.

"No!" Lt. Shaw leaned back in her seat, away from Joe.

His heart fell. She didn't want him to go. He kept his eyes on the road as Lt. Shaw turned her head toward the window.

Everyone was quiet until they reached the park. Then Joe and the captain grabbed the baskets and led the way to a picnic table with the women walking behind them.

Once they started eating their sandwiches and apples, the awkwardness in the car faded, and the four of them watched two sailboats racing on the lake and predicted which one would win. After they were done eating, Captain Russell and Lt. Madison headed down toward the water's edge.

Once they were gone, Lt. Shaw stood and motioned toward the trail along the lake, away from where the other couple had gone. "Want to go for a walk?"

Joe nodded.

Once they reached the trail, Lt. Shaw said, "I'm sorry I reacted that way in the car."

Joe wasn't sure what to say, so he ended up changing the subject. "I'm sorry if you felt tricked into spending the evening this way."

She stopped and looked up at him. "What do you mean?"

"The three of you are officers."

"Don't be ridiculous," she said.

He met her eyes. "You've been awfully kind to me."

"I like you, Joe. We all do. Like I said before, you're a good man. And you act as if you belong—" She smiled. "I was going to say 'even though you don't.' But that's not true. You *do* belong. You've been a good friend to all of us."

"But you don't want me to go to France."

She looked beyond him toward the lake. Clouds billowed on the horizon where the water met the sky. Her eyes met his again. "It's not because you wouldn't be an asset. It's because I don't want you going off to war. You're Amish. You should be in Lancaster County farming—not in France driving an ambulance through battlefields."

"You shouldn't be going off to war any more than me. You grew up Plain too."

"But I signed up, and I knew what I was getting into," she said. "You should stay here in Chicago and return home as soon as possible. Please don't pursue this anymore."

He exhaled and then confessed, "I already have. I mailed off letters to the AFS and to the Lancaster County Selective Service Board last week. I hope I'll hear back from them soon."

"But what about your father? And sisters?"

"They'll have to trust God," Joe said. "That's what we'll all have to do."

Joe sounded confident in his decision, but he wasn't. Being accepted by the AFS could change his life in ways he couldn't possibly anticipate. And even though he'd prayed about his decision, he wasn't sure if he was following God's will. Perhaps he was doing the exact opposite.

On a muggy afternoon in late July, the day before Lt. Shaw and the others left for New York, Joe received two letters. One was a notice from the Selective Service Board that he was released to drive ambulances for the American Field Service. Relief rushed through him. The last line of the letter read, *Your orders will arrive within a month.*

Then he opened a letter from his Dat. *I'm getting by but long for the day you come home. I know God is using you where you are, but I look forward to having you by my side again.* Joe swallowed the lump in his throat. He'd write his Dat that evening and update him about the upcoming change as far as his service, explaining that he didn't have orders yet, but he would notify him when he did. He'd be honest that he'd sought out the position, but he didn't expect his Dat to understand that he longed to do more to help the injured soldiers on the battlefield.

He headed to the cafeteria, hoping Lt Shaw would be there.

She wasn't, but Lt. Madison was, with a group of other nurses. She spotted Joe right away. "Are you looking for Lt. Shaw?"

His face grew warm. Was he that obvious?

Lt. Madison flashed a smile, her lipstick bright red, and said, "She went for a walk."

Joe hurried out to the front of the hospital and along their usual route. After several blocks, he saw Lt. Shaw coming toward him. He wanted to wave his papers, but he knew she wouldn't be as excited as he was.

He strode toward her. She walked slowly until she saw him, then she swiped at her face. When he grew near, he could see that her blue eyes were rimmed red.

"What's the matter?" This time, he didn't fight the urge to put his arm around her. Against his better judgment, he did.

She leaned her head against him, fitting against his shoulder. "I'm sad about leaving."

"Sad about leaving the city?"

"No."

"You'll be with the others—Captain Russell and Lt. Madison."

She turned her head up and met his eyes. "I won't be with you."

Joe stopped walking. She stepped back, but kept her gaze on his.

He cleared his throat. "What do you mean by that? That you'll miss me or . . ." His voice trailed off.

"I mean I'll miss you. I'll miss the man who finally put his arm around me, when I've been longing for that since the day we met."

Joe cleared his throat again, not sure what to say.

Tears welled in her eyes. "Like I said before, I know we have no future. In fact, our friendship ends today."

He pulled her close again. "We don't know what the future holds." His heart raced as he spoke, and he feared she'd hear the tremble in his voice. "But I know I'll miss you too." He held up the envelope in his free hand. "Maybe I'll see you in Europe though."

"The Selective Service Board approved the transfer?"

He nodded.

Tears flooded down her face. "I wish you hadn't."

"But I did." He took out his handkerchief and wiped her tears. Then he wrapped her in a full hug, pulling her to his chest, which felt like the most natural thing in the world. "I'll write to your APO address. I'll let you know where I am, as best I can. If you're anywhere close, I'll find you."

She pressed her cheek against his denim shirt. He held her even tighter.

— 11 —

Leisel

The next morning as I changed Caden's diaper, I thought of Dawdi Joe falling in love with Lt. Shaw, going against all that he'd anticipated for his life.

I'd never meant to fall in love with Nick either. We'd been acquaintances and then we were friends. And then one night while studying in the library toward the end of my second year of nursing school, I glanced at him from across the table. He had his head bent over his books and his hair fell over his forehead, covering one of his eyes.

I swallowed hard as my heart began to race. Then he looked up at me and smiled.

Grabbing my books, I stuttered, "I need to go."

"Why?"

"I have a group meeting." It wasn't for another hour, but I had to get away from him.

"What about tomorrow?" he asked. "Want to study after church?"

"Maybe." We both had the day off from work, which didn't happen very often.

The next morning, I considered not going to church but couldn't skip. It was hard enough leaving the Amish—I couldn't forego the practices of my faith altogether.

I slipped in late and sat in the back. I quickly spotted Nick a few rows ahead of me, near a side aisle. He'd left room for me. My heart lurched again.

I don't remember the music from that day. But I do remember the scripture, right before the sermon. It was from Ecclesiastes 4: "And if one prevail against him, two shall withstand him; and a threefold cord is not quickly broken."

It wasn't as if Nick and I kept warm together. No, that wasn't us. But we did encourage each other. I considered scooting up the aisle and sitting next to him. But would I seem too obvious?

I exhaled. Just because I had feelings for him didn't mean he did for me. Surely he wouldn't even connect me sitting beside him with those verses. So what if I had a crush on him? We could stay friends. Nothing would change.

As the pastor bowed to pray, I made my move.

As I slipped into the pew, he gave me a sideways glance. He had the sweetest smile on his face, which practically sent my heart into AFib. Did he care about me too? Did he love me in the way that I realized I loved him?

I bowed my head, determined to listen to the pastor.

"Lord," he prayed. "We need you, but we also need each other. We need community, we need friends. We know some are called to be single, and others are called to be married. Those people need spouses in this life. I ask that you'd make that happen for them, Lord. . . ."

My nervous system responded involuntarily, causing the

capillaries of my skin to widen. In other words, my face had grown warm. And red, I was sure.

Caden began to squirm, and I secured the last pin and then wiggled him into his plastic pants, making a mental note to buy a box of disposable diapers. Marie preferred cloth, but washing them in Mamm's wringer washer was going to take forever.

I stood Caden up, pulled up his pair of little-boy jeans, and kissed the blond fuzz on top of his head.

"Mama?" he asked.

"Let's call Mama," I said, "and see if we can talk to her, but we'll need to go outside." It was a gorgeous day, perfect for playing in the backyard.

As I shifted Caden to my hip and traipsed through the living room, Aenti Suz was finishing up the morning dishes.

"I'll meet you outside," she said.

Caden waved as we passed by. As we stepped out on the front porch, I thought of my state boards. I'd check online tomorrow to see if I'd passed. Just the thought of it made me clammy all over.

Once we were in the backyard, Caden pointed to a sparrow on the back fence.

"*Fokkel*," I said, knowing Marie hoped he would learn Pennsylvania Dutch along with English.

"Bird!" he chirped.

"Jah." I laughed. "Fokkel."

He squirmed in my arms and pointed at another bird as I headed all the way over to the gate by the old oak tree, far away from Mamm or Arden, before I FaceTimed Marie. Thankfully, she answered. I held the phone up to Caden's face as Marie came on the screen.

"Hi, *Boppli*," she cooed.

"Mamamamamamama," he squealed.

For a moment I feared seeing Marie might make things worse for Caden, but he chattered away with sounds and squeals as the breeze blew through his fine hair. I couldn't help but smile at the two of them.

Marie told me she'd call later once she'd spoken with the doctor. After we all said good-bye, I pointed to the tree and said, "*Bohm.*"

"Bohm!" Caden shouted.

I hugged him tight, and when we reached the yard, I lowered him to the grass and he toddled along. Aenti Suz met us at the sandbox.

Once I had the cover off and situated Caden with the toys, she told me she'd been thinking of ways for the farm to earn some extra money.

I turned toward her, shading my eyes from the morning sun. "Such as?"

"Well, we could set up a baked-goods stand on weekends and during tourist season."

I nodded. Arden might go for that.

"And offer tours of the farm."

Arden definitely wouldn't go for that.

"And rent out the Dawdi Haus."

"Are you serious?" I couldn't imagine Arden being all right with that in a million years.

"Lots of people do it around here. In fact, I heard a family over in the next district uses an Englischer to help with the bookings. He has photos of their farm and the apartment above their barn on a website. Of course, they pay him to handle those details, but they still make a good amount of money."

"But where would you stay when the Dawdi Haus was rented out?"

160

"In the big house. I know Arden and his family will move in sooner or later, but I might as well stay there with your Mamm until they do. We have so much room to spare—it's ridiculous that I'm still in the Dawdi Haus."

That was true. It really wasn't the Amish way to waste so much space. If Amos hadn't moved away and had instead lived on the farm, Arden's family would probably already be in the big house, instead of the house on the far end of the property, and Amos would be in theirs. Or if Silas had stayed working on our farm, then he, Jessica, and Ruby would live with Mamm. But they'd take over the farm on Garden Lane from John Stoltz.

Or if Marie had married an Amish man without a farm or family business, they would have lived with Mamm.

Or if I'd married an Amish man . . . Yeah, that wasn't going to happen either.

"So, what do you think?" Aenti Suz asked. "Do you like my idea?"

"You'd be giving up your home."

She shrugged. "I lived in that big house the first chunk of my life. I'd be happy to live there again."

"You should talk to Jessica about it."

"That's what I was thinking," Aenti Suz said. "I thought I'd stop by the family in the next district who rents out the apartment and find out the name of the Englischer who does the website. Maybe I can get an idea of how much of a profit we could make."

"I think it's a good idea," I said. "But I don't think Arden would allow it."

Aenti Suz just shrugged. "You never know."

I woke the next morning to a feeling of dread. The score for my test would be posted online by the end of the day. But before I could work myself into a panic, Caden pulled himself up in his crib and grinned at me, drool cascading down his chin.

"*Guder Mariye*," I cooed as I scooped him up in my arms. I washed his face, changed his diaper, and wriggled him into a pair of sweatpants and matching T-shirt.

As I held him again, he put his hands on each side of my face and gave me a slobbery kiss on my lips. His trust stopped me. He had no doubt that I'd care for him. Change him. Bathe him. Feed him. Love him.

And I would. I'd do anything I could to care for him. Did I trust anyone the way Caden trusted me?

Jessica arrived about an hour later to stay with Caden so I could go check on Marie in the hospital. I followed her over to the big house and so did Aenti Suz. As I readied to leave, our aunt pitched her idea about renting out the Dawdi Haus as they stood in the kitchen with Ruby and Caden.

Mamm overheard and stepped out of her sewing room. "Goodness," she said. "Is the dairy doing that badly?"

"It's touch and go," Jessica said. "Dairies all through the county—actually all through the country—are struggling."

"Why?" Mamm asked.

"The price of milk is down," Jessica answered. "People aren't drinking as much, including in the Englisch schools."

It seemed so odd that what went on in Englisch homes and public schools could affect my family's livelihood, but it did.

"There's talk of opening a processing plant in Lancaster County, which would help," Jessica explained. "It's all about supply and demand. Should we hang on until the supply goes down? Or the demand goes up? Or sell and get into another line of farming?"

"But we could make money in other ways to tide us over," Aenti Suz said.

Mamm shook her head. "Not if it means renting to strangers. I can't imagine having Englischers around."

"It would be a very practical way to earn extra money, Bethel," Aenti Suz said. "And it wouldn't take any resources other than what we already have, besides what it takes to maintain the website."

Mamm stepped back toward her sewing room. "Arden would never agree to such a thing."

"I'll talk with him about it," Jessica said. "In fact, I'll take the kids outside and go find him. We still haven't decided what we should do as far as the dairy herd, so we need to figure that out too."

The day was overcast and rain threatened, but I doubted that would deter Jessica or the children.

While Aenti Suz went to harness her horse, I helped Jessica give the kids a quick snack and then wrestle them into their jackets. She headed out the back door with Caden and Ruby, and I grabbed my purse and dug out my phone once I got in the car.

One text. From Nick. No surprise. *Today's the day. I'm sure you passed with flying colors. Let me know when you find out.*

Again, my stomach flopped. I quickly checked the website on my phone, just in case, but the scores weren't posted yet.

After I put my phone back into my purse, I looked up to see Bishop Jacobs coming toward me in his buggy. He stopped when he reached my car, and I lowered my window. "Is Suz around?" he asked.

"She's getting ready to run an errand," I said.

"Oh, here she comes." He pointed toward the barn.

I watched as the two buggies met. Bishop Jacobs climbed down out of his buggy and walked over to Aenti Suz's window.

Her face was hidden by the reflections on the windshield, but it seemed they were in some sort of heated exchange. My Aenti was the exact opposite of my mother. Mamm was fearful. Aenti Suz was fearless.

When Bishop Jacobs marched back over to his buggy, I drove away, embarrassed that I'd been, essentially, spying. My guess was Bishop Jacobs didn't want Marie staying with Aenti Suz.

As I headed into Lancaster, I wondered what would happen if Bishop Jacobs forbid Marie from staying at the farm. I could sleep on the couch in Marie and Gordon's apartment, but the flights of steep stairs would be hard for Marie, no matter what. If Randi's kitchen wasn't torn up, that would be an option. But taking care of Marie and Caden while washing dishes down the hall in the bathtub didn't sound like fun.

Several miles up the road, I passed the turnoff toward Nick's parents' house. Normally, I saw them when I came back to Lancaster County, but I hadn't had a spare moment to do so. My thoughts returned to the church service on that eventful day when the pastor had prayed for spouses for the single people in the church. As we'd walked back to his truck, Nick had reached for my hand. The gesture seemed as natural as breathing. Just like that, we'd entered a new phase of our relationship.

I met his parents for the first time about a month after Nick and I officially began dating. We'd come home to Lancaster for a weekend after classes ended, and I was staying with Mamm. He'd stopped by and told me he'd spoken to his parents about us and that they both hoped to meet me.

He'd met both Marie and Jessica, and Aenti Suz too, during my first year of nursing school, after Jessica had an ectopic pregnancy and Aenti Suz had been injured in a bus accident on the way home from Pinecraft. He drove me home so I could see them. And then Marie moved to Pittsburgh and lived with me the next summer for a couple of months until she realized how much she loved Gordon and returned to Lancaster.

My sisters and Aenti all suspected I cared for Nick more than what I'd let on, but I hadn't felt nervous about them meeting him. However, I felt incredibly nervous about him meeting Mamm, so I'd avoided that. And I'd also felt nervous about meeting his parents. What if I wasn't who they wanted for their son? His sisters were fourteen and sixteen, at the time. Perhaps I wasn't who they'd expected for Nick either.

The day I agreed to go meet his parents, Nick arrived at Mamm's house to pick me up. I hurried down the steps before he reached the porch, but then Aenti Suz called out my name.

She came around the side of the house, and when she reached us, she clasped his hand and said, "I'm so happy to see you again."

We chatted for a few minutes and then continued on our way. As we reached the pickup, the curtain in the front window fluttered. Mamm stood there, watching us. I was both terrified she would come out—and a little hurt she hadn't. She could have said hello, as Aenti Suz did, but of course that wasn't her style.

Fifteen minutes later, Nick had pulled into the driveway of a two-story house that was probably close to one hundred years old and sat on a few acres of land. An old minivan was parked in front of a shed. There was a garden with corn and sunflowers to the left of the house. A bench sat on the porch under the front window, and a wreath of silk pansies and greenery hung next to the front door.

Nick paused for a moment, staring at the house, and then said, "My parents purchased this place about six years ago. Until then we lived in apartments. They saved like crazy for a down payment on a home of their own." He turned toward me.

"I'm really proud of them," he said. "But I don't ever want to be as financially strapped as they were."

By the time we'd climbed out of Nick's pickup, a middle-aged couple had stepped out onto the porch, followed by two girls. All shared Nick's dark hair and eyes. His mother was thin like Nick. His sisters were too and dressed in shorts and tank tops.

"Leisel," his mother called out. "Welcome."

They met us at the bottom of the steps, and Nick quickly introduced me. His parents were Barbara and Doug, his sisters Stephanie and Kaylee. All smiled and greeted me warmly. His father gave me a hug after he shook my hand. Normally I would have balked at the affection, but it seemed natural here.

"We're barbecuing out back," his mother said. "Would you like to join us?"

"Sure," I said. I'd left Mamm a note and said I wasn't sure what time I'd be back. I doubted she had much planned for supper.

I followed the family through the house. It had hardwood floors, and built-in bookcases flanked the fireplace in the living room. The dining room table was covered with books, and the kitchen counter had plates, hamburger buns, chips, and a bowl of grapes on it.

I could smell the burgers on the grill through the open door. In the backyard a large area was paved with slate and bordered by trees and bushes. Containers of pink geraniums were scattered all around, and there was a gazebo in the middle with a picnic table under it. Along the fence, lawn furniture was arranged in the shade under a weeping cherry tree. His parents had turned their home that they had waited so long for into their own little paradise.

"How about a glass of lemonade?" Barbara asked.

"That sounds great."

Barbara poured drinks for all of us while Doug and Nick headed to the barbecue. Barbara, the girls, and I sat in the shade. The girls told me about their school and their baby-sitting jobs for the summer. When the burgers were done, I stood to help, but Barbara told me to sit. "They'll take care of everything."

Sure enough, within a few minutes Doug and Nick had moved all of the food to the picnic table.

"Come and get it." Doug gestured toward the gazebo.

Once we were all sitting, he led us in a prayer. Then, as we ate, he asked me about my family's farm, and Barbara asked how often I was able to visit home. Then Kaylee asked if my family was sad I didn't join the church.

Stephanie kicked her under the table.

I smiled. "It's okay." I explained that some in my family were sad, but because I'd never joined the church, I hadn't been shunned. They asked me more questions about growing up Amish, and I answered them, mostly giving short answers because I hated being the center of attention.

At a lull in the conversation, I asked a few questions of my own, trying to shift the attention off me. Nick's father worked in maintenance at Lancaster General, and his mother worked as a teacher's aide. Each spoke some about their work, which I enjoyed hearing. Because of Nick's character, I'd suspected that his parents were good people—and I was right. But they were also easy to be around.

After we'd finished eating, everyone helped with cleanup. By that time it was six thirty, and Barbara said she needed to drive the girls to church for a youth group meeting. We told them good-bye, and then Nick and I left too.

With each visit, I opened up more and more and came to love the whole family. I valued having his parents' influence in my life, even though I was sure they were unaware of how closely I observed them.

As I glanced at the turnoff in my rearview mirror, my heart constricted and left me with a queasiness in the pit of my stomach. I couldn't imagine not having a relationship with Nick—or his family. If everything hadn't been so chaotic with Marie, I would have enjoyed stopping by to see them.

As I neared the Lancaster city limits, my thoughts soon landed on my state board results, but I tried to put it out of my mind. There was a chance that Marie would be discharged, and I wanted to be there to help her and Gordon if that happened. I wanted to be completely focused on her—not whether I passed or not.

When I arrived at the hospital, Marie hadn't heard from the doctor yet, and the nurse hadn't received an order for her discharge. Gordon had gone home to shower.

Just as Gordon returned, Dr. Turner entered the room. He greeted each of us individually, and then turned toward Marie. "We'd like to discharge you today. What support do you have at home, both for your son and for yourself?"

Marie explained she'd be going back to our family farm—I decided there was no reason to tell her about Bishop Jacobs's visit—and that in addition to me, her aunt and her older sister would also be available to help.

"Great," Dr. Turner said. "In that case, if Leisel can take responsibility for changing the dressing on your wound, then we can discharge you today." He said he needed to see her next week for a follow-up appointment. Then he turned toward me. "How did your state boards turn out?"

"Fine," I said, not wanting to admit how worried I was. "I should know by the end of the day."

"Great. You can let me know next week."

I nodded and tried to smile. What if I didn't pass? What would I tell him? The queasiness in the pit of my stomach returned.

Dr. Turner smiled at me as he made a point of telling me good-bye, sending a shiver up my spine. Why couldn't Nick be Mennonite? If he was, he wouldn't be contemplating joining the Air Force. We wouldn't be at this impasse.

After he left, Marie raised her bed and turned to me. "Will you help me get dressed so we can get out of here?"

I nodded toward her IV. "It's not that easy," I said. "You'll have to wait for your nurse to take that out. Then you'll have papers to sign and orders to take home with you. The nurse may have special instructions about the wound—"

Marie groaned and lowered the bed. "I hope Caden still remembers me by the time I get back to him."

"He will." I smiled. "And he'll be so glad to see you."

It wasn't until early afternoon that Marie was discharged. I took the prescriptions and said I'd fill them while Gordon drove Marie out to the farm. She was tired and there was no reason for her to wait at the pharmacy.

She'd asked me to go by their apartment too and gather more of her clothes. She needed her robe and loose nightgowns that wouldn't rub against her incision.

I went to the pharmacy in the hospital first. After I'd submitted the prescriptions, I sat down and then decided to check for the score on my boards again. I considered texting Nick to ask him if he would check for me. But then I decided bad news would be harder to take from him than straight from the source.

I entered my ID and password, my heart racing. I stared at the screen as my results popped up.

Failed.

I stood and walked to the window, logging out of my account as I did. I fought the panic rising inside me, mentally acknowledging that it was just adrenaline doing its thing. I didn't need to give into it. I attempted to take a deep breath, but it caught in my diaphragm.

Just then the technician called out Marie's name. Somehow I managed to navigate through the waiting room to the counter.

I'd intended to pay for her meds—and I would, for the moment—but perhaps I'd have her reimburse me after all. I'd have student loans to start paying in six months. What if I didn't have my license by then? How could I manage the bills I had now, plus more?

I pulled out my debit card and paid, then listened to the pharmacist go over the instructions and warnings. The pain meds were important for her comfort but should only be taken as needed. I nodded. She needed the antibiotics to prevent infection. If she experienced an upset stomach when she took them, yogurt could help. I made a mental note to pick some up on the way home.

I shook my head as the pharmacist asked if I had any questions. I stuffed the bag in my purse and headed toward my car. How could I have failed?

My phone dinged. It was Nick, checking in. I ignored it.

Numb, I drove to Marie and Gordon's apartment. I hadn't felt such loss since Dat died. No, that wasn't true. I'd felt it with Marie's diagnosis. I'd just been fighting that feeling, trying to ignore it. But now with all my plans destroyed by not passing my state boards, I felt despair.

Mr. Weber had died alone without his daughter at his side. I'd missed all the signs of Marie's cancer. I hadn't been able to save the man in the diner. Perhaps this was God's way of telling me I wasn't meant to be a nurse. Maybe I'd been wrong all along.

I found a place to park about a block away from Marie and Gordon's apartment. Gray clouds hung heavy overhead, threatening rain. I stepped into a store on my way and purchased yogurt and disposable diapers. Then I continued on to the apartment building, walked into the lobby, and then climbed the flights of stairs, thinking of Marie lugging Caden and bags of groceries up the steps.

The apartment had one bedroom, with an alcove for Caden's crib. It was all they could afford, but Marie had made it into a cozy home. A shadow quilt she'd made covered the secondhand loveseat. The oak table was small but sturdy. There were several photos on display—one from their wedding day, a few of Caden. A bookshelf lined one wall of the living room. There was no TV, but there was a computer on a desk in the corner.

I headed to the bedroom. Another quilt, a log cabin design, covered the bed, and a smaller one was draped over the side of the crib.

I gathered the items Marie wanted and then more clothes for Caden. I found a cloth grocery bag in the kitchen and placed the items inside. As I finished, my phone dinged again.

Of course it was Nick. *Can you call me?*

I sank down on the edge of the bed, as if in prayer, debating what to do. I'd have to tell him sooner or later. Better now than when I was back on the farm.

He picked up after the first ring. As he said hello, I burst into tears.

"Leisel," he cooed. "It will be all right. Lots of people have to retake the test."

I sobbed, unable to say anything.

"Where are you?" he asked.

For being a girl who didn't cry, I was doing a lot of it lately.

I managed to answer him, and then said, "I'll head back to the farm in just a minute."

Nick told me he could help me study when he was home. "And I can take off more time if needed."

I took a deep breath. "We'll talk more tomorrow, after I have a chance to decide what I should do."

"What do you mean?" he stuttered.

"Maybe I'm not meant to be a nurse."

"Of course you are," he said. "You have a God-given gift. You were made for this."

"What if I wasn't following God's leading after all? What if I made a terrible mistake by leaving the Amish?"

"What are you talking about?" Nick's voice fell lower than normal. "Tell me what you're thinking."

I took a raggedy breath. "I'm not sure," I answered. "I need some time. To sort this through."

"Look," he said. "You took the test after your sister was diagnosed with cancer, after her surgery. You were stressed and sleep-deprived. You didn't have time to review. Don't beat yourself up about it. And don't second-guess your future because of it. It's simply a six-week delay. You'll get through this. In a couple of years, this will be a distant memory."

I appreciated his pep talk, but I wasn't convinced. "I'll call you tomorrow," I said. After we said our good-byes, I leaned back on the bed and cried more, the tears sliding down the sides of my face.

If Marie didn't have cancer and I'd never come home, would I have passed the test? But Marie did have cancer, and now I was back in Lancaster County. And Nick wanted to join the Air Force. I felt as if I were losing everything.

Perhaps I was never meant to be a nurse, never meant to leave the Amish, never meant to be on my own. Maybe Mamm was right. Maybe God was punishing me for leaving in the first place, then for becoming so prideful that I thought I could succeed in the Englisch world. I'd been courageous my entire life. Until now.

Each tear that slipped down my cheek took more of my confidence with it. Nick and Pittsburgh and all the dreams we'd had together felt so very far away.

— 12 —

The next morning, after Gordon left for work, was the first chance I had to ask Aenti Suz what Bishop Jacobs had said when he'd stopped by in his buggy.

"Oh, that." She stood at the sink, filling the kettle with water. "I'd nearly forgotten."

"So, what did he decide?" I scooped up another spoonful of cereal with chunks of banana for Caden, who squealed happily in his high chair.

"Well, he hasn't come to a final decision yet."

"What do you mean?"

Most people's faces turned red when they were upset. Aenti Suz's turned white. "Oh, he didn't realize he needed more information, which I gave him. I told him to think it through again."

Only Aenti Suz could get away with that sort of thing. I gave her a puzzled look.

"What's he going to do?" Aenti Suz said. "He can't kick me out of my house—I own it."

"He can discipline you. Force you to go before the congregation. Shun you. Kick you out of the church."

She shrugged. "I'm not worried about it."

174

I continued feeding Caden, not sure what more to say. Aenti Suz was a force to be reckoned with. I'd felt confidence like hers just a few weeks ago. Not anymore. No one had asked me yesterday whether I'd passed my state boards, and I wasn't about to bring it up.

After breakfast, Aenti Suz went to run errands. Caden played on the floor while I tended to Marie's wound.

"Oh," my sister said. "I forgot to ask about your test."

I cringed.

"What did you find out?" she asked.

I struggled for a moment, trying to find the right words. "I'll have to take it again."

"You didn't pass?" Ach, Marie could still be as direct as ever.

"That's right." My wounded pride welled up inside of me, and it felt a lot like grief.

"I'm so sorry." She squeezed my hand as I pulled her loose nightgown over her dressing. "You would have passed if it hadn't been for me. Your studying and routine were totally disrupted. I'm so sorry."

"I'm not," I responded. "Even if I knew I wouldn't pass my test, I still would have come home to care for you. And there is no way to know if I would have passed if I'd stayed in Pittsburgh, not for sure."

"When will you retake it?"

"I have to wait six weeks."

"Then we'll need to make sure you have time to study. Perhaps Jessica can help more."

"Let's give it a couple of days," I answered. I didn't want her to know I was struggling with what to do next. "I haven't told Jessica and Aenti Suz yet, but I will."

"All right." Marie promised she wouldn't share my news before I was ready to. Then she said, "You're already such a good nurse, regardless of what a test says. You're empathetic but not enabling, which has really preserved my dignity."

I appreciated her affirmation, but I still felt defeated.

While Caden napped, I hauled the dirty laundry down to Mamm's basement and put the diapers to soak in a large bucket of bleach water, thankful I'd bought the box of disposables. I feared I'd never catch up on the laundry if I hadn't.

I filled the wringer washing machine and started a load of towels. After they'd washed and rinsed, I fed them through the wringer and hung them on the line. Then I started on the diapers. By the time I got them out to the line, Aenti Suz had returned from her errands and helped me pin them.

As we worked, she told me she'd stopped by the office of a man who ran a website that advertised Amish lodging opportunities for tourists.

"He thinks we'd do really well renting out the Dawdi Haus. He believes he could book it through most of the summer, and on weekends during the spring and fall too." Aenti Suz grabbed another diaper. "Has Jessica spoken to Arden about it yet?"

"Probably." I rubbed my chin with the back of my hand. "But she hasn't said anything. She's coming back tomorrow. You can ask her then."

Aenti Suz finished pinning one diaper and grabbed another. "Did you find out about your test?"

I cringed again.

She rested both of her hands on the line. "Not good?"

I nodded.

"I'm so sorry. When can you take it again?"

"Six weeks." *If I take it again at all*, I thought to myself. She smiled at me. "You'll pass then."

"Thank you." I was touched, for a moment, by her confidence. My phone buzzed in the back pocket of my jeans. It was Nick.

"Go ahead," Aenti Suz said. "I'll finish up here."

I headed toward the fence as I answered it.

After we said our hellos, he asked how I was feeling and what my plan was as far as studying. "Do you plan to take a class? Or use a specific program?"

"I haven't had a chance to think it through yet." It wasn't like me. I always had a plan, no matter the situation.

"How can I help?" he asked.

"I don't know." I felt annoyed with him, which didn't happen very often. Which really hadn't happened at all except for his Air Force idea. And now.

"Are you still thinking you made a mistake to leave?" Did I sense a hint of fear in his voice? When I didn't answer right away, he said, "Leisel . . ."

"I really haven't had a chance to think about any of this." Except for in the middle of the night when I'd been wide awake, tormented by what had happened.

"My offer stands to help you study."

I bristled.

I could hear him exhale over the phone. "What do you think?"

"I'll get back to you."

Instead of pressing me more, he asked how Marie was doing, and I gave him an update.

Then he asked about Gordon and Caden. Then about Aenti Suz. And Mamm. Soon my mind was off the test and back on my family. By the time we said good-bye, I felt a little better.

As I headed back into the Dawdi Haus with the laundry basket, I could hear Caden fussing. I put the basket down in the kitchen and hurried into the spare bedroom, but he'd already woken Marie.

"Bring him here," she said, pushing herself up against her pillows.

After I changed his diaper, I placed Caden on the bed beside her and then scooted close to keep him from crawling on top of her. "Be gentle with Mama, Caden," I said. He reached up and patted Marie's face softly. Her eyes filled with tears as he did.

"What's the matter?" I asked.

She shook her head. "Nothing, really. It all feels so bitter-sweet."

"What?"

"Well, sweet that we have Caden. That I didn't get cancer before him. And bitter when I wonder if I'll ever be able to have another baby."

"You might," I said. "See how the chemo and radiation go, and then talk with your OB/GYN."

"You're right," she said. "I need to concentrate on getting better—not borrowing trouble."

I patted her shoulder. "It's okay to be sad. And to wonder. But don't mourn what you haven't lost yet."

"Good advice," she said, turning her attention to Caden.

I had to wonder if I could follow it myself.

That night, as I knelt beside the couch to say my prayers, nothing came out. Not even a plea that I'd pass my boards if I took them again. I was completely mute. Maybe God hadn't heard any of my prayers. Maybe He had stopped listening to me when I'd left the Amish. I climbed into my makeshift bed and stared at the ceiling for a long time before I finally fell into a restless sleep.

When Jessica arrived the next morning, I watched Aenti Suz hurry over to her when she'd parked her buggy. Our aunt was persistent, if nothing else. I admired her determination to bring in extra income for the farm.

It was a beautiful day, and Caden and I sat in the sandbox while Marie rested in the living room. Perhaps Jessica hadn't spoken with Arden after all because soon Jessica was stepping into the barn and Aenti Suz was headed back toward us with Ruby in her arms.

Aenti Suz lifted Ruby high in the air, and the two began to laugh. Caden started to wave when he noticed Ruby.

Aenti Suz had always been poised and stylish—well, for an Amish woman anyway. She had a confidence about her that intrigued me. For being in her late sixties, she still moved with grace and seemed to carry Ruby without effort.

As they approached, Jessica and Arden left the barn together and headed toward the pasture. Aenti Suz slowed, probably hoping to overhear their conversation. But Arden spoke loudly enough that we could all hear him. "I told you before that it's a terrible idea."

"You said you'd think about it," Jessica said.

He stopped, crossing his arms over his barrel chest. "I don't want Englischers traipsing through our property."

"They'd be staying in the Dawdi Haus—not having access to all one hundred and forty acres," Jessica responded.

"Absolutely not," Arden said. "We'll sell the dairy herd and the woods before we do that."

Jessica put her hands on her hips. "This could be what we need to tide us over. If we can hold on to the herd for another year, things may turn around. Perhaps the competition won't be as fierce."

Arden shook his head and continued toward the pasture, where Milton was dragging the field.

"This discussion isn't over!" Jessica called out after him. "We need to come to a consensus!"

He waved his hand as he stalked away, his long beard blowing to the side.

My heart sank. It was such a good idea.

Aenti Suz reached us and lowered Ruby into the sandbox. The children hugged each other, and Aenti Suz sank to her knees beside me. "Goodness, I was hoping that would go better than it did." She sighed. "I was looking forward to serving Englisch guests. When Marie and I were in Florida, our landlady was so kind and caring. I was hoping to do the same."

"Don't give up." I nodded toward Jessica, who was walking our way with her classic determined expression on her face. "I don't think this fight is over."

When she reached us, she knelt too. "I'll keep talking with him," she said, confirming my suspicions. "It's a good idea. If we can get through the next year or so, hopefully things will change."

I patted her shoulder.

She cooed a hallo to Caden and then asked where Mamm was.

I shrugged.

"Is she helping more?"

I shook my head.

"Where's Marie?"

"Reading on the couch," I answered. "You should go sit with her. I thought I'd do some weeding." I nodded toward the garden. "I can keep an eye on the kids at the same time."

"I'll grab the tools," Aenti Suz said. When she returned from the shed with a hoe and a weed puller, we headed to the garden.

As we worked the rows of beans, I asked Aenti Suz what she thought was wrong with Mamm.

"In general? Or specifically?"

Before I could answer, Aenti Suz continued. "She had a rough childhood—I don't think she ever got over it. Losing her first-born exacerbated all of that."

I knew little about Mamm's childhood. She was the youngest of a large family, and her mother and father had died while she was still a girl. Then she lived with an older brother until she and Dat married.

Aenti Suz continued, "And then, far as what's specifically wrong now, I think her heart is still broken over losing your Dat."

Mamm never talked about Dat. I was never sure what exactly attracted them to each other, but if I'd learned anything in life it was that you could never know what went on between two people. "It's been four years," I pointed out.

Aenti Suz shrugged. "Sometimes it takes a lifetime."

I stopped hoeing and stood up straight. "Really?" Most Amish didn't stay heartbroken. Had Aenti Suz never recovered from losing her sweetheart? "Is that why you never married?"

She smiled, just a little. "No. I would have married if I found the right man. I never did."

"What about David?"

She sighed. "I was quite fond of David. More than any man I've known since Jake."

"And?"

She shrugged again. "The timing wasn't right."

"Did you write him back?" I asked, remembering the letter that had arrived weeks ago.

She shook her head. "It wasn't necessary."

Puzzled, I continued with my hoeing, glancing at the children every so often. My mind wandered to my failed test, and then to Marie's appointment the next day with Dr. Turner. I groaned inside. Hopefully he wouldn't ask me if I'd passed or not. I wouldn't lie, but I didn't want to talk about it while the pain still felt so raw.

Dr. Turner didn't forget. It was the second thing he asked, after how Marie was feeling.

He must have been able to tell by the expression on my face before I even opened my mouth. "I'm sorry," he said. "It's not unusual to fail the first time. I've known other nurses who have—and they're some of the most qualified I know. You're not alone."

"Thank you for telling me." I didn't know many doctors who would be so encouraging.

"I hate to admit this"—he glanced at Marie—"but I failed the third step of my exams the first time I took them. I was devastated at the time, but it kept me humble and made me a better doctor. The extra studying I had to do definitely put me ahead as far as my knowledge in the long run."

Hope rose within me. I really appreciated his transparency.

He quickly turned his attention to Marie, asking her general questions and checking her incision. He was pleased with how her wound was healing.

"What about the pathology report?" I asked.

"The cancer has spread to the nearby lymph nodes," he explained. "We anticipated this, and that's why chemo is the next step." He looked at Marie. "I spoke with your oncologist this morning, and he said you have an appointment today."

She nodded.

"Then you'll soon have a plan in the works for that." As the appointment ended, he extended his hand to Marie. "I'm so sorry for the circumstances," he said, "but it was a privilege to care for you. I'll continue to pray for you and your family."

My heart melted at his words. He was exceptional. Marie shook his hand, and then he turned toward me. I shook his hand too and thanked him profusely.

"I'd like to help you." He released my hand. "If you'd allow me to."

Puzzled, I tilted my head.

"I've heard nurses talking about the best study program for the licensing exam. I'd like to buy it for you."

I stifled a gasp. "Oh no. I couldn't accept that."

"Please," he said. "As one Anabaptist in medicine to another." He smiled. "Don't you think we should stick together?"

Before I could answer, he slid a notepad my way. "Just write down your information and I'll set up an account for you."

"No." I crossed my arms.

"It would be my privilege," he said. "A family friend helped me out when I was in your position. I'd like to pay it forward."

I glanced at Marie, who just shrugged.

I hadn't decided, for sure, what I planned to do—take the test again or figure being a nurse wasn't God's will for me after all. Dr. Turner met my gaze and smiled. I couldn't help but smile back. In that split second, I decided I'd take it again. I'd do all I could to be prepared and do my very best. If I failed a second time, that would be it. I'd know for sure God was trying to redirect me.

"What do you think?" Dr. Turner asked.

The study program certainly wouldn't hurt. "Thank you." I pulled the notepad toward me and wrote down both my email and my cell phone number for registration purposes. "That's very kind of you." There wouldn't be any strings attached—it wasn't as if I'd ever see Dr. Turner again.

He smiled. "Check your email later today and you'll find directions on how to log in and access the program."

I smiled back, feeling relieved. Now I had some clarity on what to do, a plan. I thanked Dr. Turner one last time and we left.

Marie and I went straight from that appointment to her oncologist, who was the exact opposite of Dr. Turner. He was abrupt, rushed, and insensitive. He didn't ask how Marie was doing or what support she had. His waiting room was full, so perhaps he was behind on his appointments, but I believed he could have used a better bedside manner, regardless. Marie would start chemo in a month. After that, the doctor would decide whether she needed to do radiation too.

On the way home, Marie held a pillow across her abdomen and pressed her head against the back of the seat.

"It's time for your pain meds," I said gently.

"I'll take them when we get back to the farm," she said. "After I spend some time with Caden."

I turned off the highway and on to Oak Road. As I approached the farmhouse, Nick's truck came into view, parked where I usually parked my car.

And there he was, on the porch in Dat's rocking chair. I hadn't expected him this soon. Mamm sat in her chair, a scowl on her face, while Aenti Suz sat on the far end of the porch with Caden as he played with some blocks. Nick quickly stood and started down the steps once he saw my car.

I parked next to Nick's pickup, and before I could climb out he was at my door, holding it open for me. Then he went around to get Marie's door.

Caden started yelling, "Mama!"

As Nick and I walked on either side of Marie, she asked him what brought him to Lancaster.

He answered, "To help Leisel study."

"Oh, that's nice." She turned her head toward me. "You'll have to get away though. There's too much chaos around here."

It was painful to watch Marie slowly navigate the steps up the porch. "I'll sit next to Mamm." Marie gave me a sly look. Mamm wouldn't treat her coldly with Nick around. Once Marie settled into the rocking chair, she placed the pillow against her

LESLIE GOULD

abdomen and then said she'd try holding Caden. Aenti Suz helped get him settled against his mother, and Marie smiled. Then she addressed Mamm. "Leisel's going to go spend some time with Nick. Can you help?"

Mamm frowned.

"Bethel, let's give Leisel some time away," Aenti Suz said. "I'll make supper for all of us."

Mamm didn't agree, but she didn't protest either.

"Go get your things," Marie said to me.

I grabbed my laptop and backpack from the Dawdi Haus, and it wasn't long until Nick and I were on the way to a bakery and coffee shop in Bird-in-Hand. We both ordered large coffees, black, and then settled down at a table in the very back.

"Have you thought about using a study program?" Nick asked, pulling out his laptop. "I know a few that are useful. I'd be happy to purchase one for you."

My face grew warm. "I already have one," I confessed. I hesitated, but then said, "Marie's surgeon paid for it."

Nick went still. "What?"

"He insisted. He said someone had helped him out when he failed one of his tests, and he wanted to pay it forward."

"Is this the Mennonite doctor you were telling me about?" Nick's eyes narrowed.

I nodded. I powered up my laptop, logged into my email, and then clicked on the link to the program. I had no reason to be embarrassed. I barely knew Dr. Turner.

Nick continued to watch me as I pulled my notebook out of my backpack and then dug through the pocket of my backpack for a pen. I found one—and also the phone number from the woman whose husband died. The one I couldn't save. I double-folded it and put it back.

I began plowing through study question after study question,

185

Nick helping me whenever I didn't understand the answer. We worked until the barista came around and said, "It's seven. Time to close."

"Oh goodness." Where had the hours gone? I thanked the barista and then looked at Nick.

"Time flies when you're having fun." He grinned. "Right?"

There were all sorts of clichés that he'd taught me through the years. And I'd usually respond with an Amish proverb, whether it made sense or not. The one that came to mind wasn't entirely inappropriate, but I said it anyway: "All that you do, do with all your might. Things done by halves are never done right."

He laughed. "I guess that means we'll study together again tomorrow?"

"Sure." I didn't feel the distance I had when we'd talked on the phone last, but I didn't feel the closeness we normally shared either—perhaps because we still hadn't talked about the Air Force.

Nevertheless, I did appreciate his help studying. Between Nick and Dr. Turner, maybe I had a chance at passing the second time.

As we headed to his pickup, he asked if I'd be willing to stop by his parents' house on the way back to the farm. "I know my folks would like to see you. They've been asking about you."

"Sure." Guilt swamped me that I'd repeatedly driven past the turnoff to his house and hadn't visited once. Of course I had a good excuse, but it wasn't like me to stay away.

He grinned. "Good. Mom said she has a pan of leftover lasagna we can eat."

—13—

Barbara and Doug both greeted me as we came through the door, and then Stephanie and Kaylee came running down the stairs to say hello too. Both were in college now. Nick and I filled our plates with lasagna and bread, and then we all headed out to the backyard.

The mosquito zappers were working overtime, and a string of lights hung over the picnic table. Even though the sun hadn't set yet, the lights created a cozy ambiance. The Jordans' home made me feel safe and secure, and stepping into their backyard made me feel like I was on vacation—not that I'd ever been on one. But the yard was so beautiful in the summer with its flowers, shrubs, and trees that it was an oasis away from the chaos surrounding me.

Barbara asked about Marie, and I gave them all an update. Then the girls wanted to know how Ruby and Caden were doing. They'd always been interested in my niece and nephew and had asked a couple of times when they could meet them.

One time Nick asked if his parents could meet Mamm and my sisters, and even Arden and his family, but I hadn't been ready for that. Nick had barely met Mamm and Arden and his family.

We chatted about the weather, about the end of the year at Barbara's school, and about a recent electrical outage in surgery while Doug was working at the hospital. Luckily, the generators had turned on immediately.

No one mentioned that I'd failed my boards, but I wouldn't be surprised if Nick had told them. Barbara did ask how long I planned to stay in Lancaster.

"I'm not sure." I left it at that.

As I took my last bite, Doug turned toward me. "So what do you think of Nick's idea to join the Air Force?"

"Dad." Nick shook his head as he spoke.

Doug's face reddened. "Sorry," he said. "It appears I misspoke."

"How about some ice cream?" Barbara said quickly, reaching for Nick's plate and then mine.

"No, thank you. I should be getting back," I said. "I ought to help Aenti Suz get Caden to bed." Honestly, Gordon was probably in charge of Caden by now, but I would rather be anywhere else at the moment.

As we headed into the house, Barbara asked Kaylee to grab a foil pan out of the refrigerator. By the time we reached the front door, Kaylee appeared, handing me the pan.

"I made an extra lasagna," Barbara said. "You can put it in the freezer or use it in the next day or two. I know you're doing a lot right now."

Touched, I took it from her. She put her arm around me. "I'm praying for Marie and for all of you," she said. "We hope you'll come back and visit us soon."

Next, Doug gave me a half hug and whispered, "Sorry to butt in where I shouldn't have."

"It's fine," I answered. "Don't worry about it." His intentions were good.

As I climbed into Nick's pickup, a wave of exhaustion swept over me.

Nick started the engine. "I mentioned the Air Force to Dad a couple of months ago. I didn't think he'd bring it up in front of you."

When I didn't respond, Nick continued. "But speaking of—are you ready to talk about it?"

I shook my head, and we were both silent until he turned onto Oak Road and asked, "What time should I pick you up tomorrow?"

"How about one? I'll have Caden down for a nap by then." I'd ask Aenti Suz to be in charge of him when he woke up.

"How about if I come tomorrow morning and help with the garden? I noticed the weeds were getting high."

I hesitated. "You shouldn't spend all of your time off helping me."

"I'd like to."

"All right." I really could use his help with the garden—that way I could tackle the laundry. I welcomed his help in the present as long as I didn't have to talk about the future.

For the next week, Nick came every day to help me with chores—even with the laundry—and then we studied in the afternoon. He always had me back by five, in time to help Aenti Suz fix supper. As it turned out, Mamm hadn't stepped up to help.

A couple of times, Aenti Suz roped Nick into helping her in the Dawdi House. It was soon obvious that she was deep cleaning, in hopes that Arden would change his mind. Nick moved an extra bureau to the barn and several boxes too, along with helping Aenti Suz rearrange all of the furniture. He also helped her wash windows and repair the flower boxes. Arden walked by at one point with a frown on his face, but he didn't say anything.

The Dawdi Haus looked great. There was absolutely no clutter—not that there had been much before, but now there was only the couch, a table and chairs, a bookshelf in the main room, and the beds and dressers in the two bedrooms, along with Marie and Gordon's belongings, for the time being.

"What about electricity?" I asked as Aenti Suz, Jessica, and I surveyed the newly arranged living room. "Most Englischers aren't going to be able to unplug completely."

"I was thinking about buying a battery-operated blow dryer and a battery-operated phone charger. Plus, battery-operated lamps. Do you think they'll mind making coffee and tea the old-fashioned way?"

"Probably not." She had a propane stove, and it was easy enough to heat up a kettle of water. "You could always buy a French press for the coffee. That will make it easier."

Jessica folded her hands as if she were praying. "This really is a good idea. And I don't know why Arden is so set against it. He won't be anywhere near the Englischers."

I guessed he was probably against it because Jessica was for it.

"Well," she continued, "I'm going to go over the accounts with him later today. Perhaps that will convince him."

That afternoon, Nick and I headed to the bakery for our last study session. We each ordered a coffee and decided to split a cinnamon roll. And then we got down to business, making the most of our time. We concentrated on the physiological integrity section, focusing on pharmacological therapies, the risk potentials, and adaptations.

As I went through the practice questions, Nick helped me research any follow-up information I needed and came up with clever mnemonics.

At four thirty, I drained my third cup of coffee. I knew the material, but I'd been overconfident about answering the multiple-choice questions. "I feel like I'm doing much better now. I'll probably go ahead and schedule my second attempt, I'm so grateful to Dr. Turner for this study program."

At the mention of Dr. Turner, Nick paused, his cup of coffee halfway to his mouth. He sighed and set it back down on the table.

"Leisel, we still need to talk," he said, his fingers gripping the handle of the mug. "I have to tell you—"

"I need to get back to the farm." I didn't meet his gaze. I couldn't think about our future until I'd taken the test again. And I certainly didn't want to hear another pitch from him on why it would be a good idea for him to join the military.

As we approached the farm, a man I didn't recognize was sitting with Mamm, Aenti Suz, and Caden on the porch. As Nick and I walked up the steps, the man stood. When my nephew saw Nick, he started waving with gusto.

"This is David," Aenti Suz said. "He surprised us."

We all shook hands. David's eyes sparkled as he told me he'd heard all about me. "All good things," he quickly clarified. "It's a pleasure to finally meet you."

David seemed sweet and endearing. Why in the world had Aenti Suz ditched him? Perhaps this surprise visit would help her come to her senses and court him after all.

Aenti Suz turned toward me. "I have supper ready and Gordon will be home soon. You and Nick should go out this evening."

"I think that's a great idea," Nick said before I could respond.

I didn't. I didn't want one last chance to talk things through. But I didn't feel as though I could turn down Aenti Suz's offer.

"All right." I turned to Nick. "Someplace casual though. I don't have anything but jeans."

We ended up at the Japanese restaurant where the different plates of sushi passed by on a conveyor belt. The first time I'd eaten there with Nick a few years ago, I was sure there was nothing in the world more different from Amish food than sushi. I still thought I was right about that. However, I'd grown to like it.

"I don't remember you mentioning David before." Nick grabbed a tuna roll off the belt.

As we ate, I told him about David, hoping to keep the conversation off us. Then about Aenti Suz's boyfriend, Jake, who'd died in Vietnam. I explained that Jake hadn't joined the Mennonite church and that Dat hadn't joined the Amish church, but that they were both conscientious objectors and ended up going to Vietnam to work in a Mennonite clinic. Before I knew it, I was telling him about my grandfather going off to Chicago to work in a hospital during World War II.

"So, how would that be different from me joining the Air Force?"

I glanced down at my tiger roll. "My grandfather was forced to," I said. "He didn't have any choice." It was an entirely different situation.

"Leisel, there's something I have to tell you."

I looked up.

His root-beer-colored eyes appeared troubled. "I know you don't want to talk about the future, but I can't keep this from you any longer. I've put it off all day because I was trying to find the right time to tell you, but I'm being deceptive—and it's killing me."

My heart began to race. Had he cheated on me? That was one thing I'd never worried about. Not once.

"Nick, what are you talking about?"

"The Air Force."

I breathed a sigh of relief that I didn't have to worry about him being unfaithful. But then I was filled with absolute despair as his words sank in. My chopsticks clattered to the table. "You didn't."

He nodded. "I did. The recruiter said if I want my loans paid off, it was time to do it. I leave for officer training next week."

After a silent ride home, Nick parked next to my car and turned toward me. "Leisel," he said. "I'm sorry. I expected you'd be upset—but not this upset."

I reached for the door handle.

"Where do we stand?" Nick asked.

Did I have to spell it out? I turned toward him. "We don't."

"What do you mean?"

"We're done." I opened the door.

"Wait."

I could hear the tears in his voice and couldn't bear to look at him. "I'm sorry." I stepped down, keeping my eyes on the ground. "There's nothing more to talk about."

I hurried around the side of the house and then retreated to the pond, listening for Nick's truck. Finally, he drove back up the lane.

It was the warmest summer evening yet, and the sun was just setting over the tops of the trees. The wavelengths of the light and the size of the particles in the atmosphere must have been optimal because it was gorgeous. Pink and orange with streaks of lavender. I couldn't take my eyes off of the sky as the sun slipped behind the west end of the farm and the woods became a cluster of silhouettes. It was all so beautiful, but I found no joy in it. No miracles.

Jah, I wanted to wallow in self-pity, which Dat would have told me wasn't adding anything to my own life. It was only taking away the joy I could share in the lives of those I loved.

I'd share in their joy tomorrow.

I chastised myself. Marie was battling cancer. I was only battling my pride. Well, that and my conscience. I couldn't marry a military man.

I picked up a stone. *How could he?!* I attempted to skip it across the pond. Instead, it fell with a single splash and immediately sank. That was exactly how I felt. I picked up a bigger rock and hurled it into the pond.

Why would Nick betray me like that? It hurt deeply that he would go behind my back. It wasn't as if we talked things through exhaustively like some couples did, but I had thought we were honest with each other. Granted, I hadn't been willing to listen to him the last two months or so. I'd only wanted to focus on graduating . . . and then Marie . . . and then my boards. Perhaps I'd neglected him and his struggles with figuring out his future. Our future. But he shouldn't have made such a life-changing decision when I wasn't ready.

Someone called my name from the backyard. Aenti Suz. In the moment, I didn't even want to speak with her.

She headed toward me. "When did you get back?"

"A few minutes ago," I said. "Where's David?"

Her voice was light. "Sitting on the porch with your Mamm. I think he plans to leave soon." She grew more serious. "Where's Nick?"

"Gone," I answered.

"What's the matter?"

"He's joined the military," I said, my voice flat. "He's leaving in a week."

"Oh dear." She paused thoughtfully before saying, "Come have a cup of tea with me. Marie, Gordon, and Caden have already gone to bed. I'll tell you more of your Dawdi's story. That will take your mind off the present."

Would it? I did want to hear more about my grandfather and his time during World War II, but contrary to Nick's thinking, the two had nothing in common. Well, little in common. It then dawned on me that Dawdi Joe had joined the AFS as an ambulance driver partly to be near an army nurse.

But that was different. Nick was joining to help himself. I exhaled. That wasn't true either. In his mind, he thought he'd be helping me too. But since I couldn't marry him now, that was a moot point. Or was it?

Noticing my hesitation, Aenti Suz took my hand and I followed her back through the gate. "There, there," she said as she held open the door to the Dawdi Haus. "Come on in. I think you'll really enjoy the next part of the story."

— 14 —

Joe

Even though the sun shone every day and the weather was hot and humid, Joe's life seemed dreary and gray after Lt. Shaw and the others relocated to Fort Drum for training. On all of his shifts, Joe had to put up with Karcher, who was more sullen than ever. The man targeted Joe, challenging him on several decisions he'd made while caring for patients, and a couple of times he even wrote Joe up for insubordination.

Thankfully, Joe still had Ali, with whom he spent most of his free time. One day as they walked along the lake, Ali said, "Boy, you really have it bad."

Joe stopped, pretending to be watching a sailboat on the water as he realized he'd been lost in thoughts about Lt. Shaw. "What are you talking about?"

"Love," the man answered.

Joe shook his head. "I'm just restless, is all."

Ali laughed and slapped him on the back.

Joe had received three letters from Lt. Shaw filled with details about their training. *It turns out I'm an expert marksman,* she wrote. *Who would have guessed?* They also had long marches in the woods. And field hospital exercises. *How are you doing? I've been praying that you won't get orders. . . . I know that's not what you want, but it's what I want for you. I haven't changed my mind.* She signed each letter, *Your friend* . . . Friend. That's all he could hope for. He'd be satisfied with that, as best he could.

Day after day, Joe expected his orders and a train ticket. But nothing arrived. By late August, as the entire city sweltered, he feared they never would.

He, along with all Americans, breathed a collective sigh of relief as the French forces and US Infantry Divisions liberated Paris after more than four years under Nazi rule. Joe wondered if the war would soon be over. Perhaps Lt. Shaw wouldn't go to Europe after all. Perhaps he wouldn't either.

But then, in early September, Joe had a fourth letter from Lt. Shaw. She said she was doing fine, that she was enjoying the crisp fall nights, and that *what we expected will happen soon.*

He knew she couldn't write that she would soon ship out or tell him where she was going, but it was her way of communicating she would soon be leaving. She concluded the letter by writing, *The days I spent with you in Chicago were the happiest of my life. I hope we will meet again.*

He slipped the paper back into the envelope. He hoped so too.

In late September, when Joe had practically given up hope that he'd ever get orders, he pulled a letter from his Dat and an envelope from the AFS out of his mail slot. He opened the missive from the AFS first. In it were his orders to drive an ambulance for a British division in France, along with a ticket to New York and documents for passage on a ship to England. He'd leave on a train in three days.

Next, he opened the letter from his father, written in response to Joe's letter explaining that he'd been accepted by the AFS. His Dat wrote, *Forgive me for taking so long to answer your letter. I've been mulling over what to write. I fear your pride has gotten the best of you. Don't think you can save the world. Only our Lord and Savior can do that.*

A hollow feeling grew within Joe's stomach as he read. *But I appreciate your determination and your honesty in telling me. You could have hidden your intentions. I appreciate your respecting me enough to reveal your plan. I know God can keep you in the States, if He so desires. As always, I'm praying for His will for your life.*

Joe hated to disappoint his father, yet he appreciated Dat's honesty too. He sat down immediately to write his father again, giving him the details he'd promised in his last letter. Once he outlined the plan, he added, *I hope I can serve the soldiers better in France than Chicago. So many of the men I've cared for have stories of fellow soldiers who died in the field because there weren't enough ambulances. I pray I can make some sort of a difference.* Of course, he didn't tell his father that he hoped he could find Lt. Shaw in France too.

He put his father's letter in his pack, although he would mail the other ones from his family home for Charity to keep safe. The letter was a reminder that his Dat knew him better than he knew himself—and loved him anyway. But hopefully only God knew his secondary motivation was to be as close to Lt. Shaw as possible. Well, Ali most likely suspected that too. And Captain Russell. Joe couldn't help but smile.

When word got around that Joe was heading to Europe, Karcher confronted him on the ward on Joe's last day of work.

"You're good for nothing, Bachmann," he said. "Wait until you get on the front—you'll be crying to return to your Dutchy ways." Obviously Karcher, who wanted to go to Europe, resented that Joe would soon be on his way.

For a moment, Joe felt as if he were fourteen again, watching the slash pile burn out of control. But then he squared his shoulders, stared the man in the eyes, and remained silent.

Karcher quickly grew flustered. "Get out of my sight," he bellowed.

Joe continued to stare him down. He'd done nothing wrong. He wouldn't be intimidated.

It seemed Karcher had had enough because he lunged at Joe, pushing him with both hands. Joe stumbled backward an inch but held his ground. A new doc on the floor, a major, yelled, "Lt. Karcher, I've been watching you this entire time. Stand down. Now."

Joe breathed a sigh of relief and left the floor.

When Joe arrived in New York, he hoped, by some miracle, that Lt. Shaw would be on the same ship. But she wasn't. He crossed the Atlantic in early October. The ship was full of soldiers. There weren't any nurses or other women on board. Everyone worked, except for those who were too ill to do so. Thankfully, Joe wasn't seasick after the first couple of days. He was put on mess hall duty and slept on the floor, wrapped in a blanket. He worked from morning to night, washing dishes, cleaning tables, and sweeping the floor.

As often as he could, Joe would slip up to the deck and enjoy the fresh air, looking east and wondering if Lt. Shaw had already reached England.

The ship landed in Liverpool in the middle of October. The servicemen were sent to a training camp in England, while Joe boarded another ship to cross the Channel. Once he landed in

France, he was directed to join up with the British Twenty-First Army, which was operating in northern Belgium and southwestern Netherlands with the Canadian and Polish armies. They'd been fighting the Nazis since the first of October in the Battle of Scheldt, but that was now winding down.

For the next month, Joe stocked the ambulances with supplies and transferred the wounded from battalion aid stations to field hospitals and then on to transports out of the area. Besides caring for those wounded during the battle, Joe also transported soldiers injured in truck accidents and those who had fallen ill. He'd gone from Lancaster County to Chicago to Europe, a world he'd never imagined. He kept his head down and worked hard, exactly the way his Dat had taught him. Jah, everything had changed. But doing his work heartily as to the Lord hadn't.

He was constantly on the lookout for Lt. Shaw and the others and asked about them frequently, but no one had any information on their unit.

In the middle of December, after the Germans attacked the Allies in a surprise advance on the western front, Joe and his ambulance crew were sent to the Ardennes Forest, where German bombs rained down on the British and American armies.

Joe had never imagined such destruction, and the only thing that kept him going was getting the wounded, four at a time, from the battalion aid stations to the field hospitals, which were mobile units with four hundred beds. As he drove over the slick roads of the forest, he faced horror after horror. But as he was tested more and more each day, he felt relieved that he had the courage to keep going. He wasn't the failure that both Faith and Karcher predicted he would be. He was saving the lives of men who would hopefully get back to their families and their pre-war lives.

Joe believed he was doing the work God had for him, yet he appreciated the nonresistant views of the Amish more than ever. If only the entire world believed the same. The war wasn't taking Joe away from his beliefs—if anything, it was cementing them in his mind and heart.

The loss of life weighed heavily on him, as did the soldiers' debilitating wounds. Every single day men and marriages and families were altered forever—and that was for the soldiers who survived. Other men, marriages, and families were completely destroyed.

Not once did a soldier harass Joe for not fighting though. All seemed grateful for the ambulance drivers and the work they were doing.

He asked in each field hospital he went to about Captain Russell's unit. Finally, at the beginning of January, Joe came across a doctor who knew Captain Russell. "He's Major Russell now," he said. "We came over on the same ship. They're with the Eightieth Division. Last I knew their field hospital was near the village of Bavigne."

When Joe got back to his headquarters, he looked at a map. Bavigne was in Luxembourg, south of where he was located in Belgium. There was no reason for him to go down there.

But when Joe's supervisors asked for an ambulance driver to drive into Luxembourg and procure supplies from the Americans, near Mecher, Joe volunteered immediately. He knew the field hospitals leapfrogged over each other as the front line moved east. Hopefully Major Russell's hadn't yet.

With a map and the help of his partner, a Quaker named Wallace Allen who was from Ohio, Joe navigated the ambulance from Belgium into Luxembourg. They passed bombed-out farmhouses and barns, abandoned jeeps and tanks, and dead Germans along the way. They shivered through the freezing January day, both from the wind that blew through the ambulance and from the carnage all around them.

When they reached Bavigne, Joe slowed to a crawl. It was filled with American soldiers. Although houses and buildings had been bombed, the church steeple was intact, along with the few shops along the main street. As they left the village, a field hospital appeared around a curve, situated along a river.

Joe pulled the ambulance to the side of the road in front of the first tent. He turned to Wallace and said he'd be right back. "I need to ask about someone here." Wallace said he'd look for a cup of coffee in the mess tent and meet him back at the ambulance.

Joe jogged toward the first tent and asked about Major Russell and his unit.

An orderly answered, "Yep. They're here. Check the tent at the end, closest to the river."

Joe hurried through the field hospital, weaving between people and tents until he reached the last tent. He ducked through the flap and squinted his eyes. One of the nurses turned toward him.

"Joe?" It was Lt. Madison, her voice soft. She had dark circles under her eyes and looked as if she hadn't slept in a month. Then she said a little louder, "Look who's here."

Major Russell turned toward him. And then Lt. Shaw. Even in the dim light, he could tell she was pale and thin. Major Russell came forward and shook his hand. Joe complimented him on his promotion, and Major Russell simply nodded at the acknowledgment.

Lt. Shaw approached, a smile on her face, tears glistening in her eyes. "Are you all right?" she whispered.

He nodded, stepping as close as he could without touching her, but he longed to take her in his arms. "How about you?"

"Better, now that I know you're okay."

"How long can you stay?" Major Russell asked.

"I can't." Joe explained he was on his way to Mecher.

"Can you spend the night on your way back?" the major asked. "You're going to have to sleep somewhere—besides in the back of an ambulance."

Joe shook his head, although he wished with all his might he could. "We need to head right back."

For a moment, in the middle of the gathering of his friends, he could almost forget there was a war all around them.

"Go ahead and walk out with Joe," Major Russell said to Lt. Shaw. "We'll cover for you."

Joe didn't want to leave Major Russell and Lt. Madison, but his desire to be alone with Lt. Shaw was greater. He told the others good-bye.

Once they were outside the tent, Lt. Shaw leaned toward him and Joe took her in his arms, tucking her head under his chin. "I've been so worried about you," he said.

"I've been fine." She shivered. "A little cold."

Joe lifted her chin to look into her eyes. "And wet and hungry?"

She smiled. "You too?"

"Not anymore." He pulled her close again. He couldn't bear the thought of ever loving anyone but her. After a short time, he said, "I need to get going. I have to pick up supplies in Mecher."

"I wish you could come back tonight."

"Me too."

"Do you have any R&R coming?"

Joe shook his head. One of the other ambulance drivers had been allowed a few days of rest and relaxation, but Joe didn't see any in his future.

"Lt. Madison and I do," Lt. Shaw said. "Major Russell ordered it. Lt. Madison has been unsettled. Shaky and out of sorts from all the bombings."

"When will your R&R be?" he asked.

"In about a week and a half—the last week of January, unless something changes."

"Where?"

"Longwy. It's a French village in Lorraine. Could you come see me?"

"I'll do my best," he said, thinking Longwy was where the ambulance driver he knew had gone for R&R. "But I can't guarantee anything, especially if the battle doesn't end before then."

"I'll pray." She hugged him tighter.

"I will too." He kissed the top of her head.

"I've missed you, worse than I even thought possible."

He put his hands on her shoulders and stepped back, locking his eyes on hers. He felt the same way.

"Is this real to you?" she asked.

His voice thickened as he stuttered, "This?"

"What's between us. What feels like—"

"Love?" The word flew out of his mouth.

She nodded.

"Jah," he whispered.

She fell back into his arms for a moment, but then pulled away. "You need to get going. God willing, we'll see each other soon."

He hugged her again, his heart racing. Then she tipped her face upward, and his lips met hers. *Love.* This was what it felt like.

While the war was only making his nonresistant beliefs grow stronger, Joe's feelings for Lt. Shaw were threatening all he'd anticipated for his future. He knew he couldn't rely entirely on his emotions. He'd heard soldiers talk about war-time romances. He had to be pragmatic. On the other hand, he couldn't imagine ever feeling the way he did for Lt. Shaw for any another woman. He'd never imagined feeling this way was even possible.

Joe didn't put in for any leave until the battle ended on January 25 and the Germans fled east. He was given permission to go two days later. He prayed Lt. Shaw would still be there.

Of course, he couldn't take an ambulance, so he had to hitch rides as best he could, starting on the back of a troop truck and then in a jeep with a couple of officers who were also headed to Longwy, to the R&R facility.

When they pulled up outside an old hotel in the center of the village, Joe grabbed his bag, thanked the officers, and climbed out of the jeep. He noticed a curtain flicker on the second floor, and he ran toward the entrance. By the time he reached the lobby, Lt. Shaw was coming down the steps of the open staircase. She wore a black skirt and a blue sweater that matched her eyes. A moment later, she was in his arms as the two officers came through the door and tipped their hats.

One of them laughed and said, "No wonder you were so eager to get here."

Joe and Lt. Shaw stayed up half the night talking in the corner of the lobby near the fireplace. He put log after log on the fire, but the drafty room remained cold. Finally, he scooted closer and put his arm around her.

As she melted against him, Lt. Shaw lowered her voice. "War is horrible—worse than I even dreamed. I thought I was prepared after taking care of the boys back in Chicago, but I wasn't at all. I wonder how the soldiers can bear all of it, actually being on the battlefield." Her eyes welled with tears. "You too.

Scooping the wounded up and into an ambulance. It's all too close and real and horrid."

"It isn't too bad for me," Joe said. "I just have to get them to a field hospital—you have to put them back together.'"

Lt. Shaw snuggled even closer. "What's to become of us, Joe?"

He tightened his grip on her shoulder. At the moment, he believed he'd do anything to be with her. Marry her. Move to Chicago. Never join the Amish. Lancaster County felt as if it were a universe away.

"What's wrong?" she asked, leaning away from him.

He pulled her back. "Well, for one, I'm younger than you. I don't want to lead you to believe that I'm more than I am. I've been told that I'll never amount to anything."

She met his gaze. "I know you, Joe Bachmann. You're a good man. The best I know. Put those foolish predictions out of your mind. And two years? What will that matter . . . ?" She stopped.

He coaxed her to go on, but she waved her hand and shook her head, tears flooding her eyes again. He tried to smile.

"What will it matter . . . when we're old?" she whispered.

He held her even tighter. Not sure how to phrase the next item, he hesitated bringing it up. He'd never been good at discussing hard topics, but it was essential that they did. Being with her here and now, he knew his feelings for her were true. But how could he be sure she really cared for him? Enough to commit to him—for life?

"I've heard soldiers speak of war-time romances," he said carefully. "Where two people pledge their lives before really even knowing each other. I want to make sure that's not us."

"I understand," Lt. Shaw answered. "I've thought about that too, especially as I've missed you so much these last several months." The light from the fire flickered across her face. "But don't you think people get to know each more deeply in times like these? We saw each other every day in Chicago, caring for others in difficult situations and dealing with adversity. Some people could be married for years before they witnessed each other in such trying times." She looked him directly in the eyes. "I'd feel this way about you regardless of our circumstances. But what we've gone through has allowed me to get to know you faster—and more thoroughly—than I ever would have otherwise."

He nodded. He felt the same. Finally he could ask her the question he'd longed to voice since seeing her coming down the stairs of the hotel. "Will you marry me?"

She sank her face against his chest. "When?"

Without pausing, he said, "As soon as we can."

She pulled back again. "But what about you being Amish?"

"I'm not," he said. "I haven't joined the church yet."

"But you will."

"Not necessarily."

"You would leave for me?"

He nodded. "Jah, I would."

"And not regret it?"

Leaving would mean abandoning his Dat and sisters. And giving up the land. He hesitated for a moment, searching for the right words. "I can say that I'd never regret marrying you."

"What about your faith?"

"My relationship with God won't change. And wherever we settle, we'll become part of a church, hopefully in a Mennonite community, that will help us grow in our faith."

She took his hand in hers and ran her finger along each of his. "Are you serious about getting married as soon as possible?"

He nodded.

"There's a chaplain here. He was joking at dinner that he's officiated more weddings in the army than he did back home."

"But you need permission from your commander," Joe said. Her eyes sparkled in the shadowy light. "How did you know?" His face grew warm, even in the cold lobby. "I asked around."

She laughed, the first time she'd done so all evening. "So did I." She pulled a piece of paper from the pocket of her skirt. "It started as a joke." She unfolded the paper. "But Major Russell gave this to me, just in case."

Joe took the piece of paper. Sure enough, Major Russell had given his permission and signed the document. If they married tomorrow, they'd have one night together before they both had to return to their assignments.

"What about you?" Lt. Shaw asked. "Do you need permission?"

"Not that I've been able to find out." He clasped her hand and asked her again. "Will you marry me?"

"Yes." She beamed. "Yes, I'll marry you. Meet me in the dining hall for breakfast. We can talk with the chaplain then."

After only two hours of sleep, Joe made his way to the dining hall, which was a long, narrow room with dark paneling and heavy drapes. Soon after, Lt. Shaw arrived. She pointed to a man who appeared to be in his early thirties. "That's Chaplain Higdon," she said.

Over homemade bread and plain dark coffee, they talked with the chaplain, who was a Baptist preacher from North Carolina. He asked them if either had been married before. Both shook their heads.

"I'll take you on your word," Chaplain Higdon said as he stared at Joe. "You look like you just started shaving, so I believe you." Then the man slapped him on the back, and Joe could tell the chaplain was joking—most likely anyway.

Chaplain Higdon said that because they were under US jurisdiction, there was no need to get a French marriage license. Then he pointed out that had Joe been an orderly in the army, he couldn't have married the two, as Joe would be Lt. Shaw's subordinate. But, the chaplain continued, there were no regulations against a member of the AFS marrying a US Army officer.

Relief filled Joe to have what he'd been told confirmed.

Next, the chaplain asked Joe about his religion. He seemed surprised that Joe was Amish, and then even more so that Lt. Shaw was Mennonite. "Well, I grew up Mennonite," she clarified. "Obviously I'm not anymore or I wouldn't have joined the army."

"What about once the war is done? What will the two of you be then?"

"Mennonite," Joe said.

He was surprised when Lt. Shaw didn't agree with him. Instead, she simply said, "We'll figure it out. That's the least of our worries now."

Joe wondered what exactly she meant but didn't press her.

Chaplain Higdon said he was happy to marry them. He opened up a leather attaché case, pulled out a document, and held it up. "*Voilà*," he said. "A marriage certificate." He wrote their full names and then called two people from the next table to sign as witnesses.

"I can marry you right now, if you'd like," he said.

Lt. Shaw looked at Joe, who shrugged his shoulders. "I'm fine with whatever you want."

"Wait just a few minutes then," she said. "I need to go get Lt. Madison."

A waiter must have overheard their conversation because just as Lt. Shaw walked out the door the manager of the hotel appeared and called her back to the table. In perfect English, he said, "If we are going to have a wedding, we must at least attempt to have some semblance of decorum. Wait until noon. We'll have the ceremony in the lobby, and I'll speak with the chef about a wedding dinner."

Lt. Shaw smiled in relief. "*Merci.*"

At noon, they gathered in the lobby of the hotel. Lt. Madison stood up with Lt. Shaw, and one of the doctors Joe hitched a ride with the day before stood up with him. Joe wore his uniform and Lt. Shaw wore hers, a skirt and tailored jacket. Someone had made a bouquet of paper flowers that Lt. Shaw carried, along with her Bible.

Of course, the service was much different from what Joe was used to. There was no two-hour sermon beforehand. At Joe's request, Chaplain Higdon read from 1 Corinthians 13: "And now abideth faith, hope, charity . . ." It was a nod to his family. Joe hoped they would be gracious to him when they found out what he'd done.

Then the chaplain had Joe repeat the vows. "I, Joe, take thee, Martha, to be my wedded wife, to have and to hold, from this day forward, for better, for worse, for richer, for poorer, in sickness and in health, to love and to cherish, till death do us part, according to God's holy ordinance; and thereto I pledge thee my faith and myself to you."

The vows were different from an Amish wedding, but it didn't matter. The meaning was the same.

— 15 —

Leisel

Wait." I scooted forward on the couch. "Lt. Shaw's first name was Martha? That was Mammi's name."

Aenti Suz nodded.

I gasped. "Was Lt. Shaw your mother?"

Aenti Suz smiled. "You have to hear the rest of the story to find out."

Flabbergasted, I said, "Why didn't you mention that her first name was Martha at the beginning of the story?"

"He didn't call her Martha until after they married. There was no reason to introduce her that way."

"But what happened after that? It's only the end of January in 1945. There's still over three months left of the war. What happened? I mean, obviously Dawdi Joe ended up returning to Lancaster County and joining the church. Did Lt. Shaw come with him?"

Aenti Suz started to yawn and covered her mouth. Then she said, "Caden will be up early."

211

"I'll get up with him," I said. "You sleep in. You have to tell me the rest."

She shook her head. "I'm going to contact the man who runs the website about taking some photos of this place tomorrow."

She'd successfully distracted me. "Even without Arden's blessing?"

She shrugged. "I think the math will convince him. He's looked into selling the herd, but it would be at a huge loss."

No doubt farming was full of risks. So was war.

Giving up any chance of hearing more of Dawdi Joe's story, I followed Aenti Suz into the kitchen to wash our mugs, feeling a little better until I remembered Nick and the pain he'd caused me. After Aenti Suz retreated to her room, I knelt beside the couch to pray. But once again, no words formed. If only I could let tomorrow worry about itself.

I stayed awake late into the night, tossing and turning. Thinking of Dawdi Joe made my heart ache. I thought I'd had that sort of love, but obviously I didn't. Here my grandfather had married an army officer, while I'd just lost the love of my life to the military. The irony cut to my heart.

Then again, I didn't know how his story ended. Perhaps he regretted his rash decision. Perhaps something unexpected happened.

On Saturday morning, I awoke to Caden's cries and a hollowness in my soul. Gordon had him out of bed before I managed to get off the couch. He said he planned to go help his mother with her kitchen and would take Caden with him. I wasn't sure how much he'd get done with a toddler in tow, but I decided not to point that out and use the free time to go back to the coffee shop and study.

However, I had a hard time concentrating. Nick had joined the Air Force without telling me. In the end, I hadn't mattered enough to him. I felt a pressure in my chest. Shortness of breath. Sweating. So much for thinking I'd soon feel numb.

My *Hatz* was breaking. Funny that I thought of the word *heart* in Pennsylvania Dutch instead of English. But it was more than my heart. The core of me was breaking. There had to be a cure for this, just like there was in medicine. Being the nurse that I was, or that I hoped to be, I Googled what to do about a broken heart. *Appreciate your independence. Detach from your ex-partner. Laugh when you can. Help someone else.*

Sure, it was all good advice, but I was too heartbroken to even comprehend it. Nick knew how I felt about the military long ago. If he joined, regardless of my feelings, then he didn't care about me the way he said he did. We didn't share the same vision for the future.

That evening, Marie insisted she wanted to go to church the next morning before she started chemo, afraid she might feel poorly and not be able to go for the next several weeks.

I said I'd go with them and look after Caden in the nursery, if needed. Marie loaned me a dress of hers that I could wear with a pair of sandals. Many of the women at Gordon and Marie's church wore *Kappa*, but not all of them. I figured I wouldn't stand out too badly.

And I didn't. Caden ended up being fine in the nursery, so I stayed in the service the entire time, sitting next to Marie and Gordon in the very back row. We planned to leave as soon as possible to keep Marie from being exposed to unnecessary germs. My mind kept wandering during the service. First to my Dawdi Joe's story. And then to Martha. Whether she was related to me or not, she'd grown up Anabaptist and had then joined the army. Of course, from there my thoughts landed on Nick.

When the service was over, we left as quickly as possible.

Gordon headed to the nursery to get Caden while Marie and I started for the car. Ahead of us was a man checking his phone.

"That's Dr. Turner," Marie said.

"Are you sure?"

"Jah," she answered.

The man stopped at a Honda Accord. A nice car, but not flashy by any means.

"Hello," Marie called out.

He turned. "Marie," he said. Then he saw me and smiled broadly. "Leisel." He quickly directed his focus back on my sister. "How are you feeling?"

"All right. I wanted to come to church in case the chemo makes me sick and I have to miss for a while."

"Good idea," he said, turning back to me. "And how are you, Leisel?"

"Good," I answered, wishing I could think of something more to say.

"How's the studying going?" he asked.

"Really well." *If I don't count yesterday.* "The program has been a big help."

"I'm so glad to hear that."

Marie reached for my arm for support as she said, "I didn't realize we attended the same church."

"We don't," he said. "This is my first time here. Meeting the two of you inspired me to start looking for a home church." He smiled kindly.

"Well, that's wonderful," Marie answered. "What did you think?"

"I liked the service," he answered. "It's similar to the church I grew up in." He held up his phone. "I need to get going. I'm just glad I was able to sit through the service."

"Have a good rest of your day." By the way Marie clutched

214

my arm, I could tell she was tired. As we walked toward the car, I glanced over my shoulder and watched Dr. Turner drive out of the parking lot. It felt serendipitous that he'd attended Marie and Gordon's church the same day that I had.

"Don't get any ideas," Marie said.

"What do you mean?"

"About Dr. Turner. You and Nick are perfect together."

I hadn't told her about our falling out, but I did now.

She shook her head stubbornly. "Well, that doesn't mean the two of you are finished."

"No, it does," I said. "What he did is a deal breaker for me."

Marie leaned against the car. "You know, you're so empathetic and understanding toward everyone but Nick."

"What?"

She nodded. "Have you looked at this from his point of view?"

"Jah," I answered. "I have. He wants to have someone else pay his student loans. I get that. But he put finances first."

"And do you think, just maybe, you're putting your ideology before him?"

"My ideology?"

She nodded.

"To not support war? It's kind of a biggie."

"But Nick's your best friend. Your soul mate. You think that's easy to find, but it's not. You should try to work things out with him."

I crossed my arms. I certainly didn't think a soul mate was easy to find. Perhaps I'd never find another one in my entire life. "Marie," I said. "You don't know the whole story. I told him how I felt about the military and he joined anyway."

"Did you really tell him? Explicitly? Or did you do it in that way of yours where you tiptoe around the conflict?"

I inhaled sharply.

Gordon approached, carrying Caden, who started chanting, "Mamamamama." Obviously our conversation had ended. Hopefully for good.

On Monday morning, Gordon took Marie to her first chemo appointment while I drove to Pittsburgh to clean out my apartment. I didn't bother to let Nick know I was in town. It didn't take me long to pack the rest of my things, clean the bathroom and kitchen, and dust and vacuum the rest of the place.

After I hauled my cleaning supplies to my car, I stood in the doorway and looked around one last time. Regardless of its size and musty smell, the apartment had served me well. An important chapter of my life was ending.

Before I left Pittsburgh, I stopped by the care facility to talk with Rita. The conversation with Mr. Weber's daughter still haunted me, even though I hadn't heard anything more from her. I expected that if she really planned to sue me, Rita would know.

"Leisel," she called out as I stopped in the doorway to her office. "I hope you want your job back."

"Nope." I smiled. After I asked how she was doing, I asked if she'd heard from Mr. Weber's daughter lately.

"Oh, that," she said. "She told me she talked with you. I should have given you an update." She motioned toward the chair in front of her desk and I sat down. "I doubt she would have pursued a lawsuit, but once I explained all of the rules and regulations to her, she backed off."

"Oh." I'd been worried about it for no reason.

"This happens more than you'd think," Rita said. "Families have a really hard time after a loved one dies. They want to blame someone, want it to be someone's fault. For some reason, it seems to help them in their grief. Takes their thoughts off of who they lost."

"Weird." That certainly wasn't the way the Amish handled death. "But," I said, "the morning Mr. Weber died, you seemed to be suspicious of my actions too, because I hadn't charted the incident yet. That wasn't uncommon. We all would chart after our shift had ended when we needed to."

"Oh goodness," she said lightly. "I was probably just cranky that morning." She held up her coffee cup. "Maybe I hadn't had enough caffeine."

We chatted for a few more minutes, and then I left. I should have felt better, but instead I felt even more defeated. I'd really cared about Mr. Weber. His death seemed to be the start of my decline—the beginning of my disappearing confidence.

As I drove east, I didn't stop at the diner for coffee. I drove right past the exit and stopped farther along the route. There was no reason to remind myself of another one of my failures.

When I reached the farm, it was late in the evening, but I began unpacking my car anyway. I headed to the barn with the first load, deciding I'd leave everything but my clothes in the storage room in the back, where I'd already stashed my kitchen supplies.

As I pushed open the door, I heard voices. "Hallo," I called out.

"Aenti Leisel?" It was Milton. He stepped out of a stall, Luke beside him. "Dat told us to give one of the new calves another bottle. She hasn't been gaining enough weight."

"What are you doing?" Luke asked.

"Unloading my car," I answered.

Milton ran his hand through his hair. He was seventeen, not much younger than Dawdi Joe had been when he married. "Are you moving back?"

"Jah."

Luke stepped forward. "Do you plan to join the church, then?"

"Probably not," I answered. "I'm more likely to become a Mennonite."

He frowned.

I headed on down to the storeroom, stashed my things, and returned to my car for another load. When I opened the door, I heard my phone chime with a voicemail. If it was Nick, I had nothing to say. But when I glanced at the phone, I saw it was an unknown number.

After I'd finished unloading my car, I sat on the Dawdi House steps and listened to the message. "Hi, Leisel, this is Stephen Turner. Dr. Turner. Would you please call me back? I have a question for you." I quickly programmed his number into my phone.

It was after nine, so I decided to wait and call him in the morning, just in case he was already asleep. Surely, his question was about something in the area, or perhaps a question about the Mennonite church, which I wouldn't be able to answer anyway.

Again, I wished Nick was Mennonite. That would solve all of my problems.

After I had Caden changed and fed the next morning, we headed out to the sandbox. Then I left a cheery message for Dr. Turner and told him to call back anytime. I didn't tell him I wouldn't be able to answer if I was around my mother or brother, but I could always call him back. *Phone tag* is what I think Autumn called it.

As Caden played, Marie joined us, sitting in a lawn chair. I headed to the garden to weed as Aenti Suz returned from an errand. She waved from her buggy as she headed toward the barn.

Twenty minutes later, she approached the garden. "Dan is coming over today to take photos."

"Dan?"

"The website designer."

"Oh," I teased. "The two of you are on a first-name basis now?"

She smiled. "He's such a nice young man. You'll really like him."

Dan turned out to be maybe twenty. He took numerous photos without hardly saying a word, but he seemed comfortable around Aenti Suz and complimented the Dawdi Haus, saying he thought it would get a lot of business.

"I'll load everything tonight," he said. "I'm guessing you'll have the place booked by next weekend."

That would be the third weekend of June. Tourist season would definitely be in full swing.

Dr. Turner—Stephen—called me back that evening as I was weeding. Heading toward the fence line, I answered the phone as I passed Marie, who was sitting near the garden while Gordon gave Caden his bath inside. She gave me a questioning look. Did she think it was Nick? Fat chance.

After inquiring about Marie, Dr. Turner asked if I'd like to get dinner with him Saturday evening.

Surprised, it took me a long moment to respond.

"Leisel?"

"I'm here." I quickly added, "Sure. I'd like that."

I said I could meet him in Lancaster, but he insisted on picking me up. A real date. I felt a twinge of something. Nick would be leaving for officer training any day. We'd broken up. Why did I feel guilty?

As I returned to the garden, my phone tucked away in the pocket of my sweatshirt, Arden approached Marie, saying he wanted to speak with Aenti Suz. "I'll get her," Marie said.

When Aenti Suz appeared, Arden met her on the porch.

"I've thought more about you renting out the Dawdi Haus," he said. "And I've asked around. It appears you could make enough money to make it worth it."

Aenti Suz nodded. "That's what I've discovered too."

Arden tugged on his beard. "I just wanted you to know you have my blessing."

I stifled a laugh, but Aenti Suz didn't give anything away. "Well, thank you. I really appreciate your change of heart. Of course, I won't rent it out until Marie is ready to go home."

Arden scowled. "I was surprised to still find her here. Didn't Bishop Jacobs talk with you?"

Aenti Suz smiled sweetly. "He did. Thank you for checking."

"And?"

"We'll be talking again soon, I'm sure."

As Arden turned, I dropped my head and lunged for a weed between the rows of peas. He marched by without acknowledging me.

At dusk, a buggy came around the big house. Bishop Jacobs. I shook my head. It wasn't a coincidence. When Arden left the Dawdi Haus, he must have gone to the barn.

Aenti Suz came out of the Dawdi Haus when she heard the buggy and met the bishop over at the hitching post.

Determined not to eavesdrop again, I headed into the Dawdi Haus, but Gordon and Marie were cuddling on the couch with Caden. I didn't want to intrude, so I headed back outside and collected the gardening tools, taking them to the shed. When I stepped out of the shed, I was surprised to find that Marie was approaching Bishop Jacobs and Aenti Suz.

"How is Elijah?" she asked. She dated the bishop's son for a time, and the Jacobses had hoped the two would marry.

"He's all right," the bishop answered. "Last we heard, he was living down in Miami." That was a long ways from home, or even from Pinecraft. "Listen," the man said. "I've been thinking about you staying with Suz. Now, I was wrong to blame you for Elijah not joining the church, but I don't believe I'm wrong for not allowing you to stay here. In fact, I've been too lenient. I should have put a stop to it a month ago."

"We're leaving," Marie said. "In a few days."

I gasped. Why hadn't she told me?

Bishop Jacobs seemed relieved but not happy. He tipped his hat. "I guess I'm done here then."

"I guess you are." Aenti Suz turned back toward the house without telling him good-bye.

Marie walked beside her, and I jogged to catch up. "Who's going to help with Caden?" I asked.

She shrugged. "I'm not sure, but there are a few girls I'll call tomorrow."

"Marie . . ." I didn't want her to leave.

"We need to get back to our home." She put one arm around Aenti Suz and the other around me. "You two have been so good to me. Gordon and I both appreciate everything you've done, but it's time."

"I can come help at your apartment," I said.

"How about if you drive me to chemo once a week and study the rest of the time?" she countered. "I don't want it to be my fault if you fail again."

"Listen." I knew I sounded as if I were joking, even though I wasn't. "If I fail again, I'll take it as a sign from God that He doesn't want me to be a nurse." I added, "Maybe I'm meant to join the Amish."

"Don't you dare," Marie said. "How can you and Nick get married if you do?"

I stopped and her arm fell away from me. "I'm not marrying Nick," I said. "I already told you we broke up."

Marie put her hand on her hip while I started walking again. "Come back here!" she called out. "This minute!"

"Goodness," Aenti Suz said. "I thought you all had gotten past the bickering stage. . . ."

I thought we had too. I kept walking.

On Saturday, Marie, Gordon, and Caden were just leaving to return to their apartment when Stephen arrived to pick me up. I'd hoped they would be long gone by then, but Gordon had ended up working that day. Because I had thought they'd be back at their apartment, I hadn't told Marie I was going on a date with her surgeon. Of course, she figured it out as soon he arrived.

"You're pathetic," she whispered as I brushed past her toward Stephen's car, which he'd parked between mine and Gordon's.

I wore a skirt, blouse, and sandals. Thankfully, he was dressed casually in black jeans and a white button-up shirt.

He called out a hello to me as he climbed out of his car and then one to Marie and Gordon too. It was the first time he'd seen Caden. We all ended up gathered around our cars, with Mamm peeking out of the living room window. Stephen was so charming, so attentive to Marie and her family, that I couldn't understand why Marie wouldn't be thrilled for me to date him.

We spent the ride into town talking about how Marie was doing with her chemo. I told him she was tired and weak but determined to stay as positive as possible.

He pulled up to an Italian café not far from Marie and Gordon's apartment. He was all manners—opening my car door and the restaurant door, pulling out my chair. The place was nice but not too nice. The perfect spot for a first date.

He asked how my studying was going and then where I planned to live after I passed my test.

"Wherever I can find a job," I answered.

"So, around here then?" He smiled.

I smiled back. There really was no reason for me to go back to Pittsburgh. I had no apartment. No job. No Nick. My heart lurched.

Stephen ordered *Caprese salat* for both of us as an appetizer, and then I ordered linguine and he ordered ravioli. Neither of us ordered wine.

I had to admit, even though he grew up in a fairly liberal Mennonite community, he felt familiar to me. And comfortable.

After dinner, we walked along Prince Street, by the old Fulton Opera House. "I really love Lancaster," he said. "I've been at the hospital for four years now and I can't imagine living anywhere else."

We strolled around the downtown area for a half hour and then he took me home, which was now Mamm's house. I'd moved my bag and backpack that morning. Aenti Suz would soon be living there too because the Dawdi Haus was rented out for the weekend.

As he walked me up the steps to the front door, he said he had a good time and would like to have dinner again, if I'd be willing.

"I would," I said, adding that I enjoyed our time together too. We said a quick good-bye as he patted me on the shoulder.

I stepped inside the house as he returned to his car. But I stood at the living room window and watched the taillights of his Honda Accord disappear down Oak Road as he headed back to the highway.

I wasn't one to fall for a guy right away, obviously. It had taken me a couple of years to realize I had feelings for Nick. And I certainly didn't think of Stephen in a romantic way. I barely knew him. But there were definitely things I liked about him. He worked in medicine. He grew up Anabaptist. He was kind and caring.

Nick hadn't grown up Anabaptist, but, then again, he was raised in a good home. And had found a church to attend as soon as he moved to Pittsburgh.

The truth was, Nick and Stephen had a lot in common. Except that one was now at officer training school while the other hoped to stay in Lancaster County forever.

The next two weeks passed by with me taking Marie to chemo, studying as much as I could, and having dinner with Stephen four more times.

I had more texts from Paisley and Autumn. Finally, one came from Autumn that read, *What is going on? You haven't texted back in weeks and weeks. And I just heard that you and Nick broke up. Are you all right? Asking for a friend. Literally. And myself. Is your sister doing okay? Text me or Paisley back or we're going to come hunt you down.*

I fessed up to them in a group text that I'd failed my boards and that, yes, Nick and I broke up, but I was okay with that. *I'm retaking my boards the first of July. I think I'm better prepared this time.* Then I asked how they were doing and if they'd both passed.

Why did you break up with Nick? Is this for real? We heard you broke his heart. You two were perfect for each other, Autumn texted.

So good to hear from you, Paisley texted. *Don't listen to Autumn about Nick. I'm sure you had a good reason . . . although I CAN'T imagine what it might be. As far as the test, I failed mine too. But Autumn passed. Go figure!*

That made me laugh. Honestly, Autumn was the least likely to pass out of all of us—or so I thought. At one time. Hopefully, I was done with those sorts of assumptions.

Yeah, go figure! Autumn texted and then, *Please come see us. We miss you! Praying for a quick pass when you retake your test. Same for you, Paisley!*

I laughed again at that last sentence because Paisley and Autumn were roommates and were most likely texting as they sat in the same room together.

I texted back that it was great to hear from both of them, and I hoped to see them sometime soon. I didn't know when I'd be back in Pittsburgh, but I didn't want to lose touch. They'd been good friends to me. The camaraderie I had with them was probably what Dawdi Joe experienced with Lt. Shaw, Captain Russell, and Lt. Madison. Although, minus a war going on, of course.

I went back to the Mennonite church. The dresses and Kappa began to appeal to me, as did the services. I sat with Stephen, and he seemed to be heading back to his roots too.

Soon, I found myself bargaining with God. If I passed the test, I'd join the Mennonite church and begin dressing more conservatively again.

If I passed the test, I'd take any job He wanted me to. I didn't need to work in an emergency department. Or an ICU. Or go on to school to become a nurse practitioner or nurse anesthetist. I could stay in Lancaster County, close to my family. And Stephen.

I began to thank Him that I failed the test the first time. Obviously, He'd needed to catch my attention, I thought. He wanted me to make my way back home.

When July rolled around, I took my boards in Lancaster, just north of downtown in an office complex. Stephen texted me first thing that morning to cheer me on.

I texted him back quickly, thanking him. As it turned out, I finished the test in seventy-five questions. Either I'd done very well or horribly. Either way, I'd trust God. If I failed, that would be it. I wouldn't take it again. I'd get a job as a CNA and put everything I could toward my student debt. I could get jobs at two different facilities if I needed to. I could easily work sixty or more hours per week.

If I did pass, I'd look for a nursing job close by. Hopefully, Mamm would be all right with me living with her for a couple more months until I could get a place of my own.

Because my test ended so early and Aenti Suz was in charge of Caden for the day, I decided to drive out the Lititz Pike, past the Lancaster Airport, and on to the village of Lititz. I parked and decided to walk around with the thousands of tourists who had the same idea.

The first time I'd spent any time in Lititz was with Nick, after we'd finished our CNA class. I hadn't joined the church, so technically I was on my *Rumspringeh* then, although I didn't run around—except with Nick. Which didn't count. It wasn't as if we snuck around after dark and went to parties or anything.

Marie, of course, towed the line completely. She spent all of her teen and young adult years, until she left the church, worried about what Bishop Jacobs thought of her. Such ideas never entered my head. And I had no qualms about leaving the Amish either.

But perhaps I should have.

One of the places Nick took me in Lititz was the Wilbur Chocolate Company. I stepped into Wilbur's and purchased a bag of the sweet-and-salty bark, for old times' sake. As I walked back to my car, my phone dinged. It was a text from Nick. *I'm thinking this is the day of your test. I'm praying for you. Hope all goes well!*

Tears stung my eyes, surprising me. I missed him! More than I realized. I tucked my phone back into my pocket without responding. The sooner I forgot Nick Jordan the better.

Two days later, I checked the licensing exam site on my phone. I'd passed with flying colors. But instead of texting Nick, I texted Stephen. He took me out to dinner that night to celebrate. As we ate, he told me about a clinic east of Lancaster that served a lot of Old Order Amish. "I know you had an emergency or intensive care job in mind, but they'd love to have a nurse who can speak Pennsylvania Dutch," he said. "I spoke with one of the doctors this morning, and they'd like to interview you."

I did want to work in a hospital . . . but then I remembered my promise to God. No doubt this was where He wanted me.

After our dinner ended, we drove out of town and through country roads until we reached the Safe Harbor Park on the Conestoga River. Stephen parked his car, and we walked down to the river's edge and watched the sun set over the treetops. Just as it disappeared, Stephen reached for my hand.

For a second it all felt so wrong. Nick was gone. Another man held my hand. But then the feeling passed, and my hand felt safe in Stephen's, and we walked back to the car, together.

The next morning, I texted Paisley and Autumn to let them know I'd passed. They were both ecstatic. And then I interviewed at the clinic in the afternoon and was offered the job on the spot.

Mamm said I could continue to live with her until I had saved enough to get my own apartment. I called Marie to let her know, and she said Gordon or his mom, if it worked between her music lessons, would take her to the rest of her chemo appointments and her upcoming radiation, or she could take an Uber, if needed. She then thanked me profusely for my help. "I don't know what I would have done without you," Marie said. "You've served all of us with such love and care."

I knew she was sincere, and yet I felt a rift between us. She'd said I wasn't empathetic toward Nick. She felt I'd dumped him without reason. Weren't sisters supposed to stick up for each other?

I accepted the job and started the next week. The first day went well. Several of the older Amish patients had diabetes. One of the teenage boys had strep. A little girl had fallen off a hay wagon and broken her arm. I explained everything to her in Pennsylvania Dutch, which seemed to help.

When office hours were over, both doctors thanked me. Then the older one asked if I would consider wearing a dress and bonnet to work.

"A Kapp?" I asked.

He blushed. "Sorry. I wasn't sure what they were called."

I looked down at my navy blue scrubs.

"Those are fine," he said, "but it seems our Amish patients would feel better if you dressed more like they do."

I said I'd consider dressing in a Mennonite dress, but not Amish.

"That'd be great!" The doctor grinned from ear to ear.

On the way home, I debated what to do. Stephen had told me recently that his mother and grandmother both wore dresses and Kappa. I certainly wasn't opposed to it.

But for a moment, I wondered how long I'd have the job. I could tell, even on day one, that it wasn't going to be exactly challenging. Well, trying to get overweight Amish men to alter their diets would be, but there wasn't going to be any trauma at this job, which, of course, I'd known from the beginning.

The farm seemed so quiet with Marie, Gordon, and Caden gone. After Mamm, Aenti Suz, and I ate and I cleaned up the dishes, I ventured out to the front porch while Aenti Suz ran some clean towels out to the Dawdi Haus. We had a family from Virginia staying there tonight.

It was hot on the porch too, and there wasn't much of a breeze.

Aenti Suz soon joined me. "Goodness," she said, "with so much going on we haven't had a chance to sit in weeks."

"Jah," I said. "I've been wondering about the rest of the story. Do you have time to finish it now?"

"I do." Aenti Suz leaned back in the rocker. "Martha and Joe had just married, correct?"

"That's right. They were both on R&R in the village of Longwy in France. You hadn't even gotten to the part where the chaplain said, 'You may kiss the bride.'"

Aenti Suz smiled. "Jah, that was a surprise for Joe. No one does that in an Amish wedding." She laughed and then launched back into the story.

— 16 —

Joe

After the chaplain pronounced them man and wife and told Joe he could kiss his bride, he gave Martha a confused look. She nodded and then smiled. He leaned forward and kissed her. The Englisch had such funny ways.

The hotel put on a wedding dinner in the dining hall, illuminated by candles. Besides making beef stroganoff that was mostly noodles and not much beef, but delicious nonetheless, the chef managed to procure a bottle of champagne—an unnecessary touch for two Anabaptists, but they weren't going to offend the man by refusing it. Instead, they both drank a glass and then managed to dance with the others to a Glenn Miller album on an old phonograph. Joe held Martha close, having no idea what to do.

She must have had a little experience with dancing, even though she'd told him back in Chicago that she didn't dance, because she seemed to at least know how to sway to the music. No one seemed to pay any attention to them after a while, and as soon as they could, they slipped upstairs to their third-story room.

Neither one of them had a moment of regret. But they didn't talk about what their future would hold either. They said their good-byes that next morning just before Joe left in the jeep with the two doctors. Both put on a brave face, but when Joe climbed into the jeep and looked back, Martha was crying.

He couldn't talk for most of the return trip to the field hospital where the doctors were stationed, but it was too loud and cold to speak anyway. It took him an hour to find a truck going toward his headquarters, but eventually he found a ride.

None of the other AFS ambulance drivers believed him when he said he'd gotten married until he showed the marriage certificate, signed by Martha, himself, and Chaplain Higdon.

"Well, congratulations!" Wallace said. "Will there be a baby soon?"

Joe's face grew warm at the thought. He doubted it. And hoped not. That would be too much for Martha. Taking care of soldiers and herself was more than enough. Embarrassed, he simply grinned and didn't answer the question.

He folded the marriage certificate and slipped it back inside the pocket of his wool coat, where he kept all of his important documents.

If he thought his mind was on Martha before, she was on his heart every second of the day—and night—now. He prayed for her continually. For her safety. For strength. For enough food and warmth and sleep.

He wrote to his father and each of his sisters, sending individual letters. He explained that he'd fallen in love with a wonderful woman and that they'd married. He said he couldn't wait for them to meet her. He didn't mention that he didn't know when that would be or that they had no idea where they'd settle once they were reunited. There was no reason to alarm them.

Since 1752, the Bachmann family had owned their Lancaster

County land. But God could have different plans for him. And for the land too. Perhaps a cousin would want to farm it. Or a man one of his sisters would eventually marry. The land could continue in the family yet. As much as he would like to stay on the farm, he knew his decision to marry Martha most likely meant he wouldn't. A year ago, he never would have believed such a thing was possible.

Every chance he got, Joe asked soldiers, officers, doctors, and nurses about Martha's unit and if they'd moved east. The Allies were pushing the Germans farther and farther. He had no idea where Martha might be.

Finally, a doc he quizzed said he'd heard the Eightieth Division had crossed into Germany. Joe prayed harder.

A letter arrived from Charity, obviously written before she'd received his about marrying Martha. She said they'd had winter storm after winter storm. *Dat's been feeling poorly. He's had a cold and a bad cough that's lingered for several weeks.* That didn't sound good. *Several branches broke on the oak tree. Abe Yoder helped with the cleanup.*

It was odd that Charity wrote more about Abe than Faith did. Although, to be accurate, Faith had only written one letter. A short one. With no mention of Abe. No doubt, Faith would write soon enough and claim he'd fulfilled all of the predictions she'd ever made about him.

Charity's letter continued. *The pond is frozen, of course, and Abe came over to skate with us just last night. Hope thinks Abe and Faith will marry, but I don't think so.* Joe could hardly comprehend that he'd married before any of his sisters and breathed another prayer for their reaction to his letters. He expected four letters of admonishment any day.

The first week of February, all of Martha's letters caught up with him, including one written just a couple of days after their

232

wedding. He read that one over and over. He was a married man. He'd never been happier in his life, even in a war zone. But his heart ached for his wife. He wanted to protect her. He wanted her to go home. He wished he could take her place and send her to the farm to stay with his father and sisters. He'd join the army if he could, if it meant Martha would be safe.

That same week, the temperatures dropped well below freezing and more snow fell. Locals said it was the worst winter in memory. The conditions of the roads grew even worse, and an AFS ambulance driver was killed when his ambulance collided with a truck in northeastern France. A French officer and a stretcher-bearer were badly injured. Joe mourned the man and vowed to drive as carefully as he could.

In late February, Joe and Wallace followed orders to head southeast with the Twenty-First Army, leaving the Ardennes and heading toward Germany during a snowstorm. The ambulance slid several times on the slick roads, and Joe struggled to keep it from tumbling down the steep bank. By the time they stopped for the night, he feared he was too frozen to walk, but he managed to park the ambulance, and together he and Wallace set up their tent. Then he ventured into the field hospital and again asked around about the Eightieth Division.

"They jumped ahead of us a few days ago," a nurse said. "I heard they're only five miles down the road, south of here."

Joe's heart lurched. Was Martha that close? He could walk there in a little over an hour and be back before he needed to report for duty the next day.

He told Wallace he'd be back soon and began hiking down the road. The snow had been packed down with all of the traffic, but it was still high on both sides of the road. Joe wore two stocking caps under his helmet, but he still shivered for the first mile. As he clapped his hands together hard enough to try to keep the blood flowing, his body heat began to regulate. He hoped Martha was staying warm. He wished he had a blanket or an extra pair of socks to give her, but of course he didn't.

Darkness had fallen by the time he reached the field hospital—he guessed it was actually more like seven or eight miles—but the reflection of the stars and moon on the snow lit his way.

He spotted Major Russell in the medical tent, which had been patched on one side. Joe glanced around, but didn't see Martha. He stayed calm. She was probably off duty. He called out a hello to Major Russell.

He turned toward him. "Joe!" The major looked as if he hadn't slept in weeks.

"How is everyone?" Joe asked.

The major shook his head. "Not well."

Joe's heart sank.

"I sent Lt. Madison home. She came down with pneumonia and wasn't recovering."

Joe couldn't help himself and rushed his next question. "How about Martha?"

"She's ill too, although not as bad. I gave her the night off. She's in her tent."

Both relief and concern swept over Joe. "How are you?" he asked the major.

"I'm all right. Tired and cold, like everyone, and I wish you were working with me as an orderly instead of driving an ambulance."

He couldn't have married Martha if he was an orderly, but at least he'd have been close to her and better able to care for her. Perhaps he should have joined the army after all.

The major slapped Joe on the back. "You look good."

Joe responded, "Jah, I'm doing fine. I'm just down the road from here, so I thought I'd walk over."

"Walk?"

"Jah, it didn't take long." Troops hiked ten or fifteen miles all the time.

"How long can you stay?"

"Just long enough to say hello to my wife." Even in his worry for Martha, he was grateful for Major Russell helping them to be able to marry. "Thanks to you."

Major Russell smiled for the first time. "You both seemed as if you were meant for each other from the very beginning. I don't know how it'll all work out, but I'll leave that to the two of you."

"Believe me, we'll manage."

When Joe reached the outside of Martha's tent, he said her name softly. When she didn't respond, he opened the flap a little and said it louder.

A flashlight turned on. "Joe?"

"Jah, it's me."

By the dim light he could see the surprised expression on Martha's face as she sat up on her cot, but then she began to cough. It sounded horrible.

"Is anyone else in there?" he asked. "May I come in?"

"I'm alone." She swung her legs over the cot. "And, yes, please come in."

She wore a long wool coat over her bathrobe. He sat down beside her and put his arm around her shoulders, suddenly feeling shy. But she leaned into him with such abandon that it brought tears to his eyes.

He wrapped both arms around her and buried his head against her, relief flowing through him.

But then another coughing fit seized her and the force pulled her away. She leaned forward.

"Do you have anything to suppress the cough?" he asked.

She shook her head.

"I'll go get tea and honey from the mess tent."

"They don't have honey," she answered.

Of course they didn't. "I'll get you some tea."

Fifteen minutes later he came back with tea, a bowl of thin chicken soup, and toast.

As she sipped the tea, she told him she'd heard about an ambulance driver who'd been killed. "I was so worried." Her eyes met his. "When I heard your voice outside the tent, I was afraid I was hallucinating."

"Ach, I'm fine," he said. "It's you we need to worry about. We don't want you getting pneumonia like Lt. Madison."

"I'm not running a fever," she said. "It's just a bad cough. Most likely bronchitis."

He coaxed her to eat all of the soup and most of the toast. When she'd finished, he told her he needed to get back.

"Can't you stay a little longer?"

He longed to, but he couldn't risk it. "I'll come back," he said. "I'm just up the road. I'll walk down as soon as I can."

Their kiss was interrupted by another cough. Once it passed, he took her hand and led them in a silent prayer for her health, for her safety, and for the war to end quickly.

As he tucked her back into her cot, he thought of the gift of the time in Longwy to marry. But it was just as much a gift to be together for an hour now. *In sickness and in health.*

He stopped by the tent on the way back and asked Major Russell to get a message to him if Martha's health worsened. Then he told his friend good-bye, thinking of their drives along Lake Michigan last summer. What a contrast to where they were now.

As he hiked back, truckloads of American soldiers drove by, headed east. He moved as far as he could to the bank of snow and hoped the drivers would see him. As the trucks passed, he gazed at the soldiers crammed in the back under the canopies. He couldn't help but wonder what awaited them. And when the war would end.

About a mile from the battalion aid station, just after a truck passed him, it slid to the right, toward the ditch. Joe gasped. The driver pulled out of the skid, but just as he did, the truck was rocked by an explosion. Joe ran toward it as soldiers poured from the back of the bed. Joe asked if any were injured. They shook their heads, but they were clearly shaken. As he reached the cab, the driver stumbled out. He had blood flowing down the side of his face and he was holding his arm. The passenger in the cab didn't move. Joe yelled at the soldiers to grab the litters from the back of the truck and instructed the driver to sit down in the snow where he was and stay put. Joe reached into the truck and dragged the passenger out the driver door, not wanting to risk detonating another mine.

The passenger was unconscious, but at least he was alive. He was bleeding from superficial cuts, and Joe couldn't find any deep wounds. A sergeant appeared with a radio but couldn't get it to work. He said they were the last in the caravan. Joe told him the field hospital was about a mile away, and they could use a radio there.

Joe led the way, carrying the front of the passenger's litter. It was midnight by the time they reached the hospital and nearly two by the time he crawled into his tent.

When he and Wallace got up a few hours later, all of the soldiers were gone except the two injured men. Joe and Wallace headed to the battalion aid station and spent the day transporting the wounded back to the field hospital.

In the afternoon, they took a minute to get cups of coffee to try to warm up when two litter bearers began running toward them with an injured soldier as gunfire peppered the field. The rear litter bearer fell. The first one kept dragging the wounded soldier, but he was hardly gaining any ground. Joe, with Wallace behind him, ran to help as the *rat-a-tat* of gunfire continued. Wallace rolled the soldier back on the litter and grabbed the back handles while Joe scooped up the injured litter bearer, throwing him over his shoulder. But as Joe lurched forward, his right leg buckled. He struggled forward, dragging his leg as he continued on. The man he carried gasped for breath, and Joe gritted his teeth from the burning pain in his leg. It felt as if it were on fire.

Allied soldiers fought back, and Joe made it to the station. Orderlies came and took the litter bearer from him, and a medic directed Joe to a table. He reached down to his leg. It was sticky with blood, flowing from a gaping wound.

"I don't think it's so bad." Joe couldn't be sent home, not when his wife was on the front lines.

The medic just shook his head as he cut away Joe's pant leg.

A little while later, Joe rode up front with Wallace on the way to the field hospital, while the litter bearer, the soldier on the litter, and two other wounded men rode in the back.

"My wound is not that bad, right?" Joe gritted his teeth.

Wallace answered, "It looked pretty bad to me."

"But they should be able to patch me up in the field hospital. I'll be able to drive soon."

Wallace kept his eyes on the road and shrugged his shoulders. "I'm not a doctor, so I can't say, but I wouldn't get my hopes up if I were you." Wallace shook his head, a wry smile on his face. "So many would be rejoicing with a wound like yours since that's their ticket home. But you want to stay."

More than anything. Martha was so close. He couldn't be sent home now.

238

The medic in the aid station had stopped the bleeding and wrapped his leg. But hours later, Joe still hadn't seen a doctor. He clenched his jaw the entire time, unable to speak. Wallace returned to the aid station and then came back to the field hospital with more injured.

When the doc finally approached him, Joe realized with a start that it was Karcher. However, it took Karcher a moment to recognize Joe. When he did, he sneered, "I'm not surprised that you managed to get yourself shot. It's a wonder you didn't get yourself killed."

Joe gritted his teeth. "How'd you manage to get orders over here?"

"Oh, after you and your ilk left, the higher-ups realized what I had to offer."

More likely they wanted to pass him on to someone else, Joe thought. "How long have you been here?" he asked.

"This is my first week," the man answered, just as the hum of a German bomber flew over them, heading north.

"Take cover!" someone yelled.

Karcher ducked under the table. The bomber wasn't close enough to cause them any harm, but as a distant explosion shook the tent, Joe said a prayer for whomever the bomb had landed near—or on.

A minute later, Karcher reappeared. "Well," he said. "That was close."

"Not really." Joe cradled his helmet in his hands.

Karcher grimaced. "I'm going to send you on to England."

"Shouldn't you examine me first?" Joe asked. "I'm pretty sure the bullet is embedded in my tibia, which means the bone is at least splintered."

"Then we can't set it anyway." Karcher lifted Joe's pant leg. "They'll do that in England."

239

"How long will the healing process take?"

"Months." Karcher smirked. "Guess you won't be able to stick around."

Joe choked back his tears. He couldn't cry in front of Karcher. He'd have to leave Martha. The wounded soldiers. Wallace and the litter bearers and medics.

Karcher called a nurse and told her to take over. The doc patted the nurse on the back, and she shot him a sullen look as he stepped over to the next patient.

"Watch out for him," Joe cautioned, his voice low. "I knew him back in Chicago."

"He's not a very good doctor," the nurse whispered back.

"Or man," Joe added.

"Thank you for the confirmation." Her eyes looked as weary as he felt. "I'll stay away from him—and warn the others too."

After the nurse gave Joe a shot of morphine, she splinted his leg. When Wallace returned to the field hospital a third time, Joe asked him to get word to Martha or at least to Major Russell. Wallace found a piece of paper and a pencil, and Joe penned the hardest letter he'd written to date. *Dear Martha, I am fine but injured*. He briefly explained what happened. *I'm so sorry to be leaving you. I'd give anything to stay, but I'm being shipped to England. I'm no use to the AFS—I can't drive or carry a litter. My recovery could take months.* He stopped, not wanting to write the next line. But he had to.

I'm guessing I'll be sent on home. I can hardly bear the thought of being so far from you. He went on to say that he was praying for her health and safety and that he would write to let her know where he ended up. *I'm praying you'll be home soon too. Then we'll settle wherever is best. Just let me know where you are, and I'll meet you there as quickly as I can.* He included the address of the farm, and then signed the letter, *Your loving husband, Joe.*

He folded the paper and handed it to Wallace. The men shook hands and again emotion welled in Joe's throat. He'd only known Wallace a few months, but the man had been like a brother to him.

As two orderlies carried Joe out of the tent, they passed Karcher examining a soldier with a head wound. At least Karcher wasn't with Martha's unit. Joe said another silent prayer, one of thousands, that the war would end soon.

He spent three weeks in a general army hospital in England. In all that time, he didn't have a letter from Martha or from anyone else. He wrote his father and sisters to let them know he'd be home soon—and prayed they'd received his letter about marrying Martha.

The bullet remained in his tibia. The surgeon couldn't remove it without damaging the bone even worse. Instead, his bone was stretched and casted, and he was given a pair of crutches. A few weeks later, he was loaded onto a ship bound for New York. This time he had no KP duty, which gave him far too much time to think. He tried to pray instead of fret, but the struggle grew harder every day.

He disembarked in New York City on the first of April and spent a few days in an army hospital outside of the city, where his cast was removed. He was given a cane for the train trip to Philadelphia and then on to Lancaster. He limped along with his few belongings, including the marriage certificate, strapped on his back.

When he limped from the train into the Lancaster station, wearing the denim jeans and shirt Faith had bought him a year ago, he was a different man than when he'd left. He'd been tested beyond what he'd ever imagined. He'd turned from a boy into a man. And he'd been sent home far too soon.

He asked several others getting off the train if anyone was

headed toward Leacock. Fortunately, he found a middle-aged Amish couple who looked familiar. They had just picked up their daughter, who was dressed Englisch and had come to visit from Philadelphia for the weekend. She appeared to be around Joe's age or a little older. The man told Joe they were headed to Groffdale and would drop him off on the way.

As they stepped out of the station into the sunshine, it took a moment for Joe's eyes to adjust. The day was warm and bright with a cloudless blue sky. For the first time since he left Europe, the snow and mud of France seemed far behind him. His heart lurched, and he hoped letters from Martha would catch up with him soon.

He hobbled along behind the couple and their daughter, his cane thudding along the sidewalk, until they reached an open buggy. The man took Joe's pack and put it in the back, along with the daughter's suitcase. Joe sat in the front with the man while the women sat in the back seat.

The man asked Joe who his people were and quickly placed him on the Bachmann farm. The man introduced himself as Elmer Mast. "I know of your Dat and exactly where your farm is," he said. "The big one on Oak Road."

Joe nodded.

"I'm sure I've seen you at auctions and that sort of thing through the years," Elmer added.

Joe nodded. No doubt they'd been at the same places many times.

"Where have you been?" the man asked.

Joe hesitated a moment. "England."

"Is that where you were injured?"

He shook his head. "France."

"But you're not a soldier," the daughter said from the back seat.

"That's right. I was an ambulance driver."

"You didn't fight?"

"No, ma'am," Joe said, turning to look over his shoulder at her when he answered.

The young woman's voice rose some. "My husband died in France."

"I'm so sorry," Joe said. "When?"

"D-Day," she answered.

"He was a foot soldier," Elmer said quietly. "It broke our Martha's heart. . . ."

Joe's heart lurched. *Martha.* He exhaled and then said again, "I'm so sorry."

"Are you going home to your wife?" this Martha asked.

"No," Joe answered. "To my father and sisters. My wife is still in France. Well, in Germany by now." In the land of the Third Reich, where all of this devastation had started.

Martha gave him a questioning look.

"She's an army nurse," Joe answered. "I had to leave her. . . ." His voice trailed off.

"We'll pray for her safety," the woman said.

"Denki," Joe said. He mourned for her loss. It felt like too much for her to bear.

Elmer's voice was low again as Joe turned back to the front. "She left us a few years ago. We're hoping she'll return. . . ." The man's voice trailed off. That was every Amish parent's prayer. Soon it would be his father's too.

For the first time, his prayer for his own Martha caught somewhere in his frazzled soul. So many had lost so much. Did he have the right to hope she'd return unharmed?

He dozed after that, rocked to sleep by the sway of the buggy. But when the man turned onto Oak Road, Joe woke, taking in the view of the farm. The pasture needed to be dragged and the corn hadn't been planted yet, but the grass was the vibrant emerald green that took his breath away each spring, and the oak tree had leafed out, along with the trees in the woods.

The man stopped the buggy in front of the house and Joe managed to slink down to the ground, dragging his bad leg along, and rested on his cane while the man retrieved his pack.

The younger woman leaned toward him from the back seat. "So will your wife join the Amish?"

"I'm not sure." Joe met her eyes. "Will you?"

"I'm thinking about it," she answered and then leaned back against the seat.

Joe smiled at her and then thanked the man and his wife. "*Gott segen eich*," he said.

"God bless you too," the younger woman answered.

Elmer handed Joe his pack, and he slung it onto his back. Then he started toward the house, choosing his steps carefully. As he reached the front steps, the door flew open.

"Joe!" Faith froze in the doorway for a moment and then rushed toward him. "Thank the Lord you got our letters and came home. Dat is hanging on by a thread. You've made it home before he passes."

— 17 —

Leisel

That's all for tonight." Aenti Suz stood.

"No!" I gasped. "You have to tell me what happens. Which Martha is my grandmother?"

Aenti Suz shook her head. "You'll have to wait. I'm going to get to bed. Our guests are leaving in the morning, and I need to clean the place before the next group arrives tomorrow afternoon."

"You can't," I said.

She smiled wryly. "Of course I can. I'll tell you the rest soon enough. Just be patient." She headed inside, calling out, "*Gut Nacht*," over her shoulder.

I stayed on the porch. I was shocked that Dawdi Joe had been in the thick of battle. And I still couldn't get over that he'd rushed into marrying an Englischer. Thankfully, I'd been sane enough to step back from Nick and see things clearly once he'd decided to join the military. Dawdi Joe had been young and away from home. It was his first time falling in love.

Obviously, Lt. Shaw wasn't my grandmother. The other Martha had to be, which meant Lt. Shaw must have died in Europe. Probably from illness, but perhaps from a bomb or an accident. I shivered. I'd grown to like her and obviously Dawdi had loved her. Life was full of heartache. That was all there was to it.

For a moment, I felt a deep longing for Nick. What was officer training like for him? I wouldn't be surprised if he would soon be studying to become a nurse practitioner. Many of those programs were now doctoral level.

I thought of my professional life and how I'd changed in the last three months. I was just so thankful I'd passed my test and could pay off my student loans now that I barely thought about what my professional goals used to be. What had changed? My shaken confidence? Nick betraying me? Meeting Stephen? My deal with God?

Perhaps all of those things together. At one time, Nick had referred to me as a golden girl, saying I had the ability to succeed at anything I attempted. I'd never agreed with him, but whatever I'd had at one time I'd lost.

I sighed as I stepped into the house. Life was all about change. Nothing stayed the same. Desires came and went. It was all part of growing up and accepting reality. But if that was true, why did I still feel numb, even when I knelt beside my bed at night to pray?

The next day at the clinic no one mentioned my scrubs, but after work I stopped by Marie's on the way home. Her teenage helper had taken Caden to the park, and Marie was playing her keyboard and singing "Amazing Grace" when I knocked on the door. It was the first time I'd heard her sing since she'd been diagnosed.

When she answered the door, I asked if she had a Mennonite dress I could borrow until I could make one.

"What in the world?"

"And a Mennonite Kapp," I added.

She pointed toward the couch for me to sit. "Leisel, what's going on?"

I explained to her what the doctor requested.

"And you're happy to go along with that?"

I shrugged. "I've been thinking about joining your church, and I can understand his point, as far as it making the Amish and Mennonite patients more comfortable."

"Well, jah, that makes sense. But what about you? What makes you feel comfortable?"

I smiled. "Well, I did grow up Amish. Wearing a Mennonite dress won't be a big deal."

She had an odd expression on her face.

"What is it?" I asked.

"Oh, I was just remembering when you came home from Pittsburgh that first Christmas wearing a pair of jeans, a sweatshirt, and a beanie over your long blond hair." She sat on the opposite side of the couch. "Of course, at the time, I was judgmental and thought you looked awful, but the truth was you looked completely at ease. Totally natural. Like that was the way you were meant to dress all along."

I bristled. "I thought you'd be happy to have me dressing more conservatively."

She exhaled and then said, "It's not as if you dressed immodestly in your jeans and sweatshirts. What I'd really like is for you to be dressing a certain way for the right reason."

"And you don't think putting patients at ease in the clinic is the right reason?"

"I'm not even sure if I think you working in the clinic is the right thing. It seems as if you gave up a lot to come home and care for me."

I squirmed under her steady gaze. "What?"

"Have you heard from Nick?"

"No!" I crossed my arms.

She sighed. "I'll loan you a Kapp and dress. You might look on Etsy to buy your own, if you don't want to make them." She gave me a sassy look. "I remember how much you like sewing."

I tried to smile. "I was hoping Mamm would help me. Or maybe you."

"Don't count on our mother helping you—I think you'd have to join the Amish to get a positive reaction from her. And, honestly, I buy my dresses now."

"You're kidding."

"Nope. I'd rather spend my time playing with Caden. Or spending time with Gordon. Or playing my keyboard. As much as I used to like sewing, my priorities have definitely changed."

I began wearing a cape dress and Kapp to work the very next day. The doctors both thanked me. However, I didn't see that it made a big difference with the patients. Speaking Pennsylvania Dutch really seemed to be the bigger factor. But still, I wore the dresses.

I confused all the guests who stayed in the Dawdi Haus. They'd see me come home wearing the dress and then later see me in my jeans. Each time, I explained my predicament. I'd grown up Amish but hadn't joined the church. I now attended a Mennonite church and would probably join. I worked at a clinic that served the Amish. I was sure they saw me as wishy-washy.

Over time, I stopped changing into my jeans and just kept the dress and Kapp on. Mamm seemed to like that, although every once in a while she told me she still had faith I'd join the Amish.

David started coming down every other week to see Aenti Suz. At least that's what I thought, until one Saturday afternoon, Aenti Suz excused herself to go clean out the Dawdi Haus for guests who were coming in the next day. Instead of asking David to accompany her, she suggested he play a game of Scrabble with Mamm.

That surprised me. The next time David came down, he seemed as attentive to Mamm as he did Aenti Suz. And Mamm seemed to brighten a bit. She became more talkative and didn't spend as much time in her sewing room.

One afternoon after work, in mid-September, I came home to find Mamm in her rocking chair, crying. Fearing something horrible had happened, I rushed up the stairs. "Is it Marie?" I asked. She'd just finished her radiation and had a PET scan the week before. We were waiting for the results.

Mamm shook her head. "It's nothing, really. I've just been thinking."

I sat down in Dat's rocking chair. "What about?"

"Your father."

My heart melted a little. She never talked about Dat.

"I have so many regrets," she said.

I froze. Did she want me to ask more? Or simply pat her hand and leave her alone? Shifting into Nurse Leisel mode, I decided to act as if she were a patient. "What do you regret?"

"Not appreciating the life I had. Not realizing you girls would be grown so soon. Not thinking your Dat would die so young."

"You couldn't anticipate Dat dying when he did," I said. "And I think most parents probably are surprised by how quickly their children grow up."

"Your father tried to warn me that you three would be adults in no time, but I was so focused on making sure you didn't stray that I barely appreciated how strong and determined you were becoming." She turned toward me as tears rolled down her cheeks. I'd never seen Mamm cry, not even when Dat was so ill. Not even when he died. I was taken aback at first, not sure what to do. But then I thought of her as a patient again and simply took her hand, hoping she'd keep talking.

"He invited me to go to Haiti with him. I used you girls as an excuse, but Suz would have watched over you. Back then, I simply didn't want to go, so I didn't. But now I wish I'd at least considered it."

I squeezed her hand. "Why do you think you didn't back then?"

She remained silent for a long time, and I began to wonder if I'd insulted her. Finally, she said, "Fear, I suppose. Every time he went away to serve somewhere, I feared he wouldn't come back, that he'd be harmed somehow. I was afraid if I went too that something might happen to both of us—or to you girls."

Mamm was admitting to her fear. I nearly fell off the chair. "Because when you left to go to the hospital to have Jessica something did happen to Rebecca?" I asked.

She nodded. "But it was more than my fear for our family. I was afraid to go to Haiti—to see so many people hurting. I felt I'd be more of a hindrance than a help." She rocked faster.

Honestly, I couldn't see Mamm helping in a disaster zone like that, and I wondered why Dat would have even suggested it. Perhaps simply to give her the chance to serve in such a way? Or perhaps he wanted to share the experience with her.

But I'd never seen her excel in a crisis. When Dat was dying, I dreaded when she came into his study, where we'd put the hospital bed. She would worry out loud in front of him: How would the finances of the farm work out? What should she do about me taking my time to join the church? She'd bring up silly details too, like the barn needed to be painted and the garden plowed. He was so patient with her, explaining where he kept all of the paperwork and that he would talk with Arden about painting the barn, which couldn't be done until summer, and plowing the garden, which could be done in a week or so.

One time, Dat told Mamm how sad he was to be leaving her behind. "Bethel, I'm sorry I won't be here to help you."

Mamm just nodded. She had seemed far more focused on her growing loss of security than she was on Dat's pain.

"Your father was the first person I felt safe with." Mamm stopped rocking. "I was never sure that my own father could care for me, and then he died when I was still a *Youngie*, which furthered my insecurity. Afterward, my older siblings did care for me, but I often felt unwanted. Like a burden. Your Dat changed all of that for me."

I could definitely see the impact Dat had on her life. But although I loved my mother, I couldn't see how she impacted his life. She was fifteen years younger than he was, a homebody, fearful, and not inquisitive about the world or the farm or healthy living or really anything. She spent all of her spare time quilting—which was valuable but didn't make for a lot of conversation.

I wasn't sure what to say to her. She was being transparent with me for the first time in her life, and I was dumbfounded. Eventually, she got up to go check on supper.

My conversation with Mamm did inspire me to do something else I'd been meaning to do for a while. I took my laptop to the coffee shop and signed up with an organization called Mennonites Serve to volunteer during emergencies. I filled out a form online and included that I spoke Pennsylvania Dutch and was a registered nurse. A week later, I headed to an orientation meeting at a Mennonite church north of Lancaster, admiring the cornstalks swaying in the breeze and sunflowers bowing from the long stretch of hot days as I drove through the countryside. I wasn't sure when I'd be able to serve, as I wouldn't accrue any vacation time for a while, but I was determined to do something. Whenever that might be.

Soon I was wearing a Mennonite dress and Kapp all the time, and I'd spoken with the pastor at Marie's church about taking the membership class and joining. By the end of September, I'd found an apartment not far from the clinic. It wasn't furnished, and I asked Mamm if I could borrow some furniture from the storage room in the barn. She pursed her lips and said, "No. Milton will be setting up house soon."

True, I'd seen him with a young woman in his courting buggy a few times in the evenings. But because Arden couldn't take the Dawdi Haus from Aenti Suz, it wasn't as if there was a house for Milton. Maybe he and his bride would move into the big house with Mamm, but that was completely furnished.

Mamm, even though she'd opened up with me some, still saw me as a disappointment, that was certain. I visited a couple of secondhand stores and bought what I needed.

Stephen borrowed a pickup and helped me move. After we'd gotten everything into my apartment, he drove to Wal-Mart so I could pick up more cleaning and laundry supplies. I had to admit, I was happy to have an electric washer and dryer again.

As Stephen pushed the cart and I walked beside him, I spotted Nick's father up ahead, and I resisted the urge to duck down the next aisle. I got a hold of myself, and when we reached him I said hello and introduced Stephen.

Doug said how happy he was to see me—and meet Stephen.

Then he asked if I'd rejoined the Amish. I shook my head. "But I'll be joining the Mennonites sometime soon."

"Well," he said, seeming to search for what to say, "congratulations, then."

I thanked him and then asked how Nick was doing, even though I felt I was stepping into dangerous territory.

"Good." He smiled, but sadly. "He just finished officer training. He'll be home for a few days before his first assignment at Dover Air Force Base in Delaware."

"Tell him hello." I took a step backward.

"I will," Doug answered. "He'll be glad to hear from you."

My heart lurched. I managed to stutter, "Tell . . . tell Barbara hello too. And the girls."

"Oh, I will." Again, it seemed he tried to smile, but it came out as more of a grimace.

A couple of aisles later, Stephen asked, "What was that all about?"

I hadn't told Stephen about Nick. "Doug is the father of a friend of mine who recently joined the Air Force."

"Why would he do that?"

"To pay off his student loans and get an advanced degree."

"I guess that makes sense. What's his field?"

"He's a nurse."

"So you met him in school?"

"Actually before that. He's the one who got me interested in becoming a nurse." I pointed toward the shortest line before Stephen could ask me another question about Nick. "Let's get going," I said. "You need to drop me off at the farm and get the truck returned. And I need to get my apartment set up so I can have you over for dinner tomorrow."

He grinned. "Sounds like a good plan."

When he dropped me off at the house, Mamm and David were

on the porch with the two Englisch ladies who were renting out the Dawdi Haus for a week. Aenti Suz wasn't anywhere to be seen.

I greeted all of them, and the women explained they were friends, one from Kentucky and one from Ohio, and they loved meeting in Lancaster County and seeing all of the sights.

"You're not Amish," the one with shorter hair said.

"That's right," I answered. "I'm going to join the Mennonite church." The script was getting old to me, but it was a revelation to each new guest. I sat down on the steps and explained that I'd never joined the Amish. Mamm frowned, but I doubted the women noticed.

It seemed Mamm was determined to change the subject because she pointed out that one of the women was a teacher and the other was a nurse. "Leisel is a nurse too," Mamm said, which surprised me. She sounded matter-of-fact though, not as if she were proud of me or anything. I wouldn't expect her to, not as an Amish mother. Especially not as my mother.

The woman asked me where I practiced, and I told her about the clinic.

"Fascinating," she said. "What a perfect fit."

I smiled but didn't agree. The truth was, it became less and less of a challenge every day.

It turned out that she worked in the emergency department in a big hospital in Cincinnati. "I've been working there since I was your age," she said. "My husband keeps hoping I'll retire, but I love it. There's never a dull moment."

"Cathy's an adrenaline junkie," her friend said and then laughed. "Some people think teaching is a challenge, but I can never top her stories."

"Oh, teaching has its own challenges—and stories," Cathy said. "Don't sell yourself short. I just always knew I was called to do this. I wouldn't trade it for anything."

The conversation soon shifted to the women's favorite spots in Lancaster. David asked several questions, and I wondered if he wanted to do some sightseeing. By the time I'd grabbed the last of my things upstairs and come back down, the women were gone, but Aenti Suz was now on the porch. I told Mamm and David good-bye and then turned to Aenti Suz, who said she'd walk me to my car.

"Where were you earlier?" I asked.

"Washing a load of towels," she answered.

"I'm sad to be leaving before you told me the rest of Dawdi Joe's story."

"Me too. We've both been so busy. I'll tell you the rest soon." She added, "I promise."

I nodded back toward the porch. "David doesn't mind you leaving him to fend for himself?"

"Oh, I don't think David is coming down to see me anymore. I think he's coming to see your mother."

I whirled around to get a view of the porch again. "What?" David and Mamm were deep in conversation and didn't notice my outburst.

"Shh," Aenti Suz said. "I may be wrong about him and your Mamm, but I made it clear to David that I didn't want to court him."

"Why not?"

"I don't love him."

"Are you sure?"

She nodded. "It's been fifty years, but I remember what love feels like."

I turned back around. "Do you think Mamm is serious about David?"

Aenti Suz shrugged. "You should ask her."

Mamm couldn't marry someone else, not when we all missed

Dat so badly. But the truth was, she could. Many Amish widows married only a year after their husbands died, and it had been four for Mamm. And David was a good man. It would be a blessing for both of them.

Still, I couldn't imagine it.

– 18 –

The next morning, rain pelted the window of my bedroom as I dressed for church. When a weather alert on my phone chimed, I suspected it was a flash flood. I was wrong. It was a tornado in Chester County. I wondered if David had gone home last night. Most likely so.

Shortly before Stephen was going to pick me up, a woman from Mennonites Serve called, asking if I could be at the Mennonite church in north Lancaster, where we'd had the orientation, in half an hour. "We have a van leaving for Chester County," she said. "There have been casualties, including in the Amish community."

"Of course," I said, although I suspected any seriously injured people would have already been taken to the hospital by the time we got there. However, I also knew that stress-related illness increased after a tragedy, particularly panic attacks and heart attacks, plus there were always related accidents.

I called Stephen and told him not to pick me up for church.

"What about dinner?" he asked.

"We'll have to reschedule," I said, wriggling out of my dress. I'd wear jeans, a sweatshirt, and my hiking boots. "I may be

257

back tonight but at least by tomorrow. I'll call and let you know."

I went ahead and put a change of clothes in my backpack, along with a few apples and oranges, granola bars, and a couple bottles of water. I'd taken the next day off work to unpack, so that meant I could stay overnight, if needed. I added my stethoscope to my bag and tied my sleeping bag to the bottom. Then I hurried to my car and drove north toward the church.

As I parked, an older Amish woman climbed out of a car in front of me. As she turned, I realized it was Aenti Suz.

I grabbed my backpack, jumped out of my car, pulled the hood of my coat over my head, and ran toward her as the rain pelted us both. "What in the world are you doing here?"

She smiled when she saw me. "I've been wanting to do something more to help others. I signed up about a year ago, but this is the first time I've gotten a call. Milton heard the phone while he was finishing up the milking. I hadn't left for church yet, so I called a driver to bring me here."

We climbed into the back of the nearly full van. The others quickly introduced themselves to us. There was a paramedic, a carpenter, a psychologist, another nurse, and a retired doctor, all of whom were Mennonite. There was also an Amish farmer and an Amish man who did small engine repair. The leader of our group was the woman who did my orientation. As the driver started up the van, our leader explained that we would be headquartered at a Mennonite church near Coatesville and would be joining a team from that area in serving those affected by the tornado.

I asked Aenti Suz if David went home the night before.

She nodded. "He hired a driver to take him back to his farm."

"Where exactly does he live?"

"In the heart of Chester County, so near where we're headed. Hopefully the tornado didn't tear through his farm."

I nodded in agreement.

When we arrived at the Mennonite church, located on the edge of town, it was abuzz with activity. Several buses were parked in the lot, and people milled around, many of them disheveled and clearly traumatized. We quickly helped unload the supplies into the fellowship hall and then met with the facilitator for assignments. Aenti Suz would stay at the church to feed those who were arriving in the buses—mostly women, children, and the elderly, a mix of Plain and Englisch. The other nurse, the doctor, the psychologist, and I would all go to a location along the swath of the tornado.

Hundreds of houses had been damaged and destroyed, along with schools, businesses, and vehicles. Thankfully the tornado had hit before both Plain and Englisch families left for church, so there weren't many people on the road. Unfortunately, some people were still in bed when it hit and had missed the warning. Incredibly, only one death had been reported so far, and all of those seriously injured had been transported to the hospital. But there were people with minor injuries and those who were feeling shaky who needed to be examined.

The rain had completely stopped and rays of sunlight were coming through the clouds as we left the church. The nurse next to me asked if I was nervous. I told her I wasn't, and for a moment I felt my old confidence returning. But then I remembered the man in the diner. What if someone had chest pains?

At least there would be other medical professionals to help.

It was obvious when we'd reached the swath of the tornado. First we saw a car on its side in a field. Then a fence that had been ripped in two. Paper was scattered everywhere. Tree after tree after tree was uprooted. A house was missing its roof and one exterior wall. We could see right inside where the rain-soaked belongings were in a chaotic display for everyone to view.

I'd seen photos and videos of the aftermath of tornadoes and the training I took covered the topic, but nothing prepared me for the destruction all around. I felt a tightness in my chest at the sights and couldn't imagine what the people who'd actually gone through it were feeling. My confidence waned more as adrenaline surged through my system.

We reached a sheriff's blockade. After the driver explained our mission, we were allowed to proceed. Ahead, firefighters used chainsaws to cut a tree that was lying halfway across the road. They paused as our driver steered the van over to the narrow shoulder and around the tree.

We passed a house with several Amish men out front, one who carried a large blue tarp in his hands. A corner of the house had been torn away, and the roof was collapsing. Clothes, food, books, furniture, and toys, along with chunks of window frames and glass, were strewn across the yard. A girl stood at the edge of the house, holding a little boy's hand.

Just past that property, we pulled up to an Amish school. Amazingly, the tornado hadn't touched it. We quickly climbed out and unloaded our supplies, including the bottles of water, brown-bag lunches, fruit, and snacks that had been packed at the church. The door was open, and we could see people inside. Outside, on the edge of the building, a canopy had been set up. We took the food and water there, where others would distribute them, and then headed inside.

Desks had been pushed to the front, along the chalkboard, and chairs were grouped around the open space of the schoolroom. There were several elderly people in the very front, where a man and a woman in Red Cross vests were assisting them. To the side was an Amish woman with a boy and a girl with no one attending them. As I stepped toward them, the man in the Red Cross vest at the front of the school turned toward me. I froze.

It was Nick, the last person in the world I expected to see in Chester County.

I concentrated on the Amish kids, chatting with them in Pennsylvania Dutch, totally ignoring Nick. He'd seen me. And it was obvious he was just as surprised as I was.

The children and their mother lived in the house next to the school, the one with the collapsing roof. The family had gotten into the basement before the tornado hit, but afterward the oldest boy had been scraped by a branch on the side of his face, and the little girl had tripped and skinned her knee. I asked about the girl and boy back at the house.

"Jah," the woman said. "That's our oldest and youngest."

The woman was worried about her husband, afraid he'd go into the house and try to salvage as many belongings as possible. I assured her that all of the men, as well as her other daughter and son, were away from the house when we drove by.

"We'll need to stay somewhere else," she said. "Perhaps with my in-laws."

I nodded. In the Plain community, there wouldn't be much need for assistance with housing.

The woman nodded toward the elderly man who Nick was attending to. "That's our neighbor. He doesn't have any children around, or other relatives. Where will he stay?"

I assured her that the Red Cross would make sure he was housed, perhaps in a hotel.

She sighed. "That's too bad. If our house wasn't so damaged, we'd have him stay with us."

I patted her hand and then cleaned up her son's scraped

face first and then her daughter's skinned knee. As I worked, I tried to get them to talk more about what the tornado was like for them.

"I'd heard before that it sounds like a roaring freight train," the woman said. "That's exactly right. We could hear it even though we were in the basement. We only went down there because our neighbor warned us." The woman nodded toward the older man again.

"He came with us," the little boy added.

That warmed my heart, thinking of all of them huddled together.

After I was done, I checked with our van driver to see if he could take the woman and children to her in-laws, along with the two other kids, if the roads were passable.

The psychologist who was with us spoke with the elderly man once Nick was finished with him. I moved on to another Amish group who'd just come in—a middle-aged woman and her elderly parents. The father was having chest pains, which had started about an hour ago.

Nick must have overheard because he said an ambulance was on its way back to the school. "But call 9-1-1 and tell them what's going on so they can inform the paramedics before they arrive."

I thanked him and made the call. Then I took the man's blood pressure. 165/110. Definitely high. His pulse was rapid too. I opened the collar of his shirt and asked him if he had a history of heart disease. He said he had periodic angina and took nitroglycerin for it, but he didn't have any with him. It was in his house, which was unsafe to enter. I assured him the paramedics would have nitroglycerin tablets or spray with them.

The paramedics arrived ten minutes later and transported the man to the hospital as a precaution. I sighed in relief. I moved on to an Englisch woman who'd been driving through the area when the tornado touched down. She had a couple of cuts on her face and hands from when the windows of her car broke.

The day continued with all of us doing triage. I felt shaky on the inside as I helped person after person, but I also felt stronger. Houses and barns could be replaced. These lives were precious—I thanked God for each one.

When Nick was attempting to treat an Amish woman who was quite upset, he asked for my help. "I think maybe she'll feel more comfortable talking with you."

I found out the woman was a widow without any children and had been staying at her sister's house when the tornado struck. Her sister and brother-in-law were both injured and taken to the hospital. She was concerned about them and didn't know what to do.

I called the hospital, got her through to her sister, and they spoke on the phone. She started to cry. After she finished the conversation, I asked if she had a place to stay for the night. She said that the Dawdi Haus on the property hadn't been damaged, and she'd go back there so she could do the chores and tend to the animals. I then sent her out to the canopy to get a brown-bag lunch and told her we'd arrange for a ride for her.

After the woman left, Nick asked me how I was doing. "Fine," I said. "How about you?"

His root-beer-colored eyes grew large. "This is wild. I've never done anything like it. I'm so sorry for the circumstances, but I feel privileged to be able to help."

I totally agreed.

"We've been invited to step into one of the worst days of these people's lives," he said, his eyes growing even more intense. "Just like with nursing."

Not the nursing I did, I thought. I only stepped into viruses, infections, scrapes and bruises, and every once in a while, a broken bone. I changed the topic. "How'd you get up here so fast?"

"I'm home for a couple of days and left as soon as I got a call this morning. I signed up with the Red Cross last year."

"How was officer training?" I asked.

"Good," he answered. "I think it's a good fit. I'll apply for more schooling soon—probably next year."

"Do you plan to make a career out it?"

He shrugged. "It's too soon to know. Right now, I'm focused on getting my loans paid off and giving back enough to make it worth it to the Air Force to invest in me."

I tried to smile.

"How about you?" he asked. "Autumn and Paisley told me you passed your boards. Where are you working?"

I sighed before I could stop myself. I smiled to try to make up for it and then told him about the clinic.

"That's great," he said. "What are your long-term plans?"

I shrugged.

"Are you going to apply at a hospital? Go back to school?"

I shook my head.

"Leisel." He reached out to me, but I stepped back. His arm fell to his side. "What's wrong?"

I managed to smile. "Nothing," I answered. "Everything's fine."

An Amish woman with a baby in her arms and a toddler by her side approached us, giving me the perfect excuse to step away from Nick—again.

Nick left before I did, without saying good-bye. I thought my broken heart had healed, but maybe not. But knowing Stephen was waiting for me made me feel a little better.

As I rode with the others in the van back to the church, I

figured Nick had headed back to Lancaster County. But when our group returned to the Mennonite Church, his old Chevy pickup was parked out front.

I groaned, imagining Aenti Suz had been thrilled to see him. Perhaps she was serving him dinner and asking about everything he'd been doing since she last saw him. I considered waiting in the van until he left, but then our leader opened the door and instructed us all to go inside.

"The driver will be taking a group back to Lancaster in an hour, but if anyone can spend the night and work tomorrow we'd really appreciate it."

"I can," I said.

"Great!" she said. "Your aunt said she'd stay too."

We followed her into the church and back to the fellowship hall, where both volunteers and displaced people were seated at the tables. Sure enough, Aenti Suz was sitting across from Nick. I could have ignored Nick—but not my Aenti.

As I approached, she appeared weary but smiled and pointed at Nick. "Look who's here!"

I nodded. "We saw each other out in the field."

She smiled even wider. "What a surprise!"

I agreed. "How are things going here?"

"Good. We arranged rides for all of the Plain people who needed to get to relatives' houses and worked with the Red Cross to find lodging for others who are displaced. Plus, we fed everyone who came through." She pushed her chair back and stood. "And now I need to feed the two of you."

I started to follow her.

She quickly put a hand on my shoulder. "No, you stay here. I'll be right back with two plates of spaghetti."

Nick and I stared at each other for a moment after she left. Then we both spoke at the same time.

He said, "You first."

I shook my head. "You go ahead." There wasn't really anything I wanted to say to him. I just felt uncomfortable with the silence, which was unlike how I used to feel around him.

He swallowed, his Adam's apple bobbing in his throat. "I just wanted to say that it's really nice to see you."

I wrinkled my nose. "I have to admit I was shocked to see you."

We stared at each other again, and then, thankfully, Aenti Suz arrived with our food.

The smell made my mouth water. I hadn't realized how hungry I was. Spaghetti with meat sauce, salad, and garlic bread hit the spot. Nick and I both bowed our heads to pray silently, and then a couple of minutes later, Aenti Suz returned with a plate for herself and three bottles of water.

As we all dug into our food, my phone dinged. Stephen. I quickly texted him that I'd call in a few minutes.

Aenti Suz asked Nick where he was headed next.

"Dover Air Force Base," he answered. "I'll be working at a hospital, in the ICU."

"Do you plan to travel while you're there?"

He nodded. "Washington, DC. New York City. I might take the train up to Boston. Maybe even Maine. My family didn't travel when I was growing up, so I'm looking forward to seeing as much as I can now."

I tried to hide a wince. When we were dating, we used to talk about traveling together.

"Will you serve overseas?" Aenti Suz asked.

He smiled. "I hope so. I know of people who have served in Italy and, of course, in the Middle East too."

I felt shaky inside again. Would he be close to any of the major conflicts?

266

"Well," Aenti Suz said, "it sounds as if you are at the beginning of a great adventure."

He nodded, although his expression fell a little and he grew quiet.

"Are you staying tonight?" Aenti Suz asked. "Or heading back to your folks?"

"I'm going to stay the night. How about the two of you?"

"I am," Aenti Suz said.

I wished with all of my heart I hadn't committed to staying. "I am too," I answered as I stood. "Excuse me. I need to make a phone call."

After dumping my plate in the garbage and putting my empty bottle in the recycling, I slipped out the side door of the fellowship hall. I dialed Stephen's number and turned west toward the setting sun. He was home, just hanging out. I explained what I'd done all day.

"Are you headed back tonight?"

"No," I answered. "Tomorrow. Probably in the evening."

"There's that big of a need?"

"Yes," I answered. "The damage is really bad. Besides the loss of homes and outbuildings, we had people coming in with minor injuries and stress-related complaints all day."

"But all pretty insignificant complaints?"

"Well, not to them," I answered. Nor to me either.

"All right," he said. "Text me tomorrow and let me know what time you think you'll be back."

I assured him I would.

When I returned to the fellowship hall, both Nick and Aenti Suz were gone. I found her in the kitchen washing pots and pans, and I stepped in to help.

"It's so nice to see Nick," she said. "What a coincidence that he's here."

I nodded.

"He seems to be doing well."

I nodded again. He did, and I was happy about that. But my heart hurt. Even though I was pleased to be helping people, I would have never chosen to be around Nick, especially not in this sort of setting. It brought out the best in him, and it was hard to be reminded of the relationship we had.

After we finished the dishes, Aenti Suz and I stepped back into the fellowship hall. Nick was back, deep in conversation with a middle-aged Englisch man wearing overalls and a baseball hat. Nick was listening and nodding his head from time to time.

Another stab of pain sliced my heart.

"Want to go for a walk?" Aenti Suz asked, following my gaze. "Before we settle down for the night?"

"I would," I answered. "If you feel up to it."

"I do. I feel both weary and wired at the same time. I think a walk will do me good."

I knew exactly how she felt. "You can tell me the rest of Dawdi Joe's story."

She shook her head. "There's not much left to tell."

"What do you mean? I don't even know which Martha was my grandmother—the nurse or the young widow."

"Oh goodness," Aenti Suz said. "I did leave you in the lurch, didn't I?"

"And there's more after that. I want to hear about you and Dat as children and your growing-up years. And your relationship with Jake. I want to hear everything you're willing to tell me."

Aenti Suz sighed and opened the door, and we stepped out into the warm evening. I turned on the flashlight app on my phone and led the way down a side street.

After a long moment, Aenti Suz said, "I can tell you what I remember. I'm not sure if it's what you want to hear or not."

I couldn't imagine there was anything I wouldn't want to hear. "Please, just tell me the rest of the story, as it happened." I shone the light on the sidewalk ahead of us and matched my stride to my aunt's as I said, "Faith had just greeted Joe on the porch, exclaiming that God had answered their prayers to bring him home, and telling him that their Dat was close to the end."

— 19 —

Joe

As Faith led Joe through the living room, his cane thumping against the wood floor, she asked what had happened to his leg.

"You didn't get my letters?"

She shook her head. "We haven't had a letter from you since November."

Then they didn't know about Martha.

Faith stopped at the doorway to the bedroom off the kitchen, where they'd cared for their Mamm when she was ill, and motioned for Joe to enter. The shades were drawn and the light was dim. Dat was in the single bed, curled up like a child.

Joe limped to the straight-back chair beside it. He leaned his cane against the wall, sat, and then touched his father's shoulder. "Dat," he said. "I'm home."

His father stirred.

Faith stepped to the side of the bed. "Joe's here. All the way from Europe." His sister seemed to have changed. She was the kindest she'd ever been to him.

Dat turned his head, blinked his eyes open for a moment, and extended his hand. Joe took it. It was bony and the skin was paper-thin. Tears welled in Joe's eyes. So much had changed in the last year.

Dat whispered, "Joe," and squeezed his hand, but then he fell back to sleep.

Faith slipped out of the room while Joe continued to sit with their father. She returned a half hour later with Hope.

"Come out to the kitchen," Faith said to Joe. "You need some food. And we all need to talk."

After he'd washed up, Faith served him a bowl of pea soup with bits of ham in it and a biscuit. Nothing had ever tasted as good, not even his Mamm's cooking.

His sisters sat down across from him at the oak table, cups of tea in their hands.

"Where's Charity?" he asked as he ate.

Hope glanced at Faith.

Faith shook her head a little. "That girl. She ran off with Abe Yoder."

Joe nearly choked but managed to swallow and said, "But Abe was courting you."

"So I thought," Faith said.

"That's what Charity wrote to me." Joe didn't mention that Charity seemed to think Faith was unkind to Abe.

"Believe me," she said. "I was as surprised as anyone." She took a sip of tea.

Hope reached over and patted Faith's shoulder. Faith gave her a kind smile and then met Joe's gaze. "I don't hold it against Charity. Or Abe. I've done some soul-searching, and the Lord has been teaching me things I needed to learn about myself." She shrugged. "Hard things, but necessary."

Joe held his empty spoon above his bowl, not sure how to

respond. When his oldest sister didn't say anything more, he asked, "When did they marry?"

"December," Hope answered. So Joe hadn't been the first child in the family to marry after all.

"They're living south of Quarryville, on his uncle's farm," Faith added, "even though we need their help here."

"We can't keep up with everything," Hope said.

Joe agreed. "I noticed the corn hasn't been planted."

"We're going to try to do that this coming week," Faith said, sighing.

"Jah." The sooner the better. "I won't be much help for a while, not for another month or so. I've been told not to put all of my weight on my leg until then or it may never heal."

Hope asked what happened, and he gave them the short version of the story. Then he took a deep breath and said, "I wrote to all of you, but it sounds as if my letters never arrived." He paused a moment and then added, "I wrote about something else too. Something even more important."

Hope leaned toward him. "What?"

"I'm married."

Faith nearly spit out her tea. "You can't be."

"I am. I married a woman by the name of Martha Shaw. She's an army nurse."

Hope leaned back. "Where is she?"

"On the front line." He put down his spoon, suddenly exhausted.

"When did you marry?"

"January 29." He wouldn't add he'd only seen her once since their wedding and hadn't had a letter since. But then again, there seemed to be lots of problems with the mail, going both ways.

"That's not like you, Joe, to be so impulsive," Faith said. "That's more like Charity."

He wanted to laugh. She certainly thought he was impulsive when he was younger. "I wasn't impulsive, not this time," he said. "I worked with her in Chicago and knew her well. Then I had the entire crossing of the Atlantic to pray and think about it. Then, when the opportunity came in France, I couldn't take a chance and lose her. You'll understand when you meet her."

"But will she be willing to move here? To be a farmwife when she's used to a city?"

"She grew up Mennonite, with her grandparents," Joe explained. "And lived with her Amish aunt and uncle during the summer."

"So you'll live here on the farm, then?" Faith crossed her arms.

"We haven't talked all of that through." He couldn't imagine Martha would want to be a farmer's wife. It pained him, but he'd make the choice all over to marry her, a thousand times, even if it meant giving up the land. "We'll talk as soon as she comes home."

Faith leaned back in her chair. "And when will that be?"

Joe shook his head. "If I only knew." Once the war ended in Europe, he knew medical units would be needed in the Pacific.

He stood, leaning on his cane, and reached for his bowl and plate, but Hope grabbed them first. "You go sleep," she said. "Can you make it up the stairs?"

"Jah," he said. "I can."

First he checked in on his father again, whose breathing was still labored. Then he slipped his bag over his shoulder and started the climb to his childhood room.

The next week, Elmer Mast stopped by the farm. Joe was in the field with Hope, helping plant the corn. His leg hurt as he stumbled along the furrows, doing his best not to put his

273

weight on it. Elmer yelled from the road, and Joe made his way over to him.

After they chatted for a moment, Elmer said, "It looks like you could use some help."

"We could," Joe answered. "There just isn't much around." With so many of the young Amish men off serving with the CPS and the older men struggling to get their own work done, Joe didn't have anyone to turn to.

"I'll be back tomorrow with a few extra hands," Elmer said. "We'll get it planted in no time."

True to his word, he showed up the next day with four other men, all in their late fifties or early sixties. The three men worked hard. At dinnertime, Elmer's wife and his daughter Martha arrived with food to feed everyone. Martha wore a cape dress and Kapp. It seemed she'd made her decision. Faith welcomed them into the house and added their food to what she'd prepared.

Joe sat with Dat while the others ate, and then he took his turn at the table. Martha asked if he'd heard from his wife.

Joe shook his head and didn't say anything more. He'd read about the battles in Germany in the newspaper, and he feared for his Martha's safety. Or that she was having second thoughts. He longed for a letter from her. And he longed for her to be on the farm with him, willing to join the church, dressed as this Martha was. But he wouldn't expect it from her.

At the end of the day, the corn was planted. Joe thanked Elmer and the other men, grateful for what they'd done for him. He'd felt the same sense of camaraderie with them as he had working in the hospital in Chicago and driving ambulances in Europe. He'd felt it many times among the Amish—he'd just been surprised to find it among the Englisch too.

He'd also felt that camaraderie his entire life with his father and continued to as Joe sat beside his bed late into each night.

Joe knew he wasn't loved any more than his sisters, but his Dat had been happy to have a son who loved farming.

Joe told his Dat about his work in Chicago and about falling in love with Martha and learning to drive along Lake Shore Drive. He told him about his passage to England and then the trip across the Channel. He told him about his time in Belgium and Luxembourg and France. And then about marrying Martha. "You would really like her, Dat. She's kind, gentle, and honest. She might not be who you and Mamm would have chosen for me, but I'm convinced she's who God selected."

Some days Dat would take a few spoonfuls of broth and sips of water. Other days he wouldn't. Every once in a while, Dat would seem as if he were listening to Joe, but most of the time he seemed far away. Nevertheless, Joe kept talking. He shared memories of his childhood, of learning to drive the team of mules when he was eight and bucking bales of hay by the time he was ten. He remembered taking turns at the ice-cream maker crank with his sisters and catching lightning bugs every summer.

He thanked his Dat for caring for him and teaching him through the years. "You and Mamm were faithful," he said. "You showed us how to live. I'm grateful for those lessons."

Joe sat for a moment, thinking of the names his parents had given their children. He thought of the twists and turns in life. Dat, as a young man, figuring he'd never have children, that he'd never have a son to pass the farm down to. And then, late in life, he did have a boy.

Joe shivered at the thought of what twists and turns life might still have for him. He'd have to trust as his Dat had done. He'd need to be faithful, to live by hope, and to show charity. That was his prayer for himself.

Two weeks after Joe arrived home, Dat died. Faith, Hope, and Joe all stood around his bed as his heart beat its last. He'd left the farm to Joe, as everyone expected, with the stipulation that he provide a home for his unmarried sisters.

Charity and Abe came home for the service. At first Charity seemed wary of Joe's reaction to her, but he patted her shoulder and told her all was well. "In fact," he said, "we need your help. Abe's too. Won't you come back to the farm?"

"Faith would never have it," Charity said.

Joe smiled. "No, it's what she wants too."

Charity's eyebrows shot up.

"She's forgiven you—and she said she learned some things about herself."

"Like how critical she is of others? Including Abe?" Charity's chin quivered.

Joe shrugged. "You should talk with her."

He never knew if Charity and Faith talked or not, but a week later, on the first of May, Charity and Abe came home. Then, on May 9, a Wednesday, Elmer arrived at the farm again around midmorning as Joe and Abe repaired the pasture fence.

Elmer yelled from the driveway, "Have you heard?"

Joe shook his head. "What's going on?"

"It's over. The Germans surrendered."

Joe's knees grew weak, and he leaned heavily on his cane. Was it true? Could the war really be over?

Elmer assured him again and again that it was. Then, seeing that his words were not enough, he took a newspaper out of his buggy. The headline read *War in Europe Ends!* Finally, Joe believed him. Warmth radiated through his entire body.

That night he wrote another letter to Martha. *I hope you'll be coming home soon and not going to the Pacific. Every day I pray for you. And for a letter from you. I pray you are well and not regretting your decision to marry me. I love you more each day and long for you. I'll never understand God sending me home before you, but I'm trying to trust His ways, which I know are not my own.*

Every day, as soon as the mailman arrived, Joe checked the mailbox. In the middle of May, all of his letters from November to February to his father and sisters arrived. Then, a week later, a letter from Martha arrived.

Dear Joe,

It took Wallace a month to get your letter to me, but he did. I'd feared you no longer cared about me, but it all makes sense now. I'm praying your leg will heal completely and soon. I'm glad you'll be going home. I thank God for that. I pray we'll be together soon.

Your loving wife, Martha

Relieved, he held the letter to his chest. She still loved him. God willing, they'd be together soon.

By late May, Joe was getting around better and able to do more of the farming. Working with Abe wasn't the same as farming with Dat, but he was grateful for his help. His sisters all seemed to be getting along, and it only seemed right to have Charity and Abe back on the farm. A couple of times, Elmer Mast, usually with his daughter Martha, stopped by to see how Joe was doing. He appreciated their concern, but he wasn't sure Martha had made the right decision to come back to the Amish. Although she was always friendly and polite, she didn't look happy. Then again, it was probably her grief for her husband that made her sad.

One day, Elmer stopped by alone. Joe asked about his wife and daughter. Elmer, his eyes heavy, said that Martha had returned to Philadelphia. "She said that living Amish wasn't the right thing for her. She has friends in the city who will help her. We're praying she'll be all right."

Joe assured him she would be. Soon, he would be living Englisch too, or at least Mennonite. He hoped he and Martha would find the help they needed in their new community.

By early June, the corn was coming up in the field, the pasture was flourishing, and Joe had most of the fence repaired. He no longer used his cane in the house and was getting around better outside too. The weather had turned hot, and the pasture was lush with grass for the horses and the handful of cattle. If Joe were to stay, he'd look into starting a dairy herd, but of course there was no reason for him to plan for that now. It would be Abe's decision, most likely.

Joe felt strong and capable again. Being home with his sisters had brought healing. Their strength had seen him through a difficult transition. Now all he needed was Martha and the chance to get on with their lives.

That evening, Faith asked if she could talk with him. As they sat out on the porch, she said, "I need to ask your forgiveness."

He clasped his hand around the knee of his good leg but didn't respond.

"I was too harsh with you when you were a boy—right up until the time you left. I was too harsh with Charity and Hope too, but not as bad as I was with you. I didn't realize it until after Abe ran off with Charity." She went on to say that the man couldn't take her negativity—and she couldn't blame him. She believed she was teaching everyone, challenging them to be better with her criticism. She paused for a moment and inhaled sharply. "But I was tearing all of you down. It was one of the last things Dat spoke with me about. He told me I needed to stop trying to control others and instead trust God with them." She smiled a little at the memory. "You know how much I hate to be told I'm wrong, but I listened to him. And he was right. I'm doing my best to change my ways. Will you forgive me?"

Joe looked sideways at his sister. What if he didn't have Faith in his life? What if he didn't have Hope or Charity either? He wouldn't have had anything to come home to except a dying father. "Of course I forgive you." He reached over and patted her shoulder as she wiped away the tears rolling down her face.

In the days that followed, Joe realized that Faith seemed more settled than she used to be, not as easily irritated. Perhaps she feared before that her younger siblings wouldn't grow into capable adults, and she felt responsible to teach them. Now that she was learning to trust God, she was able to let go of them and enjoy life. She wasn't motivated by fear anymore.

On a spectacular Saturday two weeks later, with a sapphire-blue sky warming the farm, Joe had finished repairing the trough in the barn and was on his way to the house when he spotted a Pontiac coming up the road.

He walked quickly around the side of the house. The car stopped, and a woman climbed out of the back seat while the driver retrieved a bag from the trunk.

The woman's blond hair hung loose and wavy around her shoulders, and she wore a skirt and sweater.

"Martha!" he yelled, running toward her as much as he could with his cane.

She turned toward him, her mouth forming the word *Joe*.

When he reached her, he dropped his cane and wrapped his arms around her. "You're here!"

"Jah," she answered. "I am. I'm finally home."

Martha *was* home. Out under the oak tree in the pasture, she told Joe she didn't want to return to Chicago—or Illinois at all.

As the sun lowered in the western sky, she took his hand. "I want to join your church with you."

His heartbeat hadn't slowed since he'd seen her step from the car, but now it raced even faster. "Are you sure?" He'd never felt so alive in his entire life.

She squeezed his hand. "The reason I'm not on my way to the Pacific is because you're going to be a daddy."

Joe gasped.

"The baby is due the end of October. Nine months from our wedding night."

He wrapped her in his arms again, feeling as if his heart might burst. She was safe. They were going to be parents. A baby. A miracle that had brought Martha back to him. He felt as if he must be dreaming.

Joe's leg healed day by day, while Martha's middle expanded. Faith, Hope, and Charity became sisters to her and came to love her as much as they did Joe.

They all celebrated, in a quiet way, when the war in the Pacific ended in August 1945. But they were shocked that nuclear bombs had been dropped and wondered what that held for the future of the world. Both Joe and Martha hoped that their friends, including Major Russell, would soon be coming back to the United States.

The devastation from the fighting around the world was horrific, and the recovery took years. For Joe and Martha, each day on the farm and in their Amish community brought healing from what they'd seen on the front line. Baby Augustus, named for Martha's father, was born the end of October, just as Martha had predicted. They called him Gus. She and Joe joined the church the next spring and Charity and Abe moved out soon after that, going back to help Abe's uncle.

Hope began courting a man from New Holland who had

fought fires with the CPS in Montana. They married the next year. And just when it seemed Faith might remain with Joe and Martha forever, she started courting a widower with four children. It was the hardest for her, out of all the sisters, to leave the Bachmann farm. But she did, marrying the man, mothering the children, and having three more.

Major Russell tracked Joe and Martha down in 1948, showing up at the farm on a cool spring day with Lt. Madison, who was now Mrs. Russell. The two had married and were on their way to Philadelphia, where the major had been assigned to an army hospital. Lt. Madison seemed surprised to see Martha in a cape dress and Kapp, living without electricity and, at that time, without an indoor toilet, but after a tour of the farm, including the new dairy herd, they both praised them for their hard work. Through the years, the couples exchanged cards and saw each other from time to time.

Baby Suzanne, named after Joe's mother, was born when Gus was four. Martha had several miscarriages and a stillborn baby after that, which nearly broke her heart. Martha never worked as a nurse again, but she served neighbors, friends, and family with her advice and skills. Many times she and Joe were called when there was a farm accident. Other times she went alone to care for someone who was ill. Gus learned from both his parents about medicine, and as he grew older, Joe taught Gus all about farming and caring for the land too. And Gus and his father loved to sing, including Englisch hymns and other songs.

Meanwhile, Suz learned from her mother about cooking, canning, sewing, quilting, and gardening. When Suz fell in love with Jake, a Mennonite boy, her parents, aunts, and uncles all hoped it was a passing fancy.

When Gus, who was twenty-four and hadn't joined the church yet, decided to go with Jake to Vietnam to fulfill both of their conscientious objector duties, both Martha and Joe grew concerned. They worried about Gus's safety and also his emotional well-being. Both knew the horrors of war and didn't want their son to witness what they had. They were non-resistant, so of course they were against the war, but they were also against sending boys to fight in a conflict they believed the United States had no business getting involved in.

They pleaded with Gus to join the church and stay home, but in the end they left the decision to him. He chose Vietnam, where he and Jake worked in a Mennonite clinic in the highlands of the country. In the fall of 1970, the Viet Cong attacked the clinic, and Jake was killed. The clinic was immediately closed and Gus returned home, a traumatized young man, while Suz was left with a broken heart. Their parents cared for both of them, giving them time to heal.

A couple of years later, Gus joined the church and then married Missy. Arden and Amos were born in 1974. Gus built the Dawdi Haus for his parents and Suz moved in with them. Even though they were still relatively young—in their early fifties—both Joe and Martha had health problems.

Although Martha cared for others and encouraged them to live in a healthy way, her own health failed. Eventually, the doctors diagnosed her with congenital heart disease. She died soon after. Joe died a few years later.

Their lives seemed too short, but they were devoted to each other and to others. And they passed on their strengths to their children. The pain of what they saw during World War II never left, but instead of scarring them, it compelled them to do all they could to love and serve those around them.

— 20 —

Leisel

A enti Suz stopped under a streetlight in the church parking lot as we completed the loop back to the church.

"So my grandmother was a nurse." I sighed. "I'm so glad she survived the war. They were so in love."

"Jah," Aenti Suz said. "World War II brought my parents together and changed all of our lives."

I nodded in agreement. It had set our family on a new trajectory. Jah, they stayed on the farm, but I couldn't help but wonder how Martha's influence had shaped my Dat and Aenti Suz, and, in return, influenced my sisters and me. Still, I was surprised Martha chose to live Amish, especially when Joe was so willing to leave.

"Did she ever regret it?" I asked.

"Oh, I'm sure there were times she did. Once I saw her looking longingly at an Englisch woman driving a station wagon." She laughed. "And once she mentioned how nice it would be not to hang the wash out in the winter, but you have to remember that she grew up with no electricity and with a wringer washing machine. And her grandfather never had a car, of course. It wasn't as if living Amish was a drastic change for her, not like it would be now."

"But wasn't it hard for her to give up her nursing career?"

"No, it really wasn't," Aenti Suz said. "Back then, most women stopped working once they married."

"What about the Amish in the community? Did they accept her right away?"

"At first people in the community were suspicious of her, but then a neighbor mangled his arm in a hay baler and she saved his life. Another time, a neighbor was horribly ill and Mamm went over with her stethoscope, diagnosed him with pneumonia, and contacted an Englisch neighbor to take him to the hospital. She probably saved his life too. Others in the community sought her out after that. Sometimes, when we were old enough to stay by ourselves, she and Dat would go out in the middle of the night to check on a neighbor. Or Gus would go with Mamm instead of Dat."

"What about you?" I asked. "Were you interested in medicine?"

She shook her head. "No. For the longest time I fainted at the sight of blood. I got over that, but I was never good in an emergency. I'm better now, I think."

"How about Jake?"

She smiled a little. "He wasn't exactly made for medicine either. But it was a better match for him than fighting, so he did his best."

I thought of Joe and Martha and their years together on their farm. They'd both died long before I was born, and I really hadn't been told much about them over the years. Now I wondered if Mamm had discouraged talk about them because of their service during World War II. I know she didn't want

Dat talking about his time in Vietnam or Haiti or any of the other trips he took.

"Will you tell me more about them? And about you and Jake?"

Even in the dim light, I could see Aenti Suz's face contort.

"I'm sorry," I said.

"No, it's fine." She turned toward the front door of the church. "It's hard for me to talk about him, but I'm fine answering your questions."

"Do you have any regrets?" My voice was low. "About Jake?"

Aenti Suz shuddered a little. "Do I have any regrets? Jah. The problem is, I'm not sure if I have one or a million."

"What would the one regret be?"

"That I didn't go to Vietnam with him."

"What do you mean?" I asked.

"There were other Mennonite women working at the clinic. I wish Jake and I had married and gone together."

The idea shocked me. "Is that what Jake wanted?"

"We'd talked about it." She clasped her hands together. "Things were so odd during that time. Jah, Vietnam was a war zone, but missionaries and medical people came and went all the time. Other people did too. Businessmen. Adoption workers. It wasn't prohibited in any way. There had been an incident nearly a decade earlier when some American and Canadian medical providers had been kidnapped, but the compounds where the clinics were located were relatively safe—or at least that was the thinking when Jake and Gus decided to go."

"Did your parents not want you to marry Jake and go to Vietnam?"

"They were surprisingly resigned to letting me make that decision. They knew I didn't plan to join the Amish. They knew I planned to marry Jake. They didn't seem to think we should wait."

"So why didn't you marry and go with him?" I asked. "Were you afraid?"

Aenti Suz shook her head. "I wasn't afraid of the danger—I was afraid of being judged."

"By whom?"

"Our community."

"But you were leaving it."

Aenti Suz smiled a little. "It doesn't make any sense, I know." She exhaled. "I didn't know any women who'd ever done such a wild thing."

"Except your mother," I challenged.

"Right," Aenti Suz said. "But I had no idea of her story at the time."

"What do you mean?"

"Well, I knew she was an army nurse, but I didn't know any of the details. It wasn't something they talked about or that the bishop wanted them to talk about."

That made sense. "But what about the ancestor Marie told me about? Annie, right? The one who cared for soldiers during the Civil War and then married a man who was Brethren." I snapped the fingers of my free hand. "And how about that great-great-Aenti who Ruby is named after? Didn't she go to Valley Forge? And then marry an Englischman? They both took huge risks too."

Aenti Suz nodded. "You're right. But I didn't know about those stories at the time either."

I took a step backward. "When did you find out about them?"

"My Mamm and Dat told me their stories after we buried Jake. And then my Aenti Faith told me about Ruby and Annie sometime after that. They were all so worried about me, and I think they were just trying to distract me. They didn't realize that the stories reinforced my wish that I'd married Jake and gone with him."

I reached for her hand and squeezed it.

"Because I didn't have any examples to follow, I felt going with him would further ostracize me from my community."

I still didn't understand.

"Jake's folks had a farm not too far away, so I would be living close by," she continued. "The folks in our community already looked down on me for courting a Mennonite boy. I had this idea that everyone would talk less behind my back if I did everything as normal as possible, meaning waiting to marry until Jake returned."

"You never seemed to me like the type of person who cared what people thought."

"Oh, I did back then," she said. "Not enough to deny my love for Jake, but enough to draw as little attention to myself as possible. I wanted to wait out the year he was gone, living with my folks, and then Jake and I would both join the Mennonite church together when he returned."

"What made you decide to join the Amish church instead?"

"At first, I wasn't sure I would. I had this idea I'd go ahead and join the Mennonites anyway and then travel with different mission groups, in honor of Jake. But then his parents were so heartbroken when he died that they sold their farm, moved to Indiana, and retired in a Mennonite settlement there. My Mamm's health grew worse, and I began caring for her. Gus married and had the twins. About ten years after Jake died, I realized I wasn't going anywhere."

"How about when Dat went off to places to serve? Did you want to go with him?"

"At first I did, but I had our parents to look after. And then after a while I grew complacent and it didn't seem as important to me."

I inhaled deeply, thinking of how much I enjoyed assisting

Dat as he recommended vitamins, supplements, and healthy eating to friends and neighbors who sought out his good advice. And how much, at one time, I'd looked forward to serving with Nick. I hadn't realized I would be following in a family tradition.

My grandparents had both served in a medical capacity during World War II, yet I wouldn't have anything to do with Nick when he decided to serve in the Air Force. Was I that closed-minded? Would I be content working in a clinic forever? Or being a doctor's wife and not working at all?

Aenti Suz started walking again, and I shone the light at her feet. In the distance, the front door to the church was open. Nick stood in the light. I'm not sure if he saw us or not, but my heart ached at the sight of him. After a moment, he turned around and closed the door.

He was certainly following his dreams. At some point, I needed to figure out my own.

When had they changed?

Or, more accurately, when had I?

The next morning, as I washed my face in the ladies' room, I thought about Aenti Suz and Jake and the tragedy of his death. My heart seized again, just as it had yesterday at the sight of Nick.

A few minutes later, I pulled my phone out of the pocket of my backpack and the slip of paper with the number of the wife back in Somerset came out with it. I groaned. Was I ever going to deal with that? I was sure she hadn't forgotten me, just as I hadn't forgotten her. Hopefully, she hadn't gone back to the diner and found out I actually had her number. I really was the queen of avoiding conflict.

Aenti Suz was already in the kitchen, cooking scrambled eggs for the crew. I was surprised to see David flipping hotcakes. I greeted him and asked if the tornado had touched down on his farm.

"No," he said. "We were a couple of miles north of its path."

"Did you just happen to show up? Only to find Aenti Suz here?"

He smiled and shook his head. "Your Mamm left me a message. She said Suz was headed up here to this church. I hired a driver this morning to see how I could help."

I was surprised Mamm had called him. Did she contact him often? Nick sat at a table with the other nurse and the doctor who had stayed too.

After I filled my plate at the counter between the kitchen and fellowship hall, I stepped back to the stove to eat where Aenti Suz was scrambling another skillet of eggs, not wanting to join Nick's group. Aenti Suz gave me a funny look but didn't say anything.

When it was time to get our assignments, our leader sent me to the school, along with the doctor and Aenti Suz, while David stayed back at the church. Nick and the other nurse were sent to a different site.

We had one more day of triage. Aenti Suz greeted people, offered them a snack, and kept up with the paperwork as I examined patients. I continued to feel a surge of adrenaline, but not as intensely as the day before.

A boy had stepped on a nail while helping to clear debris. His mother had no idea when his last tetanus shot had been, so we sent him on to his general practitioner. Then we had a man who'd sprained his ankle. Most of his barn had been blown into his field, and he fell off the foundation as he was trying to untangle the remaining boards.

Just after noon, Nick joined us. He said the other nurse had headed home. Aenti Suz asked him when he needed to leave. "I'll stay until supper," he said.

"Until after supper, I hope," she added, before he could answer. "In fact, I insist."

He smiled at her. "Thank you. I will." He glanced from Aenti Suz to me. "How late are the two of you staying?"

"We're leaving when the van goes."

"Tonight?"

I nodded. "I work in the morning."

We continued on with our tasks. I asked Nick for a second opinion on a cut to a little Amish girl's leg—if butterfly bandages were enough or if I should send her to a clinic to get it stitched. After we both consulted with the father, he decided butterfly bandages would do the trick.

After I'd finished, Nick stepped over and complimented me on how I'd handled the situation. "You let the parent make the decision with the necessary information," he said. "Good job."

It wasn't a big deal, but still his comment warmed me. I remembered how encouraging he was, how he made me feel as if I could do anything. A lump formed in my throat and I simply nodded.

When we returned to the church for supper, David was flipping hamburger patties in the kitchen. After we washed up, Aenti Suz and I filled our plates, and once we were sitting down and eating, Nick joined us. He bowed his head and prayed before taking a bite of his burger.

As we all ate, our leader approached us and asked if Aenti Suz or I could stay another night. Aenti Suz quickly volunteered. I explained I worked the next day and couldn't.

"You rode here in the van, right?"

I nodded.

"Oh dear," she said. "I'll need to go speak with our driver."

Before she stepped away, Nick said, "I can give you a ride. No problem."

The leader sighed. "That would be great. I'd hate for our driver to have to go all the way to Lancaster and then back again."

I wasn't thrilled with spending so much time with Nick, but I didn't say anything. After our team leader left, I asked Nick what time he planned to leave.

"As soon we're done eating," he answered.

"All right," I said. "I just need to grab my things." I finished before he did and left while he and Aenti Suz were talking. When I returned with my backpack and sleeping bag, David had joined them. He sat next to Nick, across from Aenti Suz.

"Leave your plate," Aenti Suz said to Nick. "I'll clear it."

We told Aenti Suz and David good-bye, and then we headed out to the church parking lot. The sky was overcast and a misty rain fell. I slipped my pack and sleeping bag behind the seat of Nick's pickup and noticed his things were already stashed on his side.

As I climbed in, I thought of when he'd given me that first ride home from class. Then I'd learned to drive in this pickup. I'd arrived in Pittsburgh for my new life in it. I'd had my first kiss, outside my apartment, in it. A thousand jagged memories shattered my heart all at once.

Neither of us spoke as he turned onto the highway. A beam of light from the lowering sun shone through the clouds, and the raindrops on the windshield glistened until he turned on the wipers and they were swiped away.

"I hope you'll have some time with your family tonight," I said.

Nick smiled a little. "I'll hang out with Mom and Dad. The girls are pretty busy, but I'll be in town through the weekend."

"Are they proud that you joined the Air Force?"

He gave me a sideways glance. "Honestly?"

I nodded.

"Dad was pretty mad at me."

"Why?"

"Because I didn't talk it through with you first."

I didn't answer.

"I know you don't want to talk about this . . ."

I kept quiet, expecting him to say more. But he didn't.

We rode in silence for a long stretch, and then he said, "Dad said he saw you at Wal-Mart on Saturday."

"Jah," I answered. "It was good to see him." I didn't say anything more about that either.

"Dad said you wore a Mennonite dress."

I nodded. "I've been going to Marie and Gordon's church. I'll probably join in the spring."

"Oh."

There was another stretch of silence. Then he cleared his throat. I knew what was coming next.

"Dad said you were with a guy."

I nodded again, even though the light was so dim now that he probably couldn't see me. "Stephen," I said. "He goes to my church."

"Dad recognized him from the hospital."

"Jah, Stephen works there. He's a surgeon."

Nick leaned back against the seat. "Is he the doctor who bought you the study program?"

I hoped the dim light would hide my wince as well. "Jah," I whispered.

More silence.

"Are you happy, Leisel?" Nick asked a few minutes later. "Because I've been rehearsing a speech in my head for the last three months that I'd like to say to you, but if you're happy, I'll keep it to myself."

I looked straight ahead. "I'm happy."

His voice was an octave deeper than usual. "Are you sure?"

"Yes," I snapped.

We rode in complete silence after that, until we were a few miles from Lancaster. "Your car's parked at the church, right?" His voice was low and quiet. "Just north of town?"

"That's right."

My car was the only one in the parking lot, and Nick pulled up next to it, under a streetlight. He turned the engine off and climbed out of the pickup. I opened my door before he could reach it, but he held it as I climbed down and retrieved my things.

"Thank you for the ride." I unlocked my car and dropped my pack in the back seat.

"You're welcome." Nick's eyes grew watery and he looked away. "I really hope for the best for you, Leisel."

"Thank you." I fought the urge to run as fast and far as I could. "I wish the same to you."

I tried to swallow the lump in my throat, but it only lodged itself more securely. "This is . . ." I started to turn toward my car, not sure what to say.

"This is confusing?" He didn't move. "Frustrating? Awkward?"

I nodded. "All three." But it was more than that. I reached for the driver's-side door handle. "I need to go. Thank you for the ride."

He stepped back by his truck, and I slipped into my car. He waited for me. As I drove away, he waved. I expected the expression on his face to be angry, but it wasn't. He was still fighting back tears.

The next morning I thought of everyone in Chester County who would be clearing away debris and repairing houses.

Then my thoughts turned to the conversation on the ride home. I hadn't lied to Nick. I was happy. But I was also still in grief. It appeared we both were. But time healed all wounds and it would ours too.

By the time I reached work, the sun was shining and the day was warming up. And so was I. I texted Stephen. *How about dinner tonight? As long as you don't mind boxes stacked around my apartment.*

He texted, *Of course not! 8?*

I texted back, *Perfect. See you then.* That would give me time to go to the store and then get dinner cooked.

"We have a packed schedule today," one of the doctors said to me after I'd stowed my purse in the employee closet and readied the exam rooms. "All the regular appointments, plus a virus seems to be making the rounds already. And we had several cases of strep yesterday."

"Good to know," I said.

The day progressed like all the others. I truly enjoyed the people, but honestly my most valued skill was that I knew Pennsylvania Dutch. *Jah*, I could draw blood and give shots and all of that, but it wasn't as if I were learning anything new. Or doing anything challenging. It was fine work. Important work. It would have been the perfect nursing job for lots of people. But it wasn't satisfying to me.

It wasn't that the work I did in Chester County over the weekend was a lot different, but there was an unpredictable element to it. I liked that. It kept me on my toes.

During the last appointment of the day, I found myself yawning just before I gave an Amish toddler her booster shots. I covered my mouth, changed my latex glove, and then explained to her what I was doing in Pennsylvania Dutch. As she screamed and screamed anyway, I tried to soothe her, but of course her mother did a much better job.

As I stepped around the table, my skirt got caught on the corner of one of the metal trays that jutted out a little. It had happened before but this time the skirt stuck. As I stepped forward, it tore a little.

"What a shame," the mother said.

I nodded. It was. And wouldn't have happened if I'd been wearing scrubs.

After work, I stopped by the store and bought chicken breasts, a jar of artichoke hearts, veggies for a salad, a loaf of French bread, ice cream for dessert, and a needle and thread to mend my dress.

The first thing I did when I arrived home was change into my jeans. Then I put together my specialty chicken dish, popped it in the oven, and assembled the salad.

I timed everything to be done by eight. And it was. And then I waited. A half hour later I had a text from Stephen that he was on his way. Then I waited some more. From my clinicals in hospitals, I could imagine Stephen being called back for another question or another order or another emergency. I knew he couldn't help it.

As I mended my skirt, my phone dinged. Autumn had texted Paisley and me. *Passed my boards! Doing a happy dance!*

We both congratulated her. She'd taken her time before taking it a second time. I understood her trepidation.

Then she texted me to tell me she had a job waiting at the hospital in Wilmington where Paisley was working. *You'll have to come visit us.*

I responded that I'd love to.

She texted back and asked how Lancaster County was and what I was up to that particular night.

I made the mistake of telling her I was waiting to have dinner with a doctor.

What?! she wrote, practically unleashing on me. *You're dating already?! How could you do that to Nick?!*

When I didn't answer because I couldn't figure out what to text back, she apologized.

I told her it was okay, that I understood her confusion. And the truth was, I did.

Finally, Stephen arrived.

As I opened the door, he said, "Only an hour late." He grimaced. "It could be worse."

I nodded.

As we ate the dried-out chicken and the wilted salad, he talked about his day. He'd had an emergency appendectomy at four thirty in the morning, then appointments at his office, and then rounds at the hospital.

After a while, he asked me how my day was. "Pretty boring," I said. "Especially compared to volunteering after the tornado."

"Oh, that's right! How was that?"

I gave him a quick synopsis of my two days in Chester County, leaving out that I'd seen my ex-boyfriend.

Then I said, "I'm thinking about applying for a job at Lancaster General. I saw a position is open on the neuro floor."

He leaned back in his chair. "But I thought you really liked working at the clinic."

"I'm not learning anything new."

"Oh. There aren't many people who are nurses and speak Pennsylvania Dutch though, right? Don't they really value you?"

"I think so." I scooted my half-empty plate forward. "But I can't make my career choices just by what language I speak. I made a big investment in nursing school. I'd like to keep learning and growing."

He smiled kindly. "Well, that's great." His face grew more serious. "But don't you think that would be awkward for us to work at the same place?"

"The position is on the neuro floor. All of your patients are on med-surg, right?"

He took a drink of water and then said, "Well, sure. I mean, if the census is high, I might have a patient go to that floor. But, you know, because we're dating . . ." He smiled again.

I shook my head. "I don't see that there's any conflict."

He glanced at his watch. "I can help with the dishes before I need to get going. I have another early morning tomorrow."

I waved him off. "Go ahead. It'll only take me a minute to clean up."

He thanked me for dinner, gave me a hug and a quick kiss, and then dashed out the door.

Before I washed the dishes, I pulled my phone out of the back pocket of my jeans. My life had changed so much in the last year. I thought I'd be working in a hospital. Marrying Nick. Going to grad school. Maybe relocating to somewhere like Montana.

I slipped my phone back into my pocket. I missed Nick, but it would be crazy to contact him. No good would come from it. I didn't have many more pieces of my heart left to lose.

— 21 —

Marie asked me to go to her oncology appointment with her on a Friday afternoon in the middle of October. It meant leaving work early, but the office manager had scheduled two fewer patients for the day, which made it possible. My wanting to forego my Mennonite cape dresses at work was short-lived. Jah, I sometimes changed into jeans after work, but mostly I wore the dresses. Today I had on a purple print that I'd bought on Etsy.

It was a gloriously warm day. The landscape of Lancaster County always took my breath away, but this was a particularly beautiful day. The sky sparkled from the bright sunlight, unmarred by a single cloud. As I drove into town, I passed an Amish man driving mules pulling a plow. A collie ran alongside the team.

On a day like today, I could truly imagine staying in Lancaster County. Joining the Mennonite church. Marrying Stephen. Working at the clinic.

I hadn't applied for the job at the hospital. It wasn't that I'd decided not to—I just hadn't managed to get my application done before the deadline, which wasn't like me. I must not have wanted the position after all.

But now there was another position posted, this time on the med-surg floor. Where I'd see Stephen all the time. I hadn't mentioned it to him yet.

I double-parked outside of Marie's apartment and called to tell her I'd arrived. A couple of minutes later, she came out the door, juggling Caden, his car seat, and his diaper bag. "My sitter got sick," she said through my open window. "Hopefully he won't be too restless during the appointment."

I jumped out of the car and took the baby so she could install the car seat. Soon Caden was safely secured, and we were heading to the doctor's office.

"How have you been feeling?" I asked. Marie had more color in her face and looked as if she'd put on a few pounds, which she'd needed to. She'd gotten so thin.

"Better. I'm sleeping more, and I'm able to keep up with Caden for longer each day," she said as I drove down Duke Street. "Hey, why didn't you tell me Mamm is courting?"

"Is she? For sure?"

"Jah. And David, of all men." Her eyes were wide. "Jessica thinks they'll be married by Christmas."

"Wow."

"She'll move to Chester County with him."

I let that sink in. That meant Arden and Vi would move into the big house with their kids. Perhaps they'd rent out their house until Milton married. That would help with the finances.

"But where would Aenti Suz live?" I asked Marie.

"She'll have to stop renting out the Dawdi Haus."

Mamm and Aenti Suz were as different as could be, but they'd miss each other. And I'd miss Mamm too.

Caden began to fuss, and Marie turned around and wiggled his foot, causing him to giggle. "How are things going with Stephen?"

"Good," I answered. We'd gone for a hike the Saturday before. We hadn't talked much, but it had been nice to spend time with him.

"Have you heard anything from Nick? Since Chester County?" she asked, turning back around in the seat.

I shook my head.

I realized she was staring at me.

"What?" I asked.

She shrugged. "It's none of my business." After a long pause, she said, "I've been thinking how fun it would be to have a sisters' night. At my apartment."

"What about Gordon and Caden?"

"They could spend the night at Randi's house. And Ruby could stay home with Silas. We could sit around and talk. Bake cookies. Don't you think that would be fun?"

"What if we gather at the farmhouse? Before Arden takes over? One last night in our old home."

"That would be perfect," she answered. Hopefully we'd have good news from her oncologist to celebrate by then.

Marie's appointment went well. The PET scan found no cancer and the doctor was hopeful. She would have a PET scan done every three months for the next year and then every six months after that.

The doctor also said there were certainly cases of women who went on to have babies after stomach cancer, although it wasn't exactly common, and time would tell if that would be her experience or not. "But there's no reason not to try," he said.

On the way home, as Caden fell asleep, Marie seemed more carefree than I'd seen her since before the diagnosis. Maybe ever. "I'm going to hope for the best," she said. "If I don't have any more children, I can accept that. I'm just so thankful to have my health, a good husband, and a wonderful son."

I patted her leg, too choked up to say anything. What had

been a horrible year had just gotten a whole lot better. Marie was cancer free. That's what mattered most.

As I dropped Marie and Caden off at their apartment, I told her I planned to go see Mamm.

"Oh, tell her my news, would you? And ask her about us having a girls' night."

I promised I would do both. When I reached the farm, Mamm sat on the porch in her rocking chair while David sat in Dat's. It was after six, and they'd probably already eaten their supper. The sun was setting, and it was beginning to grow chilly. They both wore coats. Mamm stood as I came up the steps and greeted me warmly. "I'm so glad you stopped by," she said. "I have some news."

She turned toward David, and he stood too. "David and I are planning to marry, right before Thanksgiving."

"Congratulations," I managed to say, thankful Marie had warned me. "That's wonderful." I meant it, but it was still a big change.

She nodded, a hint of a smile on her face. "I'll be moving up to Chester County, and Arden and Vi will move in here."

Just as we'd expected. Now, the sisters' sleepover seemed more important than ever, so I broached the topic. "Can we stay here next Friday or the one after?"

"I'll be in Chester County meeting all of David's children and grandchildren in two weeks—I'll be staying at his oldest daughter's house."

I couldn't help but smile at her nod to propriety.

She frowned. "Marie would be coming too?"

"Yes," I answered, stopping myself from saying anything more. She did have three daughters.

She pressed her lips together and then said, "I suppose that will be all right."

Relieved, I realized I hadn't shared Marie's good news and quickly explained the results of the PET scan.

Mamm blinked a couple of times. "Well, isn't that something."

David spoke, a broad smile on his face. "Thank God," he said. "We have so much to be grateful for." He met Mamm's eyes and she smiled a little. Perhaps the man could change her in ways Dat never could.

"Is Aenti Suz in her Dawdi Haus?" I asked.

"No, she's here," Mamm said. "She has guests out in her place this weekend. A couple from Tennessee."

"I'll tell her hello before I go." I stepped into the house, squinting in the dim light. Aenti Suz stood at the sink, wringing out a dishcloth. The dish rack was full.

"Who are you?" I asked as I approached, nodding toward Mamm and David on the porch. "Cinderella?"

She laughed. "I sent them out. With so few of us, the cleanup is fast."

I stepped around the island, leaned against the counter, and told her about Marie's appointment.

"Oh, what a blessing." She grabbed a towel. "Did your mother tell you her news?"

I nodded and grabbed a second towel. "What do you think?"

"I'm over the moon for both of them," she said as she dried a plate. "And your Dat would be pleased. He knew David way back when and always respected him."

"Oh?"

Aenti Suz nodded as she put the plate in the cupboard.

For a moment I suspected that she'd played matchmaker. Did she think Mamm needed a husband more than she did? I exhaled. Surely she wouldn't have done that. But then again, I wouldn't put it past her. "So what are you going to do?" I asked as I dried another plate.

She shrugged. "I'd like to keep renting out the Dawdi Haus, but I doubt Arden and Vi will want me to keep living in this house."

I doubted that too.

"I've been toying with the idea of doing some sort of service work."

"Really?" I felt a tinge of jealousy and hoped it hadn't come through in my voice.

"I've talked with the director from Mennonites Serve. She's pulling some information together for me."

"You're thinking something long-term?"

She smiled, grabbing a handful of forks. "Perhaps. If I'm ever going to do that sort of thing, I'd better while I still can."

I asked her to let me know what she found out. If I didn't have student loans to pay back, I'd be tempted to go with her.

She pulled the silverware drawer open and began putting the forks away. "Have you heard from Nick?"

I exhaled, maybe a little too loudly.

"What?"

"Oh, it's just that Marie asked me the same thing today." I hung up my towel. "I haven't. Not a word."

"Have you contacted him?"

I leaned against the counter again. "No. Why would I do that?"

Aenti Suz met my eyes. "Because he's your friend. A very good friend, I might add. Probably the best friend you've ever had."

"I'm dating Stephen. And I'm going to join the Mennonite church. Nick ran off and joined the Air Force, remember?"

"Well . . ." Aenti Suz hung up her towel. "I hope you'll forgive him someday. And once you do, I hope you won't neglect him." Her eyes met mine. "True friends are hard to find."

Tears stung my eyes, catching me off guard. I blinked them

away. At least I still had my sisters. And Stephen. But Aenti Suz was right. Nick was the best friend I'd ever had.

⁂

The Friday night that worked best for Jessica was the one where Mamm was away. I did the grocery shopping after I got off work, then I picked up Marie, and together we went out to Jessica's house. She came out with her bag in one arm and Ruby in the other and then asked me if I'd go over to John and Mildred's Dawdi Haus with her. "You too, Marie," Jessica said. "Mildred's taken a turn for the worse. Her doctor has written an order for hospice, but she doesn't want to start it yet."

I wasn't sure what Jessica wanted me to do, and she must have sensed I was puzzled because she said, "She's impressed you're a nurse and has heard good things about your work at the clinic. Maybe you could just talk with her for a few minutes and give her your opinion."

"All right." Mildred had been diagnosed with breast cancer five years ago. She'd been very ill a couple of times and then rallied, and she'd gone into remission once. But her chances didn't sound good now.

Clouds scuttled over the horizon as we walked across the driveway. Ruby reached for me and I took her, giggling as I jostled her along. John and Silas stepped out of the barn and waved. Jessica called out that we were all going to say hello to Mildred.

Silas approached me and reached for Ruby. "It's just you and me this weekend," he cooed in Pennsylvania Dutch.

She fell into his arms, laughing as Jessica kissed her good-bye.

When we reached the Dawdi Haus, Jessica knocked softly and then opened the door. Mildred sat on the couch, wrapped in a quilt. She wore a scarf instead of a Kapp.

304

"Leisel is here," Jessica said. "And Marie too."

"Oh, Marie," Mildred whispered. "I can't tell you how relieved I am that you're better. I've been praying for you every single day."

"Denki." Marie stepped closer and knelt in front of Mildred, taking her hand and gently stroking her thin skin. "How are you feeling?"

"Not well." She raised her head a little and met my eyes. "I'm hoping you can help me decide about hospice, Leisel."

I knelt beside Marie.

"I've heard there are preachers who work for hospice—who aren't Amish, of course," Mildred said, "who might come out and try to minister to me."

"Not if you don't want them to." I took her other hand. "You have your own people to minister to you. What you need are the aides and nurses to come in and bathe you and give you your medicine and help manage your pain. I worked with hospice nurses at the care facility in Pittsburgh. They really helped alleviate the pain of patients and the stress on their families too."

Her eyes filled with tears. "I'd like to stay at home. . . ."

"They should be able to make that possible," I answered. "Unless a complication makes it necessary for you to be transported to the hospital."

"Do you think it would be a big help to John?"

"Absolutely." I peered into her eyes. "It will make the time you two spend together higher quality because he won't have to be trying to do everything on his own. He'll still have plenty to do, but he'll have others to share the work. I think it's a good idea, and if you're having a hard time with daily tasks, such as getting enough nutrition, bathing, and toileting, then it's best to start as soon as possible." Doctors usually wrote the orders when they believed a person had six months or less to live. My guess was that Mildred had a few weeks to a month or so. It was past time to start hospice.

She nodded her head slowly. "I'll talk with John and have him make the call then."

"Please let Jessica know to contact me if I can help," I said. "It would be my privilege."

She took my hand. "You're so much like your Dat." She smiled weakly. "And like your grandparents too—I knew them when I was a girl."

My heart swelled at her words, connecting me to all three of them. All because of Aenti Suz's story.

We told her good-bye, and then I flagged down John by the chicken coop and told him what I'd told Mildred. He assured me he'd keep my offer in mind.

Jessica hesitated about leaving and asked John if he preferred that she stay.

"*Nee*," he said. "Go be with your sisters. I'll get Silas if we need anything."

We all climbed into my car, sad and subdued. By the time we reached the farm, it was completely dark. We gathered up all of the groceries and bags and headed up the front steps. A lamp shone in the window, which warmed my heart.

Marie opened the door and we stepped inside to the savory smell of soup and homemade bread. The big old oak table was set for three with a big green salad in the middle.

"Do you think Mamm did this before she left?" Marie asked, her voice hopeful.

I didn't. "My guess is Aenti Suz."

—22—

Aenti Suz was staying in her Dawdi Haus for the weekend, and we had to beg her to join us for dinner.

"No, no, no," she said. "This is a time for you three sisters."

We begged her some more. "You've been such a blessing to all of us," Jessica said. "You know more about us than we know about ourselves. Please join us."

She relented.

As we sat around the table, we talked about Dat. Jessica shared stories of working with him on the farm. Marie talked about his harmonica that Gordon now had. And I spoke of friends and family coming to him with their ailments and him offering them supplements and advice.

"He really impacted all of us," Marie said.

Aenti Suz cleared her throat. "Don't forget the role your mother played in your childhood too."

Nothing came to mind immediately.

"She made it possible for your father to do the things he did."

That was what all Amish wives did—supported their husbands.

"She took good care of you girls."

Marie gripped her spoon. "She did. But she also taught us a lot of fear and legalism."

Aenti Suz smiled. "Jah, she was fearful in many ways. But I think, considering her childhood and the loss of Rebecca, she did her best." Aenti Suz tipped her head back. "We all make mistakes that have ramifications that last a lifetime. I hope, in time, all of you will be able to forgive your mother for holding everything and everyone too tightly. She never learned to open her fist, to let God take the burden from her."

Jessica spoke first. "You're right. I've forgiven her. I have no reason not to."

"So have I," Marie said. "I know I hurt her deeply, which wasn't my intention. All in all, she's reacted exactly the way I expected her to. But I couldn't live my life for her."

All three looked at me. I shrugged. "I haven't really thought about if I have anything to forgive her for or not."

Now they were staring at me. Marie's eyebrows shot up. "What?"

Jessica sighed. "Avoiding conflict again? With yourself?"

I laughed, as if I thought she was joking. Aenti Suz stood and started collecting plates. I jumped up to help.

Aenti Suz stopped with a plate in each hand. "I'm totally changing the subject, but I have a favor to ask all of you."

"Anything," Jessica said.

"Pass the stories I've told you on to the next generation in the family. To any who are willing to listen."

We all nodded in agreement.

"Make sure they know the value of this land. And the brave men and women who came before all of us. And what your father meant to all of you."

"And you too," I said.

"And Mamm," Marie added.

We sat for a moment in silence, but then Aenti Suz, heading to the kitchen said, "I made a peach cobbler."

I followed her. "I'll start a pot of decaf."

"And then I'm going out to the Dawdi Haus." She glanced over her shoulder. "I'm so glad you have this time together."

I had a wonderful time with Jessica and Marie. We all crashed in our old bedroom, and then stayed up too late. Several times they tried to get me to talk about Stephen, but I evaded their prodding. Then Marie tried to get me to talk about Nick. I managed to redirect the conversation that time too.

But late Saturday afternoon as we sat on the porch, Jessica asked about Stephen again. Perhaps my guard was down after spending so many hours with them.

"Do you love him as much as you loved Nick?" she asked. When I didn't answer, she said, "Leisel . . ." the way she used to when we were young, when she really wanted to know what I was thinking.

"Does it matter if I do?" I asked. "Nick joined the Air Force. I can't support him in that. Jah, I left the Amish, but I didn't give up my beliefs of nonresistance."

"Perhaps he didn't understand that."

"He should have. I told him."

Marie chimed in. "That still doesn't mean he understood."

"Right," Jessica said. "Maybe you just implied it."

"That's not the way it happened," I said.

"Really?" Jessica propped herself up on her elbow. "Because you left a note for Mamm when you went off to nursing school. And you wanted to be a trauma nurse, but now you're working in a clinic. And you've avoided talking with us about Stephen this whole weekend."

All were true.

Marie wrinkled her nose. "Are you sure you can marry Stephen when you loved Nick more?"

"I didn't say that."

"You didn't deny it either," Jessica quickly pointed out.

It wasn't often that my sisters ganged up on me, but they certainly were now. I wasn't going to affirm or deny it with my sisters—not when Stephen might be their brother-in-law someday. "Look," I said. "Stephen is Mennonite. He's in medicine. He's kind and good."

"And handsome," Marie chimed in.

"That's true."

Marie added, "But he's not that supportive of you having a career."

I shrugged. "I'm guessing he'll come around to that."

"Have you applied for a position at the hospital like you talked about?" Marie asked.

"Not yet. . . ." Why had I confided in her?

"So, basically," Jessica said, "you gave up someone you love because he didn't understand your ideas, and now you're willing to compromise your dreams for someone you don't love."

"No," I said. "I do love Stephen."

"But not the way you did Nick."

"It's different is all—but isn't that the way love is? You don't ever love two people the same, right?"

Jessica stopped rocking. "I thought I loved Tom."

"And I thought I loved Elijah," Marie added.

"Well, maybe I thought I loved Nick but realized I didn't once I met Stephen."

Jessica shook her head. "I think you really are avoiding conflict with yourself."

"Or else you're in denial," Marie said.

I exhaled sharply. "I don't know what either one of you is talking about."

"We're talking about a girl who used to have stars in her eyes," Jessica said. "And a boy who would do anything for her—and did. Including taking a week of vacation to study with you so you'd have the confidence to take your test again." Jessica stood. "Stephen wouldn't do that. He bought you the program, yes, but it didn't cost him any time—just money. I bet once you're married, he'll want you to quit working as a nurse. Or at least once you're pregnant."

"I won't be able to," I said. "I'll have my student loans to pay back."

"He'll pay them for you." Jessica inhaled. "That way he'll have more control."

"Jessica." I stood too. "He's not like that."

She crossed her arms. "Why can't you see what's happening? What changed for you? What's behind all of this?"

For a moment the two of us stared at each other, at an impasse. I was always the one who got along with both of my sisters. I'd never gotten into a spat with Jessica. Why was she being so pushy?

Her face fell. "I'm sorry. I've said too much. I didn't mean to be such a big sister." She reached out and touched my shoulder. "Will you forgive me?"

"Of course," I said.

"We should get going," Marie said. "I told Gordon I'd be home by five."

"And I should check on Mildred," Jessica added.

"All right," I said. "Let's pack up the car."

The mood of the last twenty-four hours was restored as I drove them both home, but after I dropped them off, I considered what Jessica had said. Had I really chosen my ideology, one I shared with Stephen, over my love for Nick—and his love

311

for me? I swallowed hard, fighting back my feelings. Avoiding conflict with myself.

~~~

I thought about those feelings after Mildred died two weeks later. John was absolutely heartbroken, even though I knew he trusted the Lord. They never had children, and Mildred was his everything here on earth.

During the service, I watched him in the front row as his shoulders shook, moved by the display of his deep love for his wife. I'd heard once that grief was the price we paid for love. But it was also the continuation of love, the evidence that love never dies.

After the service, Ruby scampered across the aisle, her pigtails bouncing up and down, and climbed up onto John's lap. He sat there for a long time holding her. Once again, I thought of the wife of the man from the diner. I said a prayer for her, but as I did guilt washed over me. *Lord, I need to call her, don't I?* But there was so much pain from that season of my life that it was hard to revisit it.

Jessica launched straight from Mildred's funeral into planning Mamm's wedding. I offered to help, but Mamm declined, and she refused help from Marie too, although she did invite us to the wedding.

I met Stephen at the hospital cafeteria for dinner a few days before Mamm's wedding. We hadn't seen each other for a while and it was the best he could manage. I'd been looking at jobs again and mentioned one in the emergency department.

"Do you think you're ready for that?" he asked. "You don't have any experience."

I shrugged. "I thought I'd apply and see what happens." He hadn't known me when I was confident and ambitious.

I thought Stephen would have to work on the day of Mamm's

wedding, but he took it off so he could accompany me, saying he wanted to see what an Amish ceremony was like.

I told him the service would be held in Pennsylvania Dutch and German. He knew a smattering of both but not enough to keep up. He assured me he'd enjoy it anyway. It warmed my heart that he wanted to attend with me.

He asked about my plans for Christmas. I exhaled. Honestly, I wasn't sure. I doubted I'd spend it with Mamm and David. Or Arden and his family. Hopefully, one of my sisters—or both— would invite me to spend it with them.

People in Mamm's district helped clean the house from top to bottom, pack up the things she was taking to David's house, and clean out the rest of our things so Arden and his family could move in. I stopped by on Wednesday after work to see if I could help.

As Milton and Luke moved the furniture Mamm wasn't taking to David's house out to the storage room in the barn, I asked if I could have Dat's desk.

"Definitely not," she answered. "I'm leaving that for Arden."

When she was distracted by Aenti Suz asking about the rocking chair, I slipped into Dat's study for one last look. Mamm had packed up all of her material and quilting supplies. Dat's desk and chair were pushed against the far wall and all of the bookcases were empty. Even the set of encyclopedias was gone.

At one time, when it was Dat's study, the room had been the heart of the house for me. Now, I stood in the middle of it, overcome with grief.

As I stared at the empty bookcases, I thought of my missing copy of *Gray's Anatomy*. Perhaps it had turned up when Mamm went through everything. I couldn't imagine her giving it to me if it had. More likely, she stashed it somewhere.

Dat had a row of built-in cupboards on the left side of the room. I checked each one, but they were all empty. I was sure

Mamm had cleaned out the desk, but I decided to open the drawers anyway. She'd left pens, pencils, and unused notebooks for Arden in the top drawers. The right bottom drawer was completely empty, but as I opened the left one, I could tell by the weight of it that it wasn't.

I pulled out the drawer. There were several books inside. I took them out, one by one. Dat's Bible. An old, fragile copy of *Martyrs Mirror* that had been in the family for generations. An *Ausbund* hymnal. A collection of family directories. And then, at the very bottom, there it was. My copy of *Gray's Anatomy*—oversized with a white cover and a medical illustration of a body from the shoulders up.

I lifted it from the drawer and sat on the floor, cradling it, remembering all of the conversations Dat and I had based on the information inside. I opened it carefully.

I leafed through it, soaking in the familiar illustrations once again. Bones. Muscles. Arteries. Organs. I stopped at page 258 and stared at a piece of white paper, folded in two and wedged in the center of the book, next to an illustration of the right atrium and ventricle of the heart. *Leisel* was written on the outside in Dat's handwriting.

My own heart raced as I pulled the paper from the book and opened it, feeling both the loss of not finding this until now and the blessing of finding it at all.

Dear Leisel,

If you are reading this, then I am gone and your mother has given you the book we both love so much, with this note tucked inside. I hope you will come across my message sooner rather than later. I'm praying for God's timing.

Eighteen is young to lose your father. I'm so sorry to be leaving when your adulthood is just beginning. Your care for me has made the last months bearable. I've known for years that God has given you a special gift—I just never thought He would use it to serve me.

In writing this, I am not being a good Amish father, and I know Bishop Jacobs and others in our community would not approve, but if you decide to leave for other pursuits, please don't second-guess your decision. Don't believe God will punish you, no matter what others say. Please continue listening to God and His story. Those who don't end up writing their own—with added superstitions. Please do all you can to avoid that situation.

I'm praying for wisdom for you, that you know when to speak up and when to stay quiet. But know that confronting others is sometimes a good idea. I'm afraid I haven't always set a good example for you when it comes to that. Which brings me to my next point:

Don't give in to fear. Trust. Move forward. Take risks. Whether you stay or go, find a way to use the gift God has given you, and find a husband—God willing—to support you in whatever you decide to do.

Do your best to stay connected to your mother. Life has been harder for her than most. Be gentle with her and kind. Encourage her to love again, to trust. To give up her fear. Always remember that she cares for you.

Most important, know how much God loves you. He perfectly designed you. Live for Him. Love for Him. And serve for Him.

Yours, Dat

I struggled to breathe. Dat had written the letter over four years ago. Whatever he had planned for it, Mamm hadn't followed through. Had she leafed through the pages and found the note? And then hidden the book from me?

I turned on my heels to go find her, the book in one hand and the note in the other. She was on the back porch, directing Milton and Luke to bring in the church benches. I held up the note. "Look what I just found."

She wrinkled her nose. "Your book?"

"The note from Dat. The one he wrote to me before he died."

"Oh, that." She held the porch door open wider for the boys to come through.

"Why didn't you give it to me?"

"Your father said he prayed you'd read it at the right time—it hasn't come yet." She shrugged. "I don't think now is the right time either, but perhaps God has a different plan." Obviously, she didn't think it would ever have been the right time.

I hugged the book to my chest. Why hadn't Dat just given me the note? Why had he tucked it inside the book and relied on Mamm? Perhaps in his foggy state he hadn't been thinking clearly. On the other hand, he wasn't known for his directness. Had he avoided conflict? Was that where I got it from?

He'd asked me to be gentle and kind with Mamm, to know she cared for me. Right now, I wanted nothing to do with her. But it was the day before her wedding. I couldn't honor my father and tear into her at the same time.

She turned away from me and headed out the back door toward the church wagon. I muttered good-bye and left through the front.

What would the last four years have been like if I'd had Dat's note? Would I have been walking an imaginary line, trying to straddle both the Anabaptist world and the Englisch world as best I could? Coming up with my own rules to keep God from punishing me? Would I have been more willing to listen to Nick? To understand his point of view?

Feeling ill, I drove home, the note tucked into my purse and the book on the passenger seat beside me.

❧

I picked up Marie at five o'clock the next morning and headed back to the farm. Jessica was already there, but in the bathroom, when we arrived. I heard a retching noise and knocked on the door. "Are you all right?"

She didn't answer, but the toilet flushed and then the water ran. When she opened the door, she was pale.

"Morning sickness?" I whispered.

She nodded.

I couldn't help but grin.

She put her finger to her lips. Perhaps she wanted to wait to tell Marie, although I was sure our sister would be as happy as I was.

We cooked breakfast while the men did the chores. After we'd all eaten, we started finishing up the details for the meal. Stephen arrived at eight and helped put the aluminum pans full of meatballs that we had made the day before into the ovens to warm, while Marie and I put out the plates and silverware for the meal.

Jessica was back in the bathroom. Marie gave me a questioning look, and I shrugged. She smiled at me in return. I directed Stephen to sit by Arden on the men's side when it was time for the service. Once Jessica came out of the bathroom, the three of us girls, along with Ruby, slipped into the second row on the women's side. Gordon had arrived with Caden and sat in the back.

Bishop Jacobs led the service, first preaching about marriage and then calling Mamm and David up front.

Both of my sisters had had difficulties with the bishop, but I never had. He did write me a letter after I moved to Pittsburgh, outlining his concerns for my soul if I didn't join the Amish. Honestly, I felt unsettled about it. But at the time it wasn't enough to make me question leaving.

I never wrote Bishop Jacobs back or responded in any way.

Now he said a few more words about marriage, and then about second marriages in particular, and then took Mamm's and David's hands in his. I was happy for my mother, I truly was. David was a good man. I just hoped she wouldn't let fear control her second marriage the way she had her relationships with all of us.

For a moment, I wondered what Mamm and Dat's wedding had been like. Dawdi Joe and Mammi Martha would still have been alive, although not for much longer. I thought of them and Dat. Their stories would live on. We would not forget them. Even though they were no longer with us, they were still a part of our *Samling*, our gathering, because I'd never forget what they'd lived for and what they'd taught their children.

Bishop Jacobs asked if all of us would support Mamm and David in their marriage, and I joined the others in saying I would. And I meant it, which also meant at some point I needed to confront Mamm about her fears.

After the ceremony, we worked in the kitchen while the men, including Stephen, set up the tables. As I watched him, I thought of Dat's letter to me. *Don't give in to fear. Trust. Move forward. Take risks. Whether you stay or go, find a way to use the gift God has given you, and find a husband—God willing—to support you in whatever you decide to do.* I don't remember ever being fearful around Dat. Why would he caution me not to give into fear?

David's family pitched in to clean up after everyone was done eating, and then it was time for all of them and Mamm to leave. She'd ride with David in one of the three vans his children had hired. For a moment she seemed flustered as she turned toward us. But then she collected herself and said good-bye. It was never her way to be affectionate, which was the norm, but she did pat each of us on the back and say, "I'll write once I'm settled."

We followed Mamm and David and his family out to the vans and watched as Mamm climbed in and disappeared, and then we waved as the vans headed up Oak Road. Mamm was in the first one, and I knew she couldn't see us any longer, but we still stood there until the last van was out of sight.

I swallowed back my tears. My childhood was over. And I was all alone.

Stephen stood a few feet away beside Gordon. I inhaled sharply. Why had I assumed Stephen could take the place of Nick? Paisley and Autumn would have told me that I was in a rebound relationship, an unhealthy one. And they would have been right. Aenti Suz had tried to tell me. And Jessica and Marie. But I hadn't been able—or willing—to do anything until now. Panic seized me. That old adrenaline rush and the urge to flee, which I usually did. After Jessica and Marie and their families left and Aenti Suz went out to the Dawdi Haus, Stephen and I sat down at the old oak table for another piece of rhubarb pie and a cup of coffee.

He took a bite, savored it, swallowed, and then smiled. "What a treat. It reminds me of home."

I took a bite too, but I was afraid my face was sour.

"What's wrong?" he asked.

"I'm sorry." I put my fork down. "I can't do this anymore."

He held up his fork, which was loaded with another bite. "You don't like rhubarb?"

I exhaled. I had more choices than fight or flight. I could trust. And move forward.

And talk.

"No, I do like rhubarb. That's not it. I can't do our relationship. I've been unfair to both of us. I don't love you."

He put his fork in his mouth. Swallowed. And then took another bite. He swallowed again and said, "This probably isn't the best time to talk."

Obviously he hated conflict as much as I did. "No, it is," I answered.

He pushed back the chair. "Is there another guy?"

There had been another guy, but there wasn't anymore. However, the memory of him, plus Dat's note, made it clear Stephen wasn't right for me. But it didn't mean Nick was.

I told Stephen about finding Dat's note and realizing that I needed more. "I've given up my dreams this last year," I said. "I need to get them back."

I'd finally stepped up and spoken my truth.

Perhaps I'd overestimated how much Stephen cared for me because he honestly didn't seem that upset. It wouldn't be long until he found another woman to date. He wouldn't be alone for long, whereas I might be alone for the rest of my life. But that would be better than marrying a man who wouldn't challenge me and who wasn't willing to take risks with me. A man I didn't love.

— 23 —

The next day, sitting on my secondhand couch, I texted Paisley and Autumn and invited myself to see them in Wilmington the next week, if possible. Both had to work the night before Thanksgiving, so they wouldn't be going home to Philadelphia, but they both had the next day off.

Plan to be here by late Thanksgiving Day, Paisley texted back. *We can hang out on Friday.*

The next thing I did was pull out the piece of paper from the diner in Somerset. I stared at the number for a long moment, guessing it was the woman's cell phone number. I hated making phone calls. I was tempted to text her—but I couldn't do that. I'd been awful enough as it was.

I dialed the numbers slowly. A woman answered. "This is Shari."

"Hi," I said and then quickly explained who I was.

"Oh, hello. I'd given up on you ever calling."

"I'm sorry," I said, dreading what she'd say next. Would she blame me for her husband's death? I fought back against my fear and kicked into Nurse Leisel mode. "I'm so sorry your husband didn't make it."

"His name was Sonny."

321

I said I remembered. "What did he die from?"

"A massive heart attack."

There wasn't anything I could have done to stop it. I hoped she realized that.

She continued, "The doctor said even if he'd been in the hospital when it happened, they probably couldn't have saved him. He had severe blockage. Ninety-nine percent."

I winced. "Did he have any symptoms? Prior to that night?"

"Looking back, yes. A few times he'd had shortness of breath. And he thought he had the flu a few days before, but not much more than that."

"He was so young," I said.

"Yes," she answered. "And he had no family history of heart disease, that we know of." She paused a moment and then said, "Do you remember he had a heartbeat when the ambulance arrived? Because of the CPR?"

"Yes." I swallowed, not trusting myself to say any more.

"He was still alive when he reached the hospital—at least his heart was beating. They put him on a ventilator to keep him breathing until his parents arrived. His daughter from his first marriage, who is twenty now, and his ex came from Cleveland. And my parents also, although they live close. We all got to say good-bye. . . . It meant so much. And, you know, I hope it meant something to him too."

I read between the lines. He was brain-dead by then. The blockage had been bad enough that it prevented any oxygen from getting to his brain, even though the CPR brought his heartbeat back. But she was right—at least it got him to the hospital and onto a ventilator.

"We were all able to tell him good-bye because of you."

"But I couldn't save him," I said.

"No. But I was able to run my hand through his hair one

last time. To hold him." I could hear the tears in her voice. "All three of his kids curled up on the bed beside him. I used to have a strained relationship with his ex, but not anymore. We're the best of friends now. And our children will always have each other."

Tears stung my eyes.

"We all thanked God that you stopped by the diner that evening. The pastor even talked about you at the funeral, saying that even though things didn't work out the way we wanted, God put you there to ease our pain and make letting go of Sonny a little bit easier."

I swiped at my eyes with my free hand.

"So thank you," Shari said. "And please don't feel bad about him not surviving. You have a gift. I felt that as you worked on Sonny, as you directed those other men, as you did your thing. And as you spoke with me and my children." Her voice grew stronger. "And it means so much that you called today, it really does."

I didn't want to burden her with all I'd been through the last six months, especially when it paled in comparison to her own pain, but I did manage to say, "You can't know how much this means to me, to hear your story."

Her voice was strong as she said, "Life is so unpredictable. If there's someone special in your life, hold him close."

I sighed. "There isn't."

"Well," she said, "when there is, don't ever take him for granted." I thought of Mildred and John. Joe and Martha. Jessica and Silas. Marie and Gordon. Even of Mamm and Dat. And now Mamm and David. Marriage had been wonderfully designed. It was a blessing.

After we said good-bye and ended the call, I felt a freedom I hadn't since Jessica called to tell me Marie was in the hospital.

God had been at work the evening I stopped at the diner. His ways weren't our ways, but He hadn't abandoned Shari and her children. And He hadn't abandoned me either.

Years ago, when I was fourteen or so, a woman in our district had come to see Dat. Her husband had died in a buggy accident the year before, then her oldest son had been arrested for selling drugs. She'd been caring for her mother who had dementia, along with her younger children too, trying to make ends meet. She believed God was punishing her. There wasn't anything specific she believed God was angry with her about, just generally who she was.

Dat reminded her of the story of Job. Then he quoted from Matthew 5:45, ". . . for he maketh his sun to rise on the evil and on the good, and sendeth rain on the just and on the unjust."

He explained to her, "Sometimes we're tested, but that doesn't mean we've done anything wrong. You need to take care of yourself as best you can to get through this." He talked with her about watching her diet, getting enough exercise and sleep, expressing her feelings, and reaching out for help. After she left, he went out to the barn. I was sure he'd gone out there to call the bishop to arrange more support for her. The next day, I noticed that Marie made a meal for the family. Men in the district soon put a new roof on her house. Dat went and visited her son in jail. And I saw the woman sitting on her porch, writing in a notebook. Perhaps that was her way of expressing herself.

What did it mean for me to take care of myself? I reached for my laptop. The professional challenges I'd longed for were missing from my life. I had to apply for a different job. I opened my computer, logged onto the Lancaster General website, and then applied for a job in the ICU. Sure, if I got it, I'd bump into Stephen now and then, but the job would be worth it.

As I closed my computer, I felt a little less numb. A little more alive.

I pulled Dat's letter out of my purse and read it again, slowing down as I reached the end. And then reread, *Don't give in to fear . . .*

Did he see me avoiding conflict because I was fearful? Had I, like Mamm, written superstitions into my own story?

Perhaps we had more in common than I thought.

Marie, Gordon, Caden, Aenti Suz, and I all went to Silas and Jessica's for our Thanksgiving meal. John joined us. Afterward, during dessert, Aenti Suz said she had an announcement to make. "I'm going to be leaving in two weeks."

I smiled. "Where?"

"The mission organization your Dat went to Haiti with also works with an orphanage that needs help right now. I've also contacted a nonprofit that helps support an orphanage in Vietnam. I may go there next."

With wide eyes, Marie asked, "What does Bishop Jacobs say?"

"I have his blessing," she answered. "I'll fly, of course, but he allowed your Dat to fly to Haiti too, so it wasn't as if he could tell me I couldn't. Arden and Jessica will be renting out the Dawdi Haus full-time."

"Will you come home?" I asked.

"Jah," Aenti Suz answered. "Eventually."

"She'll stay here." Jessica grinned. "We have plenty of room."

Aenti Suz nodded.

"And I'll mainly be the one looking after the Dawdi Haus," Jessica said. "I'll clean it and change the sheets and towels and all of that while Aenti Suz is gone."

"What a wonderful thing for you to do," John said to Aenti Suz.

As the conversation continued, my heart fell a little. I wished I could go with her. Perhaps I could sometime for a week's vacation. But once I had my student loans paid off, I'd have more opportunities to do that sort of thing.

Jessica was giving Marie and Gordon an update on the farm and the finances. "I've convinced Arden to wait a year as far as selling the herd. Supply has gone down, but we might make it with the help of the income from Aenti Suz's endeavor. If not, I'm willing to let go of the dairy."

Aenti Suz began telling all of them about when her father added the current dairy business back in the late 1940s. I smiled at the thought of Joe and Martha building up the farm. Soon it would be Milton taking charge. The Bachmann farm would continue, with its joys and challenges, one generation at a time.

I left soon after that and headed for Delaware. Rain poured from a dark, dark sky as I drove, and my car was shaken every now and then by blasts of wind, but at least it wasn't snowing. When I stopped for coffee and a break from the weather, I noticed I'd missed a call from David's number in Chester County. Had Mamm called to wish me a happy Thanksgiving? That surprised me, but maybe she was missing her daughters. I figured she'd already left the phone shed as I called back to leave a return message. But to my surprise, she answered.

Without even saying hello, she said, "I just got off the phone with Jessica—we'd planned ahead to talk today. She told me you broke up with Stephen."

"That's right," I answered.

"What were you thinking?"

It wasn't as if she really knew him. "What do you mean?" I asked.

326

"He was Mennonite. Didn't that matter?"

"I thought you wanted me to marry an Amish man," I teased.

"I gave up on that," she said. I guessed it was easier for her to tell people I was going to join the Mennonite church and marry a doctor than to say I was Englisch. At least then I was still on that imaginary line, straddling both worlds.

"I'm not going to join the Mennonites," I said, surprising us both with my sudden decision. "I'm sorry, Mamm, that I'm a disappointment to you, but I've been living in fear ever since I moved back from Pittsburgh, and I don't want to do it anymore. I don't want to feel as if God is going to punish me at every turn, and I don't think you should either."

"I don't feel that way," she said. "The Bible tells us not to fear."

"That's right," I said.

"It also tells us not to be unequally yoked. I hope you don't go back to dating that Nick."

"I wouldn't be unequally yoked if I did—"

"You're acting just like before. You're not listening to me."

I sighed. "Could we start again?" Before she could answer, I said, "Happy Thanksgiving! How are you and David doing?"

Her voice softened a little. "Just fine. We had a good dinner with his kids. . . ." She told me about his infant grandson and how she'd sat in the rocking chair with him for half of the afternoon.

I let her go on for a while and then said, "Well, I need to get going. I'm on my way to Wilmington to see Paisley and Autumn."

"Englisch friends?"

"That's right," I said. "Let's talk soon. Or maybe I'll come up to visit. Would that be all right?"

She hesitated, but then said it would.

After we said good-bye, I held my phone in my hand. And then I did what I'd wanted to do for the last week. I texted Nick.

Hey, Happy Thanksgiving! How is the Air Force? How do you like your first assignment?

I imagined he would reply eventually, even if tersely, although I couldn't help but think of when he texted me the second time I took my boards. I hadn't texted him back. Then again, his manners were better than mine. I was sure he'd reply.

But I was wrong. He still hadn't answered by the time I reached Paisley and Autumn's apartment. And not while we went out for Thai food. And not while we stayed up late watching old movies—*Mean Girls* and *The Princess Diaries*. Their goal was to make up for my "wacky childhood," as they called it.

All through the night, the wind continued to howl as the rain poured even harder. Friday morning, the bad weather continued with torrential rain, relentless wind, and falling temperatures as we headed out for a late brunch. Nick still hadn't texted.

"Why do you keep checking your phone?" Paisley asked.

Before I could respond, Autumn asked, "So what happened with that doctor, anyway?"

"Oh, that," I answered. "It's been over for forever." I gave her a sassy look. "Over a week."

She laughed. "And how is Nick?"

I sighed. "Your guess is as good as mine."

We ate at a café in downtown Wilmington that reminded me of the one up the street from where I'd lived in Pittsburgh, which of course made me think of Nick again. Afterward, as we walked through shops, my phone buzzed.

"Oh, good," Autumn teased. "Maybe it's him."

It wasn't. It was an alert from Mennonites Serve. There was flooding in northern Kent County, Delaware, along the river, and they were sending a team because there was an Amish settlement in the area. Availability was down because of the holiday weekend, and they needed all the volunteers possible.

I quickly texted back, saying I could meet the team there.

Perfect. The team lead texted me the address and said she'd see me soon.

I explained to Autumn and Paisley what the text was about.

"That's cool," Autumn said. "Let's head back to the apartment so you can get your stuff."

A half hour later, I was on my way south, wondering if Nick was at his folks' in Lancaster County or at Dover Air Force Base. As a Red Cross volunteer, he might have been summoned to the flooded area too.

The going was slow because of the wind and the rain, and there was standing water across the road in several places with detours in place. Once I neared my destination, the traffic signals were all out, as were the lights in the businesses and houses. I saw several trees toppled across houses and cars. I drove on through the howling wind and rain, hoping it hadn't been foolish of me to come.

— 24 —

When I arrived at a tent set up in a strip mall parking lot, I checked in with the woman holding a clipboard. She directed me to work on the far side of the tent. There were a couple of portable heaters running, but I kept my coat on. I also scanned the area for Nick. Of course he wasn't there—my wishful thinking had gotten the best of me.

The first person I examined had a possible concussion. He was a sixty-two-year-old man who'd woken up to water rushing into his first-floor apartment. He'd fallen and hit his head on a table while he was trying to get out. I recommended he go to the emergency department.

The next patient was an Amish man who had sliced his hand on sheet metal in his flooded barn.

Several people came in who were chilled. As I wrapped one in a blanket, more volunteers showed up. I recognized a few from Lancaster County and searched the group. I smiled when I spotted Aenti Suz. Once I was done with the patient I was examining, she gave me a quick hug and then said she'd had a visitor at the Dawdi House that morning.

"Who?" I asked, thinking maybe Stephen had stopped by, looking for me.

"Nick."

I exhaled. Why would he stop by the farm but not text me back?

"In fact, he gave me a ride to the church to get on the van." Her eyes sparkled.

"Interesting." I crossed my arms. "So did he stop by to see me? Or you?"

She just shrugged, and then said she was continuing on to go to the church, which was about a mile away, to help prepare the meal.

I kept on with my work, feeling unsettled about Nick, but feeling much more comfortable serving than I had the day of the tornado. Most things in life got easier the more we did them.

I thought of the final line of Dat's note to me: *Live for Him. Love for Him. And serve for Him.*

If only Nick were serving with me.

When my shift was done, I headed to the church. The parking lot was full, and once I found the fellowship hall, it became obvious to me that more than just the workers were being fed. I headed to the kitchen and, after I washed my hands, helped Aenti Suz butter loaves of French bread. Spaghetti was on the menu again. It was the perfect meal to feed to a crowd.

Aenti Suz instructed me to take a tray of bread out of the oven. As I positioned it on the counter, several people stepped into the fellowship hall. One of them wore a down jacket and a beanie. As he took the beanie off, I realized it was Nick.

He glanced around the hall for a moment, and then his eyes fell on me. He gave a half wave and started across the room. As he grew close, he asked, "Do you have a minute?"

Curious, I replied, "Are you volunteering?"

He shook his head. "No. When Suz said she was coming here,

I took the chance that you were too. I'm on my way to Dover."
His brown eyes were as deep as ever. He gestured toward an
empty table at the very back of the room. "Could we talk?"

Aenti Suz nudged me. "Go on."

I followed him.

As we sat, I asked if he'd gotten my text.

He grimaced. "I recently got off my parents' plan and got a
new number. I would have sent it to you except—"

My eyebrows shot up.

"I thought you were serious about the doctor. But then I
stopped by your farm today. I was just driving by and thinking
about you . . ." He exhaled. "And I stopped."

"And saw Aenti Suz?"

He nodded. "She told you?"

"Only that you stopped by." I folded my hands on top of the
table. "What did she tell you?"

"That you broke up with the doctor." His eyes were kind.
"I'm sorry."

I tried to swallow the lump in my throat. "Don't be," I managed to say. I wasn't.

He leaned forward, his forearms flat on the table. "I need to
apologize to you. I was wrong. So, so wrong."

"About what?"

"About joining the Air Force the way I did, without us talking it through."

I felt a hint of sympathy for him. "I wasn't exactly making
it easy for you to discuss it. I'm sorry about that."

"No," he said. "It wasn't your fault. On one of my sleepless
nights after we broke up, I finally researched nonresistance. I
don't know that I totally get it, but I understand that it's essential to your upbringing, to your faith. It's why the Anabaptists
were persecuted in Europe and why your ancestors came to

America, and Pennsylvania in particular, in search of religious freedom. I get why you didn't want to be associated with the military."

"I should have explained it to you better," I said. "I was so focused on graduating, and then Marie, and then my boards, and then retaking my boards." My voice wavered. "And I didn't take the time to really listen to you either, about your financial worries and interest in pursuing an advanced degree." Marie was right. I'd been empathetic to everyone but Nick. I'd taken him for granted. "I'm so sorry too."

We both had tears in our eyes as we offered forgiveness to each other.

I spread my hands out flat on the table, and Nick reached and took both of them in his. And then we talked. I told him about my work in the clinic. He told me about his work in the ICU at the base hospital. He asked about Mamm getting married. I told him about Aenti Suz's plan to go to Haiti.

"Did your Aenti Suz finish telling you your grandparents' story?" he asked. "She can't leave if she hasn't."

I told him how Dawdi Joe's and Mammi Martha's wartime story ended, and then about my note from Dat. "I learned," I said, "that I was living in fear, just like Mamm. I was walking an imaginary line, afraid God would punish me, as Mamm predicted, if I fell too far over on the Englisch side. I feared marrying a military man would do that." I met his eyes. "But my Dawdi and Mammi's story showed me that life, even an Anabaptist one, isn't as black and white as the life I thought I needed to create."

Nick squeezed my hand. "What now?"

"Could we start again? Where we left off?" I asked.

"Even though I'm in the military?"

I nodded. "It isn't what I would have chosen, but I don't want to give up you and what we had because of it. I don't want to reject what God has for us. . . ."

As my voice trailed off, he said, "I won't make a career out of it. I'll meet my commitment and then get out, I promise."

I smiled. "I can live with that."

He unzipped his coat and reached into an inside pocket, taking out a small white box with a battered lavender ribbon tied around it. He handed it to me.

I held it in my open palm as my heart began to race.

"I've been carrying it around for a while," he said a little sheepishly.

"Since the night before my graduation?" I remembered him patting his coat pocket after our celebratory dinner. "For the last six months?"

He nodded, his gaze fixed on me.

My hand closed over the box as tears filled my eyes. All the nerves in my fingers seemed to be transmitting extra signals, and yet I couldn't seem to move a muscle.

"I'm sorry." He ran his hand through his hair. "Did I mess up again?"

I shook my head, only able to squeak out, "No."

"What's wrong?"

A single tear escaped. Then another. "Nothing." I brushed at my face. "I'm just so happy," I said, "to be here. With you."

He nodded toward the box and coaxed, "Open it."

I pulled the ribbon off, wound it around my wrist, and then took the little lid off the box. Inside was a simple band with a single embedded diamond. Neither the Amish nor the Mennonites wore rings. But I would wear this one. It was perfect.

His eyes met mine. "Will you marry me?"

"Yes," I answered as joy bubbled up inside of me.

He came across the table and sat beside me, taking the ring

and sliding it onto my finger. Then he wrapped his arms around me, pulling me close. He kissed the top of my head. And then my forehead. And then my mouth.

The months apart melted away, but what I'd learned would stay with me forever.

On Christmas Day, after celebrating with Jessica, Marie, their families, and Aenti Suz, Nick and I visited Mamm and David and told them our news. Mamm said it certainly wasn't what she'd been praying for. "I had faith you'd join the church," she said. "Or at least the Mennonites."

I couldn't avoid the conflict any longer. "Mamm," I said. "I wouldn't expect you to feel any other way, but I want you to know I have my own relationship with the Lord and this is where He's led me. I love Nick, and I want to spend my life with him. And I know God made me to be a nurse. I know I've disappointed you, but I don't want you to fear that God will punish me for the choices I've made." I shared what I'd learned from Dawdi Joe and Mammi Martha's story and from Dat's note. Then I told her I planned to not live in fear anymore. "That's my prayer for you too, Mamm. I want you to be free from fear. To not hold on so tightly. To trust God, with all of us."

She pursed her lips. For a moment I wondered if she would apologize for hiding Dat's note, but she didn't. After a long spell of silence, David asked if we'd like a piece of Christmas cake, made with orange juice and pecans. Over cake and coffee, the conversation turned to grandkids and new calves and the snowstorm that was predicted for the next day. David teased Mamm about her new snow boots and soon she was smiling, telling a story about when I was little and Jessica and Marie rolled me around outside in my snowsuit. It was a story I hadn't heard before.

That night, back at my apartment, I knelt beside my bed and thought about Dat again and the woman he had helped when I was fourteen. He had reminded her of the story of Job, and then we had memorized the last chapter of it together. Now I recited, "I know that thou canst do every thing, and that no thought can be withholden from thee." I hoped I remembered that the next time life seemed to take an unbearable turn.

I found a job in the cardiac critical care unit at Dover General Hospital and moved there just after the first of the year. Nick and I were married seven months later in a small evening ceremony in his parents' backyard in late July. I wore a simple white dress that Marie helped me sew.

Besides Nick's family, Autumn and Paisley attended, along with Jessica, Silas, Ruby, newborn Zachary, and John. Of course Marie, Gordon, and Caden came too. All of those people I expected. The others who attended surprised me. Amos and Becca flew in from Colorado, and Aenti Suz flew up from Haiti. The other surprises were from closer to home—Arden and Vi and even their children arrived at the last minute, along with Mamm and David.

My family was far from typical, but I was thrilled to have us all together.

Doug and Barbara, along with Stephanie and Kaylee, had turned the backyard into a wonderland, with lights strung from the fence to the house and in the tree branches too. They placed potted plants and flowers all around the courtyard and a trellis covered with ivy in front of rows of white wooden chairs.

It was under the trellis that Nick stood, waiting for me, along with the chaplain from Dover, who'd befriended Nick and was performing the ceremony. I couldn't help but think of Dawdi

Joe and Mammi Martha and their wedding in France. I was grateful for our gathering of love.

I walked down the aisle by myself, and we'd chosen to stand alone, although Autumn and Paisley had signed the marriage certificate.

The chaplain began the ceremony by reading the verse from Matthew we'd chosen: "For where two or three are gathered together in my name, there am I in the midst of them."

I marveled that God *was* in the midst of us, that He'd orchestrated our paths and guided us to this point as two separate families and, most important on this day, as a couple.

Then the chaplain, in honor of my grandparents and great-aunts, read all of 1 Corinthians 13, ending with "And now abideth faith, hope, charity, these three . . ." but the greatest of these is love.

Out of the corner of my eye, I could see Aenti Suz sitting between my sisters, dabbing at her eyes. Jah, the past was always with us. As was the present. But then I noticed Mamm was wiping away tears too.

Nick reached for my hand. This time there was no lump in my throat. Only a smile on my face.

I'd be forever grateful for the faithfulness of my ancestors—and the gathering of my family. And most of all, for the man beside me.

Acknowledgments

A big thank-you to my husband, Peter. His support on research trips, deadlines, and throughout life is invaluable to me. I couldn't do this without him. I'm so glad he's always willing to join in on the fun!

I'm also thankful for the support of my four adult children—Kaleb, Taylor, Hana, and Lily Thao—and for all the ways that they've expanded my world.

My friend Marietta Couch deserves a big shout-out for the ongoing role she plays in my life. Besides encouraging me in so many ways, she generously shares her Plain living experiences with me and has answered countless questions of mine about the Amish. (Any mistakes are my own.)

I'm grateful for all of the doctors, nurses, and other medical professionals I know, both military and civilian. You've all inspired me with your knowledge, dedication, and compassion.

I'm also very thankful for the fabulous crew at Bethany House Publishers, including my gifted editors, Jennifer Veilleux and Dave Long.

Three books, in particular, aided my research for this novel: *The CPS Story: An Illustrated History of Civilian Public Service* by Albert Keim; *The History of the American Field Service, 1920–1955* by George Rock; and *G Company's War: Two Personal Accounts of the Campaigns in Europe, 1944–1945* by Bruce E. Egger and Lee McMillian Otts. Bruce Egger was my father, and it was moving to think of him and his World War II experiences as I wrote this story.

I'm also grateful for the many teachings God has given us about fear, including Isaiah 43:1b, "Do not fear, for I have redeemed you; I have summoned you by name; you are mine" (NIV).

Lastly, I'm thankful for my readers, including my Street Team. I'm so grateful for the encouragement and support they all offer, and for the reviews of my novels and word-of-mouth sharing. You are simply the best!

Leslie Gould is the #1 bestselling and award-winning author of thirty-one novels, including the COURTSHIPS OF LANCASTER COUNTY series and the NEIGHBORS OF LANCASTER COUNTY series. She holds an MFA in creative writing and enjoys research trips, church history, and hiking, especially in the beautiful state of Oregon where she lives. She and her husband, Peter, are the parents of four adult children.

Sign Up for Leslie's Newsletter!

Keep up to date with Leslie's news, book releases, and events by signing up for her email list at lesliegould.com.

More from Leslie Gould

Returning home for her father's funeral, Jessica faces the Amish life—and love—she left behind. As she struggles with regrets, she learns about a Revolutionary War–era ancestor who confronted similar choices. Will she find peace along with the resolution she hopes for?

A Plain Leaving
THE SISTERS OF LANCASTER COUNTY #1

You May Also Like . . .

Marie Bachmann has always been the good Amish daughter. But when two men, a Mennonite farmhand and a bishop's rebellious son, show interest in her, she finds herself at a crossroads. On a journey to Florida and back, she grapples with her heart, finding inspiration and hope for the future in the story of a brave Civil War–era ancestor.

A Simple Singing by Leslie Gould
THE SISTERS OF LANCASTER COUNTY #2
lesliegould.com

When Iraq veteran Joel Beck and his family move next door to an Amish family in Lancaster County, their lives are linked in unexpected ways. Eve Lehman, who keeps house for her brother, befriends their new neighbors, but life becomes complicated for both families when Joel's handsome army friend pays a visit.

Amish Promises by Leslie Gould
NEIGHBORS OF LANCASTER COUNTY #1
lesliegould.com

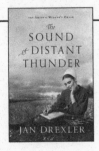

After a young Amish man from Weaver's Creek takes his brother's place in the Civil War draft of 1862, the sacrifice may take everything he holds dear—including his sweetheart's love.

The Sound of Distant Thunder by Jan Drexler
THE AMISH OF WEAVER'S CREEK #1
jandrexler.com

BETHANYHOUSE